THE BARCLAY FAMILY THEATRE

THE BARCLAY FAMILY THEATRE

JACK HODGINS

MACMILLAN OF CANADA
A Division of Gage Publishing Limited
Toronto, Canada

Canadian Cataloguing in Publication Data
   Hodgins. Jack. 1938-
       The Barclay family theatre

   (Laurentian library ; 74)

   ISBN 0-7715-9597-2 bound
   ISBN 0-7715-9765-7 pbk.

   I. Title.

   PS8565.O34B37   C813'.54   C81-094882-6
   PR9199.3.H63B37

This is a work of fiction. The characters are
products of imagination and do not represent
actual persons, living or dead.

First printed in 1981
First Laurentian Library edition 1983

Macmillan of Canada
A Division of Gage Publishing Limited

Manufactured in Canada by Webcom Limited

I guess a man who's sent seven
daughters out into the world has
launched just about every kind of
invasion you can imagine. Now let's
close down this show and go home.
There's cattle and cut hay and real
life to be faced tomorrow.

. . . J. G. Barclay, towards
the end of the seventh
wedding reception.

for Katie Murphy Blakely

Contents

THE BARCLAY FAMILY THEATRE

1

The Concert Stages
of Europe

Now I know Cornelia Horncastle would say I'm blaming the wrong person. I know that. I know too that she would say thirty years is a long time to hold a grudge, and that if I needed someone to blame for the fact that I made a fool of myself in front of the whole district and ruined my life in the process, then I ought to look around for the person who gave me my high-flown ideas in the first place. But she would be wrong; because there is no doubt I'd have led a different sort of life if it weren't for her, if it weren't for that piano keyboard her parents presented her with on her eleventh birthday. And everything — everything would have been different if that piano keyboard hadn't been the kind made out of stiff paper that you unfolded and laid out across the kitchen table in order to do your practising.

I don't suppose there would have been all that much harm in her having the silly thing, if only my mother hadn't got wind of it. What a fantastic idea, she said. You could learn to play without even making a sound! You could practise your scales without having to hear that awful racket when you hit a wrong note! A genius must have thought of it, she said. Certainly someone who'd read his Keats: *Heard melodies are sweet, but those unheard are sweeter*. "And don't laugh," she said, "because Cornelia Horncastle is learning to play the piano and her mother doesn't even have to miss an episode of *Ma Perkins* while she does it."

That girl, people had told her, would be giving concerts in Europe some day, command performances before royalty, and her parents hadn't even had to fork out the price of a piano. It was obvious proof, if you needed it, that a person didn't have to be rich to get somewhere in this world.

In fact, Cornelia's parents hadn't needed to put out even the small amount that paper keyboard would have cost. A piano teacher named Mrs. Humphries had moved onto the old Dendoff place and, discovering that almost no one in the district owned a piano, gave the keyboard to the Horncastles along with a year's free lessons. It was her idea, apparently, that when everyone heard how quickly Cornelia was learning they'd be lining up to send her their children for lessons. She wanted to make the point that having no piano needn't stop anyone from becoming a pianist. No doubt she had a vision of paper keyboards in every house in Waterville, of children everywhere thumping their scales out on the kitchen table without offending anyone's ears, of a whole generation turning silently into Paderewskis without ever having played a note.

They would, I suppose, have to play a real piano when they went to her house for lessons once a week, but I was never able to find out for myself, because all that talk of Cornelia's marvellous career on the concert stages of Europe did not prompt my parents to buy one of those fake keyboards or sign me up for lessons with Mrs. Humphries. My mother was born a Barclay, which meant she had a few ideas of her own, and Cornelia's glorious future prompted her to go one better. We would buy a *real* piano, she announced. And I would be sent to a teacher we could trust, not to that newcomer. If those concert stages of Europe were ever going to hear the talent of someone from the stump ranches of Waterville, it wouldn't be Cornelia Horncastle, it would be Barclay Desmond. Me.

My father nearly choked on his coffee. "But Clay's a boy!"

"So what?" my mother said. *All* those famous players used to be boys. What did he think Chopin was? Or Tchaikovsky?

My father was so embarrassed that his throat began to turn a dark pink. Some things were too unnatural even to think about.

But eventually she won him over. "Think how terrible you'd feel," she said, "if he ended up in the bush, like you. If Mozart's father had worked for the Comox Logging Company and thought piano-playing was for sissies, where would the world be today?"

My father had no answer to that. He'd known since before his marriage that though my mother would put up with being married to a logger, expecting every day to be made a widow, she wouldn't tolerate for one minute the notion that a child of hers would follow him up into those hills. The children of Lenora Barclay would enter the professions.

She was right, he had to agree; working in the woods was the last thing in the world he wanted for his sons. He'd rather they take up ditch-digging or begging than have to work for that miserable logging company, or take their orders from a son-of-a-bitch like Tiny Beechman, or get their skulls cracked open like Stanley Kirck. It was a rotten way to make a living, and if he'd only had a decent education he could have made something of himself.

Of course, I knew he was saying all this just for my mother's benefit. He didn't really believe it for a minute. My father loved his work. I could tell by the way he was always talking about Ab Jennings and Shorty Cresswell, the men he worked with. I could tell by the excitement that mounted in him every year as the time grew near for the annual festival of loggers' sports where he usually won the bucking contest. It was obvious, I thought, that the man really wanted nothing more in this world than that one of his sons should follow in his footsteps. And much as I disliked the idea, I was sure that I was the one he'd set his hopes on. Kenny was good in school. Laurel was a girl. I was the obvious choice. I even decided that what he'd pegged me for was high-rigger.

I was going to be one of those men who risked their necks climbing hundreds of feet up the bare lonely spar tree to hang the rigging from the top. Of course I would fall and kill myself the first time I tried it, I knew that, but there was no way I could convey my hesitation to my father since he would never openly admit that this was really his goal for me.

And playing the piano on the concert stages of Europe was every bit as unattractive. "Why not Kenny?" I said, when the piano had arrived, by barge, from Vancouver.

"He's too busy already with his school work," my mother said. Kenny was hoping for a scholarship, which meant he got out of just about everything unpleasant.

"What about Laurel?"

"With her short fat fingers?"

In the meantime, she said, though she was no piano-player herself (a great sigh here for what might have been), she had no trouble at all identifying which of those ivory keys was the all-important Middle C and would show it to me, to memorize, so that I wouldn't look like a total know-nothing when I showed up tomorrow for my first lesson. She'd had one piano lesson herself as a girl, she told me, and had learned all about Mister Middle C, but she'd never had a second lesson because her time was needed by her father, outside, helping with the chores. Seven daughters alto-gether, no sons, and she was the one who was the most often expected to fill the role of a boy. The rest of them had found the time to learn chords and chromatic scales and all those magic things she'd heard them practising while she was scrubbing out the dairy and cutting the runners off straw-berry plants. They'd all become regular show-offs in one way or another, learning other instruments as well, putting on their own concerts and playing in dance bands and earning a reputation all over the district as entertaining livewires — The Barclay Sisters. And no one ever guessed that all the while she was dreaming about herself at that keyboard, tinkling away, playing beautiful music before huge audiences in elegant theatres.

"Then it isn't me that should be taking lessons," I said. "It's you."

"Don't be silly." But she walked to the new piano and pressed down one key, a black one, and looked as if I'd tempted her there for a minute. "It's too late now," she said. And then she sealed my fate: "But I just know that you're going to be a great pianist."

When my mother "just knew" something, that was as good as guaranteeing it already completed. It was her way of controlling the future and, incidentally, the rest of us. By "just knowing" things, she went through life commanding the future to fit into certain patterns she desired while we scurried around making sure that it worked out that way so she'd never have to be disappointed. She'd had one great disappointment as a girl — we were never quite sure what it was, since it was only alluded to in whispers with far-off looks — and it was important that it never happen again. I was trapped.

People were always asking what you were going to be when you grew up. As if your wishes counted. In the first six years of my life the country had convinced me it wanted me to grow up and get killed fighting Germans and Japanese. I'd seen the coils of barbed wire along the beach and knew they were there just to slow down the enemy while I went looking for my gun. The teachers at school obviously wanted me to grow up and become a teacher just like them, because as far as I could see nothing they ever taught me could be of any use or interest to a single adult in the world except someone getting paid to teach it to someone else. My mother was counting on my becoming a pianist with a swallow-tail coat and standing ovations. And my father, despite all his noises to the contrary, badly wanted me to climb into the crummy every morning with him and ride out those gravelly roads into mountains and risk my life destroying forests.

I did not want to be a logger. I did not want to be a teacher. I did not want to be a soldier. And I certainly did not want to be a pianist. If anyone had ever asked me what

I did want to be when I grew up, in a way that meant they
expected the truth, I'd have said quite simply that what I
wanted was to be a Finn.

Our new neighbours, the Korhonens, were Finns. And
being a Finn, I'd been told, meant something very specific.
A Finn would give you the shirt off his back, a Finn was as
honest as the day is long, a Finn could drink anybody under
the table and beat up half a dozen Germans and Irishmen
without trying, a Finn was not afraid of work, a Finn kept a
house so clean you could eat off the floors. I knew all these
things before ever meeting our neighbours, but as soon as
I had met them I was able to add a couple more general-
izations of my own to the catalogue: Finnish girls were
blonde and beautiful and flirtatious, and Finnish boys were
strong, brave, and incredibly intelligent. These conclusions
were reached immediately after meeting Lilja Korhonen,
whose turned-up nose and blue eyes fascinated me from the
beginning, and Larry Korhonen, who was already a teenager
and told me for starters that he was actually Superman,
having learned to fly after long hours of practice off their
barn roof. Mr. and Mrs. Korhonen, of course, fitted exactly
all the things my parents had told me about Finns in general. And so I decided my ambition in life was to be just
like them.

I walked over to their house every Saturday afternoon
and pretended to read their coloured funnies. I got in on the
weekly steam-bath with Larry and his father in the sauna
down by the barn. Mr. Korhonen, a patient man whose eyes
sparkled at my eager attempts, taught me to count to ten
—*yksi, kaksi, kolme, nelja, viisi, kuusi, seitseman, kahdek-
san, yhdeksan, kymmenen.* I helped Mrs. Korhonen scrub
her linoleum floors and put down newspapers so no one
could walk on them, then I gorged myself on cinnamon
cookies and *kala loota* and coffee sucked through a sugar
cube. If there was something to be caught from just being
around them, I wanted to catch it. And since being a Finn
seemed to be a full-time occupation, I didn't have much
patience with my parents, who behaved as if there were

other things you had to prepare yourself for.

The first piano teacher they sent me to was Aunt Jessie, who lived in a narrow, cramped house up a gravel road that led to the mountains. She'd learned to play as a girl in Toronto, but she had no pretensions about being a real teacher, she was only doing this as a favour to my parents so they wouldn't have to send me to that Mrs. Humphries, an outsider. But one of the problems was that Aunt Jessie — who was no aunt of mine at all, simply one of those family friends who somehow get saddled with an honorary family title — was exceptionally beautiful. She was so attractive, in fact, that even at the age of ten I had difficulty keeping my eyes or my mind on the lessons. She exuded a dreamy sort of delicate femininity; her soft, intimate voice made the hair on the back of my neck stand on end. Besides that, her own playing was so much more pleasant to listen to than my own stumbling clangs and clunks that she would often begin to show me how to do something and become so carried away with the sound of her own music that she just kept right on playing through the rest of my half-hour. It was a simple matter to persuade her to dismiss me early every week so that I'd have a little time to play in the creek that ran past the back of her house, poling a homemade raft up and down the length of her property while her daughters paid me nickels and candies for a ride. At the end of a year my parents suspected I wasn't progressing as fast as I should. They found out why on the day I fell in the creek and nearly drowned, had to be revived by a distraught Aunt Jessie, and was driven home soaked and shivering in the back seat of her old Hudson.

Mr. Korhonen and my father were huddled over the taken-apart cream separator on the verandah when Aunt Jessie brought me up to the door. My father, when he saw me, had that peculiar look on his face that was halfway between amusement and concern, but Mr. Korhonen laughed openly. "That boy lookit like a drowny rat."

I felt like a drowned rat too, but I joined his laughter. I was sure this would be the end of my piano career, and could hardly wait to see my mother roll her eyes to the ceiling, throw out her arms, and say, "I give up."

She did nothing of the sort. She tightened her lips and told Aunt Jessie how disappointed she was. "No wonder the boy still stumbles around on that keyboard like a blind-folded rabbit; he's not going to learn the piano while he's out risking his life on the river!"

When I came downstairs in dry clothes Aunt Jessie had gone, no doubt wishing she'd left me to drown in the creek, and my parents and the Korhonens were all in the kitchen drinking coffee. The Korhonens sat at either side of the table, smoking hand-rolled cigarettes and squinting at me through the smoke. Mrs. Korhonen could blow beautiful white streams down her nostrils. They'd left their gumboots on the piece of newspaper just inside the door, of course, and wore the same kind of grey work-socks on their feet that my father always wore on his. My father was leaning against the wall with both arms folded across his chest inside his wide elastic braces, as he sometimes did, swish-ing his mug gently as if he were trying to bring something up from the bottom. My mother, however, was unable to alight anywhere. She slammed wood down into the firebox of the stove, she rattled dishes in the sink water, she slammed cupboard doors, she went around the room with the coffee pot, refilling mugs, and all the while she sang the song of her betrayal, cursing her own stupidity for sending me to a friend instead of to a professional teacher, and suddenly in a flash of inspiration dumping all the blame on my father: "If you hadn't made me feel it was somehow pointless I wouldn't have felt guilty about spending more money!"

From behind the drifting shreds of smoke Mr. Korhonen grinned at me. Sucked laughter between his teeth. "Yust teenk, boy, looks like-it you're saved!"

Mrs. Korhonen stabbed out her cigarette in an ashtray, picked a piece of tobacco off her tongue, and composed her face into the most serious and ladylike expression she could muster. "Yeh! Better he learn to drive the tractor." And swung me a conspirator's grin.

"Not on your life," my mother said. Driving a machine may have been a good enough ambition for some people, she believed, but the Barclays had been in this country for four generations and she knew there were a few things higher. "What we'll do is send him to a real teacher. Mrs. Greensborough."

Mrs. Greensborough was well known for putting on a public recital in town once a year, climaxing the program with her own rendition of Grieg's Piano Concerto — so beautiful that all went home, it was said, with tears in their eyes. The problem with Mrs. Greensborough had nothing to do with her teaching. She was, as far as I could see, an excellent piano teacher. And besides, there was something rather exciting about playing on her piano, which was surrounded and nearly buried by a thousand tropical plants and dozens of cages full of squawking birds. Every week's lesson was rather like putting on a concert in the midst of the Amazon jungle. There was even a monkey that swung through the branches and sat on the top of the piano with the metronome between its paws. And Mrs. Greensborough was at the same time warm and demanding, complimentary and hard to please — though given a little, like Aunt Jessie, to taking off on long passages of her own playing, as if she'd forgotten I was there.

It took a good hour's hard bicycling on uphill gravel roads before I could present myself for the lesson — past a dairy farm, a pig farm, a turkey farm, a dump, and a good long stretch of bush — then more washboard road through heavy timber where driveways disappeared into the trees and one dog after another lay in wait for its weekly battle with my right foot. Two spaniels, one Irish setter, and a bulldog. But it wasn't a spaniel or a setter or even a bulldog that met me on the driveway of the Greensboroughs' chicken farm, it was a huge German shepherd that came barking down the slope the second I had got the gate shut, and stuck its nose into my crotch. And kept it there, growling menacingly, the whole time it took me to back him up to the door of the house. There was no doubt in my mind that I would come home from piano lesson one Saturday minus a few parts. Once I had got to the house, I tried to get inside quickly and shut the door in his face, leaving him out there in the din of cackling hens; but he always got his nose between the door and the jamb, growled horribly and pushed himself inside so that he could lie on the floor at my feet and watch me hungrily the whole time I sat at the kitchen table waiting for Ginny Stamp to finish off her lesson and get out of there. By the time my turn came around my nerves were too frayed for me to get much benefit out of the lesson.

Still, somehow I learned. That Mrs. Greensborough was a marvellous teacher, my mother said. The woman really knew her stuff. And I was such a fast-learning student that it took less than two years for my mother to begin thinking it was time the world heard from me.

"Richy Ryder," she said, "is coming to town."

"What?"

"Richy Ryder, CJMT. *The Talent Show*."

I'd heard the program. Every Saturday night Richy Ryder was in a different town somewhere in the province, hosting his one-hour talent contest from the stage of a local theatre and giving away free trips to Hawaii.

Something rolled over in my stomach.

"And here's the application form right here," she said, whipping two sheets of paper out of her purse to slap down on the table.

"No thank you," I said. If she thought I was going in it, she was crazy.

"Don't be silly. What harm is there in trying?" My mother always answered objections with great cheerfulness, as if they were hardly worth considering.

"I'll make a fool of myself."

"You play beautifully," she said. "It's amazing how far you've come in only two years. And besides, even if you don't win, the experience would be good for you."

"You have to go door-to-door ahead of time, begging for pledges, for money."

"Not begging," she said. She plunged her hands into the

sink, peeling carrots so fast I couldn't see the blade of the
vegetable peeler. "Just giving people a chance to vote for
you. A dollar a vote." The carrot dropped, skinned naked,
another one was picked up. She looked out the window
now toward the barn and, still smiling, delivered the argument that never failed. "I just know you'd win it if you went
in, I can feel it in my bones."

"Not this time!" I shouted, nearly turning myself inside
out with the terror. "Not this time. I just can't do it."

Yet somehow I found myself riding my bicycle up and
down all the roads around Waterville, knocking at people's
doors, explaining the contest, and asking for their money
and their votes. I don't know why I did it. Perhaps I was
doing it for the same reason I was tripping over everything,
knocking things off tables, slamming my shoulder into door-
jambs; I just couldn't help it, everything had gone out of
control. I'd wakened one morning that year and found myself six feet two inches tall and as narrow as a fence stake.
My feet were so far away they seemed to have nothing to do
with me. My hands flopped around on the ends of those
lanky arms like fish, something alive. My legs had grown so
fast the bones in my knees parted and I had to wear elastic
bandages to keep from falling apart. When I turned a corner
on my bicycle, one knee would bump the handlebar, throwing me into the ditch. I was the same person as before,
apparently, saddled with this new body I didn't know what
to do with. Everything had gone out of control. I seemed to
have nothing to do with the direction of my own life. It was
perfectly logical that I should end up playing the piano on
the radio, selling myself to the countryside for a chance to
fly off to Hawaii and lie on the sand under the whispering
palms.

There were actually two prizes offered. The all-expense,
ten-day trip to Hawaii would go to the person who brought
in the most votes for himself, a dollar a vote. But lest someone accuse the radio station of getting its values confused,
there was also a prize for the person judged by a panel of
experts to have the most talent. This prize, which was do-

nated by Nelson's Hardware, was a leatherette footstool.

"It's not the prize that's important," people told me. "It's the chance to be heard by all those people."

I preferred not to think of all those people. It seemed to me that if I were cut out to be a concert pianist it would be my teacher and not my parents encouraging me in this thing. Mrs. Greensborough, once she'd forked over her two dollars for two votes, said nothing at all. No doubt she was hoping I'd keep her name out of it.

But it had taken no imagination on my part to figure out that if I were to win the only prize worth trying for, the important thing was not to spend long hours at the keyboard, practising, but to get out on the road hammering at doors, on the telephone calling relatives, down at the General Store approaching strangers who stopped for gas. Daily piano practice shrank to one or two quick run-throughs of "The Robin's Return", school homework shrank to nothing at all, and home chores just got ignored. My brother and sister filled in for me, once in a while, so the chickens wouldn't starve to death and the woodbox would never be entirely empty, but they did it gracelessly. It was amazing, they said, how much time a great pianist had to spend out on the road, meeting his public. Becoming famous, they said, was more work than it was worth.

And becoming famous, I discovered, was what people assumed I was after. "You'll go places," they told me. "You'll put this place on the old map." I was a perfect combination of my father's down-to-earth get-up-and-go and my mother's finer sensitivity, they said. How wonderful to see a young person with such high ambition!

"I always knew this old place wouldn't be good enough to hold you," my grandmother said as she fished out a five-dollar bill from her purse. But my mother's sisters, who appeared from all parts of the old farmhouse in order to contribute a single collective vote, had some reservations to express. Eleanor, the youngest, said she doubted I'd be able to carry it off, I'd probably freeze when I was faced with a microphone, I'd forget what a piano was for. Christina announced she was betting I'd faint, or have to run out to the bathroom right in the middle of my piece. And Mabel, red-headed Mabel who'd played accordion once in an amateur show, said she remembered a boy who made such a fool of himself in one of these things that he went home and blew off his head. "Don't be so morbid," my grandmother said. "The boy probably had no talent. Clay here is destined for higher things."

From behind her my grandfather winked. He seldom had a chance to contribute more than that to a conversation. He waited until we were alone to stuff a five-dollar bill in my pocket and squeeze my arm.

I preferred my grandmother's opinion of me to the aunts'. I began to feed people lies so they'd think that about me — that I was destined for dizzying heights. I wanted to be a great pianist, I said, and if I won that trip to Hawaii I'd trade it in for the money so that I could go off and study at the Toronto Conservatory. I'd heard of the Toronto Conservatory only because it was printed in big black letters on the front cover of all those yellow books of finger exercises I was expected to practise.

I don't know why people gave me their money. Pity, perhaps. Maybe it was impossible to say no to a six-foot-two-inch thirteen-year-old who trips over his own bike in front of your house, falls up your bottom step, blushes red with embarrassment when you open the door, and tells you he wants your money for a talent contest so he can become a Great Artist. At any rate, by the day of the contest I'd collected enough money to put me in the third spot. I would have to rely on pledges from the studio audience and phone-in pledges from the radio audience to rocket me up to first place. The person in second place when I walked into that theatre to take my seat down front with the rest of the contestants was Cornelia Horncastle.

I don't know how she managed it so secretly. I don't know where she found the people to give her money, living in the same community as I did, unless all those people who gave me their dollar bills when I knocked on their doors had just given her two the day before. Maybe she'd gone into town, canvassing street after street, something my parents wouldn't let me do on the grounds that town people already had enough strangers banging on their doors every day. Once I'd got outside the vague boundaries of Waterville I was to approach only friends or relatives or people who worked in the woods with my dad, or stores that had — as my mother put it — done a good business out of us over the years. Cornelia Horncastle, in order to get herself secretly into that second place, must have gone wild in town. Either that or discovered a rich relative.

She sat at the other end of the front row of contestants, frowning over the sheets of music in her hands. A short nod and a quick smile were all she gave me. Like the other contestants, I was kept busy licking my dry lips, rubbing my sweaty palms together, wondering if I should whip out to the bathroom one last time, and rubbernecking to get a look at people as they filled up the theatre behind us. Mrs. Greensborough, wearing dark glasses and a big floppy hat, was jammed into the far corner at the rear, studying her program. Mr. and Mrs. Korhonen and Lilja came partway down the aisle and found seats near the middle. Mr. Korhonen winked at me. Larry, who was not quite the hero he had once been, despite the fact that he'd recently beat up one of the teachers and set fire to the bus shelter, came in with my brother Kenny — both of them looking uncomfortable — and slid into a back seat. My parents came all the way down front, so they could look back up the slope and pick out the seats they wanted. My mother smiled as she always did in public, as if she expected the most delightful surprise at any moment. They took seats near the front. Laurel was with them, reading a book.

My mother's sisters — with husbands, boyfriends, a few of my cousins — filled up the entire middle section of the back row. Eleanor, who was just a few years older than myself, crossed her eyes and stuck out her tongue when she saw that I'd turned to look. Mabel pulled in her chin and held up her hands, which she caused to tremble and shake.

Time to be nervous, she was suggesting, in case I forgot. Bella, Christina, Gladdy, Frieda — all sat puffed up like members of a royal family, or the owners of this theatre, looking down over the crowd as if they believed every one of these people had come here expressly to watch their nephew and for no other reason. "Look, it's the Barclay girls," I heard someone behind me say. And someone else: "Oh, them." The owner of the first voice giggled. "It's a wonder they aren't all entered in this thing, you know how they like to perform." A snort. "They are performing, just watch them." I could tell by the muffled "Shhh" and the rustling of clothing that one of them was nudging the other and pointing at me, at the back of my neck. "One of them's son." When I turned again, Eleanor stood up in the aisle by her seat, did a few steps of a tap dance, and quickly sat down. In case I was tempted to take myself seriously.

When my mother caught my eye, she mouthed a silent message: stop gawking at the audience, I was letting people see how unusual all this was to me, instead of taking it in my stride like a born performer. She indicated with her head that I should notice the stage.

As if I hadn't already absorbed every detail. It was exactly as she must have hoped. A great black concert grand with the lid lifted sat out near the front of the stage, against a painted backdrop of palm trees along a sandy beach, and — in great scrawled letters — the words "Richy Ryder's CJMT Talent Festival". A long blackboard leaned against one end of the proscenium arch, with all the contestants' names on it and the rank order of each. Someone named Brenda Roper was in first place. On the opposite side of the stage, a microphone seemed to have grown up out of a heap of pineapples. I felt sick.

Eventually Richy Ryder came out of whatever backstage room he'd been hiding in and passed down the row of contestants, identifying us and telling us to get up onto the stage when our turns came without breaking our necks on those steps. "You won't be nervous, when you get up there," he said. "I'll make you feel at ease." He was looking off

somewhere else as he said it, and I could see his jaw muscles straining to hold back a yawn. And he wasn't fooling
me with his "you won't be nervous" either, because I knew
without a doubt that the minute I got up on that stage I
would throw up all over the piano.

Under the spotlight, Richy Ryder acted like a different
person. He did not look the least bit like yawning while he
told the audience the best way of holding their hands to get
the most out of applause, cautioned them against whistling
or yelling obscenities, painted a glorious picture of the life
ahead for the talented winner of this contest, complimented
the audience on the number of happy, shiny faces he could
see out there in the seats, and told them how lucky they
were to have this opportunity of showing off the fine young
talent of the valley to all the rest of the province. I slid down
in my seat, sure that I would rather die than go through with
this thing.

The first contestant was a fourteen-year-old girl dressed
up like a gypsy, singing something in a foreign language.
According to the blackboard she was way down in ninth
place, so I didn't pay much attention until her voice cracked
open in the middle of a high note and she clutched at her
throat with both hands, a look of incredulous surprise on
her face. She stopped right there, face a brilliant red, and
after giving the audience a quick curtsey hurried off the
stage. A great beginning, I thought. If people were going to
fall to pieces like that through the whole show no one
would even notice my upchucking on the Heintzman. I had
a vision of myself dry-heaving the whole way through "The
Robin's Return".

Number two stepped up to the microphone and answered
all of Richy Ryder's questions as if they were some kind of
test he had to pass in order to be allowed to perform. Yes
sir, his name was Roger Casey, he said with a face drawn
long and narrow with seriousness, and in case that wasn't
enough he added that his father was born in Digby, Nova
Scotia, and his mother was born Esther Romaine in a little
house just a couple blocks up the street from the theatre,

close to the Native Sons' Hall, and had gone to school with the mayor though she'd dropped out of Grade Eight to get a job at the Safeway cutting meat. And yes sir, he was going to play the saxophone because he'd taken lessons for four years from Mr. D. P. Rowbottom on Seventh Street though he'd actually started out on the trumpet until he decided he didn't like it all that much. He came right out to the edge of the stage, toes sticking over, leaned back like a rooster about to crow, and blasted out "Softly As in a Morning Sunrise" so loud and hard that I thought his bulging eyes would pop right out of his head and his straining lungs would blast holes through that red-and-white shirt. Everyone moved forward, tense and straining, waiting for something terrible to happen — for him to fall off the stage or explode or go sailing off into the air from the force of his own fantastic intensity — but he stopped suddenly and everyone fell back exhausted and sweaty to clap for him.

The third contestant was less reassuring. A kid with talent. A smart-aleck ten-year-old with red hair, who told the audience he was going into show business when he grew up, started out playing "Swanee River" on his banjo, switched in the middle of a bar to a mouth organ, tap-danced across the stage to play a few bars on the piano, and finished off on a trombone he'd had stashed away behind the palm tree. He bowed, grinned, flung himself around the stage as if he'd spent his whole life on it, and looked as if he'd do his whole act again quite happily if the audience wanted him to. By the time the tremendous applause had died down my jaw was aching from the way I'd been grinding my teeth the whole time he was up there. The audience would not have gone quite so wild over him, I thought, if he hadn't been wearing a hearing aid and a leg brace.

Then it was my turn. A strange calm fell over me when my name was called, the kind of calm that I imagine comes over a person about to be executed when his mind finally buckles under the horror it has been faced with, something too terrible to believe in. I wondered for a moment if I had died. But no, my body at least hadn't died, for it transported

me unbidden across the front of the audience, up the staircase (with only a slight stumble on the second step, hardly
noticeable), and across the great wide stage of the theatre
to stand facing Richy Ryder's enormous expanse of white
smiling teeth, beside the microphone.

"And you are Barclay Philip Desmond," he said.

"Yes," I said.

And again "yes", because I realized that not only had
my voice come out as thin and high as the squeal of a dry
buzz-saw, but the microphone was at least a foot too low. I
had to bend my knees to speak into it.

"You don't live in town, do you?" he said. He had no
intention of adjusting that microphone. "You come from a
place called . . . Waterville. A logging and farming settlement?"

"Yes," I said.

And again "yes" because while he was speaking my
legs had straightened up, I'd returned to my full height and
had to duck again for the microphone.

He was speaking to me but his eyes, I could see, were
busy keeping all that audience gathered together, while his
voice and his mind were obviously concentrated on the
thousands of invisible people who were crouched inside
that microphone, listening, the thousands of people who —
I imagined now — were pulled up close to their sets all over
the province, wondering if I was actually a pair of twins or
if my high voice had some peculiar way of echoing itself, a
few tones lower.

"Does living in the country like that mean you have to
milk the cows every morning before you go to school?"

"Yes."

And again "yes".

I could see Mrs. Greensborough cowering in the back
corner. I promise not to mention you, I thought. And the
Korhonens, grinning. I had clearly passed over into another
world they couldn't believe in.

"If you've got a lot of farm chores to do, when do you
find the time to practise the piano?"

He had me this time. A "yes" wouldn't be good enough. "Right after school," I said, and ducked to repeat. "Right after school. As soon as I get home. For an hour."

"And I just bet," he said, throwing the audience an enormous wink, "that like every other red-blooded country kid you hate every minute of it. You'd rather be outside playing baseball."

The audience laughed. I could see my mother straining forward; she still had the all-purpose waiting-for-the-surprise smile on her lips but her eyes were frowning at the master of ceremonies. She did not approve of the comment. And behind that face she was no doubt thinking to herself "I just know he's going to win" over and over so hard that she was getting pains in the back of her neck. Beside her, my father had a tight grin on his face. He was chuckling to himself, and sliding a look around the room to see how the others were taking this.

Up at the back, most of my aunts — and their husbands, their boyfriends — had tilted their chins down to their chests, offering me only the tops of their heads. Eleanor, however, had both hands behind her neck. She was laughing harder than anyone else.

Apparently I was not expected to respond to the last comment, for he had another question as soon as the laughter had died. "How old are you, son?"

"Thirteen."

For once I remembered to duck the first time.

"Thirteen. Does your wife like the idea of your going on the radio like this?"

Again the audience laughed. My face burned. I felt tears in my eyes. I had no control over my face. I tried to laugh like everyone else but realized I probably looked like an idiot. Instead, I frowned and looked embarrassed and kicked at one shoe with the toe of the other.

"Just a joke," he said, "just a joke." The jerk knew he'd gone too far. "And now seriously, one last question before I turn you loose on those ivories over there."

My heart had started to thump so noisily I could hardly

hear him. My hands, I realized, had gone numb. There was no feeling at all in my fingers. How was I ever going to play the piano?

"What are you going to be when you grow up?"

The thumping stopped. My heart stopped. A strange, cold silence settled over the world. I was going to die right in front of all those people. What I was going to be was a corpse, dead of humiliation, killed in a trap I hadn't seen being set. What must have been only a few seconds crawled by while something crashed around in my head, trying to get out. I sensed the audience, hoping for some help from them. My mother had settled back in her seat and for the first time that surprise-me smile had gone. Rather, she looked confident, sure of what I was about to say.

And suddenly, I was aware of familiar faces all over that theatre. Neighbours. Friends of the family. My aunts. People who had heard me answer that question at their doors, people who thought they knew what I wanted.

There was nothing left of Mrs. Greensborough but the top of her big hat. My father, too, was looking down at the floor between his feet. I saw myself falling from that spar tree, high in the mountains.

"Going to be?" I said, turning so fast that I bumped the microphone with my hand, which turned out after all not to be numb.

I ducked.

"Nothing," I said. "I don't know. Maybe . . . maybe nothing at all."

I don't know who it was that snorted when I screwed up the stool, sat down, and stood up to screw it down again. I don't know how well I played, I wasn't listening. I don't know how loud the audience clapped, I was in a hurry to get back to my seat. I don't know what the other contestants did, I wasn't paying any attention, except when Cornelia Horncastle got up on the stage, told the whole world she was going to be a professional pianist, and sat down to rattle off Rachmaninoff's Rhapsody on a Theme of Paganini as if she'd been playing for fifty years. As far as I know it may have been the first time she'd ever heard herself play it. She had a faint look of surprise on her face the whole time, as if she couldn't quite get over the way the keys went down when you touched them.

As soon as Cornelia came down off the stage, smiling modestly, and got back into her seat, Richy Ryder announced a fifteen-minute intermission while the talent judges made their decision and the studio audience went out into the lobby to pledge their money and their votes. Now that the talent had been displayed, people could spend their money according to what they'd heard rather than according to who happened to come knocking on their door. Most of the contestants got up to stretch their legs but I figured I'd stood up once too often that night and stayed in my seat. The lower exit was not far away; I contemplated using it; I could hitch-hike home and be in bed before any of the others got out of there.

I was stopped, though, by my father, who sat down in the seat next to mine and put a greasy carton of popcorn in my lap.

"Well," he said, "that's that."

His neck was flushed. This must have been a terrible evening for him. He had a carton of popcorn himself and tipped it up to gather a huge mouthful. I had never before in my life, I realized, seen my father eat popcorn. It must have been worse for him than I thought.

Not one of the aunts was anywhere in sight. I could see my mother standing in the far aisle, talking to Mrs. Korhonen. Still smiling. She would never let herself fall apart in public, no matter what happened. My insides ached with the knowledge of what it must have been like right then to be her. I felt as if I had just betrayed her in front of the whole world. Betrayed everyone.

"Let's go home," I said.

"Not yet. Wait a while. Might as well see this thing to the end."

True, I thought. Wring every last drop of torture out of it.

He looked hard at me a moment, as if he were trying to

guess what was going on in my head. And he did, he did, he always knew. "My old man wanted me to be a doctor," he said. "My mother wanted me to be a florist. She liked flowers. She thought if I was a florist I'd be able to send her a bouquet every week. But what does any of that matter now?"

Being part of a family was too complicated. And right then I decided I'd be a loner. No family for me. Nobody whose hearts could be broken every time I opened my mouth. Nobody *expecting* anything of me. Nobody to get me all tangled up in knots trying to guess who means what and what is it that's really going on inside anyone else. No temptations to presume I knew what someone else was thinking or feeling or hoping for.

When the lights had flickered and dimmed, and people had gone back to their seats, a young man with a beard came out onto the stage and changed the numbers behind the contestants' names. I'd dropped to fifth place, and Cornelia Horncastle had moved up to first. She had also, Richy Ryder announced, been awarded the judges' footstool for talent. The winner of the holiday in sunny Hawaii would not be announced until the next week, he said, when the radio audience had enough time to mail in their votes.

"And that," my mother said when she came down the aisle with her coat on, "is the end of a long and tiring day." I could find no disappointment showing in her eyes, or in the set of her mouth. Just relief. The same kind of relief that I felt myself. "You did a good job," she said, "and thank goodness it's over."

As soon as we got in the house I shut myself in the bedroom and announced I was never coming out. Lying on my bed, I tried to read my comic books but my mind passed from face to face all through the community, imagining everyone having a good laugh at the way my puffed-up ambition had got its reward. My face burned. Relatives, the aunts, would be ashamed of me. Eleanor would never let me forget. Mabel would remind me of the boy who'd done the only honourable thing, blown off his head. Why wasn't I doing the same? I lay awake the whole night, torturing myself with these thoughts. But when morning came and the hunger pains tempted me out of the bedroom as far as the breakfast table, I decided the whole wretched experience had brought one benefit with it: freedom from ambition. I wouldn't worry any more about becoming a pianist for my mother. Nor would I worry any more about becoming a high-rigger for my father. I was free at last to concentrate on pursuing the only goal that ever really mattered to me: becoming a Finn.

Of course I failed at that too. But then neither did Cornelia Horncastle become a great pianist on the concert stages of Europe. In fact, I understand that once she got back from her holiday on the beaches of Hawaii she announced to her parents that she was never going to touch a piano again as long as she lived, ivory, or cardboard, or any other kind. She had already, she said, accomplished all she'd ever wanted from it. And as far as I know, she's kept her word to this day.

2

Invasions '79

For ten years Bella Robson's son had taught medieval literature at Harvard and lived in a three-room apartment overlooking the bridge where one of William Faulkner's characters had killed himself. He used up nearly a ton of impressive letterhead paper explaining why he intended to stay in New England for the rest of his life. Apparently a young man who'd grown up on the West Coast had a great deal of catching up to do — especially in matters of history and culture. Long, convincing descriptions of the stone houses of Cambridge, the busy excitement of Harvard Square, and the incredible wealth of books in Widener Library made it clear he was doing the only intelligent thing. Bella Robson had flown down on one occasion and, after a few days of attending plays in Boston and dining in restaurants that looked out over the Atlantic, she saw there wasn't a chance he would return to North Vancouver.

His specialty (when anyone asked) was some old poem she'd never had the pleasure of reading. Its title went something like *Toil Less and Crusade*, though she couldn't guarantee that she'd remembered it right. He'd even written a book about the poem, which everyone said would cause an uproar if it were ever published. Professors, she explained, tended to get excited about things the rest of us would hardly notice.

Professors, she might have added, were a foreign breed to her. She had no idea what went on in her own son's head. She couldn't imagine how he could devote his life to a single poem. This wasn't even his poem, either, but one that somebody else had written, centuries ago. She sometimes found it difficult to understand how a young man could be happy living as an alien in a city that was full of foreign landmarks and people with strange accents and not a relative in sight.

How, then, could she possibly understand why those letters suddenly changed their tune? "When my own country is falling apart, how can I stay away?" he wrote. "I've got to move back home." The next thing she knew he was teaching in Ottawa. How could he call that home? She knew better than to think he'd made the move in order to be close to his sister, who lived there with her husband and two small boys. He hated his sister; his brother-in-law was a moron; he thought their two little boys were a couple of vicious barbarians. He may have been Bella Robson's only son but she'd learned long ago that she would never understand what made him tick.

She also didn't understand the first thing about the academic world, he wrote. When it came to jobs you took what you could find. But she didn't need to think he intended to become a martyr, either. If he was going to sacrifice himself in the name of national unity by leaving Boston and Cambridge behind, he'd make damn sure he did plenty of travelling too. He would take advantage, he said, of every opportunity that came along to make connections with foreigners, to get himself invited on foreign lecture tours, to choose research topics that couldn't be handled at home. And in order to encourage these miracles, he had found himself an apartment surrounded by foreign embassies. The Egyptians, the Belgians, the Swiss, the Pakistanis — all were

situated within a few blocks of his door. Every time he
stepped outside he expected to meet someone who would
invite him to somewhere exotic. "From now on," he wrote,
"consider me a citizen of the world."

Bella Robson had little to say about this. Her garden was
at its most demanding stage at the time. All the borders had
to be dug for next year's bulbs. If travel would make him
happy, then let him travel — though she hoped, privately,
that he would soon meet the girl who'd become her
daughter-in-law one day, and settle down. She took it for
granted that he would stay away from the countries whose
very names had always made her uneasy. Israel, South
Africa, Russia, Cambodia — let him stay clear of those. She
watched television every night and knew what was going
on.

Friends wondered if it wasn't a little lonely for her, a
widow living so far from son and daughter both, and there
were days when she was tempted to think they might be
right. But Bella Robson liked to live her own life, undisturbed. She was convinced it was better to have them both a
good safe distance away than to have them camped on your
doorstep every day of the week, like the children of some of
her friends. She would just as soon not know all their
day-to-day problems, thank you, since there was seldom
anything that she could do to help. A person had enough to
handle, conducting her own affairs. And as far as distance
went — in real emergencies there was always the telephone,
though her daugher Iris had got into the habit of delivering
her month's call from Ottawa in such a brusque, even brutal,
voice that it wasn't always easy to distinguish what was a
crisis from what was not.

There was little ambiguity, however, when Iris called
one evening in late October. "You'd better come see this for
yourself," she said. "Your brilliant son has got himself in-
volved with the Russians!"

Bella Robson nearly dropped the receiver. Was it possible? This might be the end of a decade that had seen the
whole world trying to act like friends, but to her a word like
"Russians" still conjured up images of barbed-wire fences

and spies and firing-squads. Iris assured her it was even
worse than that. "A woman."

When Iris was mad she stuck out her jaw and pulled her
bottom lip almost up to her nose. Her mother had told her
when she was small that it made her face look like a fist, and
the comparison had pleased her so much she'd gone out of
her way ever since to exaggerate the effect, in order to make
herself as homely as possible. When Bella Robson stepped
into the airport waiting room, she could see the expression
had become a permanent one. Her daughter, standing in a
crowd of strangers with her purple knitted hat pulled down
to just above her eyebrows, appeared to be on the lookout
for someone to punch.

"Well, he's not in the salt mines yet," she said, stepping
forward to take her mother's tote bag from her hand. Her
tone of voice made it clear that she didn't expect this state of
affairs to last long. "But I can tell that his phone's been
tapped."

Bella Robson felt her heart skip a beat but she kissed her
daughter's cheek and told herself to stay calm. "If you can
tell," she said, "it must be amateurs who are doing it."

Iris lifted her eyes to the ceiling. "If it's amateurs who
throw him in jail, will that be all right with you too?"

Bella Robson had neither the strength nor the courage
yet for any of this. Flying tended to leave her drained of
resources. Whenever she was forced to travel by plane —
family crises and the funerals of friends — she expected to
find herself in little charred pieces all over the side of a
mountain. As soon as she'd strapped the seat-belt across her
narrow lap, she always looked around for someone who was
prepared to listen, from take-off to landing, while she distracted herself with nonstop talk. A trip as long as this one
exhausted her.

"Besides," Iris said, moving towards the luggage carou-
sel, "the phone-tapping is incidental. What's at the bottom
of this is that woman." These highly educated university
types, she added, could be so naive.

Because driving was a recently acquired skill for Iris,

she sat right up at the front of her blue plush seat with one
hand clamped on either side of the steering wheel and her
face pushed forward to scowl at the road. Bella Robson had
never learned to drive — one lesson, soon after she'd been
widowed, had left her a nervous wreck — but she could tell
that Iris was just barely in control of the car. Had she flown
all this way to be killed in an automobile accident? To keep
from thinking about such things, she concentrated on what
she could see outside. Though she'd left a morning rain-
storm beating down on her garden at home, where her
dark-red dahlias were still the envy of the neighbourhood,
the light here was already fading from what appeared to be
a perfectly cloudless sky. They drove through patches of
short, half-naked trees in the direction of buildings she
could see up ahead, while Iris filled her in on what she
knew of this emergency which had flung itself on the family.
"It started when that damn university invited some big-shot
visiting Russian professor to lunch and made the mistake of
including James. This woman was there as his translator."

"She works for the embassy?"

"Her father works for the embassy. She calls herself a
poet. Sometimes if they need her she translates. She hangs
around the university now, they talk about books, she's got
him convinced he wants to do a lecture tour of the Soviet
Union. Can you imagine? Obviously she's a spy."

Bella Robson ignored what she was not prepared to
handle. "And she's what? . . . beautiful?"

Iris cut her eyes so sharply at her mother that the car
dropped off the pavement onto the gravel. "He *says* she's
beautiful." She fought with the steering wheel until they
were up on pavement again. "I haven't seen her but I'll bet
she's got greasy hair pulled back in a bun, and a jaw like a
man. You know what they're like."

Bella Robson was not at all sure she was equipped to
handle this. Like any other mother, she felt her fighting
instincts rise when her son was in danger, but the fact of the
matter was that she had always been a timid woman, easily
frightened. Even when her husband had been alive, it took

no more than a threat of changing weather to make her jumpy. Uncertain profits in his import shop kept her awake at night. When he died and left the shop to her it was even worse. News of an international emergency could send her to bed with a fluttering heart, she had to sell the business. It was the price she paid for being a person who felt things deeply, she supposed, and tried to be thankful she wasn't one of those calloused women who took everything in their stride.

But one of those calloused women, faced with a son who was tinkering with dynamite, might have been less inclined to feel helpless. Bella Robson had no idea what she would do now that she was here. She wasn't even sure why she had come, except that she knew it would have been even worse to stay at home, where she would become the victim of her over-active imagination.

The only way to handle James was to let him have it with both barrels, Iris suggested as they approached the tall downtown buildings. He was too smart to be convinced by logic, and too bull-headed to admit he was wrong, and too innocent to see for himself the danger he was getting into. Though he was already at an age when most men were married, fathers of growing children, and making responsible decisions, James was just an overgrown baby and had to be shocked into realizing how dangerous the world could be. She would do it herself, of course, but she knew he paid her about as much attention as he paid to a flea. "What he needs," she said "is to have his mother come along and slap him down, knock some sense into his stupid head for a change."

Bella Robson looked at her hands. When she thought of trying to slap her big husky son with these — parchment skin pulled over bones — she had to laugh. Sometimes she believed her skeleton was actually made of ice crystals, and would shatter easily on impact, collapse in a heap of splintery fragments inside her tightening skin. "What he needs is to meet a girl," she said. "Someone with an education."

Iris looked at her mother and sucked the air through her

teeth. "That's why you're here," she said. "He's already met one."

After crossing the canal, they started down a street that was lined with trees whose leaves were a deep rusty gold. Bella Robson supposed she had arrived at the end of their famous eastern fall and ought to make an effort to appreciate the leaves. You saw so many of them in paintings and postcards and calendars that you forgot you weren't able to see them through your windows at home. What she looked for and couldn't find was sign of some flowers blooming. Front-yard gardens seemed to be nothing but black broken stalks, but surely even here there'd be something still alive. Chrysanths, she knew, would bloom after frost, or didn't these people know?

More noticeable than leaves or blackened gardens were the signs in French. She recognized the *université d'Ottawa* from James's new letterhead, but what was *L'auberge* supposed to be? Of course, she knew better than to bring the matter up with Iris; it would only provide her with an occasion for one of her remarks about West Coast bigotry. Though she hadn't been able to speak a word of French when she arrived in this city, Iris now bragged that she never watched any television channel but the French one. She called it the francophone station. Feeling vaguely threatened by the idea, Bella Robson wondered if she was losing both son *and* daughter to forces she couldn't combat.

Eventually they pulled up to the curb in front of an enormous building and stopped. "Of course, you can see he had to pick the oldest and ugliest apartment block in the city. He's the only person in it under eighty. Says it's quiet. One of these days it'll fall down on his head!"

The building didn't appear to be in much danger of falling; it looked, with its thick brown columns and yellow brick walls, as if it intended to sit there forever. Brick buildings of any kind always looked permanent and settled to Bella Robson. She reminded her daughter that James had chosen the place for its location more than anything else, in order to be close to the foreign embassies.

"Well, we know what that's led to, don't we."

Iris pointed out the Embassy of the Soviet Union just two blocks down the street, a large cement-grey building behind a black iron fence, as stark and unimaginative as a prison. Bella Robson felt a chill settle into her bones. Were there guards? If she squinted would she be able to see their guns? She had a vision of her son stepping through that gate for the last time, never to be heard from again. Did they shoot their people right on the property, or send them to Russia first?

When they stepped off the creaky old-fashioned elevator, James — who had been alerted by their buzz at the outside door — was standing in the hallway, waiting for her with his little-boy grin on his face. Though he was more than six feet tall and stocky like his father — no chandelier of bird bones like his mother — he still knew how to look like a six-year-old when he wanted to. A sheepish grin, the hangdog pose, the uncombed hair: a mother couldn't resist. Bella Robson gave a small peep and forgot her reason for coming — she hurried forward at a tilt to fling herself into his arms. It was all she could do to keep herself from blubbering.

He held her at arm's length and frowned. "Haven't you had anything to eat since I saw you last? Mother, you're as thin as a stick. Have you caught the plague?"

She'd never been any heavier than she was right now but he'd always liked to make fun. Thin as a stick indeed. "You know very well I keep myself like this on purpose. It's the skinny women who save the most at dress-shop sales." She turned and opened her coat for Iris. "This dress now, I paid a dollar for it on the junk table of a clearance sale. They figured nobody in the world was thin enough and it would have to be sold for scraps." She'd done some poor woman out of a dusting rag, she supposed, but look how nice it hung on her, with its pattern of pink petunias.

James groaned, as she knew he would, and put his hand over his eyes. Her talent for finding bargains had always embarrassed him. "You," she added, "seem to be healthy enough." And patted his stomach.

He was proud of his paunch and gave it a hefty slap. "Haven't been sick for years."

"Except mentally," Iris said. "But that's hardly news."

He twisted his mouth and rolled his eyes up to the ceiling of the hallway, as if to say he'd hoped for better from her but wasn't surprised. When the two of them had been small, Bella Robson had spent much of her time breaking up fights, but James had eventually learned to treat his sister as if she were an imbecile determined to show off her stupidity every chance she got.

"Iris may have a point, James," she said, remembering why she was here. "Am I supposed to believe what I hear about Russians?"

He chuckled and flipped his tie. You never saw James without a tartan necktie knotted perfectly at his throat. "Well, this is Ottawa, Mother, you know what I mean? Anyone with an I.Q. over sixty is in danger of dying from boredom here if he doesn't cook up an international intrigue to entertain himself." He giggled like a small boy, his body trembling. That, at least, hadn't changed.

But Iris cut his giggles short with an icy glare. "Do you still live *inside* or do you always entertain in the hall?"

Those were her last words for the evening. The apartment, when they stepped inside, was already occupied by two men and a young woman who looked up with curiosity at the intrusion. Iris hurried across the room with her shoulders hunched forward and threw herself into a corner chair. Slumped down with her arms crossed over her chest, she clamped her jaw like a fist and lowered her brows in a suspicious scowl.

Bella Robson, of course, was incapable of such deliberate rudeness. Iris's lack of manners had always forced her into situations where she had to be twice as friendly as usual, in order to make up for her daughter. She made a point of shaking hands with every person in the room. If they were professors like her son, then she knew she wasn't going to understand a word they said to her but at least they'd see that she knew how to conduct herself like a lady.

If they were students, then it could only help her son to have them see he came from decent stock.

They behaved, however, as if they didn't know good manners from bad, or care whether she was in the room or not. The long-haired woman who sat with her bare feet tucked up on the chesterfield (introduced by James as Doctor Mallory) craned her neck to see past Bella Robson in order to ask a man in a heavy turtle-neck sweater and a beard if he'd recovered yet from the death of Elizabeth Bishop. Bella Robson had never heard of anyone by that name but it was apparent from the look on the bearded man's face that her death had been an event of some importance. He would probably never recover, he said, shaking his head, nor did he want to recover. The world had lost one of the greats and didn't know it.

An emaciated young man sitting on the hardwood floor with his arms wrapped around his knees said that he had never read any of her poems, since she wasn't one of the seventeen poets he taught every year, but now that she was dead he was thinking of reading them and maybe adding her to his course. He'd been to Harvard too, he explained to Bella — but only for a year.

This apartment — what a contrast to the one in Cambridge! This was the same furniture, she could tell — the same bookshelves, the same lightweight couch — but the walls were such a dead chalk-white and the ceiling so high. The view out that one narrow window was of roof-tops and chimneys. Poor James must be missing his view of the Charles River and the Boston skyline, and that bridge.

When he sat on the arm of her chair, with his hand on her shoulder, she spoke with her voice as low as she could, so that she wouldn't be accused of interrupting the others. "I thought you'd be alone — since you knew we were coming, I understand."

James, however, didn't mind interrupting them at all. "Mother has flown in," he said, "in order to save me from a fate worse than death." He had always called her "Mother" — never "Mom" or anything else — and pronounced the

word as if it were a joke, in the way he used the word
"periodical" while holding one of her *Reader's Digests* between his fingers. "Mother is here to sabotage my plans to
wangle a lecture invitation to Russia." Everyone looked at
Bella Robson. "She thinks that once they get me there they'll
lock me up in a mental institution, force me to betray all my
country's important secrets, then march me out into the
snow to shoot me." He giggled and dropped his arm around
her neck to pull her close in a strangle-hold. To demonstrate, she supposed, that he was teasing. She tried to smile,
to let the others know she was used to being made fun of by
her son — it was part of her life.

"Oh, Mrs. Robson," the bearded one said, "you don't
want to go spoiling things for James." Was he to be taken
seriously? She couldn't tell. "He's worked so hard, I've
never seen anyone so desperate to get a free trip. Some
people," he added, cutting his eyes to the others, "will do
anything to get out of this city for a while."

While the others laughed, the barefooted woman crossed
the room to the bookcase. "Look at this," she said. "His
friend has already given him a gift. A plastic miniature of
the Pushkin Monument." She held it out towards Bella
Robson, who turned her head away. Was it feet she smelled?
It couldn't be. The girl was a university lecturer, and looked
so clean.

"Of course, we know it's bugged," said the man on the
floor, and again everyone laughed. Iris's face was tomato
red. She'd pulled her head down between her shoulders as
if she intended to imitate the exotic turtles her husband had
sleeping in the backyard mud. Her eyes smouldered around
the room and came to rest on Bella Robson, who shivered.

"Well I want you to know," Bella Robson said, looking
only at James and trying to keep her voice from trembling
too noticeably, "that I do not approve of any of this." She
clasped her hands together, in order to hide their shaking.
"International politics is not a game."

No one took her seriously. "Would you repeat what you
just said?" the woman said, holding the tiny Pushkin Mon-

ument in her face. Her feet *did* smell! "The microphone had
a little difficulty picking it up."

"Bugged by the KGB, tapped by the RCMP," the bearded
one said. "Your son is obviously an important man. You
don't want to halt a glorious career in the service of the
Motherland before it's even got started."

"Professor Robsonov!" the skinny man said. "Vot does it
mean, diss Troilus you 'ave come to our country to spik
about? Iss it a new kind of tractor for increasing the produc-
tion of Soviet wheat in the Ukraine?"

By now everyone in the room except Bella Robson and
Iris was screeching. James had his eyes squeezed shut and
his head thrown back, shaking like someone completely out
of control. When he threw himself forward, collapsed with
giggles, she could see there were tears on his face. "And . . .
and . . ." he could barely speak. "This Professor Robsonov,
hiss book iss a marvellous work of literachure, in code of
course, on bringing the glorious revolution to the decadent
campuses of North America. *'Troilus and Creseyde*, a great
Marxist tract!'" He fell right onto his knees and held his
shaking stomach.

As a child, she remembered, his talent had been for such
mockery. She'd even expected him to become an actor. As a
boy he could make himself helpless with laughter by imitating people he knew — sometimes silently behind their backs
— and then go on to put his parodies into imagined exaggerated situations that reduced himself and his howling
audience to tears. He had not changed his style in the
slightest, she saw, except to become a little more bizarre.
Certainly not what you expected from a professor of medieval literature, any more than this conversation was what
you expected to hear when university people got together.

If she wanted proof that her son had become a stranger
to her, she need only look at what he had hanging on his
walls. Bella Robson herself hung watercolours of flower
arrangements, and a collection of porcelain plates with painted scenes of gardens. Pictures were supposed to be something pretty to liven up a room. But James had put a bunch

of posters behind glass in expensive frames, as if this living room with its chalk-white walls were actually the lobby of a theatre, or an art gallery. Faces of people she didn't recognize floated behind the huge print of titles she'd never heard of — probably plays he'd seen while living in the States. Did he do this on purpose, to remind himself of all he was missing here?

There was something else, a little smaller, which required a closer look. Behind glass again, in an expensive-looking frame, above a shelf of books. A page of poetry? Since she was not interested in encouraging any more of what seemed to pass for conversation in this place, she stood up and excused herself to the bearded young man who was in her way, and tried to make out the script. It looked like the kind of thing they used to copy out in the olden-days, with fancy letters and brilliantly coloured designs around the edge.

> She seyde, "allas! for now is clene ago
> My name of trouthe in love, for evermo!
> For I have falsed oon the gentileste
> That evere was, and oon the worthieste!"

It didn't mean a thing to her, but just imagine the labour that went into such a project! "Fourteen monks died working on that thing," James said, coming up to stand behind her. Of course, she didn't believe him. Were there monks, even today, who devoted their lives to such painstaking work? She doubted it. This was more likely something done by a grateful student.

In a moment of silence, someone's footsteps creaked across the ceiling over her head. Bella Robson looked at her son. That broad forehead, those quick clear-seeing eyes — such an intelligent man — how had he let himself become so silly? "I'm panting for a decent cup of tea," she said. Perhaps these others could be encouraged, then, to go.

But their silliness continued when the tea was served. The woman wanted to know if the bakery cakes had been checked out carefully because she didn't want to go home

with an electronic tracing device in her stomach, and the
bearded man said he expected the Red Army Chorus to
knock down the door any minute and march in to sing a
little Soviet after-dinner music. "And perhaps a demonstra-
tion of peasant dancing." He squatted on his heels and
crossed his arms over his chest in order to give it a try but
fell on his behind the first time he kicked out a foot. The
skinny man who was already on the floor laughed so hard
that he choked on his cake and had to be slapped on the
back in order to start breathing properly again. James puffed
up like an important official and demanded that he be
purged from the Party at once for excessive laughter, which,
as everyone knew, was not allowed unless you were issued
a permit. The punishment, of course, was death. By the time
they'd finished their second cup of tea, Iris's face was nearly
purple and her eyes had disappeared altogether beneath her
glowering brow. Bella Robson sensed it was time to get out
of there, before her daughter decided to let fly with whatever
it was she'd been keeping bottled inside.

"I can see," she said, standing up, "that if we are to talk
at all, James, it will have to be some other time, when you're
alone."

With cheeks still wet from laughing, he hugged her and
promised they would get together tomorrow for a decent
talk. "I'll pick you up in the early afternoon," he said. They
would go for a drive up into the park, across the river, where
there'd be plenty of opportunity to talk while they admired
what was left of the leaves.

"Idiot!" Iris said, as soon as the door had clicked shut
and the two of them were alone in the narrow hallway.
"About ten years in a Siberian work camp ought to fix him
good!" She sounded as if it were something she prayed for
fervently.

Bella Robson knew, even as she headed for the elevator,
that James would already be entertaining his guests with
imitations of his mother. "I want you to know that I do not
approve of any of this." He had always been able to mimic
her in a way that made her look like a fool. Well, she hoped

they all laughed themselves sick at her expense in there; she would give him plenty more to mimic when she got him alone tomorrow in that park.

"When you get him alone," Iris said, "ask him what he will do if that woman shows up at his door and demands asylum. Ask him what will he do then, with bullets flying and the whole world watching on TV."

"Don't be silly," Bella Robson said. "It's only ballerinas do that kind of thing. For all we know she may even be a very nice girl."

She did not believe for a minute that it was possible for any Russian poet to be a very nice girl but she knew that Iris had to be dampened a bit. If she were encouraged too much to express her opinions she would simply work herself up into an unhealthy fury. Bella Robson was confident that once she had James to herself for a while she would be able to talk some sense into his stubborn head. Iris, unfortunately, tended to make him worse.

Iris, in fact, tried to stop her from going with James on the promised drive next day, when she saw through the living-room window that they would not be alone after all, that there were two other people already in the car. "He's trying to suck you right into the middle of his mess," she hissed, "and I just won't let you go."

Bella Robson was so frightened that she thought she might faint. After lying awake the whole night, imagining terrible things, she didn't have the strength for any of this. But she was also a mother and knew there were things you endured for the sake of your own son's safety. She would skin him alive, eventually, for pulling this stunt, but she would hold off on the fainting spell until later.

"Look at that creep," Iris said. "You can tell even from here that he's loaded the car with his Russians."

The young woman, it turned out, was not a Russian at all. She was an Armenian. Bella Robson had only a vague idea where Armenia was on the map but this was hardly the time to ask for geography lessons. Besides, she was too taken aback by the girl's beauty to think of anything else.

She had not been prepared for those large, shiny dark eyes, or that soft black hair, or those perfect teeth in an enchanting smile — oh, Iris was going to have a hard time with this. No greasy bun at the back of her head, no offensive smell. Instead, an absolute stunner. Hardly more than a girl — and so pretty, with just enough make-up to give an appearance of summery health to those perfect features. A woman of taste as well — that stylish black fur coat with its matching hat was exactly the kind of thing Bella Robson would want to buy if she lived in a climate like this. They made the Armenian girl look like a magazine model. If those people had sent her here with instructions to turn her son's head, they'd certainly picked the right woman for the job. Bella Robson found herself wanting to stare.

The man slouched into the far corner of the black seat, looking at her from inside a long-haired fur like a lion's mane, only grunted and twitched his long bony face when he was introduced. Vladimir Something-or-other. He was perhaps his country's most prestigious poet, James explained, just back with Marta from a two-week tour of the universities, reading his poetry. "He doesn't speak a word of English so she's been acting as his translator." Since the two of them had been visiting all the universities of the country and still not been across the river into Quebec, he said, it seemed selfish not to invite them along for the ride.

Naturally, Bella Robson thought. Why do something nice for your mother when you could be doing something nice for a couple of Soviet spies instead?

She would not say a word in the car, no matter how excitedly James rattled on about the buildings that lined the streets, or the spectacular river-view from the bridge, or the paved road that wound uphill into parkland past tiny lakes and steep humps of rock and banks of trees with only the last of their leaves still clinging to the branches. Let him go on. The girl in the back seat seemed to think it was all worth translating for the benefit of the grouch, whose only contribution was the occasional grunt. She herself was dying to turn around for a look out the back window, certain that she would see a car following them, at a safe distance of course, with two men in black hats pretending to be out for a scenic drive.

James, if he knew what she was thinking, would accuse her of too many movies. Still, when they got out of the car to admire the view from the top of a hill, she did venture a glance downhill in the direction from which they'd come. Nothing there. The two men were probably parked just around the corner. A rusty station wagon laboured up the hill and whooshed on past, but it was full of small children. Even Bella Robson doubted that these two were important enough to warrant that much camouflage. James, meanwhile, was excitedly showing off what could be seen below: right up the Ottawa Valley to their right, tiny farms and straight roads on the flat green land; the city itself to the left, with its bridges and Parliament Buildings and glass towers glittering like crystal miniatures in the sunlight. Oh, it was pretty — she was willing to admit she was looking at one of the beautiful cities of the world — but she was still too jittery to enjoy any of this.

"There it is," James said. He looked at Bella Robson and giggled. "Everything I gave up Boston for."

The girl took a camera out of her purse and clicked a picture. "To send my mother at home."

A likely story. "Mother" was the most obvious code of them all. You couldn't imagine a spy having a real mother at all.

In the parking lot below Mackenzie King's summer estate, James said he had better give the backseat passengers a short history lesson if this was going to make any sense. Why bother? Bella Robson suspected these people knew more about our politicians than she did. What they were making of all his talk about spiritualists and seances and the ruins imported from England, however, she didn't want to guess. And she had to close her eyes when she heard him admitting to these foreigners that the prime minister who'd left all these acres to the people for a park had been in the habit of consulting his dead mother on how to run the country. She imagined the big-shots in Moscow looking at one another and smirking.

Her son was an innocent, she knew, but just *how* innocent she couldn't tell. Was she a witness at this moment to his treachery? Ridiculous. This didn't happen to ordinary people. Yet, if he was prepared to make his country look foolish in front of outsiders, wouldn't he be prepared to do other things as well? She saw him being investigated by the RCMP. Already a spy? She saw him taking out Soviet citizenship. She would never see him again.

While they hauled themselves up the slope to the ruins, James hurried on ahead and greeted them from inside a semicircle of marble pillars that seemed to be attached to nothing else but the ground. Nothing, here, seemed connected to anything else. Pieces of broken walls planted here and there like sculptures on the grass. "Some of it from England," he said, "some of it from Ottawa, none of it related to this site or the man who brought them here." Chuckling, he jumped down and posed for the girl's camera in front of a piece of stone wall covered with red-leafed ivy.

The famous poet walked up to a piece of wall and took his glasses out of his pocket in order to peer at something. Was it a message carved by some earlier spy passing through? Or was he about to pass judgment on the workmanship? He pushed the top half of his body right through the window opening and examined something on the other side.

When James's eyes met Bella Robson's he was already beginning to giggle. "When I think of Boston!" The notion was apparently so funny that he threw up his hands and closed his eyes, shaking with laughter. "Oh, who needs Concord and Salem at your doorstep when you've got all *this!*" He doubled over and shook his head between his knees. Bella Robson knew what he was trying to say, but coming as she did from North Vancouver, where everything old was considered obscene and replaced by something new, she found ruins of any kind — even imported ones that made no sense — a little awe-inspiring. She placed her open hand on the rough surface of chilly stone, and shivered.

When the famous poet straightened up again, red leaves from the vines had attached themselves to the lion's mane that floated around his shoulders and a small forked twig had caught in his thinning hair. Whatever it was he said to the girl sounded like growls and snorts to Bella Robson but she supposed it was proper language. At any rate, the girl understood, because the colour of her face had definitely deepened. Had he said something embarrassing to her, or crude?

"What was that all about?" James said, trying to put a sober expression back on his face.

"Nothing," the girl said, quickly. "Nothing important."

Again an avalanche of horrible sound rolled off that tongue. This time the girl answered back, sharply, and he barked at her, even swung out one arm like a weapon.

"If that's nothing," James said, "I'd hate to see him get excited."

The girl studied the toes of her own shoes. "He says, ah, he does not think this is, ah, the most impressive tourist attraction he has, ah, ever seen."

Again laughter exploded from James. His face crumpled. "You mean it stinks." He dug into his pocket for a handkerchief and wiped the tears off his face. "Tell Vladimir that it isn't exactly the Winter Palace but what did he expect? This is Ottawa after all, you know what I mean?"

Bella Robson shivered again. The air up here was chilly. Tired from her sleepless night, alarmed by her son's reckless horseplay, she was in no condition to cope with the breath of an early winter. What she longed for most was to get home fast.

The famous poet hunched up close to the girl and spat words in her face. The girl smiled, and shook her head. "He says now he is, ah, prepared to, ah, move on to other sights. He is not the most patient man in the world."

She would pay for that comment. Probably with years of hard labour. Bella Robson had no doubt the poet understood English just as well as she did. He only wanted to be pampered. He looked like the kind of man who would pretend to be ignorant to have the pleasure of seeing others go out of their way on his behalf.

In the car, while they drove downhill through the park, Bella Robson decided to risk a few words to the girl. It would not do to have her report that West Coast people were impolite. And to tell the truth, she was beginning to feel sorry for her, having to put up with that grouch. "My son tells me," she said, turning in her seat, "that you write poetry yourself."

The girl seemed amazed that Bella Robson could speak. Colour again rushed to her cheeks, but she slipped a glance in the direction of the celebrity in the corner. "Oh yes," she said. "A few simple verses now and then. Nothing important." Hardly a trace of an accent.

"She's being modest," James said. "Her poems have been published in the best periodicals. Some have even won awards."

"My son used to write poetry," Bella Robson said.

Again the girl looked surprised, and glanced at the grouch. But James was quick to protest. "I was never a poet, Mother. I'm an academic, not an artist."

"I still have them," Bella Robson said. "Tucked away in a bottom drawer with his first shoes."

The girl smiled. "My mother too. She has my first innocent scribblings."

Bella Robson looked at the famous poet. These people heard what they wanted to hear. "James's poems were surprisingly patriotic for a small boy," she said. "He liked to write about his love of freedom and independence."

Her heart beat so hard from the shock of what she'd said — all perfectly true — that she was afraid to say another word in case her voice betrayed her by trembling. She turned around and faced the front of the car. Luckily, the grouch interrupted with another one of his long harangues full of spit and rumbling consonants. The girl leaned forward to speak to James. "He is saying that, ah, he does not want any more driving. I am sorry but he says, ah, that he wants to go back to the Embassy now."

I'm sure he does, Bella Robson thought. He may think he's got these other two fooled but he knows he hasn't convinced me for a minute. She gave him a quick steely look to show she was on to his game, the slob.

Once the two foreigners had been dropped off at the Embassy (would they have to file reports on her before they were allowed to eat?) James drove her to a restaurant decorated to look like the inside of a barn. "You can load up all you want at the salad bar," he said. Bella Robson was not much interested in food. The back of her neck ached, from the tension. She was letting herself get too worked up over this business. The best thing to do — despite the fact that she would normally drive ten miles out of her way to avoid any kind of conflict — was to have it out with him tonight, get it over with. There was no sense suffering like this any longer.

"Mother," he said, when he got back to the table with his own heaping plate. "You have the look of an evangelist about you. Have you come here to save my soul?"

"I've come here to save your hide," she said, and swallowed a slice of tomato. If she put it off now she would be putting it off forever. "Since you seem bent on risking it with your stubborn — your deliberate innocence."

"I don't believe you," he said, and raised a forkful of coleslaw to his lips. She knew that teasing look, but it didn't mean he was to be taken any less seriously. "I can see the fire of righteousness in your eyes. You've come here to straighten me out, I can tell, to save my soul from its wicked ways!"

She put down her fork. She would never be able to eat. She was on the verge of tears. Would he take nothing seriously at all? "You know very well that in all your life you've never heard me talk like that to you. You're being silly."

"Then I'm not interested in talking with you." He put his fork down and pushed his chair back and showed her his profile. "If you're not interested in anything more than saving my hide, then we have nothing to say to one another. What I need is someone with more courage than that."

She couldn't believe this. None of this kind of talk was familiar to her. He was leading her into territory more strange and frightening than any she'd been in before. It was cruel of him, to make her feel so helpless. What language did she have for saving souls?

Behind him a parade of waiters in black uniforms followed a birthday cake across the room to a table where a young woman in a white shawl put both hands up to her face to show her surprise. Feeling absolutely miserable, she watched the waiters form a circle around the table, hum a note, then roar into a chorus of the Happy Birthday song. First in English, then in French. Did they know how silly they looked?

When they'd bitten off the final note of their song and scattered to the different parts of the room, James turned and leaned his elbows on the table without looking up at her. With one hand he stirred his fork around in his lettuce. She thought she saw a few grey hairs on the top of his uncombed mop but she was reluctant to lean forward for a closer look. "Mother, I dreamed last night I was back in Harvard."

"Then go back," she said. Was the solution so simple? "At least there you weren't tempted by embassies."

"I dreamed I was back in Harvard. I dream this regularly. People were nice to me. I actually got invited to parties. I went to brand-new plays and talked to people about books that weren't even in paperback yet and met people who cared what went on in the rest of the world. I met young single women who found me attractive."

"You're too perverse to go back," she said. "You were happy there and so you couldn't allow yourself to go back. You could be just as happy here but you'd rather be a martyr. Are you in love with this girl?"

He raised his eyes to look at her, as if the question needed to be weighed. "What?"

"The Russian . . . the Armenian . . . whatsername." Her heart beat dangerously. Did she really want to hear his answer to this?

"Mother," he said. "I've been trying to tell you. I want to

like this place but I'm lonely here. A person does what he can to entertain himself. She's a beautiful woman."

"And that's all?"

He began to giggle. "You look so serious."

"This *is* serious."

He made the sound in his throat that showed he was willing to swallow his laughter. "Then Mother dear . . . ," he reached across the table to take one of her hands in his, but she snatched it away . . . "Since you refuse to wrestle with my soul and nothing more is expected of me than reassurance — yes, yes, that's all it is. She's pretty. I like pretty women. She likes my company. That's all. We've never even been out on a proper date. It's thanks to her that I haven't yet jumped off a bridge, but that doesn't mean I intend to elope."

She stood up and hurried into the ladies' washroom where she leaned against the wall and bit her lip. Was it as simple as that? She wanted to believe so. Had all her terror been nothing more than the result of Iris's imagination? She hadn't realized just how scared she'd been until she saw her face in the mirror. If she let go and started crying she'd be here for hours.

When she'd blown her nose and splashed cold water on her face and returned to the table, James pulled a white envelope out of the inside pocket of his tweed jacket. "You and I have got ourselves an invitation." He slipped a card out of the envelope and glanced over the fancy black script. "Tomorrow," he said, and handed the card to her. "This may not be the best moment to give it to you, but you've got to admit it'll be something to tell the old girls back home."

Was she making no progress at all? This thing had a gold-embossed hammer and sickle at the top. The problem was to keep herself breathing while she read it. "On the occasion of the 62nd Anniversary of the Great October Socialist Revolution . . . The Ambassador of the Union of Soviet Socialist Republics requests the pleasure . . ." She closed her eyes. Of course this must be a joke. "You can't be serious." If he only knew how her heart was beating now.

"Forty thousand horses couldn't drag me into that place."

Even her distress — surely it was obvious — was something he could chuckle about. "You want to find out what it's like to live in a capital city, then go and find out. Rub shoulders with the diplomatic set. I'll be there to rescue you if someone tries to send you to Vladivostok for a holiday. It's only a boring stand-up thing, at lunch. And later there'll be smiling-Vladimir's poetry reading at the university."

She looked at her own small hands, feeling — oh, so fragile. "You want me to go home and tell people that I attended a party celebrating the slaughter of the Czar and his family and who knows how many thousands of people since?"

"Don't be childish," he said. "We send our musicians over there to play for them, they send their poets here. Things have changed, it's not the way it used to be." He studied his hands. His father's hands. "Mother, I'll be going whether you go with me or not."

"I don't want you to go," she said, making an attempt to sound stern. Something had to stop him and it seemed to be left to her. "This game you're playing has gone on long enough, it's getting foolish." Her voice, however, betrayed her. Anyone could have told she was ready to cry.

"But I'm going anyway," he said, turning his hands over to examine their palms. "I'm going anyway without you so there's no point talking about it any more."

"Then you were lying to me?"

He laced the fingers of his two hands together and rested them under his chin. "Lying?"

"About this girl. You were lying. I can't believe you would go ahead and attend this thing when you can see how much it upsets me unless the girl means more to you than you've admitted."

"Mother," he said, and for a moment it looked as if he were having trouble breathing. He looked down, looked over his shoulder, closed his eyes. "Mother, what am I going to do?"

She felt as if a leg had dropped off her chair, or the floor had tilted. Was she about to faint? When he looked up at her now, she saw in his eyes everything she'd hoped she would never see in her life. Things were even worse than she had originally feared.

"He's in love," she told Iris, the minute she got in the door. She stood in the hallway, stunned, while Iris stripped off her coat. Then she allowed herself to be guided to a chair.

Iris looked as if she were prepared to drive her fist through the wall. "That idiot," she said. "Ask him why doesn't he read the newspapers some time. Ask him if he's never heard of Czechoslovakia. Or Hungary."

"He cried," Bella Robson said. "When we got back in his car he broke down and cried. This is horrible. The boy is in love."

"Tell him to stop reading so many of his sappy books and smarten up. Ask him where is his backbone. Ask him if he's forgotten he's got a family that doesn't want to be dragged into this." She crossed her arms and pulled up her bottom lip and threw herself so fiercely into a chair that her feet left the floor. "He's in love! Ha! A few years on a collective farm ought to cure him of that!"

Of course, Iris washed her hands of the whole affair when Bella Robson told her she was going to an Embassy party tomorrow — she *had* to go, though she was perfectly terrified at the prospect. If it weren't that James's life was at stake, she said, she would have chosen to fly home on the first plane pointing west. If she wasn't such a pushover, Iris said, she'd have torn up the invitation, laid into the girl for all she was worth, and threatened to disown James if he didn't change his ways.

Walking down Laurier Avenue the following day she would have turned and fled when she saw the newspaper photographers around the gate to the Embassy if it hadn't been for James's hand on her arm. One of those photographers was bound to be working for the police, collecting a file of people who attended a party like this. Just wait until the next time she applied for a passport. James's strong hand, however, moved her forward and guided her in through the narrow gate in the black iron fence. *Before and after*, she thought. This was one of those moments when you knew your life would never be the same again. Her whole body shuddered. Grey walls, grey steps, small identical windows. Was this how prisoners felt being led into prison — as if they were actually stepping out of their own familiar skin and into a stranger's?

This stranger she'd become was prepared for the gruff man who welcomed them at the door, and for the sullen-faced youth who showed her where to hand over her coat, but was not prepared for the sight of the little room off the foyer where a man sat watching a panel of . . . three, six, was it nine? . . . television monitors. One she could see was trained on the gate. Another on the chauffeur-driven cars that pulled up outside. There was not enough time for her to get a good look at the others. Was one of them watching the prime minister's office? Was one of them, for that matter, watching James's apartment? The man who sat staring at the tiny blue screens glanced at her for a moment, from under heavy brows, then looked away. Why wasn't he ashamed to be caught doing what he was doing? Why didn't he shut the door?

The stranger she'd become was quick to forget the sinister television monitors when she found herself herded into a line that filed past the ambassador and some other official-looking men in uniforms. It was at a time like this that she missed her husband most, though he'd been dead now for fifteen years. Why wasn't he here to endure this terrible thing instead of her? He would have known what to say to these foreigners. He'd have known, for that matter, what to say to James, to smarten him up. All she seemed able to do was tremble with fear and rub her cold clammy hands together and hope that she wouldn't say precisely the wrong thing. When her name was announced, she walked forward with her heart beating painfully in her throat and shook hands with the ambassador (just exactly what she'd expected him to be, short and bald, with a chest plastered over with medals) and couldn't think of a single thing to say. The ambassador barely glanced at her, then turned to greet James, whose name had already been announced.

"Idiot!" She heard Iris's voice in her head. She'd missed her chance to tell that cocky little big-shot how she felt. But then — why deny it? — if she'd opened her mouth and told him her fears for her son he'd only think she was crazy.

A crazy woman was exactly what she was beginning to feel like, anyway. Who else but a crazy woman would have felt enormous relief to see the Armenian poet detach herself from the crowd in the adjoining room and hurry this way, smiling at Bella Robson like any good hostess who was surprised and pleased that a very special guest had arrived? Who else but a crazy woman would feel this rush of gratitude towards the very person she was here to protect her son from? Had she allowed herself to become so terrified, then, that even the face of the enemy was a welcome sight in this horrible place, this crowd? She delivered herself over to the girl with a small whimper and went through the motions of accepting a drink, eating something unidentifiable on a cracker offered her by a young woman in an apron, shaking hands with people whose names she forgot just as soon as she heard them. Here I am, brushing shoulders with people from every country in the world, she thought. But no flame of excitement leapt to life in her, as it might have in other circumstances. Here I am, she thought, inside the belly of this big grey machine that would like to digest us all, given a chance. These ordinary-looking people she was meeting, she knew, were the real-life equivalents of those sneaky-looking murderers and torturers she'd learned so easily to hate in the stories she watched on her television set. They were hiding behind a mask of normality here, but she knew she was surrounded by cold-blooded killers, who would seduce her son and steal him away and destroy him. This wasn't a story she was watching, this was real.

Yet she couldn't deny she was glad to be led around the room and introduced to people who looked important. This one from Switzerland. That one from Peru. She didn't catch where the fat one was from, but she did like the way he kissed her fingers and admired her dress. For James's sake she resisted telling him she'd found it in a second-hand shop in West Vancouver, though it looked as if it were created just for her. An ivory background with rusty-yellow daisies. The tall long-nosed Englishman with the limp handshake seemed more interested in someone coming up behind Bella Robson, but fortunately the little man in the Red China uniform was willing to exchange a few words on the weather. It wasn't easy, in this crowd, to keep from spilling your drink down your dress, or backing into someone else, or putting your heel down on somebody's toe. "All stuffy diplomats," the girl whispered, "but maybe we can find an actor, or a musician. We have some here, you know, though not very many."

Neither the actors nor the musicians materialized, though it was enough just to know they were in the same room, or in one of these rooms. Eventually the girl left Bella Robson to her own devices while she went off to talk with James by the table of food. It was up to the officer in his pale-blue uniform and white hair to introduce himself, as he seemed intent on doing. "Colonel Viktor Kozhevnikov," he said. "Soviet Air Force." When he shook her hand, he leaned forward a little as if his instincts were to bow. When he stood upright again, light flashed off the rows of medals on his chest. They dangled like toy coins on ribbons. If she stole a quick look, would they really say "Hero" like those in the old cartoons?

Colonel? No one was going to believe this. No one was going to believe he took her empty glass from her hand and guided her, by the elbow, to the bar, where he had it refilled. No one was going to believe that, when he put it back in her hand, he said, in his perfect English, "In this crowd of stiff serious men, you stand out as so gracious, so feminine. Are you an ambassador's wife, or a new ambassador yourself that I haven't yet met? Why is it that we haven't met at these things before? Usually they are so boring, but I would remember someone like you."

Boring? When she was thumping with excitement? Was it possible for a Russian airman to be so handsome, and her own age as well? When he smiled, the skin crinkled out from the ends of his eyes. Blue eyes, exactly the colour of his uniform.

He wanted to know all about her. About her home, her family, her reason for being in Ottawa. All of it, everything she said, seemed to fascinate him. And what about him, did he have a family back home? Or were they here? He had one son who was an engineer, he told her, another a doctor. His wife was in Leningrad still. He seemed determined to tell her everything, his wife's brother's career in the foreign service, everything, but all she wanted to know about was those medals. Did she dare ask if these were Russian letters she saw on them, or pictures? Was a person allowed to ask such a thing, or touch them?

Well, why shouldn't she ask? And touch as well. "These decorations, you have so many, could you tell me what they're for?" With two fingers of her right hand she touched each one, flipped it a little to show that while she was impressed she wasn't all *that* impressed, and then felt their weight in her hand. "Did you have to risk your life for each of these?"

What had she done? Cold sweat broke out across her forehead. She couldn't hear a word that he was saying. Fingering a colonel's medals? People had probably been shot for even attempting such a thing. To his credit, and probably contrary to his training, he hadn't batted an eye at her vulgarity. Such a gentleman that he wasn't even allowing his eyes to show the contempt he must feel for her ignorance. A country woman, a westerner, a product of this soft society where familiarity had replaced respect. Her face burned. Every one of those medals seemed to deserve a long story but surely he could tell she wasn't listening.

"I must," she said, "find my son."

"You are not well?" His hand touched her arm.

"No. No. But I promised . . . I must see where he got to . . . I'll be back . . . I'll be just . . ." Oh, but she had to escape.

Luckily James was in another room, on a chesterfield pushed up against the sheer curtains of a window that looked down on a park. And a river. She was glad just to sit and pretend she was part of this conversation. He was listening to the girl, who appeared to be a little upset. What had gone wrong? "He is," she was saying, and had to search for an appropriate word. Her eyes, when they swept past Bella Robson, did not acknowledge her. "He is quite obviously a horrible man. You could see that, surely, during our yesterday's drive."

Bella Robson looked at James. Presumably they were talking about that Vladimir. But was this allowed? Wasn't she afraid the microphones hidden behind those paintings would pick up what she was saying? James, thank goodness, seemed to have the sense to keep his own mouth shut. For a change.

"He says the most outrageous things and then I'm expected to translate in a manner that won't offend. He drinks too much. All across your country. Every place we went. He said terrible things. To me, to our hosts, to the poets who had come to meet him. I wore myself out, ah, trying to think of ways of saying these things politely, in English. Politeness — politeness is so important and yet so exhausting! Fortunately no one, anywhere, seemed to understand very much Russian."

"Like what?" James said. "What kind of thing did he say?"

I don't want to hear this, Bella Robson thought. There are things I am better off not hearing. But where could she go? Back to the airman and his medals? She could stare at the embossed wallpaper only so long.

"Like this." The girl cast a glance around the room, perfectly aware that she shouldn't have been saying any of this. "In Vancouver, I find myself trying to find a polite way of saying that he thought this country was full of ignorant peasants, incapable of appreciating a poet of his own importance."

"And what did you say?"

She smiled. "That this is such a young country, so close yet to the soil, that it must be very difficult sometimes to appreciate a foreign poet who writes of very esoteric matters."

James laughed. "Well done! You'll make a diplomat yet."

"In Calgary," she said, "he told a gathering of young academics and poets that he had never seen such an ugly city in his life, nor confronted such a collection of homely faces gaping at him like stupid pigs. He does it, I think, to annoy me. He knows I couldn't possibly tell them the truth."

Then why are you telling us? Bella Robson squirmed. Was it already taken for granted that James, and she too, were insiders, sympathizers? That they would not repeat any of this?

"It would serve him right," James said, "if you translated him literally some time. Let people see what kind of a man he is."

She pulled a face to show mock alarm. "The purpose of these cultural exchanges is to promote understanding and sympathy. Do you want to be responsible for destroying that?"

"I suppose," James said, "that we have to make some allowances for genius."

Bella Robson stood up. It was time they left. Some others, she saw, had gone to collect their coats.

The girl smiled ironically, "The drunken nonsense of a giant talent may have some tragic dignity to it but the same behaviour in a man of only a tiny talent is pitiful."

"But this man . . . he is one of your best?"

"Did I say that? In fact he is barely known at home. Our best people do not get sent to the, ah, smaller countries. It is not something to be offended about, it is only natural."

A minor poet! Just as Bella Robson had suspected! Before going downstairs for her coat she made a point of searching through the crowd until she found him. There he was, in a corner, lording it over a bunch of admirers. Who was translating now? The mushroom-coloured carpet was

littered around their feet with bits of food and abandoned
toothpicks. Did she recognize a Member of Parliament in his
audience? What a stupe, to fawn over this silly impostor.
When the poet's eyes flickered her way, she cocked her nose
at him and swung on her heel. Let him see that not everyone
in this country was so easily impressed.

Before she escaped, however, the colonel left a conversation of his own to intercept her. Was he going to give her a
lecture on protocol? "I can see in your face that you are
determined to leave," he said, standing directly between
her and the door. He stuck out his hand and, before she
could think, she was shaking it. "Please," he said — and
crinkled those eyes up again, so attractively — "We will see
you later, surely, at the poetry reading?"

Flustered, she answered "Yes." She'd had no intention
of going anywhere near the stupid reading. "Yes," she said.
"I'll be there."

He still held her hand, and pumped it again, while he
gave her a little bow. The hair on the top of his head — so
white! And she could hardly believe that he wasn't laughing at her for her faux pas with his decorations. A man with
class. "I shall look for you there," he said, and released her.
God help her, she felt this urge to finger his medals again.

The man at the television monitors was still doing his
job when she stopped outside his door for James to pick up
a number of colourful travel pamphlets from a table. Somehow he seemed a little less sinister now. People who travelled in international circles surely were used to such
things. When you lived in a capital city and attended embassy parties you took such things in your stride. They
added colour to life.

So did the row of cars, lined up at the curb as far as the
corner and half a block down Laurier, though most of them
were black. All had red-and-white plates, however, and
chauffeurs who stood out in the sunshine, talking. As she
walked down the sidewalk with James, she pretended for a
moment that one of those limousines — way down at the
end — was waiting for her. One of the chauffeurs — that

chubby black man in a cap — would recognize her and rush around to open the door. When she got home, the first thing she would tell friends was about this party. Ottawa, she would say, was the only place in the world to live! Surrounded by embassies, by people in foreign costumes, by limousines with chauffeurs and red-and-white licence plates waiting at the curb. Where else could a person meet a white-haired colonel from Leningrad in a beautiful blue uniform covered with decorations, and that lovely smile? Was it only coincidence that Bella Robson, walking back to her son's apartment, saw a bank of rust chrysanthemums blooming in the garden of a Tudor house?

"So welcome back from exile, Comrade Robson," Iris said, in the hallway outside James's apartment. "I figured I'd meet you here in case you needed debriefing. Have they given you your party membership card?"

"Not yet," James said, as he searched for his key in his pockets, "but a certain air-force gentleman can hardly wait to show her the sights of Leningrad."

"You were listening!"

Well, was he? Hadn't he been in the other room the whole time after all? She couldn't tell from the way he laughed. She could tell by the look on Iris's face, however, that she must be blushing a little. Iris herself was the colour of plums.

"You flew three thousand miles to get yourself invited to there? You're as bad as *him*."

"She fell in love with about fifteen pounds of medals," James said, beginning to giggle. "I hope you didn't disturb the hidden camera when you fingered them."

Iris clenched her fists and shoved her face up close to her mother's. "If I was as wishy-washy as you two are I'd shoot myself."

"But think of all the fun you'd miss," James said, ushering them into his living room. "Your mother's only beginning to find out just how exciting this city is. Travel, as they say, can broaden the mind."

"That's only when there's a mind there in the first place."

Iris snatched a pamphlet from James's hand, glanced furiously at a few of the pages, and flung it against the wall. "Don't you two know anything? Don't you ever read? Don't you ever turn on a television set to watch the news? When I think of how they're down there right now laughing at you I want to curl up and die."

James suggested that instead of dying maybe she ought to come to the poetry reading this afternoon. "You and Vladimir," he said, "are a perfect pair." He winked at Bella Robson. "Don't you think, Mother, that once Iris meets Vladimir she too will be seduced?"

Seduced? Is that what she'd been — seduced?

"I intend to," Iris said. "It's obvious I'd better stick close to you two from now on, in case an adult is needed."

Seduced? Was James right — had that party only seduced her? Nothing else had changed, that was certain. Her son was still in love with a girl from behind the iron curtain. That was not as bad as it might have been a few years back, but still it was bad enough. She would lose him. If he didn't disappear altogether, or get himself killed, he'd end up having trouble with the police, accused of spying, never being able to escape this part of his life. It would come back to haunt him in terrible ways some day. She'd read of such things, of lives ruined. Could she allow herself to be guilty of letting it happen? Suppose, after all, that Iris was right. She would never forgive herself. Fifteen pounds of medals indeed! How many villages had that smooth old white-haired killer bombed? Did he smile his crinkly smile as he pulled the lever to wipe out hundreds of lives? If he showed up at the reading she would snub him as surely as she'd already snubbed the poet.

Yet, when she came into that university room — already nearly full — and he stood up, smiling, to shake her hand again, how could she carry through with her threat? Bella Robson, above everything else, was polite. Even fighting mad as she was now, she couldn't bear the thought of hurting the feelings of anyone who had been nice to her. Especially since he'd somehow managed to save three armchairs in the front row, and escorted her down the aisle at his side. Still, she made sure that Iris sat in the seat between them. If he thought she was so easily won over, it wouldn't hurt him to look at her across the formidable expression on Iris's clamped-shut face.

Beside her, a student in blue jeans and unlaced running shoes saw that James had been left without a seat and scrambled over the back of his chair to the row behind. "Sit down, Doctor Robson," he said, with such deference that Bella Robson turned to see if he mocked. He didn't. It was obvious the boy looked up to her son. Imagine! The first time she'd ever heard him talked to in that manner, and called Doctor too. She smiled at the boy, and nodded her gratitude. It was nice, amongst other things, to discover there were still some young people with manners.

"You can't deny she's beautiful," James said, leaning across Bella Robson to address Iris. He tilted his head in the direction of the table at the front of the room, where the poet was already seated and the girl was taking off her fur hat and shedding that gorgeous coat. "I bet you'd give your right arm to look like that. Or own that stunning dress."

Iris snorted. "Probably made from human skin."

James reddened and looked at her as he might if she'd been a worm in his salad. "When your I.Q. hits fifty, sell!" He threw himself back in his chair with such force that he tilted back almost into the lap of the student, who gently pushed him ahead.

Iris's eyes, narrowed to tiny slits, did not shift from the girl on the platform. "Human skin stripped from her own mother's hide."

Was Bella Robson about to take up her life's role as referee again? Apparently not. The bearded young man from James's apartment stood up at the front and started the introductions. He introduced someone from the embassy, a stumpy man in a striped suit standing at the back of the room. He introduced someone from the English department — the woman who'd been with him in James's apartment all dressed up in a tailored suit, with that long hair pulled back

in a bun. Was she wearing shoes? Whether she wore them or
not, they learned that she was an expert on Russian literature, and had in fact been partly responsible for the great
honour of today's visit by this leading light of contemporary
Soviet Literature. Finally, he introduced the poet himself, in
terms so glowing you could swear he was trying to wipe
that terrible frown off the old grouch's face. It didn't work.
And, of course, his translator for the occasion. Bella Robson
was sure her son would have done a better job. He would
know better, for one thing, than to pick at the seat of his
pants while he talked. She liked to believe he would also
have taken care to avoid catching his toe on the microphone
cord as he stepped aside for the poet to begin.

Whether James stayed around long enough to have the
opportunity to do such things would be up to her. When the
poet stood up behind the table, she saw the phrase *Bella
Robson vs. the Soviet Bloc* flash vividly across the front of
her skull. She crossed her arms, settled back, and tried to
control her breathing. She was afraid, of course, but she'd
once sent a husband off to war, and worked in a factory
while he was gone; she knew there were times when you
couldn't afford to listen to your timid little soul.

The poet (oh, he didn't need to think he was fooling her,
the phony) scrunched up his little pig eyes and peered at a
book. For several minutes he read, making sounds that might
have been describing the noise of a tractor breaking down.
Though you couldn't understand the words, you could have
a good hard look at the man himself — the long bony face,
the dandruff on his shoulders, the suit that looked as if it
hadn't been pressed since his wife put him on the plane in
Russia weeks ago. Bella Robson had never been to a poetry
reading before and tried to sneak a look at others around the
room, to see how they were taking it. Did the glazed-over
eyes mean they were entranced, or almost asleep? It was hot
in here, she noticed, much too hot; and everyone was shoved
so close together. People sat inside their own shed coats and
steamed.

When the poet paused and loosed the phlegm in his

throat, the girl read in English from a piece of paper. What
had sounded like a dying tractor turned out to be children
on a lazy summer day helping their father cut hay in the
field. The poet watched her as if he hoped to catch her
falsifying the translation. What he couldn't see, the old fart,
was that she read his poem more beautifully than it deserved. And looked more lovely doing it than he had any
right to expect. If James had seen her like this before, no
wonder he'd fallen in love. You'd have to be a stone not to
feel attracted to her, no matter what you thought.

"That's one down," Iris said, out of the side of her
mouth. "Three cheers for the proletariat."

The poet and the girl alternated for the next hour. Every
poem sounded the same to Bella Robson in the original
language, but it turned out that while one was about a dying
mother, the next was about a factory, and the following one
about the birth of an idea. All of them sounded to her, even
in the girl's melodious voice, a little pushy. They forced
themselves on you, as if you had no right to disagree.

About the time her bony behind was beginning to complain about sitting so long, the poet sat down and the
woman professor stood up to ask if there were any questions. So dignified and professorial now, you'd never guess
she had smelly feet. She'd decided to ask the first question
herself, she said, and naturally it was in such high-falutin
literary language that Bella Robson had no idea what she
said. The girl, however, seemed willing to take a stab at it,
and muttered something into the poet's ear. Without looking up he muttered something back. No more than three
staccato words. "He says," the girl said, "that while your
question is very, ah, interesting, it is basically irrelevant
because, ah, the literary traditions in our country and, ah,
your country are so different. To answer that question in the
manner it deserves, he says, he would have to write an
entire book." Amazing how that man had been able to say so
much in just a few little words.

Other questions were easier to understand. Questions of
rhyme, of rhythm, of imagery. Was this what it was like to be

a student? Bella Robson had a question of her own that she'd like to ask: was he his country's leading poet or in fact a third-rate has-been they'd dragged out of retirement for the sake of a cultural exchange program? Of course she would never dare.

What someone else with more courage *did* ask seemed to be giving the girl some difficulty. Would the famous poet not have preferred doing his tour in the country just south of our border? Even after the poet had finished a long complicated answer full of arm-waving and snarls, she frowned over her hands, trying to find the right words. Her face was flushed. Eventually, she looked up. "He says, ah, he says the United States of America is not number one of his list of, ah, preferred places."

James put a hand over his mouth. His body was shaking. Was he about to get the giggles again — a respected professor making a spectacle of himself in this room? The next question, unfortunately, was not the kind to sober him up. Someone wanted to know if the poet had any observations to make about his visit to Ottawa. Would he like to comment on the capital of our country?

This time the girl's discomfort was obvious. Even before the poet had finished grumbling into her ear she looked alarmed. What was he telling her? Whatever it was, apparently, was not to be shared with them. "He says," she said, and paused for a long time — were there tears in her eyes? "He says, ah, he prefers the more how-do-you-say lively cities like Paris or Rome, but that, yes, it's very pretty, he likes the leaves, he likes the park."

"Is that what he really said?" Bella Robson asked. She'd intended it for James alone, but everyone looked at her. Some laughed. Was it really her own voice she had heard?

James tugged at her sleeve. "Mother, what are you doing?" He was in no danger of giggling now. Iris on the other side had slid down to sit on her neck. The colonel leaned forward to look at Bella Robson, his blue eyes puzzled. But Bella Robson, now that her chance had come, pretended she wasn't scared to death. "Are you telling us what he said?"

The girl looked down, looked away. "Another question, please?" There seemed to be someone at the opposite end of the room that she wished to encourage.

"Yes," that someone said, from behind a dozen heads. "I was wondering if Mr., uh, Mr., uh, I was wondering if our guest had any opinions he'd like to express about the culture he's encountered during his visit to this country. In other words, now that we've admired his poetry I'd like to ask him what he thinks of our poets?"

Again the girl muttered to the poet and again he shrugged and grumbled something back. He laced his hands together and looked at his lap while she answered. "He says, ah, thank you very much, yes, he enjoyed his visit to this country." The poet spluttered something into his lap that could have been a reprimand. Had she overstated his case? "He says, ah, that he enjoyed the poetry of your, ah, mountains, and the ah, music of your, ah, plains."

"Why doesn't she tell us what he really said?" Bella Robson asked James, in a voice that everyone else seemed to hear. Someone behind told her to be quiet, so she turned and said, "Well, do you think she's telling the truth?" The polite young student looked mortified.

"Shut up, Mother," James said, between his teeth. He was sweating. His face was red. "You'll be asked to leave."

Bella Robson tightened her lips. "Well, I just think if she's going to go to the bother of translating she could at least tell us what he said."

The poet let rip with another long string of growls and snarls, spit flying as far as the front row, where one fleck landed on the toe of James's shoe. Light winked in it and went out.

"Now he is saying," the girl said, looking straight at Bella Robson. She faltered, looked down, looked up again at Bella Robson and tried again. "Now he is calling me a cretinous bitch."

Bella Robson closed her eyes. What had she done? The room had fallen silent. James's hand squeezed her arm. "You," he said. "You." It was hot in here. She could barely stand the feel of her own clothes against her skin.

The poet had more to say. Did he know the girl was translating him accurately now? He seemed to be smiling. If he really understood English, as Bella Robson suspected, this must have been what he'd been working towards throughout his entire tour. From one end of the country to the other he'd hounded her, tried to see how far she could be pushed. Now, thanks to Bella Robson, she had finally broken down.

"Now he says," the girl said, "that I am a no-talent stupid Armenian whore." This time she spoke it to the whole room, in a clear, determined voice. "He says I couldn't write a decent line of poetry if I tried for a hundred years and that my hairy Armenian armpits smell of fear. He would like to, he says, he would like to breed me to his horse."

The colonel was standing up, protesting. One of his hands messed up his white hair. His face was angry, but at whom? The stumpy man in a striped business suit hurried up the aisle and turned, right in front of the girl, to address the audience. Apologies, apologies, he said. The translator had unfortunately been under a great deal of strain recently and was not to be held responsible for her indelicate remarks. Fortunately, the poetry reading had already come to an end, anyway, and if their kind and generous hosts at the university would permit, perhaps they could adjourn now for some coffee and refreshments.

"You," James said. "You." He leapt out of his chair and rushed up to the girl, who had remained sitting behind the table staring at the pieces of paper in her hands. When she looked up at him, it was with the expression of one looking at a total stranger. Bella Robson saw him reach out, as if to touch her, then pull back. Whatever she was saying to him she said softly enough that only he could hear, but it was the stumpy man in the suit and not James who escorted her from the room. Was he her father? James, left standing at the opposite end of the table from where the poet was surrounded now by a half-dozen people with books to sign, picked up her pieces of paper and put them into his pocket.

Bella Robson remained seated. If she had done what she

believed she had done, then why didn't she feel elated? How was she going to force herself to look into her own son's face?

It wasn't necessary, however. He refused to look at her. He walked them back to Iris's car and refused to get in. Iris offered him supper (her husband's favourite meat pies, a treat) but he said he would eat alone.

"Are you all right?" Bella Robson said.

"Don't baby him," Iris said, and started her engine. "Of course he's all right. The Scholar Learns a Lesson in Real Life. Let him eat alone."

"I'm all right," he said, and turned to walk away.

When she telephoned the following day, his "Yes?" seemed full of hope, but when he recognized her voice he sounded disappointed. Yes, he was still all right, he said. No, he didn't hold a grudge. Yes, he understood why she felt the way she did and had no intention at all of throwing himself in the river. He'd been trying to get through to the girl the whole morning, he said, but they acted as if they didn't understand what he said. He'd even walked down to the Embassy and pushed the buzzer at the gate but they behaved as if the name he gave them was something they'd never heard. Her father's office neglected to return his calls. He'd driven over to her apartment block but no one had answered the ring. What was he going to do?

"Tell him it's time to grow up," Iris said in the background. "Tell him it's time he took a good look at himself. It's not everyone who can afford to fool around like a kid well into his thirties. Tell him to take up bridge."

During the following week Iris took Bella on a day-long shopping binge through several shopping malls where she found gifts to take home to friends, and clothes for herself — all bargains she couldn't afford to pass up. Together they toured the National Gallery as well as several museums and the Mint. The two of them had lunch every day in a different downtown restaurant, and in the evenings they visited friends

with lovely homes in various parts of the city. By the end of
the week there seemed to be nothing for Bella Robson to do
but fly home to North Vancouver and devote herself to
tidying up her garden for the winter. Some of her dahlias
had been broken by the weight of excessive rain and even
the hardy marigolds seemed to have suffered from her absence. Down on her knees in her yellow raincoat — $2.99 at
a Woolco sale — she was glad to dig her hands into the damp
and fragrant soil again.

When friends stopped in to talk, she confessed that her
daughter lived in what was perhaps the prettiest city she'd
ever visited. And not at all as dull as they liked to claim. She
would move there tomorrow herself, she said, if it weren't
for their famous winters — and the fact that you couldn't
find flowers at the beginning of November. She told them
she'd recognized several Members of Parliament jogging
along the side of the canal in sweat-suits, red-faced and
panting, trying to pump the blood up into their brains. She
told them about the hiking trails up in Gatineau Park, where
you were surprised by sudden waterfalls and unexpected
look-out points. She told them about helping Iris shop for
her groceries at an outdoor market where she'd found
herself a bargain in honest-to-goodness local maple syrup.
She explained that a shopping centre was called a *centre
d'achats*. Of course, she did not neglect to mention that she
had attended a Russian Embassy party where she'd rubbed
shoulders with ambassadors and politicians and movie stars
and admired the medals on the chest of a colonel in the
Soviet Air Force, a perfect gentleman with the bluest eyes.
Naturally she did not mention James's unfortunate attach-
ment to the Armenian poet.

She tried not to worry any more about James. What good
would it do him now? What good would it do anyone for
that matter, including herself? She hadn't the language for
saving anyone's soul, whatever he meant by that. Saving his
mortal hide for a while was the best she could hope to do.
But despite her intentions, she felt that somehow James and
his complicated life had moved inside her while she was

there in Ottawa, and resided in her yet, like an uncomfortable dangerous weight that she couldn't dislodge.

And there was still Iris, and the telephone, to remind her. When it rang a few days after Christmas, she was startled out of the book she'd been reading to discover a long chain of armoured tanks parading across the screen of her television set. An invasion of some sort was on, but who was invading whom was still unclear, since she'd kept the volume low. Bearded guerrillas fired rifles down out of a snowy mountain and the tanks returned the fire. It was the early evening news, not a drama, but she'd allowed herself to get lost in an historical novel over her dinner and had forgotten the time.

"Mother?" As usual, Iris was angry. "Have you seen what his friends have done now?"

"What *whose* friends have done?" Was she expected to be able to read their minds? "Have you been talking to James? Has he heard from the girl?"

"Not a word." There was some gloating in the voice. That bloody Embassy behaved as if she'd never existed, Iris said. "You should hear the big boob whining. She hasn't written, she hasn't left him a message, she simply disappeared. Good riddance as far as I'm concerned. And now this. Surely you've heard. It's on the news from morning till night in both languages — they've invaded Afghanistan."

She supposed she was watching part of it now. The rows of tanks had halted. Soldiers were out strutting around. It seemed to be desert, but covered with a skiff of snow. Was that what an invasion was like — soldiers stretching their legs and stomping around in the snow? Did it happen like that? "And James?" she said. "Is he all right now?" She was a mother still, and would worry about those Afghanistan people tomorrow.

"He jokes," Iris said. "The fool. You know how he can't take anything serious for long — even this. When I called him he didn't even want to talk, but then he wanted to know if I thought our old friend Vladimir was in one of those tanks. He giggled and sputtered, you know what he's like, a twit. 'Watch out when they hit Kabul,' he says. 'That crazy poet will go bashing down their buildings right and left and have the ruins sent over here for Mackenzie King's collection!' "

"He doesn't really think it's funny," Bella Robson said. "He's just trying to cover up how he feels. Do you think I should phone him now, to see how he is?"

"He says it's all your fault. In his giggling and snorting and acting like a little retarded kid he says this whole thing is probably just a scheme to punish that poet, this whole invasion, and none of it would have happened if you hadn't exposed him here. The weight of this whole damn thing has to rest on your guilty shoulders. What do you think of that? Your son is a moron, Mother, you better forget him."

"Yes." She could watch it happening even while listening to Iris's voice. The parade of armoured tanks was moving again, like squat mechanical reptiles, across the plain. And now, as quick as blinking, a man who looked familiar held a microphone to his face and spoke some silent message in this direction. Behind him, people in colourful desert clothes strolled past the fronts of buildings that looked like the shops and markets of a city. Were these the people the tanks were heading for? If so, the man should be warning *them* instead of *her*. Like people anywhere they seemed to be going about their business as if they didn't know they could be surprised by an invasion at any given moment of their lives. When she turned on the television set tomorrow for the news, she'd be anxious to see how they were handling themselves once it came.

3

Mr. Pernouski's Dream

No wonder this woman couldn't take her eyes off Mr. Pernouski. With her knees almost touching his, he knew she could hardly fail to notice his tremendous size. He'd come to expect this kind of attention from strangers; he'd come to depend on it. Perhaps she'd never seen a person like him before, perhaps he was the fattest man this grey-haired lady had seen. Mr. Pernouski believed himself to be the largest person ever to ride these ferries. He hoped he was. Only a few minutes before, he'd made a joke for the young woman who'd sold him his ticket: "Maybe I should sit close to the centre of the boat, in order to keep things in balance?" The young woman had laughed, and said no, that it wasn't necessary, but if the ferry sank they would know who they ought to blame.

And he didn't sit in the middle, he sat here in a window seat on the starboard side, facing this elderly couple with the mess of cigarette butts on the carpet around their feet. The gentleman wore a hat with a wide felt brim and took several pictures of the waves that splashed against the ferry below the window, but the woman lit one cigarette off the

butt of another and watched Mr. Pernouski out of pale blue
eyes that squinted against her smoke. She watched him
finish a can of diet cola and begin a second. She watched
him riffle through a newspaper he'd found abandoned on
his seat. She watched him toss back several handfuls of
salted peanuts. Then, because Mr. Pernouski believed that a
ninety-minute ferry ride across the Strait of Georgia was
wasted time if you didn't make some useful contacts with
people, he washed the last of the peanuts down with diet
cola and sat back to level a long hard squint of his own in
the woman's direction. She neither flinched nor turned
away; she wrapped one long narrow leg around the other
and hugged herself while she sucked at her cigarette. Did
she think if she stared at him hard enough she would
discover the key to his size?

"You see that little sailboat out there, with the bright
green hull?" he said. "Got one exactly like it at home but I
never have time to use her. She's been in the water just once
in more than a year."

She frowned, peered out the window at the tiny boat
that leaned its narrow sail away from the ferry, and shuddered. "I wouldn't trust my life to a thing like that. For me,
this tub we're riding on is bad enough. I'd have felt safer in a
plane." She stuck the cigarette in the middle of her mouth,
sucked noisily, then jerked it out like a plug while she
inhaled.

"You folks are new to this part of the country, aren't
you? Tourists. Myself, I'm just returning to the Island from a
convention." And then, in case she thought of him in robes
and an Arab's hat: "Of salesmen."

He took her small nod as permission to continue. "You
expect outrageous things to happen at conventions. Sometimes that's why you attend — because you know outrageous things will happen there." Mr. Pernouski chuckled
to himself, then told the woman about poor old Swampy
Grogan, who'd got so drunk last night that he'd passed right
out. A number of his friends — Mr. Pernouski included
— had carried him up to his room, which overlooked the

harbour and had seagulls screeching and swooping around the balcony. "We stripped him down to the skin and laid him out on the bed. Then we opened the sliding glass doors to the balcony — this was Mr. Pimlott's idea — and made a trail of peanuts from out there across the carpet to the bed. We also left peanuts scattered on Swampy's bed and all over his sleeping body. When he woke up this morning . . ."

"Mmmmfff," the woman said, and closed her eyes.

"Well, I can see I don't have to tell you the rest."

She removed the cigarette from her mouth and held it between two long stained fingers. "Your colours," she said, "are rude."

Mr. Pernouski knew that she couldn't be referring to the colour of his suit, which was a conservative grey, so he lifted one foot to check on his socks. They too were grey. If she meant the orange of the vinyl seats on this ferry he was prepared to agree, but he saw no reason why he should take the blame.

"No no," she said. "I mean your *colours*." She gestured with the cigarette in the direction of the window, where her husband was aiming his camera. "Your greens are too green. Your blues. It's gaudy here, people must go blind. The trees are unnatural, and look — look at those mountains."

Mr. Pernouski glanced at the mountains of the island they were approaching, but they looked to him the same as they'd always looked — like mountains. They were part of his own back yard. Something more important than an attitude towards nature's colour scheme had been uncovered here, however, and he felt his instincts pounce. "You're from the prairies," he said.

The man put down his camera and looked at Mr. Pernouski. His wife permitted the smallest smile to flicker across her lips.

"Because of the way you keep taking pictures of the waves."

The man, who had not taken off his hat, stuck out his bottom lip. "We could be from the Yukon."

"And because of the skin," Mr. Pernouski added. "In my business you learn these things. The dry skin always gives them away. You've lived all your life in Saskatchewan.''

The woman puffed out another cloud of smoke, and raised her chin. "But I was born in Nebraska.''

"And because, sir,'' Mr. Pernouski said to the gentleman with the camera, "your wife has smoked seven cigarettes in a row, sitting directly under the No Smoking sign.''

The elderly couple, apparently so impressed with Mr. Pernouski that they did not challenge his logic, looked at the carpet where the woman had been grinding her cigarette stubs and matches under her heel. The gentleman pushed his hat back and looked up at the sign that hung from the ceiling above him. His wife took another cigarette from her package and lit it off the butt in her hand. "Silly rule,'' she said, and added the new butt to the mess at her feet.

Mr. Pernouski explained that the reason he had been so quick to recognize they were from the prairie provinces was that he was in real estate. He said that he saw thousands of people like them every year. They'd left farms behind, or shops. They'd finally retired, or sold everything, and could hardly wait to find a little house on the coast, or some property to build on, in order to escape the winters back home. He himself, he said, had been personally responsible for finding many of them the little retirement place they'd dreamed of. It was one of the rewards of his job. As a matter of fact, it was because he had an appointment this afternoon with a charming couple from Calgary that he was returning a day earlier than the rest of the conventioneers.

"Now what type of home were you folks hoping to find?'' he said. "I probably have just the thing.''

The woman unwrapped her left leg from around her right and pointed her toes. "We're visiting,'' she said. "We have friends here. We'll never stay.''

The gentleman lifted his camera to his eye and took a picture of Mr. Pernouski. People all over the lounge turned to see why there'd been a flash. The gentleman leaned forward and shook Mr. Pernouski's hand. "The name's Eckhart.''

"The name's Pernouski,'' Mr. Pernouski said, and reached

for one of his cards. "Eden Realty. You might say, without
fear of contradiction, that I'm the biggest man in real estate
on the Island."

While Mr. Eckhart stared at the little white card, Mr.
Pernouski said he always offered to pay double when he
rode the ferries, on account of his size. He patted his belly
to show what he meant. "The girl in the window told me
they have different fares for the various sizes of auto-
mobiles, but lucky for me only one for humans." Since the
elderly couple seemed reluctant to show an interest in his
bulk, he decided to tell them that he understood perfectly
why so many prairie people fell in love with this part of the
world and refused to leave. He'd been everywhere himself,
he said, and knew exactly what this island had to offer. He'd
been to Saskatoon and Regina and Thunder Bay. He'd also
been to Greece once, would you believe it, not long ago.
He'd won the trip by selling the most houses that year
of anyone in the office. He'd been down to Florida, and
Mexico, and over to whatsit, Taiwan. He knew what the rest
of the world was like so he also knew precisely why everyone everywhere would give a leg to live on this island they
were approaching. Climate was only half of it.

"We haven't been to many places ourselves," said Mr.
Eckhart, but his wife was quick to add: "Well, there was
Montana." She sounded annoyed, as if she resented telling
this stranger even that much about themselves. In case the
little couple thought he was bragging when he told about
all the places he'd been, Mr. Pernouski remarked that he
wasn't the only member of his family who travelled. His
wife Christina, in fact, had been to far more places than he
had. She was in Africa right this minute, on a buying trip.
Or more precisely — he glanced at his watch — she'd started
home but was stopping for a few days in Toronto where
she'd been asked to make a speech. Because they looked as
if they expected to hear even more, Mr. Pernouski explained
that shortly before she married him, a widower with three
growing children, his wife had bought an import shop once
owned by the husband of one of her sisters and become a

successful retailer on her own. Even after their marriage, while caring for his children, she expanded her business in a dramatic fashion until she owned a string of shops right across the country and had to travel abroad in order to select the merchandise herself. She was so successful that groups of businesswomen paid her to stop on her way through their towns and cities to make speeches on the secrets of her success.

Mr. Eckhart said he must be married to a most remarkable woman, but his wife pulled a small hardcover book out of her purse, and said she was going to read. She opened the book to where she'd turned a corner down and settled back in her seat. With eyes shifting back and forth across the pages, she kept her nose in the book while Mr. Pernouski and her husband talked about the price of homes and the differences in weather between the coast and the prairies. She didn't look up again until a voice came out of the ceiling to warn them they would soon be docking. Mr. Pernouski rode down the three flights of escalators with the Eckharts in order to help them find their car, which turned out to be an expensive late-model sedan with suitcases and cardboard boxes piled high in the back seat. He estimated that they would be in the market for something substantial when they came around, waterfront maybe, or a view home high up a hill. Mrs. Eckhart looked to him like the kind of woman who would demand that her husband buy her only the best. "You've got my card," he said. "You know where you can find me if you want." Before he shut the little woman's door, however, he asked them if he couldn't have the address of their friends, in case he needed to get in touch with them for some reason or other in the next few days. Mrs. Eckhart laughed and said she couldn't imagine what reason he might have for wanting to contact them, and shut her door herself.

Nevertheless you'll be seeing me again, Mr. Pernouski thought. He had no doubts about that. For him it was a matter of principle that no ninety-minute ferry ride across the strait be wasted time. He didn't intend to let today be any exception. While he hurried forward up the ramp and into a light gusting rain, he sorted in his mind through various listings he was responsible for, in search of the one which would be exactly right for the Eckharts.

Mr. Pernouski's determination was not something he could easily explain to his son, who had only recently got into the business of selling real estate himself and had much to learn. The boy insisted he had no desire to be Number One Salesman of Anywhere like his father, he simply liked his work. He claimed that he enjoyed the company of the people he met and the satisfaction of finding them what they wanted. It was clear to Mr. Pernouski that the boy hadn't learned a thing from his father's example.

Still, he spent most of dinner telling his family about the convention. You can always count on something outrageous to happen, he said, and told them about sprinkling peanuts all over Swampy Grogan's body in his hotel room so the seagulls would come in while he was sleeping.

"EEEeeeeee!" The twins pulled faces at one another and squealed. They wanted to know if he had a shower before he came down to breakfast.

"Of course he did, but boy was he ever mad!"

Mr. Pernouski's son said that Swampy Grogan must be one hell of a grouch. No sense of humour at all. "A real son-of-a-bitch, eh, not to think it was funny to have seagull shit on his body and smeared all over his face."

Mr. Pernouski had learned long ago to ignore the sarcasm in his son's voice. He said he didn't know why Swampy Grogan ever went to these things since he certainly wasn't any great shakes as a salesman. "If he ever sells a house it's just because no other salesman's around and the customer's begging for it." Mr. Pernouski's son said he ought to be glad of that, at least there was no danger of Swampy Grogan pushing him out of the Number One spot in the foreseeable future.

Mr. Pernouski said that this year every person in that convention hall recognized him without an introduction. Even old Pimlott from West Vancouver forgot his snootiness and treated him like the star he was. They couldn't ignore him now. When you were Number One Salesman on the Island, even mainlanders had to sit up and take notice. Everybody wanted to congratulate him, as if they'd only now discovered he'd held the position for five years in a row. Everybody wanted to know his secret. He was a hero. Naturally he enjoyed every minute of the convention and nothing short of an appointment with a potential buyer from Calgary could have pulled him away.

Without looking up from his plate, his son said he was sure all of Calgary was grateful for the fantastic goddam sacrifice that had been made.

Mr. Pernouski's voice took on an impatient edge. "Look. That's exactly the difference between Number One and all those others." While he was over here selling a hundred-thousand-dollar house to a retired druggist from Calgary, he said, Number Two and Number Three-hundred-and-two were still over there having a good time.

"Oh wow!" His son pushed away from the table and took his dishes to the sink. "I imagine we can count on you to let Number Two and Number Three-hundred-and-two know what stupid assholes they've been."

Rather than call him back for an argument, Mr. Pernouski reminded himself that this was the same person who'd run away to live in a commune for six months only a couple of years ago. His first job after that had been on a tugboat hauling barges up and down the strait, where he'd turned himself into a legend by regularly stripping to the skin and parading around the deck of his boat in sunlight playing a flute. How much did you expect from a boy who behaved like that? He still smoked an incredible amount of something he liked to call "the green stuff" which he grew in an attic window. That such a boy should agree to try a job like selling real estate was something in itself to be grateful for, and Mr. Pernouski knew better than to push his luck too far. As his wife was fond of saying, you didn't count on miracles to happen overnight, you just went on trying to set a good example.

He was reminded, now, that this was the day his wife

was to make her big speech. "Think of me when I'm in Toronto," she'd written. "You know how nervous I get." While the twins washed up the dishes, Mr. Pernouski found her most recent letter and carried it into his bedroom where he sat to reread it. Her plane had been delayed by a dust storm off the Sahara, she wrote, but she'd arrived safely in Kano and spent her day wandering amongst the colourful market stalls. In all Nigeria, this promised to be her most rewarding stop. Calabashes. Carvings. Talking drums. Thornwood figures. Brilliantly dyed cloth. The place, of course, had been invaded by tourists but if you knew how to shop you could still get some bargains. The dust, the heat, were terrible! She might even adopt the local women's custom of wearing a huge colourful rag around their heads — if it didn't keep you cool, at least it would keep the dust out of your hair. She'd been nearly run down by a snub-nosed truck with bicycles and bedsprings roped to the sides and at least twenty people standing jam-packed in the back of it, in their robes, laughing at her with their huge white teeth. NO STANDING were the words painted on the sign that flapped just below their elbows. She enclosed a postcard showing the local emir on a white horse, the man so wrapped in white that only his eyes were showing. Mr. Pernouski didn't know what an emir was but he could guess this fellow was some kind of prince. The men who surrounded him in their brilliant robes, she wrote on the back, were supposed to be his eunuchs. Whether they were or not she hadn't found out for herself. "Think of me when I'm in Toronto," she added. "You know how nervous I get."

He knew how nervous she got before these things but he also knew she could handle it. She even enjoyed it. She looked forward to working herself up into a high-strung nervous state, like an actress. She would stand in the middle of her hotel room and holler at the top of her voice, over and over, that she was terrific, that she was marvellous, that she was fantastic, and that she was going to knock them dead. He knew, too, just what she was going to tell those women, all those young Christinas who came lusting after

her kind of success. She'd practised several times in front of
him. Up there behind her lectern she would give her secrets
away, her top ten requirements for the successful modern
woman of business. Necessities, she liked to call them.
Pride in yourself was one, you could get nowhere at all
without it. Flexibility too. Understanding the workings of
your business. Each of these she developed in detail for
several minutes. Independence — it came natural to her.
Caring for others. Tenacity. Planning. Honesty. Clear-
sightedness. These were her first nine. She had several
others that she used for her tenth, depending on the audience and the circumstances. The woman loved it. When
she'd explained all ten of the necessities they begged for
more; she couldn't possibly make all the speeches she was
asked to make, not if she wanted to keep her own business
growing, and pay a little attention to her family.

Mr. Pernouski wondered if sometimes, in front of those
audiences so eager for secrets, his wife was tempted to use
him as an example of what you could do. It wasn't impossible. That he was Number One in his line of work was
indisputable. Five wooden plaques on the wall of his office
proclaimed him Salesman of the Year. Last spring, with over
one and a half million dollars' worth of business, he'd won
a trip to New Zealand. Three years in a row his own company had awarded him a trip to the World Real Estate
Convention — last year in Greece. Once, he'd won a station
wagon for the largest volume of sales in just this district
— his wife still drove it — another time a mobile home for
the largest volume of sales in the mid-Island region. And if
the plaques on his office wall weren't proof enough, there
was his healthy bank account to consider, his accumulated
investments in properties that would boom some day, and
this comfortable house with the spectacular view of the
strait. And of course (most important of all) there was the
long list of buyers, sellers, and businessmen who refused to
do business with anybody else but him. If that wasn't proof
of success, what was?

A more important question he liked to ask himself was,

how did he do it? He could list the ways. He'd often done so, in fact, for the benefit of his son, but liked to go over the list in his head once a day in case he came up with anything new. Most obvious, of course, was his high profile. He was noticeable. When he was travelling as a private individual, Mr. Pernouski wore conservative grey suits to offset the attention his bulk quite naturally drew, but when he was on duty he wore a red-and-white tartan jacket and white pants and shoes, in order to take advantage of his size. People could hardly avoid him. Dressed up like that he became a presence in the town — everyone knew him. Other sales- men, who believed you should wear quiet three-piece suits in order to improve the public image of the profession, called him the Plaid Tank. Mr. Pernouski was always pre- pared to tell a joke about his appearance. He had to wear brighter clothes than most, he said, so he wouldn't get lost in the crowd, a tiny fellow like him. He said he bought his suit from Brown's Tent and Awning and rented it out to circuses on weekends when he wasn't working.

Of course there was seldom a time when he wasn't working — and that was part of the secret too. Energy. Enthusiasm. He never let up. If you turned your back or closed your eyes or put your feet up for a rest, somebody else (his eye on the Number One plaque) would grab those clients away from you. He couldn't blame them, it was part of the job, in fact he would be happy to show respect for any man or woman who deposed him as Number One, any man or woman who equalled his talent for sales and sales- manship.

Even as he drifted off to sleep that night, Mr. Pernouski was aware that despite the difference in time his wife would be still performing for those women in Toronto. Her speech would be over by now but they would be pressing them- selves on her for more, touching her, praising her success and her speaking ability and the remarkable flair with which she carried everything off. In the crowd, she would be the tallest, the most poised, by far the most tastefully dressed. One of the women, the one who was the most like Christina, would be standing back from the rest, with her eyes narrowed, thinking *Just you wait*. In his sleep this woman walked into his head and lit a cigarette and squinted at him through clouds of smoke out of Mrs. Eckhart's face.

Exactly the way Mrs. Eckhart was looking at him in real life the next morning when Mr. Pernouski stepped into the coffee shop for his break and discovered the couple sitting at the booth nearest the door. They didn't seem at all surprised. Mrs. Eckhart took a Kleenex out of her purse, blew her nose, and put the Kleenex back. "My nose has been running since I arrived," she said. "It's your damp air."

Mr. Pernouski squeezed into the bench on the facing side of their table and ordered his usual from the waitress, who looked up from behind the counter and smiled. Three doughnuts and a glass of diet cola. "A beautiful day out there," he said, unwilling to let this woman get away with her jibes. "The sun is going to break through those clouds any minute, you wait and see."

Mrs. Eckhart drew her eyebrows together in a frown. "What will people do, if it does come out? Will they hide, or fall down and worship it?" Through his laughter her husband explained to Mr. Pernouski that prairie people believed that folks out here dried up and shrivelled away like a jellyfish on the beach if it ever stopped raining.

When Mr. Pernouski had finished the last of his doughnuts, he insisted on paying for the Eckharts' coffee and buying Mrs. Eckhart a package of cigarettes. Out on the sidewalk she looked at the package as if she couldn't quite believe they sold her brand in this part of the country. "And now, since it's obviously Providence that we should meet this second time," Mr. Pernouski said, "I insist on being allowed to take you on a scenic drive of the area."

Mrs. Eckhart's head jerked up. "No!" By the look on her face it was clear that she smelled a plot. Her eyes shifted to her husband for support. "We've got things to do! Shopping! And there's Nellie's . . . you know."

Mr. Eckhart shook his head, as if to say he regretted everything, everything. "A half-hour's drive, Mr. Pernouski, would be pleasant. But after that, I'm afraid my wife is correct. There are things that must be done. We have friends here, you see, who are expecting us."

Mrs. Eckhart allowed herself to be helped into the back seat but she slouched in one corner where her clouds of smoke could escape through the open window and made it clear, almost immediately, that she intended to make a nuisance of herself. Was there an art gallery in the town, she wanted to know. Mr. Pernouski laughed. With all this beautiful scenery to look at, he said, why would anyone want to look at pictures? When he stopped his car in front of a small waterfront home with his company's sign on the front lawn so that they might admire the view of the strait and a few little islands, she blew her nose again and wanted to know what you could do with a view after you've looked at it twice. She hated views. "After a week of living along this stretch these people probably couldn't tell you whether their windows looked out on the strait or the city dump. The eyes adjust to anything." When Mr. Pernouski drove them down the lane of a small hobby farm he'd been trying to sell for a year and a half, she wanted to know what kind of tree that was whose ratty bark was peeling off like the hide of a mangy dog.

In a new subdivision high on a hill behind town he insisted they all get out of the car and admire the panorama. He led them to the edge of the gravel and remained silent while they took it in: the sharp treed slope beneath them, the town laid out around the harbour with its little islands and cluster of sailboats, the strait and the purple mountains of the mainland and the moving clouds in the sky. "And all that," Mr. Pernouski said, "is what I'm offering you."

Mrs. Eckhart seemed to find something amusing in what he'd said. "You offer us that?" She moved closer, prepared to laugh. Just by the amused and squinting look on her face she made him feel that he didn't understand a thing. "You offer us that?" she repeated, and jabbed her cigarette in the general direction of the view, laughing. "If we *what*? If we *what*? If we hurl ourselves down this cliff? If we sign away our souls to you?"

"Doris," Mr. Eckhart warned.

"I meant it only in a manner of speaking, of course," Mr. Pernouski said. "For the price of the lot behind us."

"Oh." Was she satisfied or disappointed? In either case she twitched her nose and shifted her attention to a crow which was making a racket in a fir.

Perhaps it was the altitude. Perhaps it was the sense he had that he'd just put the Eckhart woman in her place. Whatever the reason, Mr. Pernouski decided to risk a confidence and tell Mr. Eckhart his special dream. He saw all the rest of the world made up of broken-hearted people, he said, whose own dreams had failed them. Millions and millions out there who lived in squalor and ignorance and hunger and backward cultures, looking for something better. He saw mothers and fathers and hopeful children, he saw old people and sick people and tired people, all living amongst the ruins of plans that had come to nothing — wars and dead civilizations and outdated languages and old-fashioned buildings and meaningless religions. All of them, he said, dreamed of a place where they could start over again — a place that was green and clean and still uncluttered by the ruins of other people's mistakes. He saw himself — oh, he knew this was a romantic notion but wasn't it still worthwhile? — he saw himself as a person whose job it was to make all those dreams come true, to gather all those tear-stained faces full of worry lines onto this island and give them the chance they needed, provide them with a home. Nothing made him happier than to hear that a new family had landed in from India, say, so he could start looking around for a nice house painted blue with a basement large enough for all the relatives who were bound to follow soon, and of course in a neighbourhood where they would be surrounded by relatives who had already arrived before them. Prairie people were his favourites, because he knew that by the time they put themselves into his hands most of them were panting for what he had to offer. It was an impossible dream, he knew that! There wasn't enough room for the whole world here, he just wished the Island were a little bigger so that everyone who deserved to live in this place could find the room. Sometimes he felt he was offering a little piece of paradise to anyone out there who needed it!

Mr. Eckhart made appreciative muttering noises and pushed back his hat and looked out over the strait as if he could see all those homeless broken-hearted people heading this way right now. He lifted his camera and snapped a picture, perhaps to capture Mr. Pernouski's vision on film.

His wife, however, was trembling. "Sir!" She puffed her cigarette and narrowed her eyes at Mr. Pernouski. He hadn't noticed before how noisily she sucked on her smoke, how impatiently she blew it out. "Do I understand . . .?" She seemed unable to find the words she wanted. "Do I understand that you . . . that you think you're in a position . . . to offer us paradise?"

"Doris," her husband said, his face colouring. "Is that any way . . .?"

Mr. Pernouski, who hadn't even realized the woman had been listening to him, thought she must be working up to some bitter joke, in her manner. But she hunched over her crossed arms and paced along the gravel shoulder of the road and came back to squint up angrily at him through her smoke. "When you are more likely the proprietor of . . . ," her eyes searched for the word amongst stones by her feet, ". . . of hell." From her sudden smile, you might think she expected to receive congratulations for her daring.

Mr. Pernouski decided he would tell his family at the dinner table that after all these years he had finally met an honest-to-goodness madwoman, something right out of a loony-bin, or a book. "No more meat on her bones than a cat," he would say, "but she's as crazy as they come."

He would be sorry, though, that he'd mentioned her at all. Mr. Pernouski's son threw himself back in his chair and laughed. "She said you were the proprietor of *where*!" This struck him as so funny that he had to leave the table and get himself a drink of water from the kitchen sink to keep from choking on his peas. Shit, he wished he could have met this babe, he said. She must be really something.

Mr. Pernouski did not add that she'd gone on to accuse

him of wearing a jacket that made her think of a mobile billboard, a lurid advertisement for the attractions of his native land. And by his native land, she said, jabbing her cigarette into the air all around her, she did not mean *this*. He knew what she meant but he saw no point in taking advantage of the woman's mental illness for the sake of an easy laugh.

There was no harm in reporting what the husband had said to him once the woman was back in the car, however. He said she was a saint, a real saint — could you believe it? He said this little display of anger was as much a surprise to him as it was to Mr. Pernouski. He said he'd never seen anyone bring out the vicious side of her the way Mr. Pernouski had. Back home she was one of those saintly people who quietly go about looking after everybody that needed looking after in their town. She was loved, he said, by everyone.

She was also, Mr. Eckhart added — as if it were an obvious fact — the wisest woman in the world. A respected professor of fine arts in Regina.

Mr. Pernouski did not need to remind his family of how realtors looked on clients who were teachers: the bottom of the list, to be avoided wherever possible, or foisted off on some unsuspecting beginner. They were impossible to get along with. Thought they knew everything. Mr. Pernouski said he also doubted very much that she was the wisest woman in the world since she wasn't smart enough to know an arbutus tree when she was faced with one. If he had any sense he would forget about her right now. But the thing that made it impossible for him to do that was this — the husband had admitted it was only his wife who was keeping him from buying a little place and settling here. Like everyone else he had dreamed of it for years, but his wife just wouldn't budge.

"Which means?" his son said.

"Which means," Mr. Pernouski explained, "that tomorrow I'm going to sell something to those people, you just watch."

To Mr. Pernouski's surprise, this simple announcement

led to an instant row. His son said it was typical of these
bloody high-pressure gougers to act as if people didn't
mean it when they said they didn't want to buy; and Mr.
Pernouski said that some people just didn't have the sense
to know what was best for them. His son said that if a
product didn't bloody well sell itself, a salesman had no
right to try and change a person's mind, or trick him into
thinking he wanted something he didn't want. He wished to
know if Mr. Pernouski was afraid this one old lady teacher
would prevent him from being the Number One Salesman
for the sixth year in a row, and Mr. Pernouski said that with
an attitude like that his son would be on welfare within the
year, he'd never last. Because if you weren't aggressive in
this business you might as well give the country back to the
Indians and let it sit, just going to waste. Mr. Pernouski's
son became very red in the face and scraped back his chair
to stand up. "Maybe that woman's right, did you think of
that? Maybe there's more in what she called you than you
think." He left the room before Mr. Pernouski could find an
appropriate response.

But the Eckharts were not in the coffee shop the next day, or
any other place in town that Mr. Pernouski could see. He
neglected several clients — forfeited them, in fact, to a panting novice on the staff — while he went in search of them.
Shops, restaurants, business offices were full of people,
many of them quite likely visitors from out of town, but
none delivered up the missing Eckhart couple. No hotels
admitted to the name on their list of guests. Mr. Pernouski
felt ill at the thought that the Eckharts might have left the
Island prematurely, or driven on to another town. When his
son at the dinner table asked if he'd found his crazy lady off
the ferry yet, Mr. Pernouski said he could curse himself for
not insisting on the names of their friends in town while he
had the chance. Would he have to knock on doors? His son
suggested that a month of knocking ought to be enough —
aside from digging up his ladyfriend it would give him a
chance to ram expensive mortgages down the throats of

sixty thousand innocent people who might otherwise never even have thought of coming to him for the pleasure.

When Mr. Pernouski's wife telephoned from Toronto, his son picked up the receiver and told her that Mr. Pernouski had fallen in love. He was sick like a boy for the love of a wild crazy-woman out of a bloody madhouse, he said, and he wouldn't relax until he'd tracked her down and brought her home to sleep between them in the bed.

"Get out of the way," Mr. Pernouski said, and took the receiver out of his hand. A client, he said, was driving him crazy. Even at dinner, while he was talking to the children, his mind continued to walk the streets, looking for her. And her husband. He peered into shops, knocked on doors, surveyed the cars waiting at traffic lights. They'd become a damned obsession.

"Sounds like a normal day in a salesman's life," Christina Pernouski said. As for herself, she'd had a busy, wonderful day in Toronto. This woman who was herself very successful in the retail business invited her to her home for lunch today, to a lovely brick house in Rosedale with ivy growing all up the face of it and lovely Eskimo sculptures inside. They had eaten salads, which were brought in by a maid, and sipped sherry. And afterwards the woman had taken her on a walk through a park, down by a ravine, and told her she could do anything she wanted, anything. The woman told her she could spend all her time making those wonderful speeches and forget her own business if she wanted. The woman told Christina Pernouski that she was an inspiration to every modern woman in the country, an inspiration and at the same time a challenge.

"Yes," Mr. Pernouski agreed. "I'm sure it's the truth."

"She said I was a genius," Christina Pernouski said. "I've been invited to stay for a few more days. I'm afraid there are several more groups who want me to speak to them while I'm here." She added that she'd been interviewed by several magazines that day, they were really making a fuss over her back there. "Including *Maclean's*," she said. "They said I was probably one of the three best-known businesswomen in the country already, especially amongst other women, and it was about time they did a feature on me. *Chatelaine* asked me to condense my speeches into an article for them." She said a couple more days ought to wrap things up and she could get back to the Coast, she hoped, at least as far as Vancouver, where she would have to look in on her shop. She said she hoped everything else was going well at home, she missed the kids, and missed him too.

His son leaned close to the phone to say she'd better get home in a hurry, that Mr. Pernouski was so much in love with the crazy-woman he was wasting away to a shadow. Sorrowing over this wild impetuous love affair had shrunk him to skin and bones, he said. Down to four hundred pounds, he'd had to take several great big tucks in the plaid jacket. He would soon start losing interest in his job and sink to position three-hundred-and-two amongst the salesmen of the Island.

"A position just above your own," Mr. Pernouski said, waving his son out of the way. Laughing, his wife said he could fool around if he wanted, see if she cared, but he'd better have that woman out of her bed by the time she got home.

The notion was ludicrous, of course, and she must have known it. Mr. Pernouski seldom considered another woman seriously in that way, she knew that by now. His obsession with the Eckhart woman had nothing to do with that. It had little to do with real estate, for that matter, either. It had something to do with this feeling he had whenever he thought of her with that schoolteacher look on her face. He was sure she believed herself capable of doing him damage. He intended to show her she was capable of no such thing. Nor any other man or woman in this world.

Mr. Pernouski himself could hardly believe he was becoming so obsessed. All his life he'd been a sensible man, his only obsession the healthy drive to be Number One. When he'd fallen in love with the first Mrs. Pernouski it had been a quiet unremarkable affair, just as he'd expected it to

be. Their marriage had been a sensible unremarkable rela-
tionship, without rifts or ructions, as both of them desired.
When she'd died, quite unexpectedly, Christina Barclay had
come into his life, quietly, a little older than he was, but
wonderfully attractive to him and very kind to his children.
She'd been recently divorced from a runaway beachcomber
named Speedy Maclean who preferred to live on his boat. A
mother herself, of a daughter who'd grown up and left
home, she saw no reason why her remarkable success in the
business world should stop her from having a second marriage, a second family, and a second home. In seven years
they'd never had a fight, or any serious interference in
their life together.

Of course, it helped that Mr. Pernouski had always been
a sensible, reasonable, and even predictable man. He'd never
even been one to lie awake at night worrying about his
children, or to become a raving maniac when they defied
their parents — not even when his son had run away from
home to join that commune. Whatever it was this prairie
woman was bringing out in him, a streak of some kind he
hadn't suspected he had, he knew he couldn't rest, or carry
on with his job, or care again about the only ambition that
meant anything in his life, until he'd cornered her somewhere, and stared her down, and showed her he could sell
her a piece of land, or a house, despite her determination to
defy him. He dreamed at night that she was watching him
from just beyond the rim of his vision, and laughing while
she filled the air with her smoke. In the mornings his son
reported that the sound of him grinding his teeth carried
easily through the wall.

After several days of searching, Mr. Pernouski caught
sight of Mr. Eckhart's hat at a service station, where the little
man was putting air in his tires. He looked at Mr. Pernouski
as if he had some difficulty imagining why this enormous
red-and-white jacket had swooped down on him to shake
his hand and slap his back and inquire about his wife.

"Pernouski," Mr. Pernouski said. "Remember?"

"Yes, yes, of course I remember."

But nothing had changed. They were catching a ferry back to the mainland in an hour, he was getting the car ready, and no, his wife hadn't changed her mind about anything. She seldom did. Mr. Eckhart admitted that he himself would give much to buy a little place here before going home, something he could look forward to returning to, but — too bad — it was far too late now, it would probably never happen.

"She's a stubborn woman," he said. "And who knows but that she may be right in the end?"

"You'll give up your dream just like that, because of her stubbornness?"

Mr. Eckhart laughed and dragged the hose around to another tire. "I've never met a man so desperate to sell me something."

"You've never met a man so used to getting his way. I've got places to show you that even *she* won't want to leave behind. Just give me the chance, I'll turn her around."

Mr. Eckhart said it was too bad they didn't have time to look at some undeveloped property. His wife would never say yes to a house, but if he could convince her that buying a piece of land was a good investment, she might agree. He could try and convince her later to let him build a little house on it, a place they could come and stay in a while each year.

"You have an hour? Then give me half of it. Go pick her up and give me half an hour to show you something. A piece of . . ." Mr. Pernouski's mind went through his files. "A piece of waterfront. The perfect investment. You can't lose."

When Mr. Eckhart continued to look doubtful, Mr. Pernouski said he'd make it easier for him. He got into the front seat of the car. "Are you prepared to try pushing me out? Let's go, we're wasting time, we've got to pick up your wife and tramp over your brand-new piece of the world!"

No wonder Mr. Pernouski's heart was pounding. No wonder his palms were sweaty, his enormous stomach churning with excitement. His chance had come at last, she wouldn't

escape him now. The showdown, so to speak, was immi-
nent. He was about to demonstrate to that Mrs. Eckhart just
what it was he was made of. The thing was to make the best
possible choice, to show them a piece of land that would
sell itself, something that not even the little madwoman
could stand to let go. If he could show them something they
would fall in love with right away, then there was nothing
left to be done but sign the papers.

Whether he'd made the perfect choice was not immediately
clear. This was the best piece of waterfront property he had,
with a spectacular view. But it was steep. Now that he was
looking at it, it appeared to be nearly vertical. A sudden
plunge down from the road to the beach. Maybe not the
wisest choice for people who loved their flat prairie, but he
hadn't been given much time to make his choice, he'd
operated on instincts only and forgotten about the slope.

He'd also forgotten about the isolation. There was no
sign of life around, except for a couple of half-finished
houses on neighbouring lots. Once Mrs. Eckhart had dismissed the view of the pale blue strait dotted with fishing
boats and the curve of shoreline that lay beneath them, she
said a person living in a place like this would have to grow
one leg longer than the other just to keep herself upright.
"You want to turn us into cliff-dwellers — like birds?" The
cliff-dwellers of Arizona, she added, had the sense to build
their houses inside the cracks and caves of the hill. Getting
out of the car, she smiled at Mr. Pernouski. "They had
ladders they could retract — whenever they heard the real
estate developers planning to descend."

Determined to recover what he could from his mistake
in judgement, Mr. Pernouski gave the place a history. "All
this used to be part of a colony," he said, indicating with his
hand that he meant the whole stretch of land around the
bay, not just this lot. "A bunch of religious fanatics from
Australia that put up some shacks and a big high fence
around them to keep out the world. After their leader blew
his own brains out, the rest of them moved away and some

hippies took over. To do whatever hippies do when they get together."

His own son had lived among them for a while, Mr. Pernouski admitted. That was how he'd come to hear about the place and found out who owned the land and convinced his boss to make them an offer. "They practically gave it to us. Those types don't have any business sense to know what something's worth, they're just as well off up in the mountains or wherever they went."

Mrs. Eckhart looked as if she were prepared to return to the car. "You claimed it was the rest of the world that lived in the rubble of failed dreams," she said. "This paradise of yours was supposed to be fresh and new."

"Oh, that's all right," Mr. Pernouski said. "We bulldozed all the buildings down and burned them. We cleaned the place right up. You won't find a trace of any of that left here."

Mrs. Eckhart squinted at him through the cigarette smoke but said nothing.

Mr. Eckhart stood up on a stump and took a picture of a fishing boat that was throbbing by. The voices of men on board carried hollowly in to shore. "If you lived here," Mr. Pernouski suggested, "you could have your own boat. Fishing's supposed to be wonderful out where you can see those specks. I talked to a man last week who caught something that weighed twenty pounds."

"He can't swim," Mrs. Eckhart said. "He's afraid of the water."

Mr. Eckhart's face coloured. He jumped off the stump and aimed his camera down the curve of the coastline. "Maybe that's only because I never had the chance to learn," he said. "If I lived here, things might be different."

"If you lived here, things *would* be different," Mrs. Eckhart said. "You'd be living alone." Using her cigarette butt as a light, she puffed a new one noisily to life. "Now, Mr. Pernouski, do you intend us to tramp over this paradise of yours like genuine customers . . . or are you going to cut us loose to catch our ferry?"

Mr. Pernouski considered the slope beneath him. There was no question that he had to get them down to the lower edge, to the beach, if he had any hope of salvaging something from this big mistake. "What you are about to witness," he said, "is an act of pure faith. For a man of my size and weight to go down that slope is asking for trouble. I may never get back up again."

This was the first time that Mrs. Eckhart had shown amusement at one of Mr. Pernouski's jokes about himself. "A true act of faith," she said, "would be to throw yourself in that . . . that water down there. And *then* see." She turned and snatched a sweater off the seat of the car.

He saw what her grin meant. It wasn't amusement at all. Having chosen foolishly, having brought her here, he should now be prepared to surrender — this was what she was thinking. Having come this far, to the top of this slope, they both understood that it had nothing to do with real estate, or with selling. Having brought him here — how could he pretend he had anything to do with it? — she expected him now to concede, or jump in the sea.

Mr. Pernouski felt there wasn't all that much difference between jumping into the ocean and what he was about to do. They were equally foolish. To plunge down into this steep jungle of thick wet underbrush seemed not unlike a dive into dark bottomless sea. There was no way for him to enter it but to hold his breath and leap, all at once, and to hope that he didn't disappear altogether, or break an ankle, or go rolling out of control. The thud, when he landed, jarred bones up as far as his neck, and made his ears sing. With salal and tangled vines up to his elbows he turned and waved them down: "Come in, the water's fine."

Above him, the Eckharts gaped, apparently unwilling to accept his invitation. Mrs. Eckhart edged herself along the gravel until she'd found a gentler entry, and told him about it. "There's something of a trail over here . . . where you won't have to dog-paddle through that mess." She all but disappeared herself, except for her head, but when he'd waded through to her (his pants and jacket soaked, from the rainy leaves) she was standing in a narrow clearing where the ground had been dug up, or pounded bare. Below her a narrow path slashed downhill at an angle . . . why hadn't he noticed it? . . . a deer's trail, he supposed, since he hadn't heard there were mountain sheep in the area. Mr. Pernouski decided it would be best if he led the way, since a woman like Mrs. Eckhart was only too willing to snatch control away from you, and turn it into her own show.

"What's this?"

Mr. Pernouski held onto the limb of a small tree to help himself come to a stop, and turned to see what Mrs. Eckhart was up to. Bent over, with her face down around her knees, she was scraping around in the dirt with her hands. Fingers pried up something lumpy out of the ground.

"They had children," she said, looking at the object with a sense of wonder on her face. "Those people had children."

Mr. Pernouski saw that it was a small metal car of some kind, rusted and squished flat. "I don't know about that Australian bunch," he said, "but the hippies had dozens of kids, swarming all over the place. Dirty and smelly and completely wild, a pack of savages."

Mrs. Eckhart looked from the small toy to Mr. Pernouski without changing the expression on her face. "The child who played with this thing may have been your grandson, Mr. Pernouski." She stuck her cigarette between her lips and squinted through the smoke while she brushed the dirt away to get at the metal.

Mr. Pernouski turned his back to her and led the way still farther down this damnable cliff. Even holding onto the bunches of small trees and the twisted roots of dug-up stumps he felt as if he were climbing precariously down the side of something. The weight of his own body threatened to send him hurtling down the slope at any moment. Maybe once he'd got to the beach at the bottom he'd feel less insecure.

But there was nothing when you got there that you could call a beach. The water slapped against slabs of rock, which were scarred by glacier marks and cracked in a checkered pattern like old paint and in places crumbled away to a pile of stones. No sand, no gravel, no gradual slope; hardly anything even here that was close to level, where you could feel you weren't about to fall off and crack your head on the bottom. There were a few places where you could find a spot to sit, and natural steps where you might climb around the jagged lumps, and a sharp V where a small rowboat might be tied up out of the wind. A row of tangled weeds and chips and feathers and slimy kelp had been left behind by the sea. When Mr. Pernouski's shoe, with its slippery sole, slid out from under him, he was saved from crashing by Mr. Eckhart, whose hand shot out to grab his arm. For a moment, the two of them teetered above the spray. Mrs. Eckhart, behind, said, "My Lord, look how far we've come down!"

The car, when Mr. Pernouski could bear to look up, was a small bump on the sky. Everything between him and it was a green jungle wall, which could as easily have been leaning towards him as away. Only his presence here could convince him that trail was something you could walk on and not just a dark scar scratched into the side of a cliff.

"You'll never sell this lot to anyone," Mrs. Eckhart said. "Where could you tell a person to perch his house?"

Mr. Eckhart looked at Mr. Pernouski for help. Perhaps he'd been thinking the same himself.

"You get a bulldozer, Mrs. Eckhart," Mr. Pernouski said. "Have a look at those houses on either side. You get a bulldozer and make a shelf to build your house on. This is the modern world, the landscape can be altered to suit your needs."

Mrs. Eckhart jerked herself upright to look at him. "Would your wife agree to that?" she said. "Or your children? If you consult them." Before Mr. Pernouski had time to protest she glanced at her watch. "Well, I've seen all I need to see, let's go. We've got a ferry to catch."

Just like that? Mr. Pernouski would have thought she had plans for a shouting match, at least, here at the bottom.

Or a discussion of philosophies. Having brought him down
here, was she simply going to turn around and leave? "Just
hold it a minute," he said. "Have you any idea just how
much the value of this property will go up in the next few
years? You're passing up a wonderful investment."

No talk of investments, no talk of resale profits could
stop her. When he tried to paint a picture of the summer
cabin they might build there some day, with a cantilevered
patio over the rocks where she could plan her lectures
accompanied by the background sounds of waves, she said
she couldn't imagine anything worse. Right now, she said,
she was thinking of all the other cars that were getting
ahead of them in the ferry line-up. With her narrow legs
jabbing into the slope, she found it easier going up than
coming down.

Behind her, Mr. Eckhart, after only a few feet of the
climb, had to stop and puff. "There wasn't really much of a
chance," he panted down at Mr. Pernouski. "Though I thought
that, maybe . . ."

If coming down for Mr. Pernouski had been a matter of
abandoning himself to gravity, except for a restraining hand
on well-rooted trees to keep from falling, going up soon
proved to be impossible. He'd have had better hopes of
surfacing from Mrs. Eckhart's suggested plunge in the sea.
His body, after just a very few steps, refused to rise. His
heart pounded dangerously, his knees seemed prepared to
buckle under his weight, the sweat that poured out of
his skin felt hot and greasy inside his clothes. His vision
blurred. Hoisting this bulk would do some terrible damage.
He couldn't move.

He sat, and tried to laugh it off. What a ridiculous figure
he was proving himself to be!

"You can't stay there," Mr. Eckhart called down. He
sounded as if he believed Mr. Pernouski were just being
stubborn. He came down to sit beside him on the log. "You
can't just sit here."

Mr. Pernouski fanned his face with his hand. "I should
have known better in the first place. I'll never get up."

"Well, you've got to try," Mr. Eckhart said. "We have that ferry. If I pulled on you . . ."

It was worth an attempt. Mr. Pernouski stood up and let Mr. Eckhart show him how they could grasp each other's elbow for a steady grip. Mr. Eckhart grunted, leaning back, and Mr. Pernouski strained forward, eager to help all he could. But his foot pushed dirt out from under itself and he fell to his knee.

"If I got behind you and pushed!" Mrs. Eckhart shouted down.

Mr. Pernouski sat on his wet log with his knees far apart, panting, and imagined Mrs. Eckhart beneath him, pushing, while her husband pulled on his arm. Laughter bubbled up in his throat. If he fell, she could be ironed out, like a piece of cardboard, on the rocks. He felt his whole body heaving with laughter.

"Well then, if you crawled!"

Mr. Pernouski roared, and threw out his arms. If it hadn't been too undignified, he might have pedalled his feet in the air. "Crawled!" Like a great fat baby, he could get down on all fours and drag himself up the hill, from bush to bush.

He took off his jacket and tossed it over a twisted root. He hauled his shirt up out of his belt and used the wide wrinkled tail of it to wipe the tears and sweat off his face. "I can't. It would take forever."

"Yes, crawl!" Even at this distance he could hear her mouth sucking impatiently at smoke, blowing it out. Mrs. Eckhart had come down a little closer to squat on her heels. She wasn't laughing, nor was her husband, who made sympathetic noises in his mouth. "It's the only way. Otherwise we'll have to flag down a boat." She stood up straight and stuck her cigarette in her mouth and waved her arms about over her head. But all the fishing boats were tiny dots, miles away.

"My son has a boat," Mr. Pernouski said, almost before he realized he was going to say it. It sobered him up. There was nothing funny now.

"But your son isn't here, is he?" Mrs. Eckhart said.

"We could call him," Mr. Eckhart said. "We could find a phone."

Would it really come to that? A rescue mission from the sea, when he was only a hundred feet or so from the road? There were those who might still find some humour in the situation, he supposed, but Mr. Pernouski felt the first stabs of panic. It would be like his son to bring a whole flotilla with him — dozens of boats filling up the bay, dozens of people to laugh. "If I have the choice," he said, "I would rather you didn't." The truth of the matter was that he'd rather perish in great agony on this slope than live to see the grin on his son's face as he hopped out of his boat to rescue him.

It wasn't something, though, that he was willing to share with a woman like Mrs. Eckhart. Mr. Pernouski considered the alternatives. If *up* was impossible here, then how about *along*? It seemed a reasonable thought, but when Mr. Pernouski looked at the coastline on either side he realized that there would be at least four miles of stumbling over this rocky obstacle course before he'd get to an access road that could lead him gently uphill to the world.

"If I had a rope in the trunk of the car," Mr. Eckhart said.

"There's no rope in the car," Mrs. Eckhart said. "We took everything out before we packed."

"I helped this fellow pull a tractor that had gone over a bank, once. We could've put a loop around your chest, under your arms see, and pulled you up with the car."

"Surely someone in one of those houses . . . ," Mrs. Eckhart proposed, from above.

But there was no one around to help. On Sundays, builders were at home, or out on picnics.

"Walter," Mrs. Eckhart said. "If we don't *move*."

Mr. Eckhart glanced at his watch and took off his hat for the first time. He was bald. "We can't miss it, Mr. Pernouski. There are people on the other side, expecting us."

Mr. Pernouski might have suggested they phone their friends on the other side, since they'd seemed so eager to phone someone. Tell them they'd be a ferry later than expected. One missed ferry was not a tragedy. But he could think of no practical use these two might be to him if they stayed. All they could offer was company and the sound of her puffing — filling the air with the smoke of her impatient righteousness. It would be better, in fact, to have Mrs. Eckhart some place where she couldn't watch him helpless like this, a fat fool. Like a cow on its back, bloating up. Or an overturned bug, wiggling its useless legs. Go ahead, go ahead, he told them. Someone was bound to come along sooner or later. Someone with a rope in his trunk, as Mr. Eckhart had already suggested. Or one of those fishing boats coming in at the end of the day, if it came to that.

Mr. Eckhart stood up and looked all around, as if in search of some alternative which hadn't occurred to anyone yet. He shook his head, sadly, and put a hand on Mr. Pernouski's wet shoulder. "When we get to the ferry dock we'll call your home. I'll tell your son to come help you out of here."

Mr. Pernouski closed his eyes and thought of his wife — his nationally famous wife — being interviewed by magazines in Toronto. "Call my office," he said. "Call my office. They'll make jokes but they'll send someone to come pick me up." Maybe, he added, they could even get some publicity out of it — good for business. He tried to laugh. "The Plaid Tank Scuttled". He saw it in terms of headlines. "By Prairie Guerrillas". Then he put his hand over his eyes. "Don't bother my family, though. Don't phone them."

When he removed his hand from his eyes, he saw that Mrs. Eckhart had come farther down the slope to squat on her heels just above him. He knew when he looked up at her face that it would be a miracle if any phone call at all was made. "In the meantime," she said, "you'll have your paradise all to yourself." She reached for the damp tail of his shirt and wiped his forehead with it. "And you can think about things, while you're waiting to be rescued. I should imagine, at a time like this, a man has no shortage of things to contemplate. I imagine you will think, for instance, about your family, and the kind of success you have been as a family man. You will think about your career, I'm sure, and estimate its importance to you."

"Please go," Mr. Pernouski said.

She smiled. This woman who'd been described by her husband as a saint. And turned to hoist herself up the hill.

Mr. Pernouski watched the ferry approach the Island from out in the strait and then, a half-hour later, nose out into the open water again from behind the point of land. Without moving from his spot on the damp log he continued to watch, until it had become a tiny white dot in the haze. Then he put his jacket on, took a deep breath, and started to crawl up the slope. Chuckling at the picture he would make if anyone saw. And whimpering. By grabbing onto the thicker salal stems, and chunks of roots sticking out of the ground, he was able to drag himself uphill a foot, a couple of feet, maybe even three, before collapsing, heaving for air, on his side. His hands already were bleeding. It would take forever. His knees and the rocks, between them, had already torn holes into the flapping tail of his shirt. How was it possible, he wondered, to get yourself into such a mess? When he had bounced, so stupidly, down this same slope.

By the time he'd reached a point which he estimated to be about a third of the way up, Mr. Pernouski imagined that the ferry had docked and that Mr. and Mrs. Eckhart were taking off their sweaters and making themselves at home in the living room of their friends. It struck him that this might become one of those jokes he could tell on himself — a fat man without the sense to avoid going to the bottom of a hill he wasn't able to climb up. "They waited until they got to the mainland before they phoned," he would say. "And naturally, they didn't phone my office, they phoned my house. I had crawled half-way to the top, three-quarters of the way to the top, already ten pounds lighter just from the sweat I'd lost, when my son's motor boat rounded the point and roared across the bay towards me. Hey Dad, he yelled, and I staggered down to the beach to embrace him. Thank God you found me, I said, but he pushed me away. Never mind that, he said, did you make the goddam sale?"

The light had begun to fade from the sky before it occurred to Mr. Pernouski that they might not have telephoned at all, this saint and her husband. They could not possibly have forgotten such a thing, but they were capable of discussing it on the ferry and of deciding that there would be no real harm in it, that he was bound to be rescued sooner or later, if only by accident, and a little bit of a scare never killed anyone. The woman would be thinking there was some lesson in it for him undoubtedly. For the Number One Salesman of the Island. Who knew what a woman like her intended? Or even whether this indignity was intended just for him, or for everyone who lived in this place she hated, everyone who lived on this island.

When dark made it impossible for him to see where he was going, Mr. Pernouski curled up under his jacket against a charred stump and thought of his wife, Christina. Perhaps she was in her hotel room, already beginning to work on a condensed version of her speeches for the women who read *Chatelaine*. Maybe she was dreaming of that *Maclean's* article and wondering if they would put her on the front cover. Or considering the Toronto woman's suggestion — that she sell her string of import shops and spend all her time travelling, making her speeches for the hungry crowds of women who desired to emulate her example. Eventually, despite sharp stones that dug into his flesh and the wet leaves that brushed his face, he fell asleep and dreamt that rescuers came from every direction for him. Dozens of fishing boats and yachts and pleasure craft crowded into the bay, while wrecking trucks and police cars and wailing ambulances lined up along the road at the top of the hill. It was a helicopter, however, that got to him first. It hovered above him, slicing the air with its blades, and lowered a man on a ladder who strapped Mr. Pernouski into a giant sling on the end of a rope. Up into the air went Mr. Pernouski, arms and legs dangling, like an elephant being rescued from a pit, or one of those polar bears he had seen on television, being flown back to the north, tranquillized, after coming south to raid garbage dumps. With the helicopter throbbing above him he rose up over the coastline, over the trees, up over the town and the strait with the small white-and-blue ferries cutting lines on the surface, and ascended — perhaps the men in the helicopter had no intention of letting him down — to become engulfed in the clouds before breaking free to clear sunny sky.

When he awoke it was a grey dawn, and there were no helicopters, no sounds at all but the soft splash of waves. He was damp, cold; his legs ached. There were no boats either, or wrecking trucks or ambulances with sirens, no police. As Mr. Pernouski grunted to a sitting position, pushing the jungle of salal out of his way, he saw that if he were to be rescued at all from this hellish slope, he would have to do it himself, in whatever way he could manage. On his knees if necessary, though it could take all this day that stretched ahead of him, it could take all his life, with the imagined sound of Mrs. Eckhart's righteous puffing all around him as he climbed.

4

More Than Conquerors

Aw Gladdy, don't quit."

He could yell his lungs out, though, before she'd change her mind. Gladdy Roote lay there on that beach, gasping, and would have called herself an old half-dead seal foundered on rock if anyone asked.

She knew well enough that in a bathing suit she was a sight to see: flesh like slabs of goose-pimpled lard, legs all knots and cords, breasts like dead fish hanging in her black canvas suit. Still, she lay there on that flat rock — half in, half out of the water — surrounded by bits of floating kelp and wood chips, unwinding the string of seedy yellow rock weed that was wrapped around her hand.

"Aw Gladdy, don't quit, not yet."

Carl was treading water a hundred feet out, riding the wash of a ferry that had slid into the harbour across the bay.

"Go to hell," she said, and crawled farther up the slope. "I've frozen long enough." She rested, breathing heavily, on the sun-coated sandstone shelf of beach.

And just to show how little he cared, he dived under and left her gaping at nothing but heaving surface for so

long she was on the verge of whimpering; then came up
farther out, laughing. She imagined that even from here she
could see the brown snoose stains on his teeth. It wouldn't
surprise her if he was chewing now, it wouldn't surprise her
a bit to see him spit a long brown stream out into the water.
The bugger.

"Gettin' old, woman," he yelled. "Your blood's gettin'
thin."

And laughed, floating up onto his back. He'd laugh in
the Queen's face, that one. Brown teeth showing, and all
those lines in his face. Carl Roote had blood as thick and
slow as syrup.

"Drop dead," she said, and flopped over to face away
from the bay, to face straight into the cliff that rose up
seventy or eighty feet, nearly straight up, to home. A path
zigzagged up the slope, through tangled shiny salal brush
and Oregon grape and blackberry vines, right up past peeling mangy-looking arbutus and scrub oak. From down here
the houses were hidden; there might have been nothing at
all up there on top but miles and miles of bush.

"Besides," she yelled back over her shoulder. "We've
got obligations." And rolled her eyes. "A silver-engraved
invitation. . . ." That ought to knock the cheek out of him.

He swam in and came slapping up out of the water to
stand beside her. The black hairs grew right down over his
insteps and out onto every toe, to the edge of every thick
yellow nail. Dripping water, he grunted and bent to check
his watch, which was lying with the sweat-matted socks on
his towel.

"A big night," she said. "At least for some."

"Which I sure as hell wish we could miss." He flopped
down beside her on the rock. The sandstone had been
carved by the tides into smooth rolling slabs with granite
boulders embedded here and there as if in concrete.

"Well, I can't imagine a good enough excuse for *not*
going," Gladdy said, and examined her hands. "Not when
you consider." She poked with her finger down into a pocket
of trapped water and weeds left behind by the tide. "Not
when it's him."

"If one of us drowned."

She gave him a look. "I doubt even then. He never cancelled when the Payne kid — never even made noises about it — and that was only Monday. You'd've thought a thing as horrible as that happening right in the house would put him off, but no. An artist is like one of those actors, nothing's important enough to stop the show."

"And when he's your landlord, you're over a barrel," Carl said. He ran his hand down the hair on his chest, flicked the water off in her direction. "Paintings!"

It could have been a curse. Because he knew she wouldn't miss it for the world. "It won't hurt you a bit," she said, "to look at pictures for a while."

"Drowning might be easier," he said. And winked. And sent a stream of brown-gold juice sailing out in an arc to land on a piece of twisted white driftwood.

"Yes." She sat up and rubbed the towel in her hair. "The old lady, Sylvi, says its the first time he's ever done a one-man show. You wouldn't dare miss it." And dug her fingers in, to dry right down to the scalp. "Now I'll have to set and dry my hair with the electric dryer, you and your ideas."

"It was hot."

"A swim before supper. You'd think we were kids."

He slid a hand in the gaping side of her bathing suit and bounced a breast. "Kids," he said.

"Here!" she said, and slapped at him. "Get your horny paws out!" She looked up the beach to see if anyone was watching. No one was, no one ever was. The people along this part of the bay had heated pools up on the top of the cliff, they never came down to the beach. A sailboat, though, was slicing through the water in this direction. "Can't you ever think of anything else?"

"What else?" he said, and laid one arm across his eyes.

"Go on back in the water," she said, and stood up. "Another dip in that cold will freeze the ideas off you." Though she couldn't help just a glance at the wet black hairs going down his belly out of sight. Carl Roote was a thick hairy man. Her father had warned her she'd give birth

to monkeys with a husband like that, but all they'd ever had
was Sparkle, pretty and dainty as anyone could ask for.

"There's only one picture I really want to see at that
show," she said, and nudged his ribs with her toe.

He knew. "I'll feel like a fool." And squirmed.

"At least he never asked you to pose in the nude," she
said, and snorting drove her toe into his navel before heading for the trail up the cliff. While he roared at her, she
threw a towel-cloth robe over her shoulder and hugged it
tight. Didn't she know there were eyes at every window?
There always were, all along the cliff edge, every house
with its eyes watching her appear at the top of the long
steep trail and walk across the yard to her own door.

Mediterranean was what some called this place. Visitors
gasped, especially at first, and said the place was practically
like being in Naples or somewhere. All that cement and
those dripping baskets of flowers. The whole bay laid out at
the foot of the cliff, blue and shiny in the sun. Ha! She'd
Naples them, she said. What it was was a basement suite, no
matter how you looked at it. The cement patio was cracked
and frost-heaved. And how much of the bay could she see
from her kitchen window with that stupid big arbutus tree
hogging it all? What she'd like to do was take a chain-saw to
the twisted old bastard and get herself a view to match the
people who lived above. Trunks were all she saw, big and
thick and pink, busting out of their own bark once a year
and dropping curled-up skin like parchment scrolls all over
her patio.

Though who in his right mind wanted to look across the
bay to the spreading suburbs of the city? And farther off, the
white stinking smoke from the paper mill?

"Hungry enough yet?" she asked her daughter, who was
laid out on a lounge chair reading a magazine.

The girl only grunted. Sparkle Roote. Named after that
little darling daughter of B.O. Plenty and Gravel Gertie in
Carl's favourite comic strip. Some Sparkle. Gladdy had seen
more sparkle in day-old beer, when she was into one of her
snits.

It was the Payne kid that put her into the latest. The whole ugly business, it gave you the creeps, that kind of thing always did. And now those two, those Paynes, down at the funeral place, waiting.

Still waiting too, if the silence above meant anything. Not a single footstep had creaked over her head the whole day. No radio playing. No water rushing in the pipes. The middle floor was empty, empty.

Though up top, up in the real house, the A-frame building that sat on them all, old man Wainamoinen would be pacing now, biting his lip over his art show, barking orders at the poor stick of a woman he was married to, Sylvi.

Making the supper, Gladdy Roote could almost have sung out loud. Her hair was in rollers now. The new long dress she'd made herself was ironed and hanging from the top of the closet door. Big splashes of red flowers. It must've been, oh, ten or twelve years since Carl'd taken her to anything where she had to wear a long dress. He wouldn't be taking her to this either if they hadn't got that silver-engraved invitation for him being a model for one of the paintings. She could just let rip into the loudest song she knew, she was that excited. For Gladdy Roote would rub elbows with the best tonight. Maybe she'd nudge the mayor's wife and say, "That's my old man in that picture there. Lookit the gleam in the bugger's eye!"

Though of course she hadn't seen the painting yet. Not even Carl had seen the thing finished. They'd have to listen to speeches and who knew what all before they could get near it, just like anyone else.

Suddenly, doors slammed above, and footsteps creaked across over her head. The Paynes were home. Gladdy put a hand over her heart, she was scared to think what it meant. She'd tried to avoid them the past two days; people under that kind of strain didn't need nosy neighbours pushing in every time they turned around.

Though she felt, when one set of footsteps went out onto the deck, that it wouldn't hurt a bit to go outside and talk to

Sparkle, ask her to help set the table, or ask her if she'd decided yet whether she was going to come along with Carl and her tonight. And discovered, when she did, that just up above their heads, leaning on the railing was Carrie Payne.

A person had to say hello at a time like that.

Though Carrie Payne, it seemed, would never have noticed if she hadn't. Her eyes were somewhere higher.

"You look tired," Gladdy said.

Well it was true. Why not say it? A young woman like her shouldn't have purple smudges under her eyes.

"We've just come home for a bite to eat," she said. Her hand at her throat.

"Put your feet up," Gladdy said. "Get some rest. It must've seemed like the longest day in the world for you."

"Yes. I wouldn't have left but David insisted."

And then, because she just had to: "Anything happened yet?"

Sparkle's knees slapped together. "Mom!"

Carrie Payne didn't know where to look. Her eyes scurried everywhere looking for something to anchor them.

"No," she said. "No, not yet."

While Sparkle, face red, stomped past into the house. From the door she turned and gave her mother a horrible scowl.

If what you expect really happens, Gladdy thought, the newspaper writers will hound you into an insane asylum: and if it doesn't happen, the cops'll lock you in jail. They'll get you one way or the other.

It was the cheekiest she'd been since her operation. She could almost believe she was on the mend. Humming, she went back inside to get the supper out, feeling the huge curls to see if they were dry.

If Eli Wainamoinen were to let go, truly let go, who knew what might happen?

Madness, some people would guess, or greatness. Some, like his wife, thought he had already let go enough and ought to spend a little more time being normal. Wainamoinen himself suspected that he might become one of the immortals, that if he let go altogether and released all the talents swelling within him, he would quite likely soar well above the world of ordinary men and find himself in some kind of timeless place of spirit and harmony.

Not that he despised the world of man and nature.

From his balcony he could see a great deal of it, and it was beautiful. Across the top of the arbutus there was the bay-harbour, nearly encircled by the string of beaches and apartments and houses of the town that curled around its edge. The forest, too, covering the slopes and reaching up into the harsh gashes in the blue mountains of the island's backbone. It was a scene he had never painted, or ever wanted to. Too peaceful, too pretty, too pleasant. Art was an act of violence, not a sedative. Each work must begin as an assault on the pure canvas and end as a shock to the viewer's sensibilities. There were harbours in his collection but not this one, not with its comfortable ordinary calm, not where the only colours could be green and white and blue: he preferred the cramped up-island inlets with storm-wrecked docks and crimson boats that bled their reflections into dark water.

He could see the Payne woman on her deck below him. And had seen Gladdy Roote when she came up over the rim of the cliff, panting and hunched over like a sick cow. Two silly women. The incredible thing was that on this of all days it was possible for ordinary people to do ordinary things, completely unaware of how important it was to him, or how frightening. Completely oblivious to the fact that his name, if nothing else, should be enough to give pause on a day like this. You didn't have to ride a Viking ship to save the land of heroes. His namesake would have understood that. That there were other ways.

Back home, of course, this day would have come forty years sooner. But he had chosen, after all, to live here in this country, on this island, where a man had to be seventy years old before he could be sure there'd be people at his first show. They couldn't trust themselves any earlier. How could they be sure he wasn't trying to put one over on them, as they said, until he could show he'd been selling his paint-

ings to art lovers all over the continent for nearly fifty years?
Until he could list the museums that bought his work.

And yet, "The people, the people," he said.

And thought of that old composer in Helsinki.

He turned and went back inside the house, his legs
aching from tension and the slow hours of pacing. He could
be sick, he could easily be sick. But he hadn't waited all
these years just to miss out on his own first show. He would
be there even if he had a stroke between now and then and
had to crawl.

With his wife, his Sylvi.

Sylvi. The perfect wife. Who knew how to protect him.
Who stood between him and the people. There were forty
workers getting ready for the show and not once in the two
months of preparation had she let a single problem get past
her to bother him. He had been able to spend all his time
painting.

"Tired, Sylvi," he said. "You look tired." He put both
hands on her tiny shoulders and she looked up, grinning,
her eyes bright. And tilted her head to let her face rest
against his hand. "Eli," she said. And it was clear that she
would have crawled through fire to serve. With joy.

"You thought I was saving you from life on a farm, but
look . . . look what you have instead. Servant to the selfish
one."

Though the farm had been only a cow, and a field on the
side of a rocky hill.

"*Mina olen onnellinen,*" she said, and kissed the hand.

But he put a finger on her lips. They had agreed: no
Finnish, not even in private. They had done everything
possible to eliminate any trace of an accent. If he had been
Italian, he said, if he had been Spanish or Hungarian or
English he would have worked hard to hold onto a foreign
accent. It would have been a help to an artist. But not
Finnish. A Finnish accent, he said, was something these
people expected to hear in the logging camps. A Finnish
accent was for fallers and bunkhouse cooks. It could only
hurt an artist. It was better even to sound Canadian.

That he used a language of his own they would learn soon enough. In less than two hours.

"Sylvi!" he said and pulled his hand away. "Sylvi! My warm milk, please now."

"Yes," she said, a gasp. And leapt to her feet. "Yes Eli. And you sit down, in that chair."

"Sit!" He waved his arms at the sloped ceiling. "Don't be a fool, woman. How could I sit?"

Instead he paced the full length of the house, from the carved oak door at the front to the sliding glass doors at the rear. Then back. When she handed him the mug of warmed-up milk he looked at it, felt his stomach lift, and gave it back. "Too late, Sylvi, take it away!"

She took the mug and poured the milk down the drain. "Then please stop your marching, Eli, you'll drive the people below crazy."

"Already crazy!" he shouted. The Paynes. Already crazy. "And the bottom floor not much better. You should have seen that woman in her swim suit."

"Hush. Now stop. Calm yourself down. It'll all be over soon. Everything will be well."

They'd stripped the house. There wasn't a painting left on any wall. The workers had come in yesterday and, under Sylvi's direction, had taken down everything he'd painted and hauled it away to the ballroom of the hotel. Even the studio was bare, except for easels and blank canvas and pots of paint.

In Helsinki there'd been such a house. A composer's home. It too had been on a cliff overlooking the city harbour. His father had taken him there once, when he was a small boy too young for the composer to notice. He hadn't listened to them talking; instead he'd memorized the house. Every corner, every board, every piece of furniture. And he had reproduced it here, years later, when he knew in his soul that if he'd been back home he'd have far surpassed that composer in the people's hearts. Luckily the builders here were as accustomed to the proper use of wood as they'd been in Finland. And the furniture had been shipped directly from Helsinki. No North American imitation.

He touched it all now. It was something to hold onto. The cedar walls. The thick red carpet. The spiral staircase to their sleeping loft. The lamps. The teak tables. The places where paintings had hung. The door frames at the entrance to his studio.

While the windows in the house had been placed to take advantage of the harbour view, the windows in the studio were arranged for light. Made of a special glass, non-glare and very expensive, they ranged along the north wall, so all the light would be indirect, none of it ever straight from the sun.

"Sylvi! Sylvi!" he called suddenly. "What is all this nonsense I'm doing? A painter should be painting."

"No!" she screeched. But he took off his dress shirt, stripped off the pants of his rented tuxedo.

"My canvas!" he shouted. "My paints!"

So she scurried around him and brought out the easel, set up the first canvas she laid eyes on, set out his paint. "At least you'll be out of the way," she said. . . . "I'll call you when we have only half an hour left."

"Sylvi," he said, when she had almost escaped.

"Yes."

"What will you be doing?"

"My dress, Eli, I have to take it in. I've been so busy I haven't got around to it. It hangs like a sack."

"Never mind." He swung his hands in the air, beating her words away. "Leave the dress. Pray!"

She looked horrified. "What?"

"Go into the bedroom, Sylvi, and pray for me. Pray for the paintings. Pray for the people."

She put her hands to either side of her face. "And you?" she said. "What will you be doing while I'm arranging things with God for you?"

"Working," he said. And drew a blood-red line of paint down the middle of the canvas.

"I don't think He will mind if I talk to Him while I'm using a needle and thread on my dress," she said, and

wheeled away. But stopped. "He might even be persuaded
to listen to a man holding a paintbrush."

"Aggh!" he said, as she slammed the door. And slashed
red again, this time horizontally across the white rectangle.
Every painting began as a violence against the perfect canvas. You had to understand that every work of art was a
violence itself, a cry, a hand-slap to wake the hysteric to
reality.

He worked, thinking of the people who would be there,
at the ballroom, for him.

So long as none of the men were there. If any of the fellows
from the maintenance shop showed up he'd clobber that
Gladdy for talking him into sitting for that bastard painting.
There was no point in hoping nobody would come from the
paper mill; the bosses would be there, the office men with
their white hands, everybody important. Old Wainamoinen
knew where the money was in this town.

Carl Roote lay out on his back and floated, looking at
sky. A jet going somewhere drew a thin perfect white line
that began immediately to drift and shred. Seagulls glided
across, screeching. Riding air. Bastard birds, he'd be happy
to shoot every one of them, if they let him. If they hadn't
made it illegal. As a kid he used to put out food for them on
a fish-hook attached to plenty of string. Whenever a bird
swallowed the food on the hook and flew up level with the
tree tops he yanked hard and brought it down.

You had to punish greed. Seagulls would eat anything at
all and so asked for what they got. Tourists said Oh aren't
they beautiful, so graceful! But Carl thought of the way they
hounded you for food, the way they'd gobble up a fish's
bloody guts. You had to stomp on gluttony.

He lay out, relaxed, flat on his back. He would lie like
this in the back of the family pickup when he was a kid,
eyes closed, feeling the wheels beneath taking him steadily
toward some place he couldn't see. Relaxed, a sense of
motion, surprise. Smelling the dirt and sawdust and rotting
leaves that danced around him on the floor of the pickup's

bed. You trusted the truck to take you there, you trusted the Old Man to drive safely and quickly and to know where he was going. Just as you knew that if you let go, if you relaxed, the water would hold you up, keep you floating, even when the waves hit.

Then, treading water a hundred yards out from shore, he watched the ferry move out of the loading slip and pass silently along the opposite shore, heading for the open strait and the mainland. The waves would be a few minutes crossing the bay, and then they would toss him like a piece of kelp. Behind the ferry the houses in the subdivision were still and quiet in the sunlight; they might have been empty, every one. He could pick out the ones he had built, before. *Carl Roote, Building Contractor.* Before it had become necessary to get the job at the paper mill, in maintenance, patching up other people's rotten work.

Their owners would live in those houses five years, if they were like the others around here, before they moved on to another. While Carl Roote rented old Wainamoinen's basement.

He couldn't see the basement from here, but he could see the A-frame top floor standing up above the trees. And through the arbutus he could make out Carrie Payne on the middle-floor deck, looking this way. He raised an arm to her, in case she saw, but she made no gesture at all in return.

It was Kit O'Donnell who returned his wave, walking along the beach directly below the house. She was in her bikini, flapping a huge towel in the air. You couldn't help wanting to move in closer, to see. Carl Roote started to swim.

He came out of the water streaming wet, laughing, fingering back his hair. He pulled out the waistband of his trunks to let air inside, to keep the cloth from clinging like a piece of seaweed.

"Well," he said.

And "Well," she said, and spread out her towel on the stone shelf. She lived by herself down in Kennedy's boathouse and could have done her swimming there, but she liked this spot. Fewer crabs, she said, and laughed.

Skinny as a two-by-four but still that bathing suit drew the eyes. Two little pieces of rag. She twisted in the skinny body as if there was another her, inside, separate. And tossed her hair. And spoke with a phony English accent.

She was a teacher. Hardly more than a girl herself, he'd say, but still she was paid to teach teenagers older than Sparkle.

Carl Roote slapped his belly, still hard as it had ever been, though thicker, and danced on his feet on the hot stone. "Mrs. Payne is home," he said.

She looked up the cliff and of course saw nothing. "Oh," she said. Then looked down at his hairy feet.

"Stupid woman," he said.

"To see God in a bathroom mirror." She put a toe in the water, danced back. He could have counted the ribs; and the small black moles on her back.

"G'on in," he said. "It's a shock at first but you get used of it."

"I saw Gladdy earlier. The two of you were out here like a pair of seals. I couldn't resist coming down. It's wonderful that she hasn't given up swimming."

"Aw Gladdy's gone up, to get supper. She's probably gabbing away with Carrie Payne if I know her at all, or across the fence. That woman would talk to a statue if there was nothing else." He knew his own voice sounded as if he was bragging. As if he had married the only friendly woman in the country. As if nosy was a virtue.

But she didn't dash into the water, or walk in. She crossed her ankles and sat down — folded down — onto her towel, and frowned at a cluster of rocks. "I wonder if it's even possible to imagine what it must feel like to be them right now."

"The Paynes."

She nodded, then threw back her head and scanned the sky. You never knew, either, what a girl like that was thinking about. Suddenly she slapped her hand on the rock beside her to tell him to sit down.

He did, too, and tried to hide his feet down under a cluster of mussel shells and kelp. A crab brushed past his toes and scurried for new cover. "I guess it's not really all that fantastic an idea after all," he said. "My grandmother . . . they figured she was dead once and then she up and came alive again."

She looked at him. "Really?" She pulled her lips back over her teeth in a way that some speech teacher must have taught her. This was a great town for speech teachers. Kids learned to talk as if they'd been brought up in bloody Buckingham Palace.

So he was conscious of his own voice, flat and rough as a fresh-sawn board. "I was a kid at the time. She got blood poisoning from something, in her hand, in one of the fingers. She died in the hospital, the doctor even sent my grandfather home to break the news. But she revived after that, and they had to call him back."

She watched him speak, her own lips moving with his, and smiled when he stopped. "Oh but that's different. That's a doctor's stupidity."

"I could hardly stand to be in the same room with her for a long time after that. A big woman, sitting in one corner of her kitchen with that crippled hand in her lap. Like someone who knew something the rest of us had to wait for."

She drew both bony knees right up under her chin. He could see hairs curling out from under the suddenly stretched-tight bikini. "Children," she said, "see things magnified a dozen times. As I believe flies do, or bees."

"So it's not so far-fetched," he said. "And then there's that story in the Bible, that fellow."

She laughed. "Oh but such nonsense has been said about that!" When she said "nonsense" it sounded like a word she'd invented herself, a special velvet word. "Do you think if he believed even for a minute that Lazarus really was dead he'd have been able to raise him up? The only reason he could do it was he knew better than to believe in death at all."

"And so Mrs. Payne?"

"Is fooling herself."

He set his jaw and nodded. Though, somehow, it was a disappointment. You needed a little excitement now and then. Or at least the possibility.

"Anyway," he said, "that's two people won't be there at the old man's show tonight."

"The only people who won't. I heard they used the phone book to make up the guest list."

He snorted. "They didn't waste their time inviting people who can't afford to buy. But that still leaves more people than I want to have finding out I was fool enough to sit and let him paint me."

She put a hand on his knee and laughed, showing him all her teeth. "In the old days mostly they painted royalty. And the nobility." And shook her head at the thought, stirring up her hair. "Count Carl Roote!"

The hand left, went back to join the other in a bridge across the back of her neck. She didn't shave her armpits. That was one thing you'd never find on Gladdy, a single hair or even stubble under her arms. If I wanted to be a European, Gladdy said, you might persuade me to chew garlic but I'd never let my legs become jungles.

"He should of painted Carrie Payne," he said. "Her and her damn mirror!"

She didn't laugh at that. Because of course you couldn't make fun of everything in this world. A few things were beyond that.

So he said, "They're quiet enough people. If you got to have people living on top of you they're good enough. Hardly move, hardly talk. When we lost the house Gladdy didn't know how she could stand living so close to people, but she shut up about it when she saw how quiet those two are."

"And their girl."

"Was a friend of our kid's. A nice enough girl. Quiet, too, until the two of them got alone in a bedroom with a radio. Then watch out."

Then suddenly Kit O'Donnell was on her feet. "Well if I sit here all day talking to you that sun will go down and I'll never get my swim."

And ran in, squealing. On those skinny legs.

Sparkle Roote wouldn't go to the stupid old art show if they paid her. To see a bunch of dumb paintings by that old fart. What was so special about him? Personally she wouldn't walk across the street.

She ate her supper with them all right. There was no way for an only child to avoid that without causing a great big commotion. She tried not to look at her dad, who sat with both arms laid out on the table while he slurped up his macaroni without lifting his hand more than two inches from the plate. In his soiled white undershirt. Black hairs growing on his shoulders. She didn't want to look at her mother either. There was something disgusting about the excitement that flushed up her cheeks, shone in her eyes. She couldn't have stood to see her flouncing around like a lady at that art show. She'd eat her supper with her eyes on the open pages of her book *Lucky at Love* and then she'd play records all night.

There wouldn't be a person left in this building to bother. She could turn the noise up as loud as she wanted. Even the Paynes would be gone again.

She would dream of being a television actress.

Anna Payne had wanted to be a television actress too. First she wanted to be a nurse, but they said with her health it was a silly idea. So the two of them had planned to become tall and slender women who slunk and pouted through prize-winning dramas. Anna would get a part in a doctor series, she'd be a television nurse. Sparkle would be a bitch, a sex-goddess, a destroyer of men.

"By then," she said, "you won't need your medicine any more."

But Anna had shaken her head. "I'll always need my medicine. This thing is part of me. I'll have it with me all my life, to the very end. Like a twin, or a lover."

Though other kinds of lovers, too, were important.

Sparkle would sleep with every man that worked for the television company and then pick out the half-dozen she wanted to keep with her all the time. Anna would be on the verge of marrying the doctor-star of her show when a wealthy South American would fall in love with her and spirit her away to his plantation where they would live in sin. Whatever that was.

"But isn't eleven too young to be planning these things?" Anna said.

And of course Sparkle, who always knew better, said, "No, you're never too young to plan your life."

The alternative was to end up like Mom and Daddy, or Mr. and Mrs. Payne, or like nearly everyone else they knew.

She wished with all her heart that it was possible for the police to come and take Mr. and Mrs. Payne away to jail and then put nooses around their necks and drop the trapdoors open to let them snap dead like a couple of chickens. But that was not possible any more in this country and so she wished that the two of them would be put in a prison until they were old old old and would rather die than come out.

"It wouldn't hurt you a bit to come with us," her mother said.

And her dad: "If I have to go . . ."

She told them she'd rather be tied naked on an ant pile. That shut them up.

It's somewhere in the middle of the week, thought David Payne, but the day escapes me because it doesn't really matter and I'm sitting here at this table beginning to hate my wife. Trying to eat, God help me, trying to bring the fork up coldly, silently, with food I don't want and will never be able to keep on my stomach while she stares out that window and waits for me to finish. Like a parent who has taken his child to the bathroom and stands at the door, waiting, looking off somewhere else as if it doesn't matter but really saying with every line of posture and angle of bone, "Hurry up and get your business over with, so the more important aspects of life may continue."

David Payne was beginning to hate, more than anything else, the dark line of tension that creased down the centre of her forehead.

The air in the room was stagnant. All of it tasted second-hand in his mouth, warm and still and slightly sour. She had gone out onto the deck for a while and so a little of the sea air had managed to creep inside but old lady Roote had said something that sent her scurrying back inside to lock the sliding doors. She sat now on the arm of a chair by the window, like a bird ready for immediate flight. Despite the waiting, the days of waiting, the days of sitting and sweating in the heat, her white suit was still impeccable — uncreased, unsoiled, undisturbed.

Her voice, too, was as perfect and cool.

"I have no idea whether that arbutus is a blessing or not. How many people have come in here and said, 'Oh you've got to get them to cut that tree down so you'll have a better view'? But then, the tree itself is our view, isn't it David? It fills up everything and still we can see between some of its branches and watch the swimmers, follow the ferries in and out."

He had no idea what she was getting at. Three days of sitting in a mortuary had made him uninterested in anything she could say. I know what has happened to me and to her and to Anna, he thought, but no amount of sitting in the damn place waiting for something to happen will ever convince me that any of it is real. Because you don't really believe, despite the knowing and the feeling and the way you can see people all around beginning to treat you as if you've suddenly grown an extra skin of mustard yellow, you don't really believe for a moment that it could really have happened to you and that there is nothing you can do to reverse it.

"Remember Aunt Gwennie at Christmas, when she came out from the prairies, she said My word that's a leaf tree but it's still holding onto every one of them at the end of December. You said it's an evergreen despite these big leaves and she didn't believe you. She said evergreen had needles.

She said all those pine and firs and hemlocks were hard enough to get used to in the middle of the winter but this, this was some kind of freak. So you had to admit that yes, they did lose their leaves, in July. You told her they went dry and yellow and fell off like big crisp flakes all over the yard. And then you told her the special part: that not one of those leaves fell off the tree until the new ones had already opened up like flower buds on the end of every tiny twig and shone like fake wax leaves in the sun!''

He stood up and carried his plate into the kitchen where he scraped the food off into the garbage container under the sink. Then he carried the other dishes in and put them in the sink. Yesterday's dishes were still piled there, bits of food hardened, turning black. And dishes from the day before. I am an architect, he thought. Within a year I will have built up the healthiest architecture firm in this city and by that time we'll be ready to build ourselves the house we've been dreaming about and planning for a dozen years if the world hasn't fallen in around our ears before then.

Forgetting for the moment that it already had.

He returned to the living-room and saw her from behind. The back of her neck. If you want to know whether you love someone, his mother used to say, then approach her from behind and see what the back of her neck does to you. That is the most vulnerable spot, or seems it, and if you love someone you will want to weep at the knowledge of how vulnerable she is. Why do you think a mother weeps at a wedding? It isn't the music, it isn't the happiness, it isn't even the unhappiness. It's the sight of her son's bare neck turned to her and to life as if to the executioner's axe.

But Carrie's hair was up, swept up, like a girl in a brown old-fashioned photograph. Even at a time like this she made sure not a hair was out of place. And her neck with that white smooth skin made him think of something someone had laboured over for days and weeks polishing to a perfect shape and shine. But, it was a rigid thing, as marble works of art must be, and not in the least vulnerable.

"Remember how she didn't want to believe about the

bark either! How you can hear it on certain days. How the
trunk seems to have swollen too big for its casing and so the
bark on a hot day snaps and cracks and splits and curls up
like scrolls and corkscrews and springs. For an afternoon or
two it will sound as if the whole world is rustling old dry
newspaper! And there it is, the brand-new skin beneath,
pale and smooth and already doing all the things a tree's
bark is meant to do."

David Payne sat in a chair and put his feet up on a
padded stool. There was always the chance she had decided
not to go back. There was still the possibility that when
she'd stepped inside this small house full of stale air and
neglect she realized that all she was doing was wearing
herself out and that hope can last only so long.

He really did, David. He really did.

Don't.

*An unbelievable light from the mirror. I was blinded.
White as snow-glare. And His voice.*

Stop it.

*Three days. Destroy this temple and in three days I will
raise it up. Oh David, David, I know!*

He was aware that already there were some who were
calling it more than a tragedy. Each time they left the house
in their month-old station wagon there were people all
down the street who, if this had been another time, another
place, would gladly have thrown stones.

I am beginning to hate my wife, thought David Payne.
It's somewhere in the middle of the week but the day escapes me because it doesn't matter and I'm sitting here
beginning to hate my wife. At a time when she needs to be
loved, God help me, more than at any other time in her life.

"The others will be right across the street from the . . .
from the place," she said. "At the art show. When it happens they'll be right there, they'll be the first to know. After
us."

She looked at him for the first time since they'd come
home. Her eyes, her pale face, were as rigid and polished as
her neck. There was not a flush of doubt. Not a flicker of
vulnerability.

I am beginning to hate this woman, thought David Payne. And discovered that he was crying.

Carl was in one of his moods.

He'd started out by drinking three beers before supper and another two with it, despite her warning. You couldn't go to a thing like this smelling like a brewery. But he'd got glummer and poutier and redder and had barked at them both so much the kid finally got up and stomped into her bedroom.

And now he was trying to get friendly. Drying dishes beside her, for Pete's sake, something he never did. Sliding hands inside her dress. Saying let's forget the show Gladdy and head for the bed. Kissing her neck with the old whisker bristles scratching. "Get away," she said, and side-stepped, but he kept up until she threatened him with two soapy hands.

"Shoot," he said. "What fun is it?"

Gladdy would easily spend the whole day in bed with Carl. She'd more than once stayed in bed with him through a whole Saturday, when Sparkle was away staying at a friend's and it was more fun than anything, but never when he'd been drinking. Beer made him stink. She hated the smell until she'd had some herself. And it made him useless in bed, all he wanted to do was paw her and tickle her and get her all worked up without any hope of relief.

Though on his good days he could make that bed rock. The first week they were married they brought it crashing down off its legs. Carl could bring a barn down if he tried. They left the bed where it lay, on the floor, solid and quieter than some squeaky thing up on flimsy legs.

But when he got a few in him he couldn't have got a hammock swaying.

That was the first thing he told her about himself, when they met at a dull party thrown by a friend. She was hardly twenty then, working in Eaton's office. "I can keep it up all night if I'm sober, I can outlast an elephant. But put a few drinks in me and I'm useless." She told him she'd take his word for it, thank you, but she knew from her first look at those long-boned thick hairy hands that she'd be finding out for herself soon enough. She fell in love with his thick, cracked chewed-down fingernails. His left thumbnail was black, dead, ready to fall off.

Some people thought she could've done better. Her sisters. "Better than what?" she said. "He's a carpenter, a contractor. There's money in real estate." But he spends it as fast as he makes it, they said, on pleasure. On useless taste-less things, just to squander it. "He loves me," she told them. "He's crazy about me." And they had only been able to cry that oh, but he was so red and hairy!

That was what bothered her family the most. A man who looks like that, a man who can't keep his hands off you even in public! More animal than human. Some day he'll turn on you like a mad dog. But she had liked the attention he paid. To feel his hand going up the back of her leg while she was talking to someone. To have his hands inside her clothes while she was on the phone. To have him surprise her from behind when she was at the sink. Animal shmanimal, they could have their gentlemen with manners. She liked to be lusted after. She liked to have him keep every nerve in her body tingling with life, keep all of her alive and guessing. With Carl around there was never any question what she was.

Even when his business went belly-up, even when they lost the house and he was feeling so bad, he never stopped wanting her. Or making her feel like she was the most important thing to him. That was the one thing that didn't change in their life. He was as randy as ever. Not even her operation slowed him down, except out of respect when she was overwhelmed sometimes by a huge tiredness.

Though there were times, like now, when it wouldn't seem right anyway. Not when she was about to dress up and go to a high-class do. It was bad enough he got her into the ocean, ruined her hair when it was too late to do much but dry it and slap on one of her wigs. She wasn't going to let him breathe his beery breath all over her. Or keep her from a nice hot bath.

Over their heads a floorboard creaked.

"Not gone back yet," she said, and plunged her hands into water.

"You think the police?"

She closed her eyes, nodded. "Must be waiting just to be polite. One thing about the Mounties, sometimes they're not as crude as you expect police to be. They're just waiting for today to be over, so's everyone can see what a fake."

"Still, if it happens."

"It won't happen, hush up."

"Still, if it does."

"If it does you won't see me for dust. You won't see this old girl. I'd be scared to ever put my foot in this house again."

"But if it does, just think."

"Think nothing." She threw him a scowl. "You must be getting soft in the head." And tossed a whole handful of wet soapy cutlery onto the rack for him. "Can't you tell a couple of loonies?"

Carl chuckled. Sucked air through his teeth. He always did when she got arched, when the colour rose in her face and her voice strained.

Though he knew it only made her worse.

She stomped a foot. Tied here to the sink by dripping hands, she would like to have stomped out on him. The way Sparkle did. But he sucked air through the spaces in his teeth, laughing at her, and put one hand on her rump.

"Off!" she said, and swung her hip.

And "Off!" again, because it held on like a huge suction cup. She danced sideways, trying to lose him. But he held on, laughing, and put the other hand there too, on the other side, and squeezed.

"Bastard!" She brought up the hands, red and dripping with soap bubbles, and swung on him. He tried to get a kiss down into her throat but she pushed both palms into his face and fanned them like windshield wipers to cover it all.

"Ha!" she cried. "How do you like that?"

He didn't. Not at all.

"Jesus, Gladdy." And stepped back just long enough to finger soap off his eyelids, and look at her as if he was considering. A fist perhaps: he'd hit her before now, it wouldn't be the first time. He hated to be pushed away, he always hit back. Bent over like that, his legs apart, she would have believed it to see him charge at her like a bull and drive his head into her stomach. That too had happened before.

And still, she was glad she had done it. She picked up the dishtowel he'd dropped, wiped both hands dry on it, and dropped it on the counter. "It's time for my bath," she said, and dared him with her eyes to stop her. "I'll just have time to get dressed. Your suit's pressed and hanging."

"Pressed and hanging," he said. "Screw the suit. If you think I'm going to that stinkin' affair . . ."

"Go or not, please yourself," she said. "It doesn't make any difference to me. I'll be there."

But he blocked her escape. "Look, Gladdy, I don't want to go to that bastard affair. What the hell business have I got in a place like that?"

Upstairs, the floorboards creaked again. Footsteps passed over.

"No business at all if you think of it that way," she said. "But if you don't go you'll sit here and worry your gut out thinking about all those people seeing your picture. You may as well be there to look too. Sylvi told me the price on it would be eight hundred dollars."

"What?" he said, grinning despite himself. "Eight hundred dollars for this mug? Who's gonna pay that?"

"Somebody with money to burn," she said. "Somebody who'll put it in the basement to scare the rats away."

"Huh."

"Maybe your ugly face will hang in a gallery somewhere. For tourists to gawk at. They might even charge admission for the pleasure." She cocked her hip at him and walked past. Then turned. "You and the bloody Mona Lisa."

He lunged for her but she stepped aside and all he got ahold of was the collar of her dress. But he yanked on it anyway, sent buttons flying, ripped the seam open. "God damn!" she shouted, and slapped at the arm. But he pulled harder, and tore a strip right down the front. An old house-dress but one of her favourites.

He was sucking air again, through his teeth, but his face was red with anger. No one laughed at Carl Roote. Not if he didn't want a poke, or the hard thrust of a shoulder.

But she knew how to handle that. She put both hands on her stomach and grimaced. Groaned.

"Gladdy?"

She hunched across to the nearest chair and sat. Carefully.

"Is it the operation?"

She nodded. And indeed, now, she could feel the pain there. Throbbing. She put up her hand and he took it, held it tight.

She didn't even have to use her magic word, it was that easy this time. Sometimes she had to haul out the word the doctor had given her like a weapon and fling it at him to stop him dead. Hiss it at him. Make him leap back and turn away. But this time just the few groans, the doubling over, were enough.

"Aw Gladdy, are you all right?"

She was all right, yes. She nodded. And watched him. He was sober enough now. She'd scared the beer right out of him. Look at those eyes.

"All right," he said. "We'll go. You get that dress on and we'll go to their bastard art show."

She put her hand on his arm. The pain was worse, which served her right for conjuring it up in the first place. "Go get your suit on, you dumb ox," she said. "I've still got the time for a quick bath."

It was true that Sylvi Wainamoinen spent a great deal of her time dreaming of pilgrims. They came to her door, in her dreams, wide-eyed and afraid. They came down to the door from their cars, from the tourist buses, from their taxis, they came whispering across the gravel on tiptoe as if what they walked on was holy ground, they came from all over the island, from all over the country, from all over the world, with breaths held and hands tight: just to see her, to see her home, to touch her things.

So she dreamed.

Oh, she was willing to admit it. To herself, and to Aili too, soft sweet almost forgotten Aili, momma, who smelled of the dairy and cinnamon cookies. Who lived, now, like the pilgrims, only in her dreams.

She opened the door to them, she confessed, in the black rags of widowhood.

It was true, certainly, that she was spending larger and larger portions of her days on the dreams, but it had never before occurred to her that when the time came for at least part of it to come true she would be too tired to care. That her cheeks would burn from lack of sleep, that her arms would ache, her eyelids droop.

Yet she was expected to be a gracious hostess, once they got to this thing. The helpers would all turn to her for advice; she'd be expected to make it all run smoothly. And what did she know of such things? Really? Why were there helpers at all if everything, everything, must be told to her?

She would be expected to check everything over. The paintings, were they straight? Were the helpers in their places? Were the programs out? The price list posted on the walls in several places? Eli would be up on the platform with the alderman, ready for the people. She could go home at that point, if she wanted, and it wouldn't really make that much difference. Except of course to Eli. Except to insult him.

She played with her wedding ring. Plain gold. A ring was a reminder that eternity was not impossible, he'd told her, that some things could go on and on so that you couldn't tell beginnings from endings. A marriage was supposed to be like that.

There were 250 paintings. A lifetime, hanging on those walls, and on the standing screens. Some were new, hardly dry. Half of them were borrowed from the owners. She could stand there in the centre of that hall and, by turning slowly all the way around, follow the seventy-five years of her husband's life.

And could, even if he himself disappeared. His life was broken up, reflected, mirrored in these 250 rectangles. Those people out there would see nearly as much of him as she'd ever seen. If he'd welcomed them naked he'd be no more exposed than he was already.

Back home they would say, *"Miksi Sina olet nun bidas."* What took you so long? Here there were some who said, "Are you sure you're ready?" and "Is there any point? When you know that few really care?"

"Aili," she whispered, "can I confess you something once again?"

I dream of myself welcoming pilgrims, travellers who have come from all parts of the world to our house, which has become a shrine. "You," they say with emotion that closes the throat. "You are the widow? You knew the Wainamoinen? You lived with him all those years?" The house is owned by the government as a museum (can you imagine that?) and I show them through the studio, show them the unfinished canvases, let them touch the furniture in our home.

It will be easier then, Aili, much easier. Of course, I never expected any of it to be simple, living with him, but oh, so much of it has been hard.

"Oh you silly fool baby," Aili would laugh at her. "You dreamer baby. Do you really believe it's any easier for the rest of us? Can you imagine you're the only one who wants to be a widow?"

"Sylvi!"

It was Eli, calling her from the open door. Outside, she could hear the car's motor running. "Get your coat on, Sylvi. It's time to go."

"Yes," she said. "Yes." And touched the hair at the back of her neck.

"Before we go," David Payne said, "we should stop in

upstairs and wish them luck."

"Luck?" she said, and raised a perfect eyebrow. "What would a thing like that mean, coming from us?"

"Still," he said.

She smiled. "To wish good fortune for someone else you should at least have demonstrated a little of it, yourself."

So if there was no doubt in her, he thought, there was at least some bitterness. Waiting was a strain, even waiting for something you were so sure of.

He turned on the radio. "We'll go, just as soon as I've heard the news," he said. And sat back in his leather armchair in the corner. "If you insist on taking me back to that place."

There were ten minutes left, however, before any of the stations would be offering news and all he could find was music. He snapped off the switch. What kind of a union is it that falls apart this easily, he thought. Where was its strength if it could hold together through all the first twelve years of growing and planning and learning and then snap like this from the weight of its first real burden? What was the matter with him?

"If you really believed," he said, "you'd be full of joy and excitement."

She did not look at him. She spoke with her face turned away, in the direction of the window, the arbutus tree, the harbour. "Who are you to know what believing brings with it?"

Wainamoinen sat back on his chair and crossed one leg over the other. Perfectly, carefully. No one must see an old man slouched down like a pouting child dragged here by his parents. Nor see bare white leg exposed above the stocking. This was a time for dignity.

And it was too late to do anything about the red smear of paint along the side of his hand. Except to hide it, for now, in the left pocket of his suit.

As people entered the ballroom, nervously, tentatively, he tipped back his head and closed his eyes. Now, now it was happening.

Only One
Life of us all
open my eyes
only to perfection,
mine
and theirs

Why, why, they said, did you choose to hide yourself on that island? Frontier island on the far edge of a frontier country. When you could have had Scandinavia first and then Europe and finally all of the world. In a country that is only beginning to care, you hide out on an island that is not yet even aware of itself.

It was because this island was a big enough country, he told them. If he were an Irishman he'd have a country not very much bigger and it would be enough, more than enough. In Finland, too, the country is small and yet as big as one man can identify with. Insist that he become a Canadian painter, or a North American painter, and he would panic. How was it possible to identify with anything so unimaginably huge except by induction, except by seeing the small first and knowing it so well it must include all of the rest?

Should he be like his son, who had gone south to America? To become a famous movie director. Who ever heard of him? What could he show that country of itself that they hadn't had to show him first? Robert Arfie Wainamoinen, big shot.

Caroline, on the other hand, had married a mechanic and moved up-island to help him run a broken-down crossroad service station. She was poor and bone-tired from bringing up those kids in a pile of discarded car parts but she knew every inch of that piece of land and could sing of it so that you'd think she'd seen the backyard of every wife in the world.

Only One
Life of us all
open my eyes
only to perfection

What he opened his eyes to was a crowd of hushed people filling up the room, moving in close to the platform. Faces looked up at him. Frozen uncertain smiles. They might have been saying: Are you sure there is no catch to this? Are we really here for what we think we are here for? They moved in, more and more of them, closer gradually to the platform. Standing uncertain, then pushed ahead by still more coming in, then standing again. Waiting.

Their eyes flickered across him, briefly, and strained to see all they could of the paintings around the outside walls of the ballroom. Trying to look as if they were only casually interested. Men, some men, gathered in clusters and spoke agitatedly, about work perhaps, or about politics, certainly not about him; they probably weren't even quite sure why they were here, had been dragged here by their wives. Some wouldn't even be certain of his name.

There was still the red smear on his hand, which he kept hidden. This was not a crowd that wanted an eccentric. They would hate him enough for the platform, for the speeches. Age and dignity and quiet calm were closer to what was expected. An artist who was normal, who wouldn't try to cheat, who wouldn't be tempted to make a fool of you. They wanted to know that if they liked a piece of work there wasn't somewhere behind it the kind of artist who was laughing, thinking: Fool, fool, it's a piece of junk, I wiped my brushes clean on it!

What they wanted of course was not an artist at all but rather a kindly trustworthy art teacher. Dull and gentle. No affectations. Well, he could be gentle.

As his son, too, had been gentle. "My God, Dad, they're all a bunch of raving lunatics down here! They call me the dull Canadian." The dull Canadian, of course, had become even duller when faced with a public that expected madness. And so eventually he must have faded right out, respectable and grey and unnoticed. In less than five years.

Sylvi closed the door, then opened it again just long enough to let one more alarmed-looking woman come in from the foyer.

Then silence. At the other end of the platform the alderman stood up behind the microphone.

Ladies and gentlemen . . .

Most of them watched the alderman. A few, still, were looking at the paintings. Gladdy Roote was grinning at him. As if out of all this crowd she thought she was the one he'd be happiest to see! The silly woman; a cow in the parlour.

Which was hardly what he could call seeing only perfection.

The truth was, he knew, that she was probably getting more enjoyment out of this thing than anyone else. Including him. Including even Sylvi. She just didn't have the others' ability to hide it. Poor simple silly woman. She may be the only one in the room who truly loved living.

. . . who took his training under the very best teachers . . .

And Carl, who knew how to suffer. Red and sweating. Trying to look invisible. Hoping no one would notice his fingers prying the tight collar away from his neck. His coarse hard face clamped shut, his eyes shifting.

"Never mind, Carl," he thought, "when you see what I've done with that face you'll forget your discomfort. You'll see yourself for the first time from the outside."

. . . moved with his lovely wife to this island . . .

It was a face he had known for nearly five years that he must paint some day. From the day they came to look at the basement suite. And yet it had been necessary to wait all that time, watching, thinking, planning, before even asking the man. So that when the time came it had been possible simply to put down what he had already done in his mind. With Carl sitting, of course, so the light would be right.

His son had lived in the basement. Robert, with that Chinese girl. For nearly two years. A trial marriage, they called it. And Sylvi, poor Sylvi, had said at least they'll be home, they're not sneaking off somewhere, we can keep an eye on them. But the Chinese girl had gone and soon after that Robert had gone too — off to Hollywood to become a

famous director — and then the Rootes had arrived to answer the FOR RENT ad in the local paper.

... *fortunate for all of us that such a man should
choose* ...

"We saw your ad," Carl said. He made it sound as if he
were accusing them of a crime.

"A basement suite?" Gladdy said. Looking around the
place. Sniffing the air, perhaps, for flower scents and the
odours of dogs. She was ordinary, an ordinary heavy sagging woman, an ordinary face. He would quickly have forgotten her face if they'd never come back.

But he could not have forgotten Carl's. Not ever. His was
a face that would have to be painted sooner or later. Those
scowling eyes, like velvet blackberries. The bone-stretched
jaw, the skin creases. The sudden thick nose. The way a
tiniest movement of any part changed all of it, as if the light
had changed, or a mask had shifted.

"Well, can you show it to us?" he asked. It was obvious
he didn't really want to rent, not this or any other place.
"We musta been through a dozen of these bastard places."

Gladdy had explained, almost in a whisper, that they
had lost their house, that the business had gone bankrupt.
And Carl had told her to shut up, never mind telling everybody all your goddam business. Though they had clung to
each other as if they were afraid that one of them would turn
a corner and disappear.

... *ladies and gentlemen, Elias Wainamoinen* ...

He rose (one leg had gone to sleep) and walked carefully
to the mike. Head high. Aware of the heavy silence.

Forty years.

"My friends," he said.

Though he saw none of them. He spoke to the far corner
of the ceiling.

"My good friends. Around you, on every side of you, is
the evidence of my career."

Sylvi was there; there was Sylvi; standing by the door.
Her face tilted; flushed. She was tired.

"Perhaps a man's life is a journey toward heaven."

He paused, closed his eyes.

"Perhaps some people from time to time achieve moments there. Perhaps an artist is the man who can show you glimpses of those moments."

He breathed deeply, tilted forward now, almost bowing. "Thank you for coming, my friends. I hope, this evening, some time this evening, my work will give you a glimpse into the harmonious world of truth."

Not offering much is he, Gladdy thought. The harmonious world of truth, for crying out loud!

And shifted weight in her tight shoes. She hadn't worn the things since winter. So much barefoot walking in summer had spread out her feet.

The dress, though, the dress was perfect. Hung on her body like it was made in Paris for her. She looked as good as any one of these other babes, anyone could see that at a glance.

She felt flushed from excitement, but didn't look as red as Carl. The poor bugger hated to wear a suit and tie anyway, and here he was with his head the colour of a fat radish, and sweating buckets as if that collar was really squeezing. His eyes bulged, and never stopped peering around the room the whole time the speeches were on, searching for the shock of his own face looking back.

"You'd think he was a bloody Michelangelo," she whispered, out of the side of her mouth, to Carl. She nodded, smiling, at the woman who turned to let a look scorch right down the full length of Gladdy Roote.

Your face's got as much paint slapped on it as some of these canvases, Gladdy thought. And wondered if the necklace was real diamonds. In this town, who could tell?

Mercifully the ribbon was cut at last and the crowd fell apart like struck billiard balls. They spread out in every direction all over the hall, running — some of them — to get a closer look at something their eyes had picked out while they stood listening. Someone, moving, kicked Gladdy's ankle; though she swallowed the curse that rose in her throat, and smiled. This isn't a bloody $1.49 day at Eaton's, she thought. Were the rich at an art show like housewives at a bargain sale?

"Where's the picture?" Carl muttered. "So we can get the hell out of this place."

But no one was going to cheat her out of one minute of this.

"You can't just look and go."

He mopped his high shiny forehead with his handkerchief and glowered. "What else are we here for?"

"You have to mix," she said.

"Mix?"

"This isn't a department store. You gotta look at every painting like it was the only one here, and you gotta talk with people."

"Shoot, I'm not looking at 250 goddam pictures. And we don't know any of these people."

She slipped her hand in behind his elbow. "We know some. Enough." And smiled at her dentist's second wife, who had begun, after all, as his receptionist. "We'll start here," she said, "and work our way around."

Down the first wall there wasn't a single painting she'd say thank-you for. Not one she'd have in her house. A photograph cut out of a magazine would look better than any of these. A lot of trees with fuzzy leaves, and silly messed-up skies. Carl pulled her down past them too fast to see anything else but she didn't mind. What she minded was not having the time to get a good look at the people who stood there, studying. They seemed to be saying things about the paintings as if one wasn't the same as the next.

"Did you notice the prices he's got on these things?" Carl said.

"Paintings are a good investment."

"How much do you figure he pays for the canvas? Not much. And the paint. He sure as hell puts a high price on his labour."

"What else is there to a painting but the labour? You

don't think these people came here to admire the paint, do you? Or the frames?"

Carl Roote shook his head. You'd think he was looking at the biggest con job of all time. Still, he wasn't going to spoil *her* night. Gladdy stood back from a large watercolour in the corner and tilted her head. "Now that's got depth," she said.

The fat woman beside her smiled. "Yes," she said. "That man understands light."

"Yeah," Gladdy said. "You could guess exactly what time of day it is, where the sun's coming from."

The woman moved up closer, one pudgy finger out, as if she wanted to touch.

Carl said, "Maybe he knows light, but he don't know nothing about a logging claim. Them trees are all too clean and perfect. Where's the dead limbs? Where's the rotten snags and widow-makers? Where's the windfalls?"

The fat woman looked Carl over. "Have you met this, this Mr. Wainamoinen?"

"Oh yes," Gladdy said. "We know him well. Neighbours. I suppose we're what you could call friends."

The woman's face lighted up. "Really! Well he certainly is a talented man."

"My husband," Gladdy said, "modelled for him."

Carl growled. The woman's eyes darted to him, away, then back again. Clearly she didn't believe.

"We haven't seen the picture yet," Gladdy said. "We don't even know if it's a good likeness."

"Shoot," Carl said. "Let's get . . ."

"It's the first time I ever heard of a Finn who could paint," the lady said. "They don't go in for things like this. As a rule."

"Mr. Wainamoinen," Gladdy said, "has always painted."

Which ended that conversation. The fat woman tip-toed on to the next painting as if she were really invisible and had only to be silent to be undetected. As if paintings were things to sneak up on, like whispering children.

"Aw Gladdy," Carl said. "Let's see that damn thing and

get out of here. I'm dry as hell." He ran a finger around the inside of his collar. "A beer would help."

"There's a cocktail lounge next door," she said. "We could step in for a drink once we've seen it." She could have promised him anything then, her heart was so full. This was where she belonged. She could sing, she could stay forever, she could promise Carl the moon out of pure joy.

"If we go out to the middle of the room and turn around we should be able to pick it out," he said.

"In this crowd?"

"Over their heads. I'll stand on your shoulders if I have to." And put a hand on her breast. Hidden fish. For reassurance, perhaps, or gratitude.

She stepped back, looking for people who'd seen. No one had, and anyway, when she did that, he moved his hand to her rear end and bent down to whisper in her ear. "Where's the nudes?"

"The what?"

"There's bound to be some naked bodies in a few of them. All them artists get naked girls to model for them."

"Speaking of naked," she said, and watched Kit O'Donnell slither by in something scarlet and see-through and nearly indecent. Then she said, "Mr. Wainamoinen doesn't do that kind. People's heads and hillsides are his specialty. I don't expect you'll find a single nude here."

They worked their way out to the centre of the room. Carl stood up on his toes and strained to find his portrait over people's heads but he felt silly and gave it up. "We could be stuck here all night," he growled. And would have started making his way to the door if Gladdy hadn't spotted Wainamoinen himself coming toward them, his arms outstretched like she was a sister he hadn't seen in twenty years.

"Gladdy," he said, and put one hand on her shoulder. "Carl," and put the other hand on Carl's arm. He looked at one and then the other. "These people," he said, and held out both hands like someone feeling for rain. "These people, they fill me with something, with . . ." and one hand slapped back onto his own chest, unable to grasp the perfect word.

"A good-sized crowd," Gladdy said. He must've been a handsome man at one time, she thought. One of those strong slant-boned Finnish faces. With eyes that moved like glittering birds. And white even teeth that slanted in, with spaces. He was a tall man, with big thick hands that could just as easily have held a chain-saw as a brush all these years. "Yes," she said. "You never know."

"Eh?" Carl said.

"Art lovers," Gladdy said, raising her voice. The noise of people talking around them seemed to be getting louder. "You don't have to be rich to like pictures!" And straightened out Carl's red-and-green plaid tie that had got somehow crooked. From all his fingering at it probably. He couldn't keep his hands off a tie once it started bothering his neck.

"This town," Wainamoinen said, "has truly turned out to honour an old man. And to see if my hand has captured more truth than their eyes have seen." He tilted his head back and looked around. "Look well, my friends. I offer you more of the real world in this room than you may see in a lifetime of looking at cars and houses and streets and at the daily monotony of your jobs."

"I wondered if you would have music," Gladdy said. "But in this crowd, no one would've heard a note. Listen to them."

Then, suddenly Sylvi was at her husband's side. She dipped her head in a dry nod to Carl, to Gladdy.

Thinks she's his bloody watchdog. Deciding who's good enough to talk to her precious husband.

"You look lovely," Gladdy said. "Sylvi."

"And you," she said. Sweetly smiling, her dimples deepening. In Finland she would probably have become a factory worker. Tightening nuts. Tittering behind her hand in the lunch-room.

"A big night," Gladdy said. "You must've had your picture taken a hundred times for the papers already."

Again the dimples, though the eyes remained flat and

dull. "Not of me," she said. "It's Eli's night. His alone."

"Sylvi," the old man said, and put an arm across her shoulder, pulling her close.

"Of course," Gladdy said. "But you too. You must be proud."

"I'm happy at least two of our neighbours could come," said Sylvi Wainamoinen. "Because of course the Paynes . . ." And smiled, sadly.

Gladdy lowered her eyes, she hoped enough. "A tragedy."

Though Carl, the bugger, didn't know when to keep quiet. "Closer than you think," he said. "That funeral place is right across the road. Where they're waiting."

The old man looked frightened. A rosy flush burned at the edges of his eyes. "Hysteria," he said. "Stupid emotional people."

It was clear his wife agreed. Her hand went to his, clasped it. "The woman is clearly unwell, I feel sorry for the husband. Sitting waiting in that morbid place. And who could have known ahead of time?"

"Still," Carl said. "There's still the chance she's right."

Wainamoinen's eyebrows dropped like two grey wings. "Carl," he said. And looked away. "But you haven't said if you've seen the portrait."

"No," Gladdy said, quickly. "Not yet." And would happily have disappeared.

"No. 97," Sylvi Wainamoinen said, lifting a finger vaguely to her left.

The old man beamed. "At least five people!" he said. "Five people or more have shown interest. The painting will be sold before this evening is through. A beautiful thing, Carl, it's one of my best. A beautiful thing."

"Eli," his wife cautioned.

"Yes, one of my best. And the title, Carl. Do you know what the title is?"

If it says Carl Roote on it we may as well pack up right now, Gladdy thought. He would never stand for that.

But no. The old man lifted those eyebrows once again. "You'll see, I've made you immortal."

And so, suddenly, she and Carl were left standing in the middle of the room. Her bloody feet hurting. People's cigarette smoke stinging her eyes.

"C'mon," Carl growled at her. "Let's get this goddam thing over with." He elbowed a stoop-shouldered man out of the way.

David Payne, driving his car up through the web of downtown streets with his wife beside him silent and white and rigid with both hands fisted together before her mouth, wished for two things: that his day would be over as quickly as possible, and that whatever was going to happen after that would happen swiftly and with little trouble. He did not bother wishing that the dull pain in every bone of his body should go quickly or that the faint dizziness in his head should pass: such things were unimportant and would leave him anyway once this other business was over.

Wednesday. That's what it was, Wednesday. The streets were deserted, or nearly. A few people walking toward the theatre. It had been Monday morning — he'd barely settled into work at the office — when they phoned from the hospital to say it was too late, by the time they got the girl into the hospital it was too late for anyone to help her, that she had died quietly without ever regaining consciousness; and he had said, "What? What? What are you talking about? Are you talking about my daughter? Anna's at home, she was still sleeping when I left." They told him he'd better get over right away because obviously he'd been under the wrong impression and had better talk with his wife too who was sitting on a couch right there, right beside the phone. Where she was still sitting when he got there and hurled himself across the waiting room toward her and shouted out, "What's going on?" She sat, unruffled, undisturbed — he would have said uninvolved — and said Anna was dead but don't worry because she'd been promised something in three days. He said, "What?" and she said, "He promised. Destroy this temple and in three days I will raise it up."

"Don't be afraid, David," she said. Her hands, her beautiful hands, were folded in her lap. "You mustn't be afraid."

"What are we expecting?" he said. "We've never been inside any kind of a church since the day we were married. We know nothing of God. I can't recall you ever admitting even that you prayed. Who are we to expect a miracle?"

She'd looked at him as if he were a new, only slightly interesting piece of furniture someone had moved in front of her.

"There are people who refuse to believe in death," he said. "But they have their reasons and I don't pretend to understand them. There are even people who have cured people of hopeless diseases and brought them back from the edge of the grave through the power of prayer. I've read of them. But they have their reasons, they know what they're doing, they claim to understand what God is all about."

She crossed one leg over the other and closed her eyes while she pressed two fingers into the furrows of her forehead. She always looked, wherever she was sitting, like a person who was installed permanently in the chair. Or waiting for it to take her wherever it was she wanted to go.

"They don't just hope," he said. "They don't just have faith. They have reasons."

But she too had her reasons, she told him at last. The mirror, the voice, the promise.

As she had always had reasons, for everything she did. For marrying him in the first place: she was an interior decorator and it was just as easy to fall in love with an architect as with anyone else, she said, and much more practical. For insisting on living in rented suites all the twelve years of their marriage while every one of their friends had bought at least one house: she couldn't see any point in settling into anything of their own until they could afford the dream house they were capable of creating together. For refusing even to consider a second child once they'd discovered what was wrong with Anna: "Can you imagine what it would be like for her to have a *perfect* sister, a *perfect* brother?" she said, and shuddered at the thought as if only a monster would consider it. For heading off at

least once a year with the girl to some different part of the
continent seeking out every hint of a possible cure; she
believed that any doctor who practised on this island couldn't
possibly know all the latest discoveries and inventions, and
any parent who didn't at least investigate all the possibilities, no matter how remote, was cheating his own child out
of a normal life and ignoring his first duty.

He drove along the harbour where tourists in their yachts
stood talking across the floats to one another, over the still,
oily water. Then up through town and on up the hill. He
would like to press his foot right to the floor, keep right on
going up the hill, off up the mountain, into nowhere, into
somewhere else. But he drove — carefully, because here,
suddenly, cars full of young people were racing from light
to light — on up through town and onto the short street to
the mortuary. For blocks ahead the street was lined on either
side with cars, a surprise at first until he remembered that
this was Eli Wainamoinen's night, his show. "In another
country this would have happened forty years ago," Sylvi
Wainamoinen had told him. "But here, we must wait until a
life is almost over before we dare to celebrate it." David
Payne couldn't see how a gathering of a few hundred people
on Vancouver Island could be called celebrating a life, but
then he had never pretended to understand what the business of art and artists was all about.

As he pulled up in front of the Blessed Sleep Funeral
Home and parked his car in the reserved area, someone
opened the door to go into the ballroom of the hotel across
the street. Light slid out across the blacktop parking lot like
a sudden thrust finger when the door opened, then pulled
back in again and died suddenly. "It would be polite to at
least put in an appearance," he said, though he would
rather walk naked into fire than step in front of all those
eyes.

And she did not disappoint him. She breathed in, heavily. "No," she said, and exhaled. "Nobody would expect."

You could've stolen the show, he thought. Who'd want
to look at a lot of old-man paintings when there's an

honest-to-goodness fanatic in your midst? Wainamoinen would gnash his teeth in jealousy, and Sylvi — poor Sylvi — would have our furniture out on the street by the time we got home again.

Oh how nice to see you, Mrs. Payne, and isn't this the day your little girl . . .?

Yes, yes, but not a flicker yet.

Well never mind, the night's still young. I love your suit.

Dear God, he thought, and suddenly yanked on the hand brake. A police car moved slowly down the street and until it had gone out of sight the weight of pain on his chest nearly broke him.

He cracked all the finger joints of his left hand, one after the other. Then he did the same thing with the right.

"This is it," he said.

But she didn't move. "It's not as if I actually *did* something," she said. "It's not as if I hurt her."

"Or anybody else," he said. And hung his head. "Poor Carrie, you never hurt anybody in your life."

She did not move.

"Sometimes," he said, "in a particularly rainy spring the parent birds will let their children starve to death while they hover over them trying to keep them dry."

She looked at him. "Because they're afraid," she said. Then she said, "Let's go. Charlie will be wondering what happened to us."

Lost her, damn it. He'd gone and lost her. You couldn't take ten steps in this bastard crowd without your wife disappearing. People buzzed around like somebody was stirring them with a stick, the bottom of a paint can.

He would rather have been at home, where there was no one who pushed and shoved. He would rather have been back in the water again, cold as it would be by now, just lying out on his back and floating. You could trust the water, it would hold you up if you let go and allowed it. You could lie on your back and feel all of it below holding you up while you kept your eyes on the sky or closed them to watch your own dreams. You couldn't trust a crowd like that, it would even swallow your own wife.

He would have left her entirely, gone right out the door and waited for her somewhere in the foyer or downstairs in the beer parlour if it hadn't been for Kit O'Donnell.

"Carl!" she said, and broke loose from the crowd. "You look like somebody's lost little boy. Ready to cry!"

"Arrrgh," he said, and started to stomp out.

But she stood in front of him, head swivelling on that skinny neck. "Where's Gladdy? You always seem to have just misplaced her."

"Lost her," he said. "She was with me, and all of a sudden she wasn't. We was headed for the picture."

She put her finger to her lip, considered. "The place is full of booby-traps," she said, and spilled a small chain of laughter. "She could have bought a $1000 painting by the time you see her again."

"Not Gladdy," he said. "Not her." She wouldn't dare, not without asking him. She knew they couldn't afford it, even if she did see something she liked.

Though he wouldn't be surprised to hear Kit O'Donnell paid a fortune for something to hang in that boathouse shack she lived in. She'd done sillier things.

And wore clothes that no one but a husband should see. Carl didn't know where to look; the front was split open right down to her damn belly button, while her slit skirt let all the world see leg right to the hip.

He rooted around in his pocket and brought out his handkerchief, already damp, and passed it over his forehead, around his neck. The heat in this place, the heat could be over a hundred. And all these people were breathing up the air.

"What do you think?" he said, and nodded his head at all of it. She was a teacher and perhaps she could tell him what it was all about.

"Think?" she said, and raised an eyebrow as if it had never occurred to her.

"Of this, of him, of his stuff."

"Oh," she said, "that." And looked blank as if already she'd forgotten the question, or him, or both. Then, suddenly, when he'd nearly walked away, she came to life again, sucked in air.

"He puts on a good show," she said. Dismissing it, perhaps. She wasn't impressed.

"He got a crowd."

"He got a crowd. But the paintings disappear in a place like this. Side by side, hanging, you suddenly realize what they are — products. In his studio, one at a time, they can suck you in. When I sat for him he let me see just one painting a day, no more. Each was like a fist in the stomach."

"You sat? He painted you?"

She chewed on her bottom lip and studied him. One finger slid down her naked front. "A whole series," she said. "Nearly every evening for two or three months."

"I didn't know, I never seen any of them. What part of the hall are they in?"

She put fingers, hot as electric bars, on his hand. "I've got to teach in this town," she said, and slid her eyes to one side. "I asked him not to display, not this time, not here."

The old goat. Had this little girl on up there in his studio every night for three months. Didn't do nudies, eh? Didn't show nudies, maybe, but he did them all right. Like every other damn one of them so-called artists.

"No. 97," he said. "I think that's the number they said."

"For?"

"For the painting of this here mug. I may as well take a quick look at it before I get out of here."

She turned and led him through the crowd. They threaded their way past moving couples, between talking clusters, around knots of gawkers. She led him right down to the far end of the hall where the crowd was thinner, all the way down to the corner. Then she stood back for him to see, as if she were the painter.

What he saw first was Gladdy, standing alone, staring at the picture, her head cocked to one side, her long dress stretched tight across her rear end, and her tight shoes apart for balance.

Then the painting.

"Well shoot," he said. Because there must be a mistake. They were at the wrong one.

No. 97, though. And he couldn't deny the tuft of hair at his throat. Or the white stretch of forehead high into his thinning hair.

"Well shoot," he said.

Because it wasn't him at all. Not his face. Not any face he'd ever seen in a mirror. It was as if his face had been wiped partially off, then painted back on again just slightly altered so that it was someone else's, a stranger's. If he met this fellow on the street he'd pass him by without even thinking there was a resemblance.

"That looks more like old Wainamoinen himself than me."

Gladdy turned and just barely smiled and said, "Oh, it's you all right."

And Kit said, "It's not bad at all. Though a bit unusual for him."

The face which was not quite his face filled up most of the left half of the canvas. Looking out, as if the frame was actually a window through which he could watch with cold marble eyes all these people watching him. On the right, behind him, was the new foundation of a house being built on a rise of stones and weeds, and on the foundation, a few perfect pink studs stood up as if they had grown there, or been nailed down at random, though at the top of one there was a small branch of leaves still alive, curving upward: an impossibility. The sky behind was the worst; it came right down to the foundation, right down to the man's shoulders; and it was white, nearly white. As if it were both nothing at all and a terrible threat. Because there were faint shadows in it, like pale grey smoke, that might have been anything, as if you were meant to peel it away to reveal what was hidden within.

A man with that sky at his back would be cold all the time.

"Son of a bitch," Carl Roote muttered. And hoped no one else had seen him there. To guess.

"Eight hundred dollars," Gladdy cried, consulting the price list taped to the wall. Her finger moved across the paper. "No. 97. *The Builder*. Eight hundred dollars. That's what she told me."

Kit O'Donnell smiled. "He promised you immortality," she said. "Maybe what he meant was you'll be paying for it forever."

"I ain't buying it," Carl growled.

"But who?" Gladdy said, and sidled up to the picture as if she owned it already and he was threatening to give it away.

"Let some other stupid bastard pay to hang it on his wall," he said. "Right now I'm getting out of here."

In the basement suite of the artist's house Sparkle danced. Her body twisted and shook, jolted, twisted and shook, in the middle of the living-room floor. Hands flashed. Her hair whip-cracked in light.

The radio was turned up full volume, the house was solid sound. There wasn't another soul here but her — all the old creeps had gone. She was alone.

Twisted and shook, jolted, twisted and shook. Outside, the bay faded, the town translated itself into a band of yellow lights.

Hear it, hear it, she cried. Hear it, hear it.

Gladdy Roote could've bawled. Right into her pink lady. Men! She gritted her teeth to keep from speaking her thoughts.

They expected at least a clap of thunder. Or slashes of light. They thought that scales should fall.

Though she felt warm at the gaining of friendship. Kit O'Donnell had come in here with them, and argued with her against Carl's preference for the beer parlour, had ordered a pink lady too.

A corner table. Gladdy sat so that she could see, through the glass and across the foyer, the edges of movement in the wide doorway to the ballroom. And just by turning her head she could see the white stucco front of the Blessed Sleep Funeral Home through a window on the outside wall. It was a place you could sit all evening and never feel left out.

"I heard the brother agreed not to do anything to it until the three days were over," she said. "To the body."

Kit ran a finger around a stain on the Arborite table. "Is that legal?"

"I don't know, but I guess for a relative you can bend things a little."

Gladdy looked across the table at her own closest relative. But Carl, scowling, hunched over his glass of beer as if he wanted to wrap his own shoulders around it, the only thing he intended to acknowledge in this world.

"You can't deny he's attracted attention," Kit said. "For a painter."

"I suppose the papers are here."

"The locals," she said. "I don't imagine the Vancouver papers would send across a real art critic."

"It's possible," Gladdy said, and sipped. "Anything is possible."

The girl's great dark eyes travelled all around the inside of the lounge. "Yes, I imagine," she said. And laced her long hands together on the table, scarlet nails like petals of blood on the white. What Gladdy would give for nails again!

Others had come in from the art show, talking excitedly at their tables. The jangle of bracelets, the baritone laughter. Gladdy could not want to be anywhere else, she was alive here. If only they wouldn't notice the misery implied by Carl's posture.

"I should've come alone," she said. "To spare Carl."

Who grunted.

"Oh no!" the girl cried. "I'm always surprised to see one of you without the other. It never seems right. You two are one of those couples it seems impossible to imagine apart."

Carl lifted his face to look at her out of one eye. As if Kit had just now landed there, from Mars. Then he looked down and drank the beer, his third. Gladdy felt cold breezes at her neck.

"Oh, we know what it's like to be apart," she said. "We haven't always been together."

"It still wouldn't seem right."

"The operation," Gladdy said. And rejoiced at the sudden rigidity of Carl's shoulders, of his huge arms.

"The operation?"

"All that time, while I was laid out flat in the hospital he cooked like a woman, looked after Sparkle, kept house as clean as if I'd been there. All that time, we were apart."

She cocked her head.

"Mind you, he used to come up to the hospital every evening and just sit there, staring at me. And cry when he had to go."

Carl put his big hands around her wrist. "All right, Gladdy."

"But I told him it was good practice for him. I told him 'What if?' you know, 'What if?' but he said he'd never get used to it in a hundred years. He said he'd rather they cut off his privates than take me from him."

The hand jerked away. She'd gone too far. Even the little teacher was blushing.

"Well excuse me," Gladdy said, and stood up. "While I visit the powder-room."

And Kit, too, was standing. "I'll go with you." And followed. You might have thought the two of them were running away from that brooding hulk. She saw the bloodshot eyes slide up at her from under his brows. He was sulking; he would sulk for a good while yet.

Kit went for a mirror, to fuss with her hair, and Gladdy slipped into a cubicle, shut the door. "Did you ever imagine," she said, "the network of pipes there has to be under this town just to keep places like this ready for these little emergencies?"

Kit admitted that the thought had never occurred to her. She said if you started to think about all the complicated workings behind every simple part of your life you'd never be able to move.

"Ha!" said Gladdy Roote, and lowered her behind onto the black cold horseshoe seat.

Then added, "Did you see old Carl's face when he took a look at that picture? I thought he was going to drop dead out of shock, right there."

Kit's voice was high, more English than she'd thought. "He must have expected a photograph. He must have thought Eli's brushes were meant to do what a camera does."

"Eight hundred bucks for that!"

"Well, he'd probably lower the price a little if you were the ones to buy it."

"He could drop it all the way down to a dime and I know Carl wouldn't have that thing hanging in the house. Though he may be willing to pay for the right to chop it up in pieces."

And then she noticed.

A seam in her dress had opened up for a foot or so down the front. The stitching was right out, a long white thread. If she'd pulled it the gash would lengthen all the way up to her waist.

Jesus. She rummaged in her purse. For pins. For anything. You couldn't count on anything going right, it seemed. She turned over everything, all the combs and peppermints and bits of paper. She began taking everything out, one piece at a time, and laying it on the floor, but soon there was nothing left but fluff and grit at the bottom.

"What's going on in there?" Kit called. And laughed. "What are you doing?"

Throwing everything back into the purse. God damn this thing. How many people had noticed anyway? It was what happened when you had to make your own clothes, with an old machine. She'd never do it again, she'd steal first. The thought of those babes out there, noticing, laughing. She could spit.

And did. Straight into the toilet just as she pressed the lever.

"My bloody seam. Look," she said to Kit when she came out. And waited while the girl went through her own purse and came up with two straight pins, enough to get her through the evening.

"You're a doll, thanks," she said. And touched the girl, lightly, on the bare arm.

"Not at all," she laughed, and checked herself in the mirror, made a face. "You can't let a thing like that spoil your night."

"You can't let anything spoil anything," Gladdy said. "Not when you expect it will end. Some day."

Kit O'Donnell coughed, turning away. Tucking things back into her purse. Snapping the catch.

"Well," Gladdy said, and straightened everything, lifted her chin. "Let's go see if my old man's still pouting."

He was. Beautifully. His face like a brooding cloud hung over those beers. His red eyes shifted to watch them approach, then scowled again at the sudden appearance of someone else.

Eli Wainamoinen. Walking like a young man, at his age. Flushed.

Gladdy and Kit slid into their seats just as he arrived, his fingers playing with his own enormous ring. He tilted, nearly bowed; Gladdy could've snorted easily. Who was he suddenly, the Finnish ambassador?

"Carl?" he said.

Carl sat back, looked up. He showed his snoose-stained teeth.

"Carl, a gentleman has just approached me, from Victoria. He says he wants to buy *The Builder* but I told him not until I've spoken with my friend Carl Roote. In case."

"In case what?" Carl said.

"In case you want to buy it, stupid," Gladdy said. And nudged him with her elbow. "In case you don't want that someone else to own your picture."

"He likes it very much," the old man said. "He's a wealthy man, owns a huge house-building business. He told me he wants to hang the painting in his office!"

"His office!" Gladdy cried. Because whoever heard of putting out that kind of money for an office picture? Carl's office when he had one had two calendars for decoration, one of them several years old, both of them with pictures of hunters knee-deep in field-grass pointing shotguns at flying ducks.

"Well bully for him," Carl said. And drained his glass.

"I wouldn't say yes to him until I'd spoken to you. In case."

Carl looked at Gladdy, held his eyes steady on hers. "Well, Mr. Wainamoinen," he said, "you let that fellow have the bastard painting. It hasn't got nothing to do with me. It don't even look like me. And all that other shit you promised me . . . "

"Promised you?"

"All that crap. You laid out a hell of a lot of paint onto that canvas, Mr. Wainamoinen, but you never laid out no heaven. A camera could of done better."

"Jesus," Gladdy said. And shook her head. And waited.

Wainamoinen sat. He felt, suddenly, that his bones could easily have been two hundred years old. Carl Roote and Gladdy and Kit O'Donnell looked at him as if they expected him to shatter, fall apart, disintegrate.

You offered what you had to give and they did one of two things every time: didn't recognize what it was or rejected it without even looking.

"When you moved into my house I'm afraid I thought of you as my children," he said. To Gladdy. You couldn't expect Carl to look up. "I'd just lost my son and then you came along. I would've done anything. I told Sylvi she'd have to watch me, I might do anything I was such a fool. Just watch, I told her, they'll be up to complain about that tree, they'll be hollering they can't see the view just the same as Robert did, can't see anything but all those trunks. And I was willing, it didn't matter to me, we see right over the top. I would've chopped it down if you asked."

Carl looked up. His face glistened with sweat. "All we wanted was a place to live."

"Of course," Wainamoinen said. "And that is the point. I'm always trying to give people more than they want. It is a fault of many old men."

"I wouldn't've called it a fault exactly," Gladdy said.

"Oh but it is. When it intrudes. When it disappoints."

"We all disappoint," said the girl, and looked at the floor. "No one knows that better than a teacher."

"And have our faults," Gladdy said.

Though from the look on Carl's face you wouldn't think he was ready to agree.

"Still," Wainamoinen said. "There is more in that painting. If you had only looked at it. I've given you . . . given you, what you want, what you said."

But there was nothing in those faces to show they were listening. Or cared.

Then Gladdy Roote brought her hand up to her throat. "Look!" she said, and pointed out the window. "David Payne. He's coming out of that place, out of that funeral place."

Carl didn't hear the first time she said it. He was thinking of the three beers and the painting. Wishing he could be at home tipping back a bottle from his own fridge. With Gladdy in the other chair drinking beer too with him, instead of that pale stinking gin in its silly glass.

Then: "David."

David Payne, where? Where the hell did she see him?

He twisted, nearly swept the table with his elbow, strained his neck to see. Out in the almost-dark the bastard was coming down those steps, watching for traffic, running fingers of one hand back and forth across the back of his neck. He looked like he'd seen a goblin, or a ghost.

All at once, something inside Carl leapt.

"What?" Kit said. "What is it?"

"Look out, you'll knock the bloody table over!" Gladdy threw her weight to counterbalance his threat.

"Aw," he said.

He would've pushed them all.

But they jumped back, let him free. Gladdy screeching: "Watch out what you're doing, can't you. Look what you spilled on my dress!"

Wainamoinen gestured, his hands helpless, his stiff face crumbling.

"Excuse me," he said as if he'd been the one to knock the table. "Pardon me."

He stood in front of Kit. "Carl, Carl."

Carl only grunted. And pushed past, bumping one shoulder against the wall. "Shit."

If this was it! If this was the goddam thing, wouldn't they just look? These other bastards with their show, all of them, wouldn't they just sit up at the difference? What would a bunch of paintings add up to then?

In his hurry to get out into the foyer he nearly fell over someone. But he ducked aside and went across the red carpet (people turning, he couldn't say who, and saying "What's wrong?" and "Who's that?") and managed to straighten himself and slow down a little by the time he got to the oak door.

The smell of gasoline exhaust. And pulp mill. The shock of the light flashing violet neon from the sign: HOTEL ARBUTUS HOTEL. Down on the sidewalk he waited for a truck and camper to pass. "Yaw!" he yelled at the driver, a bulge-eyed American staring at him, slowing down. But the truck stopped right in front of him and the driver stuck his head out the window: "We just got off the ferry. Where's your liquor store?" Carl yelled, "Yaw," again and gestured for him to move on out of the way. "Bugger off, mister, go on out of here."

When the truck had moved, David Payne was holding onto the lamp-post at the edge of the sidewalk, hunched over and staring down at the street as if he expected to be sick.

"What happened?" Carl said. "What happened there?" His chest hummed with the possibilities, his head throbbed.

But David Payne's face was yellow, his eyes ringed with dark smudges. "Hunh?" he said. And shook his head. His hand on the post was fat and short, like mottled raw sausage.

So Carl went right on past. Though the sight of any funeral home was enough to make his stomach knot, it was plain he was going to have to go inside this one.

He had to see whatever it was that had yellowed David's

face, sent him outside. He had to face that woman and her damn coffin.

Or whatever.

Behind him, the others had come out onto the street too. He could hear. Let them come, let them follow. Let them have something to talk about tomorrow.

He couldn't help noticing someone had done a hurry-up job on the concrete steps, lousy trowel work, with ridges and hollows. It was his unthinking habit whenever he entered a new building to estimate the size of rooms by counting plywood panels or ceiling beams or imaginary paces down the length of floor, and to pass judgment on the quality of the finishing work (mitre joints of casings told the story, and cupboard doors). But when he left the foyer and walked across the second room of the Blessed Sleep Funeral Home, where a person would normally expect to find a body laid out, there was no time or inclination for estimating, there was only a vague impression of polished coffins sitting around on chrome legs. And in a third room beyond, there was only Anna Payne laid out on a small bed in the very centre, blankets pulled up to her chin like someone sleeping. And Carrie Payne, looking at him down the length of it.

"Carl," she said. You'd think it was the name of a little boy who had run to her for comfort.

He'd never before seen such a face. Swollen. Those two eyes which must've gradually been getting bigger every minute since Monday morning were looking at him now as if he should have been able to walk right on inside and disappear.

"Oh God, Carl, I think she moved."

His throat clamped. "What? Now? Just now?" Because if it was, he was running.

She shook her head. "Earlier. I was sure of it. I could've sworn she moved, just the smallest bit."

She offered it like a shy gift, but he could have puked. He couldn't even let himself look down at the girl, whose head was just inches below Carrie Payne's chin. Her hands were down somewhere underneath as if she were ready to haul that body right up into a sitting position for him to face.

"Goddamit, Carrie," he said. "Are you sure?"

"Of course she's not sure."

It was David's voice, behind, in the doorway. "She only thinks she saw."

"I was sure of it, David." Now she was someone begging for favours. "I was sure I saw her move."

Carl turned. If David Payne hadn't been in the doorway he might have run. But the little man stood there as if he expected to fall, and lifted up his face just far enough to look out from under those eyebrows. "Don't lie, Carrie," he said. "It's only because you were so sure. It's only because you expected."

Outside, a car braked, suddenly. The tires screeched, it seemed, down the full length of the block.

Wainamoinen on the steps of the Arbutus Hotel watched the car skid to a stop. Then he followed the others across the street as far as the door to the funeral home. Something heavy sat on his chest, however, and he turned to start back toward the hotel, moving slowly through the neon violet like a swimmer.

Gladdy said "Ah!" and bit her lip.

Everyone was going up those steps after Carl and David. Pushing against shoulders.

She put her hand on the pale flesh of Kit's arm. "You don't suppose?" she said. And swallowed.

"Don't be silly."

The girl had the kindness to soften the words with the quick touch of fingers.

Still, a person couldn't just turn her back and pretend. "Maybe Carl needs me in there."

The girl, though, was not convinced. Or raised an eyebrow at least to question. So Gladdy added: "Who knows what the bugger might do," and stepped forward to follow the others.

If there had been a way of avoiding this she would take

it, provided no one noticed. If she could have refused to put one foot inside that place, avoid getting the chilled skin called up by velvet and candles and polished wood. But she couldn't leave Carl like that, when his mind was thrashing about, when he might not be able to stomach it. He didn't know that you couldn't conquer it by fearing it, any more than you could by daring it or by tempting it or by accepting it.

"Well, if it happens," she reminded herself, "you won't see me for dust."

She was, too, spared the unpleasantness of witnessing. Whatever had been going on had reached an end. Someone rushed out past her, hand on his mouth, muttering, "Jesus Christ," and nearly fell over his own feet to avoid bumping her. And a woman, following, touched Gladdy's arm. "There's no point going in," she said. "Leave the poor things alone."

Clutching her purse she stepped into the room, smelled the thick heavy scent of flowers and furniture polish, felt the breathing, the shifting of feet. Was there a decent way to enter such a place? All eyes seemed happy to turn her way, to avoid whatever else there was.

But looking straight at things was one demand Gladdy Roote had always made of herself. Directly ahead was Carrie Payne, standing over a bed as if it was something she needed to defend. She glanced up at Gladdy out of one eye from under a wing of hair which had fallen.

But it was David, not Gladdy, who attacked. "Can't you see what fools we've become? Look, they're crowding in to stare at us."

At the same time, he put a hand on her arm as if to give her comfort too, or maybe just to keep from falling over. Carrie only strengthened her grip on whatever she had ahold of at the top end of the bed. A dark-suited man who must have been the brother hovering about, fluttering, looked ready to scream at the chaos which had broken out in his premises. He looked like a man who was considering a blow to the side of his sister's head to bring her to her senses.

David: "Think of the number of people who die every

day in this world. Out of all that tell me how you dare to expect one girl to be chosen for this special privilege? Do you think we are so different?"

And Carrie: "How do you know how He works? You don't know Him. I saw her move."

Gladdy's knees gave under her, she could've dropped. Something gurgled in her stomach.

David was trying to pull her hands away, trying to loosen their grip on the bed. "It's only because you refuse to admit," he said.

And Carl too, now, was getting in on the act. He placed a big hand on David's shoulder. "Leave her alone. She's got a right to expect."

But David flung him off.

Gladdy said, "Carl," and bit her lip. He didn't hear.

"She's got a right," he said. "You can't blame a person for being on the side of life. There's enough of the bastards already to take the other side."

Gladdy thought it was a laugh that lifted in her chest but it was a hiccup instead. She couldn't be sure how many heard and anyway it didn't matter because now David was trying to push Carl toward the door. "Go on away," he said. "Leave us alone." And to them all: "Leave us alone, can't you? Leave us alone."

But Carl wasn't giving in. Not yet. "That picture too," he said. "That bastard picture turned out to be nothing."

David Payne might not have heard. Gladdy didn't know whether to drag Carl out or leave by herself and let him find his own way out of the mess he was making. Now that he was getting louder.

"You'd think he'd painted the all-time masterpiece the way he carried on, the way he talked. But it was nothing. Nothing at all." He clasped a hand around the thin arm of David Payne. "You would've expected it to be something more than that."

"No," David said. "Go away, Carl. Leave us be. Go on back where you were."

So he pulled on the arm, nearly yanked the little man off

balance. His voice softer now. "But there's got to be something!" His eyes, bloodshot, toured the room until they found Gladdy. She could feel their two glances lock like the snap of a screen door closing. "Because if I lose her! Because if I goddam lose her!"

Then he bolted.

She could've cried, the way he looked at her. As if somebody had come up behind and hit him on the head with a great wooden mallet. Seeing something he hadn't seen before, or hadn't been there.

She snapped eyes at Carrie, at David, and said, "Well, if anybody's risen this day it wasn't in the flesh," before hurrying out to the foyer. She could almost have added, "Nor was it one of the Paynes, either," if there wasn't this something in her throat. She thought of rummaging in her purse, in the junk again, for a hanky . . . anything. But she found, quite surprisingly, that there was no need after all for the hanky or for anything else to stall her. She snapped the purse closed and hurried outside.

The street, a little darker now, was nearly deserted. Only a few stragglers on the other side, around the hotel doorway. Carl was seated on the top step of the Funeral Home with his back against the door frame, watching his own hands out of eyes that had shrunk down to the dull stone hardness of late-season blackberries. Like a man, perhaps, who sits amongst the leaves and sawdust in the open bed of a pickup truck, just waiting to be taken somewhere.

"When I saw it wasn't going to happen I was glad," he said. "I would've been just as scared of it as you. Scareder."

"Still, it's only natural, I guess. To want some kind of sign."

"Hell, Gladdy." His hand clamped around one of her ankles. "That's what I mean." He ran the hand up her leg. "Any bugger who's saddled with an old rip like you for a wife's got no business looking for signs. It's them other people that have to make them up. The ones that don't trust something." The hand moved away then, fanned lightly across the concrete step. "Lookit this mess, Gladdy. Too

damned rushed to do a decent trowel job of it. They couldn't
wait for it to set right."

She moved the toe of her shoe over the offending step.
As if she could feel, through the sole, the imperfections his
hand could detect almost without touch. "Let's go home."

He pulled his hand back in, started to rise, and then
slumped again. "Aw Gladdy, don't go, not yet. Sit here for a
while. Just till I catch my breath."

"Sit on cement?" she said. But sat, all the same, and
smiled. The bloody dress had already fallen apart — what
more damage could she do it?

She looked out across the street to where the HOTEL
ARBUTUS HOTEL sign splashed light down the front of the
building and out over the roofs of cars. Someone inside the
ballroom laughed. Gladdy Roote in that moment swelled,
throbbed, with the rich blood of her possibilities.

5

The Lepers' Squint

Today, while Mary Brennan may be waiting for him on that tiny island high in the mountain lake called Gougane Barra, Philip Desmond is holed up in the back room of this house at Bantry Bay, trying to write his novel. A perfect stack of white paper, three black nylon-tipped pens, and a battered portable typewriter are set out before him on the wooden table. He knows the first paragraph already, has already set it down, and trusts that the rest of the story will run off the end of it like a fishing line pulled by a salmon. But it is cold, it is so cold in this house, even now in August, that he presses both hands down between his thighs to warm them up. It is so cold in this room that he finds it almost impossible to sit still, so damp that he has put on the same clothes he would wear if he were walking out along the edge of that lagoon, in the spitting rain and the wind. Through the small water-specked panes of the window he can see his children playing on the lumpy slabs of rock at the shore, beyond the bobbing branches of the fuchsia hedge. Three children; three red quilted jackets; three faces flushed up by the steady force of the cold wind; they drag tangled clots of stinking seaweed up the slope and, crouching, watch a family of swans explore the edges of a small weedy island not far out in the lagoon.

A high clear voice in his head all the while insists on singing to him of some girl so fair that the ferns uncurl to look at her. The voice of an old man in a mountain pub, singing without accompaniment, stretched and stiff as a rooster singing to the ceiling and to the crowd at the bar and to the neighbours who sit around him. *The ferns uncurled to look at her, so very fair was she, with her hair as bright as the seaweed that floats in from the sea.* But here at Ballylickey the seaweed is brown as mud and smells so strong your eyes water.

Mrs. O'Sullivan is in the next room, Desmond knows, in her own room, listening. If he coughs she will hear. If he sings. She will know exactly the moment he sets down his next word on that top sheet of paper. Mrs. O'Sullivan is the owner of this house, which Desmond rented from home through the Borde Failte people before he discovered that she would live in it with them, in the centre of the house, in her two rooms, and silently listen to the life of his family going on around her. She is a tall dry-skinned old woman with grey finger-waves caged in blue hair-net, whose thick fingers dig into the sides of her face in an agony of desire to sympathize with everything that is said to her. "Oh I know I know I know," she groans. Last night when Desmond's wife mentioned how tired she was after the long drive down from Dublin, her fingers plucked at her face, her dull eyes rolled up to search for help along the ceiling: "Oh I know I know I know." There is no end to her sympathy, there is nothing she doesn't already know. But she will be quiet as a mouse, she promised, they won't know she is here.

"Maybe she's a writer," Desmond's wife whispered to him, later in bed. "Maybe she's making notes on us. Maybe she's writing a book called *North Americans I Have Eavesdropped On*."

"I can't live with someone listening to me breathe," Desmond said. "And I can't write with someone sitting waiting."

"Adjust," his wife said, and flicked at his nose. She who could adjust to anything, or absorb it.

On this first day of his novel Desmond has been abandoned by his wife, Carrie, who early this morning drove the car in to Cork. There are still, apparently, a few Seamus Murphy statues she hasn't seen, or touched. "Keep half an eye on the kids," she said before she left. Then she came back and kissed him and whispered, "Though if you get busy it won't matter. I'm sure Mrs. O'Sullivan won't miss anything." To be fair, to be really fair, he knows that his annoyance is unjustified. He didn't tell her he intended to work today, the first day in this house. She probably thinks that after travelling for six weeks through the country he'll rest a few more days before beginning; she may even believe that he is glad to be rid of her for the day, after all those weeks of unavoidable closeness. She certainly knows that with Mrs. O'Sullivan in the house no emergency will be overlooked, no crisis ignored.

Desmond, now that his hands have warmed a little, lifts one of the pens to write, though silently as possible, as if what he is about to do is a secret perversion from which the ears of Mrs. O'Sullivan must be protected. But he cannot, now, put down any new words. Because if the novel, which has been roaring around in his head all summer and much longer, looking for a chance to get out, should not recognize in the opening words the crack through which it is to spring forth, transformed into a string of words like a whirring fishline, then he will be left with all that paper to stare at, and an unmoving pen, and he is not ready to face that. Of course he knows the story, has seen it all in his mind a hundred times as if someone else had gone to the trouble of writing it and producing it as a movie just for him. But he has never been one for plunging into things, oceans or stories, and prefers to work his way in gently. That opening paragraph, though, is only a paragraph after all and has no magic, only a few black lifeless lines at the top of the paper. So he writes his title again, and under it his name: Barclay Philip Desmond. Then he writes the opening paragraph a second time, and again under that, and again, hoping that the pen will go on by itself to write the next words and surprise him. But it does not happen, not now. Instead, he discovers he is seeing two other words which are not there at all, as if perhaps they are embedded, somehow, just beneath the surface of the paper.

Mary Brennan.

Desmond knows he must keep the name from becoming anything more than that, from becoming a face too, or the pale scent of fear. He writes his paragraph again, over and over until he has filled up three or four pages. Then, crumpling the papers in his hand, he wonders if this will be one of those stories that remain forever in their authors' heads, driving them mad, refusing to suffer conversion into words.

It's the cold, he thinks. Blame it on the bloody weather. His children outside on the rocky slope have pulled the hoods of their jackets up over their heads. Leaves torn from the beech tree lie soaked and heavy on the grass. At the far side of the lagoon the family of swans is following the choppy retreating tide out through the gap to the open bay; perhaps they know of a calmer inlet somewhere. The white stone house with red window frames in its nest of bushes across the water has blurred behind the rain, and looks more than ever like the romantic pictures he has seen on postcards. A thin line of smoke rises from the yellowish house with the gate sign *Carrigdhoun*.

But it is easier than writing, far easier, to allow the persistent daydreams in, and memory. That old rooster-stiff man, standing in the cleared-away centre of the bar in Ballyvourney to pump his song out to the ceiling, his hands clasping and unclasping at his sides as if they are responsible for squeezing those words into life. The ferns uncurled to see her, he sings, so very fair was she. Neighbours clap rhythm, or stamp their feet. Men six-deep at the bar-counter continue to shout at each other about sheep, and the weather. With hair as bright as the seaweed that floats in from the sea.

"'Tis an island of singers sure!" someone yells in Desmond's ear. "An island of saints and paupers and bloody singers!"

But Desmond thinks of Mary Brennan's hot apple-smelling breath against his face: "Islands do not exist until you have loved on them." The words are a Caribbean poet's, she explains, and not her own. But the sentiment is adaptable. The ferns may not uncurl to see the dark brown beauty of her eyes, but Desmond has seen men turn at her flash of hair, the reddish-brown of gleaming kelp. Turn, and smile to themselves. This day while he sits behind the wooden table, hunched over his pile of paper, he knows that she is waiting for him on a tiny hermitage island in a mountain lake not far away, beneath the branches of the crowded trees. Islands, she had told him, do not exist until you've loved on them.

Yesterday, driving south from Dublin across the Tipperary farmland, they stopped again at the Rock of Cashel so that Carrie could prowl a second time through that big roofless cathedral high up on the sudden limestone knoll and run her hands over the strange broken form of St. Patrick's Cross. The kings of Munster lived there once, she told him, and later turned it over to the church. St. Patrick himself came to baptize the king there, and accidentally pierced the poor man's foot with the point of his heavy staff.

"There's all of history here, huddled together," she said, and catalogued it for him. "A tenth-century round tower, a twelfth-century chapel, a thirteenth-century cathedral, a fourteenth-century tower, a fifteenth-century castle, and . . ." she rolled her eyes, "a twentieth-century tourist shop."

But it was the cross itself that drew her. Originally a cross within a frame, it was only the central figure of a man now, with one arm of the cross and a thin upright stem that held that arm in place. Rather like a tall narrow pitcher. There was a guide this second time, and a tour, and she pouted when he insisted they stick to the crowd and hear the official truths instead of making guesses or relying on the brief explanations on the backs of postcards. She threw him a black scowl when the guide explained the superstition about the cross: that if you can touch hand to hand around it you'll never have another toothache as long as you live. Ridiculous, she muttered; she'd spent an hour the last time looking at that thing, marvelling at the beautiful piece of sculpture nature or time or perhaps vandals had accidentally made of it, running her hands over the figures on the coronation stone at its base and up the narrow stem that supported the remaining arm of the cross.

He was more curious, though, about the round swell of land which could be seen out across the flat Tipperary farms, a perfect green hill crowned with a circle of leafy trees. The guide told him that after one of the crusades a number of people returned to Ireland with a skin disease which was mistaken for leprosy and were confined to that hill, inside that circle, and forbidden to leave it. They were brought across to Mass here on Sundays, she said, before leading him back inside the cathedral to show a small gap in the stones far up one grey wall of the empty Choir. "The poor lepers, a miserable lot altogether as you can imagine, were crowded into a little room behind that wall," she said, "and were forced to see and hear through that single narrow slit of a window. It's called the Lepers' Squint, for obvious reasons."

Afterwards, when the crowd of nuns and priests and yellow-slickered tourists had broken up to walk amongst the graves and the Celtic crosses or to climb the stone steps to the round tower, Desmond would like to have spoken to one of the priests, perhaps the short red-faced one, to say, "What do you make of all this?" or "Is it true what she told us about that fat archbishop with all his wives and children?" But he was intimidated by the black suit, that collar, and by the way the priest seemed always to be surrounded by nuns who giggled like schoolgirls at the silly jokes he told, full of words Desmond couldn't understand. He would go home without ever speaking to a single member of the one aristocracy this country still permitted itself.

But while he stood tempted in the sharp wind that

howled across the high hump of rock the guide came over the grass to him. "'Tis certain that you're not American as I thought at first," she said, "for you speak too soft for that. Would you be from England then?"

"No," he said. And without thinking: "We're from Vancouver Island."

"Yes?" she said, her eyes blank. "And where would that be now?"

"A long way from here," he said. "An island, too, like this one, with its own brand of ruins.

"There's a tiny island off our coast," he said, "where they used to send the lepers once, but the last of them died a few years ago. It's a bare and empty place they say now, except for the wind. There are even people who believe that ghosts inhabit it."

But then there were people, too, who said he was crazy to take the children to this uneasy country. It's smaller than you think, they said. You'll hear the bombs from above the border when you get there. What if war breaks out? What if the IRA decides that foreign hostages might help their cause? What about that bomb in the Dublin department store?

Choose another country, they said. A warmer safer one. Choose an island where you can lie in the sun and be waited on by smiling blacks. Why pick Ireland?

Jealousy, he'd told them. Everyone else he knew seemed to have inherited an "old country", an accent, a religion, a set of customs, from parents. His family fled the potato famine in 1849 and had had five generations in which to fade out into Canadians. "I don't know what I've inherited from them," he said, "but whatever it is has gone too deep to be visible."

They'd spent the summer travelling; he would spend the fall and winter writing.

His search for family roots, however, had ended down a narrow hedged-in lane: a half-tumbled stone cabin, stony fields, a view of misty hills, and distant neighbours who turned their damp hay with a two-tined fork and knew nothing at all of the cabin's past.

"Fled the famine did they?" the old woman said. "'Twas many a man did that and was never heard from since."

The summer was intended as a literary pilgrimage too, and much of it was a disappointment. Yeats's castle tower near Coole had been turned into a tourist trap as artificial as a wax museum, with cassette recorders to listen to as you walk through from room to room, and a souvenir shop to sell you books and postcards; Oliver Goldsmith's village was not only deserted, it had disappeared, the site of the little schoolhouse nothing more than a potato patch and the parsonage just half a vine-covered wall; the James Joyce museum only made him feel guilty that he'd never been able to finish *Ulysses*, though there'd been a little excitement that day when a group of women's libbers crashed the male nude-bathing beach just behind the tower.

A man in Dublin told him there weren't any live writers in this country. "You'll find more of our novelists and poets in America than you'll find here," he said. "You're wasting your time on that."

With a sense almost of relief, as though delivered from a responsibility (dead writers, though disappointing, do not confront you with flesh, as living writers could, or with demands), he took the news along with a handful of hot dogs to Carrie and the kids, who had got out of the car to admire a statue. Watching her eat that onion and pork sausage "hot dog" he realized that she had become invisible to him, or nearly invisible. He hadn't even noticed until now that she'd changed her hair, that she was pinning it back; probably because of the wind. In the weeks of travel, in constant too-close confinement, she had all but disappeared, had faded out of his notice the way his own limbs must have done, oh, thirty years ago.

If someone had asked, "What does your wife look like?" he would have forgotten to mention short. He might have said dainty but that was no longer entirely true; sitting like that she appeared to have rounded out, like a copper Oriental idol: dark and squat and yet fine, perhaps elegant. He could not have forgotten her loud, almost masculine laugh of course, but he had long ago ceased to notice the quality of her speaking voice. Carrie, his Carrie, was busy having her own separate holiday, almost untouched by his, though they wore each other like old comfortable unnoticed and unchanged clothes.

"A movie would be nice," he said. "If we could find a babysitter."

But she shook her head. "We can see movies at home. And besides, by the evenings I'm tired out from all we've done, I'd never be able to keep my eyes open."

After Cashel, on their way to the Bantry house, they stopped a while in the city of Cork. And here, he discovered, here after all the disappointments, was a dead literary hero the tourist board hadn't yet got ahold of. He forgot again that she even existed as he tracked down the settings of the stories he loved: butcher shops and smelly quays and dark crowded pubs and parks.

The first house, the little house where the famous writer was born, had been torn down by a sports club which had put a high steel fence around the property, but a neighbour took him across the road and through a building to the back balcony to show him the Good Shepherd Convent where the writer's mother had grown up, and where she returned often with the little boy to visit the nuns. "If he were still alive," Desmond said, "if he still lived here, I suppose I would be scared to come, I'd be afraid to speak to him." The little man, the neighbour, took off his glasses to shine them on a white handkerchief. "Ah, he was a shy man himself. He was back here a few years before he died, with a big crew of American fillum people, and he was a friendly man, friendly enough. But you could see he was a shy man too, yes. 'Tis the shy ones sometimes that take to the book writing."

Carrie wasn't interested in finding the second house. She had never read the man's books, she never read anything at all except art histories and museum catalogues. She said she would go to the park, where there were statues, if he'd let her off there. She said if the kids didn't get out of the car soon to run off some of their energy they would drive her crazy, or kill each other. You could hardly expect children to be interested in old dead writers they'd never heard of, she said. It was no fun for them.

He knew as well as she did that if they were not soon released from the backseat prison they would do each other damage. "I'll go alone," he said.

"But don't be long. We've got a good ways to do yet if we're going to make it to that house today."

So he went in search of the second house, the house the writer had lived in for most of his childhood and youth and had mentioned in dozens of his stories. He found it high up the sloping streets on the north side of the river. Two rows of identical homes, cement-grey, faced each other across a bare sloping square of dirt, each row like a set of steps down the slope, each home just a gate in a cement waist-high wall, a door, a window. Somewhere in this square was where the barefoot grandmother had lived, and where the lady lived whose daughter refused to sleep lying down because people died that way, and where the toothless woman lived who between her sessions in the insane asylum loved animals and people with a saintly passion.

The house he was after was half-way up the left-hand slope and barely distinguishable from the others, except that there was a woman in the tiny front yard, opening the gate to come out.

"There's no one home," she said when she saw his intentions. "They weren't expecting me this time, and presumably, they weren't expecting you either."

"Then it is the right house?" Desmond said. Stupidly, he thought. Right house for what?

But she seemed to understand. "Oh yes. It's the right house. Some day the city will get around to putting a plaque on the wall but for the time being I prefer it the way it is. My name, by the way," she added, "is Mary Brennan. I don't live here but I stop by often enough. The old man, you see, was one of my teachers years ago."

She might have been an official guide, she said it all so smoothly. Almost whispering. And there was barely a trace of the musical tipped-up accent of the southern counties in her voice. Perhaps Dublin, or educated. Her name meant nothing to him at first, coming like that without warning. "There would be little point in your going inside anyway, even if they were home," she said. "There's a lovely young couple living there now but they've redone the whole thing over into a perfectly charming but very modern apartment. There's nothing at all to remind you of him. I stop by for reasons I don't begin to understand, respect perhaps, or inspiration, but certainly not to find anything of him here."

In a careless, uneven way, she was pretty. Even beautiful. She wore clothes — a yellow skirt, a sweater — as if they'd been pulled on as she'd hurried out the door. Her coat was draped over her arm, for the momentary blessing of sun. But she was tall enough to get away with the sloppiness and had brown eyes which were calm, calming. And hands that tended to behave as if they were helping deliver her words to him, stirring up the pale scent of her perfume. He would guess she was thirty, she was a little younger than he was.

"Desmond," he said. "Uh, Philip Desmond."

She squinted at him, as if she had her doubts. Then she nodded, consenting. "You're an American," she said. "And probably a writer. But I must warn you. I've been to your part of the world and you just can't do for it what he did for this. It isn't the same. You don't have the history, the sense that everything that happens is happening on top of layers of things which have already happened. Now I saw you drive up in a motor car and I arrived on a bus so if you're going back down to the city centre I'll thank you for a ride."

Mary Brennan, of course. Why hadn't he known? There were two of her books in the trunk of his car. Paperbacks. Desmond felt his throat closing. Before he'd known who she was she hadn't let him say a word, and now that she seemed to be waiting to hear what he had to offer, he was speechless. His mind was a blank. All he could think of was *Mary Brennan* and wish that she'd turned out to be only a colourful eccentric old lady, something he could handle. He

was comfortable with young women only until they turned
out to be better than he was at something important to him.
Then his throat closed. His mind pulled down the shades
and hid.

All Desmond could think to say, driving down the hill
towards the River Lee, was: "A man in Dublin told me there
was no literature happening in this country." He could have
bitten off his tongue. This woman *was* what was happening.
A country that had someone like her needed no one else.

She would not accept that, she said, not even from a
man in Dublin. And she insisted that he drive her out to the
limestone castle restaurant at the mouth of the river so she
could buy him a drink there and convince him Dublin was
wrong. Inside the castle, though, while they watched the
white ferry to Swansea slide out past their window, she
discovered she would rather talk about her divorce, a messy
thing which had been a strain on everyone concerned and
had convinced her if she needed convincing that marriage
was an absurd arrangement. She touched Desmond, twice,
with one hand, for emphasis.

Oh, she was a charming woman, there was no question.
She could be famous for those eyes alone, which never
missed a detail in that room (a setting she would use, perhaps, in her next novel of Irish infidelity and rebellion?)
and at the same time somehow returned to him often enough
and long enough to keep him frozen, afraid to sneak his
own glances at the items she was cataloguing for herself.
"Some day," she said, "they will have converted all our
history into restaurants and bars like this one, just as I will
have converted it all to fiction. Then what will we have?"

And when, finally, he said he must go, he really must
go, the park was pretty but didn't have all that much in it for
kids to do, she said, "Listen, if you want to find out what is
happening here, if you really do love that old man's work,
then join us tomorrow. There'll be more than a dozen of us,
some of the most exciting talent in the country, all meeting
up at Gougane Barra . . . you know the place, the lake in the
mountains where this river rises . . . it was a spot he loved."

"Tomorrow," he said. "We'll have moved in by then, to the house we've rented for the winter."

"There's a park there now," she said. "And of course the tiny hermitage island. It will begin as a picnic but who knows how it will end." The hand, a white hand with unpainted nails, touched him again.

"Yes," he said. "Yes. We've been there. There's a tiny church on the island, he wrote a story about it, the burial of a priest. And it's only an hour or so from the house, I'd guess. Maybe. Maybe I will."

"Oh you must," she said, and leaned forward. "You knew, of course, that they call it Deep-Valleyed Desmond in the songs." She drew back, biting on a smile.

But when he'd driven her back to the downtown area, to wide St. Patrick's Street, she discovered she was not quite ready yet to let him go. "Walk with me," she said, "for just a while," and found him a parking spot in front of the Munster Arcade where dummies dressed as monks and Vikings and Celtic warriors glowered at him from behind the glass.

"This place exists," she said, "because he made it real for me. He and others, in their stories. I could never write about a place where I was the first, it would panic me. I couldn't be sure it really existed or if I were inventing it."

She led him down past the statue of sober Father Matthew and the parked double-decker buses to the bridge across the Lee. A wind, coming down the river, brought a smell like an open sewer with it. He put his head down and tried to hurry across.

"If I were a North American, like you," she said, "I'd have to move away or become a shop girl. I couldn't write."

He was tempted to say something about plastering over someone else's old buildings, but thought better of it. He hadn't even read her books yet, he knew them only by reputation, he had no right to comment. He stopped, instead, to lean over the stone wall and look at the river. It was like sticking his head into a septic tank. The water was dark, nearly black, and low. Along the edges rats moved over humps of dark shiny muck and half-buried cans and bottles. Holes in the stone wall dumped a steady stream of new sewage into the river. The stories, as far as he could remember, had never mentioned this. These quays were romantic places where young people met and teased each other, or church-goers gathered to gossip after Mass, or old people strolled. None of them, apparently, had noses.

Wind in the row of trees. Leaves rustling. Desmond looked at her hands. The perfect slim white fingers lay motionless along her skirt, then moved suddenly up to her throat, to touch the neck of her sweater. Then the nearer one moved again, and touched his arm. Those eyes, busy recording the street, paused to look at him; she smiled. Cataloguing me too? he thought. Recording me for future reference? But she didn't know a thing about him.

"I've moved here to work on a book," he said.

Her gaze rested for a moment on the front of his jacket, then flickered away. "Not about *here*," she said. "You're not writing about *this* place?" She looked as if she would protect it from him, if necessary, or whisk it away.

"I have my own place," he said. "I don't need to borrow his."

She stopped, to buy them each an apple from an old black-shawled woman who sat up against the wall by her table of fruit. Ancient, gypsy-faced, with huge earrings hanging from those heavy lobes. Black Spanish eyes. Mary Brennan flashed a smile, counted out some silver pieces, and picked over the apples for two that were red and clear. The hands that offered change were thick and wrinkled, with crescents of black beneath the nails. They disappeared again beneath the shawl. Desmond felt a momentary twinge about biting into the apple; vague memories of parental warnings. You never know whose hands have touched it, they said, in a voice to make you shudder in horror at the possibilities and scrub at the skin of fruit until it was bruised and raw.

Mary Brennan, apparently, had not been subjected to the same warnings. She bit hugely. "Here," she said, at the bridge, "here is where I'm most aware of him. All his favourite streets converge here, from up the hill. Sunday's Well, over there where his wealthy people lived. And of course Blarney Lane. If you had the time we could walk up there, I could show you. Where his first house was, and the pub he dragged his father home from."

"I've seen it," Desmond said, and started across the bridge. She would spoil it all for him if he let her.

But she won him again on the way back down the other side with her talk of castles and churches. Did he know, she asked, the reason there was no roof on the cathedral at Cashel? Did he know why Blackrock Castle where they'd been a half-hour before was a different style altogether than most of the castles of Ireland? Did he know the origin of the word "blarney"?

No he did not, but he knew that his wife would be furious if he didn't hurry back to the park. They passed the noise of voices haggling over second-hand clothes and old books at the Coal Market, they passed the opera house, a tiny yellow book store. She could walk, he saw, the way so many women had forgotten how to walk after high-heeled shoes went out, with long legs and long strides, with some spring in her steps as if there were pleasure in it.

"Now you'll not forget," she said at his car, in his window. "Tomorrow, in Deep-Valleyed Desmond where the Lee rises." There was the scent of apple on her breath. Islands, she leaned in to say, do not exist until you've loved on them.

But today, while Mary Brennan waits on that tiny island for him, Philip Desmond is holed up in the back room of this house at Bantry Bay, trying to write his novel. His wife has taken the car to Cork. When she returns, he doesn't know what he will do. Perhaps he'll get into the car and drive up the snaking road past the crumbling O'Sullivan castle into the mountains, and throw himself into the middle of that crowd of writers as if he belongs there. Maybe he will make them think that he is important, that back home he is noticed in the way Mary Brennan is noticed here, that his work matters. And perhaps late at night, when everyone is drunk, he will lead Mary Brennan out onto the hermitage island to visit the oratory, to speak in whispers of the stories which had happened there, and to lie on the grass beneath the trees, by the quiet edge of the lake. It is not, Desmond knows, too unthinkable. At a distance.

The piece of paper in front of him is still blank. Mrs. O'Sullivan will advertise the laziness of writers, who only pretend they are working when they are actually dreaming. Or sleeping. She will likely be able to tell exactly how many words he has written, though if he at the end of this day complains of how tired he is, she will undoubtedly go into her practised agony. He wonders if she too, from her window, has noticed that the tide had gone out, that the lagoon is empty of everything except brown shiny mud and sea-weed, and that the nostril-burning smell of it is penetrating even to the inside of the house, even in here where the window hasn't been opened, likely, in years. He wonders, too, if she minds that the children, who have tired of their sea-edge exploring, are building a castle of pebbles and fuchsia branches in the middle of her back lawn. The youngest, Michael, dances like an Indian around it; maybe he has to go to the bathroom and can't remember where it is. While his father, who could tell him, who could take him there, sits and stares at a piece of paper.

For a moment Desmond wonders how the medieval masses in the cathedral at Cashel must have appeared to the lepers crowded behind that narrow hole. Of course he has never seen a Mass of any kind himself, but still he can imagine the glimpses of fine robes, the bright colours, the voices of a choir singing those high eerie Latin songs, the voice of a chanting priest, the faces of a few worshippers. It was a lean world from behind that stone wall, through that narrow hole. Like looking through the eye of a needle. The Mass, as close as they were permitted to get to the world, would be only timidly glimpsed past other pressed strain-ing heads. For of course Desmond imagines himself far at the back of the crowd.

("Yes?" the guide said. "And where would that be now?"

"A long way from here," he said. "An island, too, like this one, with its own brand of ruins. You've never heard of it though it's nearly the size of Ireland?"

"I have, yes. And it's a long way you've come from home."

"There's a tiny island just off our coast where they used to send the lepers, but the last of them died there a few years ago. It's a bare and empty place they say now, except for the wind. There are even people who believe that ghosts inhabit it.")

What does the world look like to a leper, squinting through that narrow hole? What does it feel like to be confined to the interior of a circle of trees, at the top of a hill, from which everything else can be seen but not approached? Desmond likes to think that he would prefer the life of that famous fat archbishop, celebrating Mass in the cathedral and thinking of his hundred children.

Somewhere in the house a telephone rings. Desmond hasn't been here long enough to notice where the telephone is, whether it is in her part of the house or theirs. But he hears, beyond the wall, the sudden rustling of clothes, the snap of bones, the sound of feet walking across the carpet. Why should Mrs. O'Sullivan have a phone? There are so few telephones in this country that they are all listed in the one book. But her footsteps return, and he hears behind him the turning of his door handle, the squeal of a hinge. Then her voice whispering: "Mr. Desmond? Is it a bad time to interrupt?"

"Is it my wife?"

No it is not. And of course Desmond knows who it is. Before he left the castle-restaurant she asked for his address, for Mrs. O'Sullivan's name, for the name of this village.

"I'm sorry, Mrs. O'Sullivan," he said. "Tell her, tell them I'm working, they'll understand. Tell them I don't want to be disturbed, not just now anyway."

He doesn't turn to see how high her eyebrows lift. He can imagine. Working, she's thinking. If that's working. But when she has closed the door something in him relaxes a little — or at least suspends its tension for a while — and he writes the paragraph again at the top of the page and then adds new words after it until he discovers he has completed a second. It is not very good; he decides when he reads it over that it is not very good at all, but at least it is something. A beginning. Perhaps the dam has been broken.

But there is a commotion, suddenly, in the front yard. A car horn beeping. The children run up the slope past the house. He can hear Carrie's voice calling them. There is a flurry of excited voices and then one of the children is at the door, calling, "Daddy, Daddy, come and see what Mommy has!"

What Mommy has, he discovers soon enough, is something that seems to be taking up the whole back seat, a grey lumpy bulk. And she, standing at the open door, is beaming at him. "Come help me get this thing out!" she says. There is colour in her face, excitement. She has made another one of her finds.

It is, naturally, a piece of sculpture. There is no way Desmond can tell what it is supposed to be and he has given up trying to understand such things long ago. He pulls the figure out, staggers across to the front door, and puts it down in the hall.

"I met the artist who did it," she says. "He was in the little shop delivering something. We talked, it seemed, for hours. This is inspired by the St. Patrick's Cross, he told me, but he abstracted it even more to represent the way art has taken the place of religion in the modern world."

"Whatever it represents," Desmond says, "we'll never get it home."

Nothing, to Carrie, is a problem. "We'll enjoy it here, in this house. Then before we leave we'll crate it up and ship it home." She walks around the sculpture, delighted with it, delighted with herself.

"I could have talked to him for hours," she says, "we got along beautifully. But I remembered you asked me to have the car home early." She kisses him, pushes a finger on his nose. "See how obedient I am?"

"I said that?"

"Yes," she says. "Right after breakfast. Some other place you said you wanted to go prowling around in by yourself. I rushed home down all that long winding bloody road for you. On the wrong side, I'll never get used to it. Watching for radar traps, for heaven's sake. Do you think the gardai have radar traps here?"

But Desmond is watching Mrs. O'Sullivan, who has come out into the hall to stare at the piece of sculpture. Why does he have this urge to show her his two paragraphs? Desmond doesn't even show Carrie anything until it is finished. Why, he wonders, should he feel just because she sits there listening through the wall that she's also waiting for him to produce something? She probably doesn't even read. Still, he wants to say, "Look. Read this, isn't it good? And I wrote it in your house, only today."

Mrs. O'Sullivan's hand is knotting at her throat. The sculpture has drawn a frown, a heavy sulk. "'Tis a queer lot of objects they've been making for the tourists, and none of them what you could put a name to."

"But oh," Carrie says, "he must be nearly the best in the country! Surely. And this is no tourist souvenir. I got it from an art shop in Cork."

Mrs. O'Sullivan's hand opens and closes, creeps closer to her mouth. "Oh," she says. "Cork." As if a lot has been explained. "You can expect anything at all from a city. Anything at all. There was people here staying in this house, 'twas last year yes, came back from Cork as pleased as the Pope with an old box of turf they had bought. They wanted to smell it burning in my fire if you don't mind. What you spend your money on is your own business, I told them, but I left the bogs behind years ago, thank you, and heat my house with electricity. Keep the turf in your car so."

Carrie is plainly insulted. Words struggle at her lips. But she dismisses them, apparently, and chooses diversion. "I'll make a pot of tea. Would you like a cup with us, Mrs. O'Sullivan? The long drive's made me thirsty."

And Mrs. O'Sullivan, whose role is apparently varied

and will shift for any occasion, lets her fingers pluck at her face. "Oh I know I know I know!" Her long brown-stockinged legs move slowly across the patterned carpet. "And Mr. Desmond, too, after his work. I was tempted to take him a cup but he shouldn't be disturbed I know."

"Work?" Carrie says. "Working at what?"

"I started the novel," Desmond says.

"You have? Then that's something we should celebrate. Before you go off wherever it is you think you're going."

"It's only a page," Desmond says. "And it's not very good at all, but it's a start. It's better than the blank paper."

Like some children, he thinks, he's learned to make a virtue out of anything. Even a page of scribble. When he'd be glad to give a thousand pages of scribble for the gift of honesty. Or change. Or even blindness of a sort. What good is vision after all if it refuses to ignore the dark?

Because hasn't he heard, somewhere, that artists — painters — deliberately create frames for themselves to look through, to sharpen their vision by cutting off all the details which have no importance to their work?

He follows the women into the kitchen, where cups already clatter onto saucers. "Maybe after tea," he says, "I'll get a bit more done."

Pretending, perhaps, that the rest of the world sits waiting, like Mrs. O'Sullivan, for the words he will produce. Because his tongue, his voice, has made the decision for him. Desmond knows that he may only sit in front of that paper for the rest of that day, that he may only play with his pen — frustrated — until enough time has gone by to justify his coming out of the room. To read one of the books he's bought. To talk with Carrie about her shopping in Cork, about her sculptor. To play with the children perhaps, or take them for a walk along the road to look for donkeys, for ruins. Desmond knows that the evening may be passed in front of the television set, where they will see American movies with Irish commercials, and will later try to guess what *an naught* is telling them about the day's events, and that he will try very hard not to think of Mary Brennan or of

the dozen Irish writers at Gougane Barra or of the tiny
hermitage island which the famous writer loved. Deep-
Valleyed Desmond. He knows that he could be there with
them, through this day and this night, celebrating something he'd come here to find; but he acknowledges, too, the
other. That words, too, were invented perhaps to do the
things that stones can do. And he has come here, after all, to
build his walls.

6

The Sumo Revisions

If number one on Mabel's list of musts for their trip to Tokyo was sitting through this Kabuki play, the only thing on Jacob Weins's list was a sumo wrestling match. All he asked was a chance to see with his own two eyes what he hadn't been able to believe on the television screen: two naked tubs of lard with greasy topknots squatting nose to nose, stomping their feet like pile-drivers and clapping their hands while pulling ugly faces at one another. When they came together at last, after their ritual dance, he wanted to be there to feel that crash reverberate in air.

Try telling a thing like that to Mabel Weins. She'd never heard such nonsense, or so she said. Had he crossed the entire Pacific with no other purpose in mind? He had no taste. Even worse, he had no gratitude. Her daughter Jill in the Embassy had put a good deal of thought and effort into this holiday for them, the least he could do was give her plan a try.

He knew he hadn't a hope. If giving this play a try was the least he could do to show he wasn't ungrateful, then giving this play a try was what he would do. The least the cast of this play could do, on the other hand, was speed things up.

Speeding things up, however, was not the Kabuki style. By the end of the first long hour the woman below had finally swallowed the poison her husband had given her, but it hadn't done a thing to quiet her down. Staggering around the stage in her hobbled bent-kneed manner, she tilted her white face up to squawk her complaints to the heavens — or to Mabel and Jacob Weins at the balcony rail — and showed no sign of expiring, or even of getting tired. Her white hands clutched at her throat, tore at the breast of her dark-blue kimono, sprang out to grab at the air. Her eyes raced along the balcony rail looking for help and stopped, almost certainly stopped, when they lighted on him. Worn out from waiting for *something* to happen, he was hardly the person to look to when you wanted some sympathy.

Mabel beside him, however, was a softer touch. "Oh lady," she sighed, "don't I know how you feel!"

The hell she did. Or was she teasing? Even given his reputation for being hard to live with, she was overstating the case. The idea that Jacob Weins could bring himself to poison her, like that strutting husband in the play, was ludicrous. Had he ever raised a hand? Or even threatened? The problem was that this theatre was primed for melo-drama — with that peculiar music and the clacking wooden sticks and that woman's unceasing falsetto voice — to the point where someone of Mabel's suggestible nature was prepared to believe almost anything. As for himself, what he was prepared to believe still waited to be revealed. As he said to Mabel, leaning down close to her ear: "Too bad the whole damn cast didn't take a swig of that poison. Save everyone a lot of trouble, including us."

Would he last the full five hours, or fall asleep like the fellow across the aisle? Neither if he could help it. He needed to stay awake in order to look for a chance to make his escape. The woman down on the stage, however, was expected to do her part. Now that she'd swallowed the poison, how long would she take to die? He would let her

death — five minutes from now or an hour — be a signal he'd
done his duty. When she dropped he would stand, when
she breathed her last he would flee; Mabel could stay here
and watch the rest on her own. It was already after noon and
somewhere out in this city there were wrestling matches
starting. It was up to this woman to give him a signal to
show he'd been freed to go see them.

That he'd chosen a foolish signal became evident soon
enough. The woman wasn't given to rushing things. From
one end of the stage to the other she shuffled, complaining;
down on her knees she went to comfort her baby, a doll with
a mechanical wail; up and swaying again she threatened to
last forever. There was little she could do with her face to
show how she felt — chalk-white with tiny dark lips, it was
painted to look like a mask. Even those eyes, under their
high thin questioning brows, seemed incapable of expres-
sing anything but her helpless innocence. Her voice kaw-
kawed those foreign words as if she were slowly measuring
out the lyrics of a song without ever getting around to
singing them. What she relied on most to get her message
across was her hands: held out to the sky they invited or
begged for mercy, up to her face they showed horror, groping around her large elaborate hair-do they seemed to be
seeking reassurance that she hadn't fallen apart. If he was
forced to sit through her slow demise — tied, so to speak, to
her fate — he might as well make an effort to understand
what she was trying to say.

The fact that she was really a man inside that kimono
didn't help. The idea, if he thought about it, could make
him sick. How any male in this world could let himself be
painted up like a doll and do that bent-kneed shuffle on the
stage like a cringing geisha was more than he was prepared
to understand. What must his father think? Not being a
father to boys himself (only to girls, including Mabel's daughter Jill by an earlier marriage) he could only imagine. And
what he imagined, if a son of his own did something like
that, was killing himself. What other choice did he have?
Listen to how that high squawking voice went on, look at

those hands. Where he came from, a man who was capable
of this would be hooted out of town, expected to drown
himself rather than show off like this on a stage for the
world to see. Not a modern attitude, he supposed, but there
you were. In Japan what you had to do was try and forget
what you knew, though you couldn't resist suspecting some
kind of fraud. Didn't a person have the right to know what
he was looking at? With a sumo wrestler, now, there wouldn't
be any doubt. Was it because they were stripped of everything but their own thick fat and a tiny cloth between their
legs that he wanted to see?

Questions of sexual fraud were obviously not on the
minds of the little old couple beside him. With bowls and
cups and little cardboard packages of food laid out on the
rail in front of them, they gave more attention to their lunch
than to the play below. Maybe they knew it by heart. The
tiny wrinkled lady held her rice bowl up under her chin and
made those chopsticks fly like a pair of knitting needles.
Slurping and sucking she still managed a bit of a bow when
she noticed that Weins was watching her. He gave her a bow
himself. If she expected to engage in conversation he wondered what he could tell them about himself that would
make any sense. Assuming they knew the language. If he
told them that back home on Vancouver Island he'd been a
mayor of a little town for fifteen years would they be impressed? What if he told them the only reason he was free to
wander the world like this at an age when most men were
still tied to their jobs was that several months of rain and a
giant mudslide had wiped his town right off the face of the
map? Would they believe him? Probably not. They'd want
to know what else he had found besides travel to take the
place of the town and the job he'd lost.

Nothing. By the time that mudslide had finished pushing his home and income and elected position into the sea
he had already started plans to sink savings and private
pension and collected debts into a truck and camper. If
permanent homes could slip out from under your feet, then
maybe mobile homes were more dependable. Out on the
road you weren't putting your faith in a single piece of the

earth. From stay-at-homes he turned them into gypsies. A little beach cabin outside Victoria served as home base when they needed one but he'd never been able to stand it there for long. Off they went through the Rockies into Alberta, to poke around in dust for dinosaur bones. Down to Montana to visit a smelly old bachelor cousin who lived in a falling shack and drooled while he talked about buffalo he'd never seen. Right across the country for a look at southern Ontario. Down to Nevada; up to the Kootenays; right up the Alaska Highway, end to end, with three blown-out tires and a shattered windshield to show for it. A few days at home between these trips and he'd get all tight, he couldn't sit still, off they would go again. Down to Mexico, across to . . . he couldn't remember them all. As soon as he got where he was going he wanted to head back home; as soon as he got back home he thought of some place else he wanted to go. Never satisfied, never content; retirement had turned out to be hell.

It was Mabel who'd got him off the road and onto a plane to Tokyo. If retirement was hell for him, she said, it was even worse for her. On top of all that ridiculous chasing around there was also the guilt she felt. When your husband was unhappy you felt there must be something you ought to do. In Oregon, when he'd set up camp in a beautiful park in sand-dune country, instead of giving in to the familiar urge to move on, he'd stripped off his clothes and plunged to the bottom of the lake. Once there, he decided to stay. With his feet dug into sand and his hands wrapped around weeds he couldn't claim that things looked any clearer there, but he did agree with himself to live, so to speak, with his fate. Dragged to the surface and revived, he discovered his fate had already been decided. After all this senseless wandering, she announced, it was time she paid a visit to her daughter in External Affairs. Since External Affairs had recently posted her to Japan, it was a way of getting him off the truck-and-camper routes. They couldn't begin to afford it, she said, but neither could they afford a repeat of this. She indicated the lake.

In the library book which Mabel had brought him to

read on the plane, a handful of tourists in Mexico sat staring into a bullring, much as he and Mabel were staring down at this stage. What went on in that smelly sandpit was a damn sight faster and bloodier than what went on on this stage, he recalled, but the people in the book saw everything *but* the bullfight they'd paid to see. They looked inward to see themselves or backwards to relive the past or sideways to make guesses about each other. No two of them saw the same thing. "There's a man in there that reminds me a lot of you," Mabel had said. Who had she meant? Nearly half-way through the book already, he couldn't imagine which of the tourists was him. If *he* had paid out money to see a matador flapping a rag at a bull he'd make damn sure he didn't miss out on a minute. You could do your dreaming later. Since what he'd paid out money to see was a woman who refused to die, however, he could forgive himself for drifting off for a while.

But he couldn't drift off for long. A voice behind him screamed out something sharp, like someone in desperate pain. Or anger. Weins grabbed the arms of the seat and swung to look. Had someone committed a murder up in the seats at the back? Almost immediately, a voice at the far end of the balcony shouted too. Perhaps a challenge. A thrill of pleasant terror ran down his back. Maybe they were about to witness a riot, right here in the theatre. For all he knew he may even have caused it himself. These people were foreigners, after all, and capable of things you could barely imagine.

Mabel laughed at his surprise. Her daughter must have warned her of this, but of course she hadn't bothered passing it on to him. "They scream out the name of their favourite actor," she told him now. "Just to let him know he's doing okay." The little lady with the chopsticks, when he looked her way, nodded her confirmation. But knowing what it was all about didn't mean you were any less surprised when the next scream hit you from behind. The next, when it came, sounded like "Enjaku!" and was flung from the back. If he knew who was playing the poisoned woman

he'd holler too, and tell her to hurry things up. As it was he
was hit by a screamed "Utaeman!" from a man who was
only a few feet away. He seemed to be the father of a row of
children who hung over the balcony rail, beyond the little
couple devouring food. When he turned to look at his tribe
his face was split by a grin. When his eyes met Weins's eyes,
however, the grin died altogether, replaced by a frown, or
was it a scowl, perhaps it was even a "face" — he couldn't be
sure it wasn't a deliberate "face". He felt the heat rise in his
throat. Had he done something that offended the man? Did
he think that Jacob Weins had no business watching this
play? Did he think, perhaps, that this big-eared grey-haired
westerner wasn't capable of understanding the distress of
the poor little housewife down there on the stage?

The poor little housewife, it began to appear after some
time had gone by, was not about to drop dead from the
poison at all. At least not yet. Instead of dying she'd only
been badly disfigured. Whatever the poison had been it
wasn't the regular kind, or any that Weins had heard of,
since it brought up a lump the size of an orange over one
eye. A bald-headed man who seemed to be in every scene
for no apparent reason — except to over-react to everything
and get a few laughs — was trying to force the woman to
take a look in the mirror. It wasn't easy. She knew she
wouldn't like what she would see. But the silly old man,
flapping his hands and leaping about, could hardly wait for
the fun of seeing her reaction when she discovered how
ugly she was.

He wasn't disappointed. Nor was the audience. For all
her over-reacting in the earlier scene, she still hadn't shown
what she was capable of doing. Now she pulled out all the
stops. Weins had never seen anyone, even on television,
carry on with such exaggerated horror. Did she think she'd
been some kind of raving beauty before, with that masculine
jaw? She glanced at her hand mirror and jumped back,
stricken; she glanced again, and threw her hands over her
face. She wailed, she complained, she took another look in
case there'd been some mistake. There hadn't. She stag-

gered in her bent-kneed swaying manner around the stage
and tried to get used to the shock. *Kaw kaw kaw* — her high
voice measured out the rhythm of her despair. Up and down
the notes of some imagined music. She held the mirror at
arm's length and eventually began to calm down, but another peek started her off again.

Down on her knees she went, with her makeup kit.
Trying to repair the damage? Forget it lady, Weins thought,
it'll take more than makeup to put you back in shape. But
no, she wasn't trying to repair the damage, she was putting
black on her teeth. The old man, when she looked at him
now, flapped his hands in horror. The audience laughed;
Weins nearly laughed but Mabel's hand and a warning look
restrained him. Did he think it was funny, she said, to see a
woman ruined?

Of course he didn't think it was funny to see a woman
ruined, or anyone else. Surely she knew him better than that
by now. How could any man who'd survived to the age of
sixty-one see any humour in that? He wasn't a vain man
when it came to his looks — he'd never had any reason to be,
with these huge ears — but he knew the fright a mirror could
give you on certain mornings. You didn't have to be a
woman with a belly full of poison to know what was going
on here.

Just as any female in the world might do in the circumstances, he supposed, the disfigured woman pulled the pins
out of her giant hair-do and let it fall long and shiny and
black around her shoulders. Sitting on her heels and gently
rocking, she began to comb it, her one remaining beauty.
Weins had seen Mabel doing the same, humming to herself
in front of a mirror, if things got tense and she needed to let
off steam. Think what she might do if she had a mane like
that. Mabel, of course, had never looked as feminine as this
woman looked when she slipped both hands under the hair
at the back of the neck and lifted the whole weight of it up
over her head to hang down in front of her face. With her
head bent low, she made each stroke of the comb a long
slow gentle caress. With chilly goosebumps rising on his

arms, was Weins supposed to believe this was really a man he was watching?

He wasn't stupid. If that woman down on the stage was really a man (with wife and kids at home for all he knew) was he any more or less disguised than the people who paid for the right to sit here and watch him perform? When he looked around at the audience, how much of what he thought he saw was genuine? Mabel herself, in fact, was a mystery. After all these years of marriage could he claim to know how much of her was real, how much disguise? When she raked through the contents of her purse as she was doing now, was she really so upset by this play that she needed one of those pills out of Dr. Lewis's free-sample drawer, or had she decided that she wanted to appear to be a high-strung sensitive matron, greatly affected by the play? In this country where you had to learn everything from scratch and nothing at all was familiar, you couldn't be sure that anyone was what he seemed.

And things down on the stage were getting worse. Weins remembered dreaming once that all his teeth had decided to fall out, one after the other, like tiny white pieces of chalk in his hand, but he'd never imagined that hair, like this poor soul's, could come away in great chunks in the teeth of a comb. Clots of it lay around on the floor. Clumps fell out of her hand. When she tossed her head back, her forehead was bald nearly as far as her crown. People everywhere gasped. Mabel beside him held her hand over her mouth; her face was wet. Another sudden shout from behind made everyone jump. The poor woman staggered around again, falling apart, while that fool of a man was making it just as obvious as he could how repulsive he found her to look at now. All over the theatre people were screaming out names.

"Sit down!" someone shouted behind him. Weins found it was himself that was standing. "Sit down!" — in the chaos of shouting names and beating clackers and the racket from down on the stage he could make out the words only because they were English. Standing, he was prepared to shout too, but why should he shout? If he hollered his own name into the din would anyone notice or care? An impatient tug at his pant leg reminded him: Mabel would notice, of course, and definitely care. She would think he had lost all his marbles, and as it was, she probably thought he was about to dive over the rail and fall on somebody's head. It was time he got out of here. Turning, he threw one leg over the back of his seat, pulled himself up into the empty row behind, and made for the closest door.

Out in the hall he didn't know which way to turn. Why hadn't he paid attention while coming in? All he knew for sure was that he had to go down a ramp, and several flights of stairs. Stalled like this, he could only gape at Mabel, who burst out through the door, her hand still rooting inside her open purse.

"Wait, just wait, just give me a minute to find my . . ." She pried open the purse for a better look. Hissing with frustration, she shook it, then moved over to the wall and squatted on her heels while she hauled out the contents and laid them on the carpet. Lipsticks and wallet and Rolaids and wadded-up Kleenex and an Instamatic camera and a sketch-pad and some pencils. Her white slacks bulged, her flowered top rode up her hips to bunch at the waist. Her tourist costume, she called it, including the pair of glasses that hung on a chain from her neck and rode the waves of her breathing bosom, and the long white scarf that was no use at all, just something she had to keep throwing back over her shoulder. Travelling, she lived in the outfit, she called it her second skin. "Just wait, I'll be with you in a minute. Wait."

What did she mean by that? "Listen, you don't want to go where I'm going."

"Ahhh!" she could smile again; the pill bottle was there after all. While she twisted off the lid she tilted her head and looked up at him steadily. "A wrestling match?" Into her mouth went a flat white disc. No need for water, she'd learned long ago how to swallow these things without. "You're leaving this for a wrestling match?"

He nodded. He knew what she thought: a disgusting

spectacle, as uncivilized as fighting cocks. When he'd told
her he wanted to watch a match on Jill's television set, she
said it should be illegal. His only hope, if he judged by the
look on her face, was to take the initiative. "I'll catch a taxi
and be back here to pick you up before this thing's even
over.

Though she looked down to put everything back in her
purse he knew what she was thinking. Or was it only that he
was thinking it himself? How could a man like Jacob Weins,
who was used to living in a little isolated pulp-mill town
of under two thousand people, expect to survive in the kind
of jungle that waited for him out there? "What you'll do if
you step out into that crowd is get yourself lost. Have you
forgotten where you are?" In case he had, she reminded
him: the largest, most crowded city in the world, where
they didn't believe in street signs. He'd never be seen again.

"So . . . ," she said, snapping her purse shut and standing to pull the flowered top back down over her hips. "If I
can't persuade you to stay, I'll have to go too." She tightened
her lips in a forced-cheerful manner, slid a look to one side,
and released her breath in a long slow audible stream down
her nose. To show her patience. And tossed back the end of
her scarf. Here was a woman who had much to put up with
in a husband.

His stomach hurt. Was she about to remind him of that
Oregon lake? It wasn't in her to be so brutal, but he saw in
her eyes the temptation: out of her sight he was a man who
could not be trusted to look after his own best interests. Out
of her sight in a city like this was worse. How could she be
sure that the next she'd hear of him wouldn't be news of a
sudden decision to swim the Pacific home? The twenty
years of their marriage had been only an introduction; it
was in the past two years of retirement that she found out
what he was like.

Weins loved this woman. He supposed that "love" was
the word. At any rate it was something to be remembered.
Whatever it was, he couldn't see her trying to hide her
concern for him without wanting to put his hand against

the soft white skin of her throat. Her own hands were as
rough and hard as roots. Brought up milking cows on a
dairy farm, those hands had raised two daughters from
different husbands, kept a garden year after year, and taken
care of minor repairs around the house. But he couldn't
imagine hands he'd rather hold. Was he a soppy sentimen-
talist? He supposed he was. Her hair was dry and brittle
from years of that reddish-blonde dye, her chin that used to
double only when she was looking down had taken on a
permanent twin, her stomach required a girdle even inside
those slacks and hidden beneath the folds of that floppy
smock, but she was a woman still, and made him aware that
what he was was a man.

If a gorgeous blonde in a string bikini were to throw
herself at him, would he turn up his nose? Since nothing of
the kind had ever happened and wasn't likely to (as long as
he kept this belly) he could only guess that what he would
do is run. So what if half his reason for running from her
would be fear? The other half would be from knowing all
that Mabel could offer him that no stranger in the world
could match. Still, though it wasn't hard to imagine giving
up a blonde for her, it was damn well nearly impossible to
imagine giving up this chance to see a Japanese wrestling
match. Or to imagine sharing it with her, when he knew
she would hate every minute, and spoil it with her distaste. "You stay where you are, see this through to the end.
Nothing will happen to me. I'll go back to the hotel in a taxi
and phone that young man of Jill's. He'll make sure I don't
get lost." Because she pursed her lips, nearly convinced, he
couldn't resist a temptation: "If a beautiful geisha tries to
seduce me I'll tell her I've got a disease!"

"What!" Horror and laughter both. Given a choice between being unfaithful and telling a stranger lies, Mabel
could only search for a third solution. But what it was, or
what she began to suggest, was sliced in two by a piercing
scream from inside the theatre. This was not just another
enthusiastic shout from the audience; something was wrong.
Weins got to the door before she did, and pulled it open.

Down on the stage the woman was disengaging herself from the point of a sword. Mabel gave him a look that said *Now see what you've caused me to miss*, and pushed right past. Blood spurted up from the wound, and spilled itself down the woman's kimono. How had it happened? The old man couldn't have done it — he was quivering at the far end of the stage, frightened out of his wits. And the woman appeared too surprised to have done it deliberately. Some kind of crazy accident. Down to the floor on her knees she dropped, a fragile heap, and lifted — tentatively — her white hands to her own pale innocent face. Unable to believe. Cringing sideways, she seemed too weak to lift her eyes. *Kaw kaw kaw* — her falsetto complaints had turned to feeble questions. After all this time, was she really unprepared for her death? When she lowered her hands she appeared to Weins to be trying to hold onto the floor — like someone who was afraid of floating upward.

He recognized the posture. The way that woman resisted floating reminded him of himself at the bottom of that lake in Oregon. All he could think of to do down there was dig himself into the sand and hold on to whatever weeds he could find. Everything in him ached to float to the surface; his hair lifted like seaweed, the cords in his throat stood out like ropes and threatened to explode to the air on their own, even his eyes felt as if they would pop out and leave him behind. Yet it had taken two divers several minutes to pry him loose from the bottom and drag him up to the world again, and air.

The baby, abandoned on the floor of the stage, began to howl. The mother, almost too weak to move, ignored the wailing doll and dragged herself into the little sleeping room in the far corner. "Look," Mabel said, "she's going to close herself in. How can she leave her baby?"

The answer was obvious. The woman who had thought nothing of making an unholy uproar when she'd been poisoned and disfigured by her husband was too well brought up to cause a fuss when she'd finally been outright killed, or to let herself die in front of an audience. It would be like having her face-paint wiped off in public, or the kimono stripped from her thin male body. Unmasked, exposed — not only would she be destroying illusions, but she'd be committing other betrayals as well.

He understood. As she slowly closed the sliding wall to separate herself from her baby, from that old man and all this riveted crowd, she turned that innocent face up to the balcony. To Jacob Weins, by the door. His heartbeat quickened, ridiculously. Was she trying to tell him something? Well, he knew what it was. That she didn't understand. It had been painted right into her face from the beginning, he could have told her, it was right in her makeup from the start of the play: she was just not able to understand a single thing of what had been happening to her here.

And he? What did he understand? That it was no accident she'd chosen him out of all these hundreds of gawking faces in the theatre? She may have recognized another victim of the masquerade. When the sliding wall clicked shut, a chilling shudder ran up his back. What had she left him with, goddamit? Whoever was clacking those wooden sticks together had gone mad again, people all over the audience were shouting. He had to get out of here fast. When a rat the size of a dog ran across the stage and dragged the screeching baby off between its jaws, he pushed his shoulder against the door. Like the silly old bald-headed man down there on the stage, Weins knew it was time to escape.

II

From this hotel window Weins could look down on the narrow street, the fenced-in yard of a private home, and the wide green stagnant water of the royal moat. He preferred the moat. He preferred, in fact, the opposite bank of the moat, the jungle of leafy trees where the Emperor apparently lived beneath one of those barely glimpsed roofs. Over there, he was thinking his royal thoughts. If he knew that Weins was thinking of *him*, would he invite him across? The two of them, if they got together, could find they had much in common. Weins had once been himself an authority figure, a leader of people, and imagined they wouldn't have trouble finding a lot to discuss.

What must it be like, for instance, to be the only person in the world to have signed a paper declaring yourself not a god? Weins was curious to know. A man with a thing like that in his past — weighing no doubt on his mind — would likely be glad of a friend. He might even leap at the chance to sneak off (in disguise of course) to watch a sumo match in a crowded arena. To clap eyes on those powerful thighs! To see those enormous force-fed stomachs in action! The former god might be interested to learn that the biblical God was supposed to have come to earth once as a wrestler. That was about all that Weins could remember from his Sunday-school days but it was something he couldn't forget. Some other Jacob rolling around in desert sand locked in combat with this superhuman stranger who refused to give out His name. Neither Weins nor the Emperor would expect to see God or gods in the sumo arena today but they might be lucky enough to see someone who was almost as famous: Wajima, the man who'd gone up through the ranks to Grand Champion in less than four years. An incredible feat. Women were crazy about him, they tacked his photo up over their beds like a movie star. Children fought for his autograph. Men worshipped the ground that he walked on. Surely His Highness would take pleasure in watching a champion at work, in the company of a friend from abroad.

Of course this wasn't the kind of thing he'd mentioned to Jill's young man. When he'd finally got through on the phone he'd kept the Emperor out of it. No use pushing his luck. Now all he had to do was wait here for Hiroshi to come down that moat-edge pathway to get him — just as soon as he escaped from the office where he spent his days listening to businessmen practising English. He wasn't a qualified teacher, he was an unemployed movie actor who was waiting to be given his next role. If you could speak the language at all, according to Jill, you could find people who were eager to pay you for it. They were desperate for the promotions that would take them to the States for conferences or a university. And this fellow Hiroshi, who'd lived in Toronto as a student once, spoke English better than Weins.

On the phone the boy had been eager to help him out. Aware of the shock he'd caused when he was sprung on them at the airport (her live-in boyfriend, Jill had called him), the fellow would break his neck in order to ingratiate himself with Mabel and Jacob Weins. Mabel had proved herself to be nearly a hopeless cause. She didn't like to pass judgment on anyone, she said, but the things that people did could still embarrass her. While Mabel tried to adjust to the things that people did, the boyfriend concentrated all his generosity on Weins. Anything he wanted, he only had to ask. Any place he would like to go, Hiroshi would see what he could do. When Weins had called to ask directions to sumo, he'd seemed to be glad of the chance to be of some help. "A good thing you did not try to go there on your own," he said. "You almost certainly would not have got in. Tickets, you must understand, are purchased ahead of time, seldom at the door. Businesses buy up whole blocks of seats for their employees and customers."

Weins, he said, would have found himself stranded there.

Did that mean he would have to go home without seeing the only thing he wanted to see in this place? Weins watched a column of schoolgirls come down the street while he waited for the youth to answer. In blue pleated jumpers and white blouses they followed a grim-faced woman in single file. "No, no, one of my students . . . I'm sure, if you could just wait." He was certain he knew someone who had tickets for today's *basho*, he said. Give him an hour to do some persuading, and then he would come by the hotel. They would go together.

But so far there'd been no sign of him. Instead, a pack of joggers thumped up the paved stone pathway in their white karate suits and headbands. Were they crazy? They had to be, to move any faster than they were forced to in this humidity. Like living in a laundromat as far as he was concerned, or being forced to spend time with the hot wet pulp in the paper mill. This beer and the rattly air-conditioning were only now beginning to cool off the sweat he'd worked up just crossing the street from the taxi.

He ought to change his clothes, get out of these sticky things. He regretted even that he hadn't some brand-new clothes to wear for the occasion, something appropriate. (If it really *were* the Emperor he was going with, could he get away with this touristy shirt and these baggy nondescript pants?) Getting himself a new suit of clothes was in fact something he wanted to do before he went home but he hadn't managed it yet. On the verge of stepping into a tailor's shop on half a dozen occasions since they'd arrived, he'd changed his mind at the last minute every time. The reason was simple. He didn't know what he wanted. Just an outfit made to measure was hardly enough to know; he couldn't begin to imagine a style or material he'd like. Since that mountain slide had buried everything he owned in the ocean he'd had nothing to wear that felt as if it belonged to him, nothing that fit him right, and not the faintest idea of what he would like to buy.

It would make a difference if he were still the mayor of Port Annie. WHERE THE FUTURE WILL GET ITS START. Printed on a gigantic banner across the road for visitors to see, that slogan had tempted fate. The future had got its start by wiping the town of Port Annie right off the face of the earth.

The trouble with slides was that they weren't content with whisking away your home out from under your feet, they took everything else as well.

He'd devoted his life to that town. Though he'd made his living from running his store, all his energy, talent, and attention had gone into dreaming up schemes that were meant to put the town on the map. Imaginative attractions designed to bring in the tourist dollars. Expensive real estate developments to help them enter the twentieth century. Mill expansions to create new jobs. None of it had ever come to much in the end, but every failure had spurred him on to even greater attempts. Who cared if his giant cactus imported from Arizona had rotted and died? No one had ever rivalled his ability to bounce back from defeat with even greater and more imaginative ideas than before. And what had happened to it all? Once that slide had destroyed the town, it dispersed the people who'd elected him and eliminated his job. How could you be a mayor when there wasn't any town left to be mayor of? Not only had that slide taken away his official reason for dreaming up schemes, but it had stolen his well-known talent for bouncing back as well.

What was even worse, or seemed it, the slide had also gobbled up his famous wardrobe. These sticky Fortrel pants and pullover shirt that Mabel had bought in some department store were not the kind of thing he liked to wear. As mayor he'd had a closetful of costumes. One for every occasion that came along in small-town life, some for no occasion at all, and every one of them felt exactly right. For holidays of an historical nature he'd had his Captain Vancouver outfit, an English naval officer's uniform complete with three-cornered hat and telescope. Who cared if it strained a little at the buttons? When he wanted to please the native population he wore his papier-mâché Thunderbird costume with its enormous wings and its beak that stuck out from his forehead. It brought back memories of all those totem poles which had been taken away to museums. On ordinary days he had a wider range to choose from — his

Dieter Fartenburg logger outfit, his Big Depression beggar's rags, his twentieth-century astronaut suit. The last was a favourite with the young. Had anyone ever suggested that he hadn't been colourful enough? Only *he* knew how necessary those outfits had been.

But a person who was not a mayor could not go around dressed as an early explorer. A person who was not a mayor could not show up at meetings dressed as a man from space. He'd felt naked ever since. He'd worn nothing but ordinary pants and shirt like these since the day of the slide, which was to say that he'd been parading a certain kind of nakedness through the world. He couldn't imagine one of those wrestlers wearing such humdrum clothes. When they weren't stripped down for the ring, what *did* they wear? A long kimono, maybe, but he doubted it. The only kimonos he saw on the streets were worn by little old ladies. He remembered seeing a photo of a wrestler once, leaning against a doorway in an alley while he held a little dog's leash. The man had been wearing nothing except his skimpy loincloth, a dirty one at that, with his stomach bare and round as a baby's in the sun. But an alley wasn't quite the same as being on the street. Surely he didn't go visiting dressed like that, or down to the corner store. Yet in a shirt and baggy pants he'd be transformed from giant athlete into pitiful slob. What other choice did he have?

No use asking a question like that of the only person out there that he recognized. Mabel's sister. Eleanor had no idea how *anyone* could live a life that wasn't the same as her own. Beneath one of the trees of the park on the edge of the moat she was draping a white sheet over a bench and tugging at corners to get it hanging just right. Who else but Eleanor would steal a hotel's sheets just so she wouldn't get dirt on her filmy white dress? A stranger might wonder if she were preparing herself for a modelling session. From a certain point of view he might be right. This woman was convinced there were unseen photographers snapping secret pictures of her wherever she went. The world for her was not only a stage, it was also a series of backdrops for

those picture hounds who couldn't resist when they saw a
mature woman of considerable beauty and class. Or who
knows? — recognized her from *Crossroads of Life*. Had that
silly day-time series been seen in Japan? Weins doubted it.
When no one had watched it at home, why should foreign
countries pay for the privilege of letting it bore them to
death?

Always on the look-out for eyes that watched, she
spotted him in the window and waved, a beckoning gesture.
Wouldn't he like to come down? Even from here at this
fifth-floor window he would see the brilliant red of her nails
as she took a cigarette from the package at her waist and
tapped it before she put it between her lips. Did she expect
him to race down four flights of stairs to light it? She would
claim there were men who had. She knew how startling she
was, in any landscape. Here, she had chosen white. Her
tanned skin, her nails, were the only colour. Even her eyelids would be the pearly-white of an oyster shell. Against a
paler background, he'd seen her decked out in scarlet, from
turban to shoes. The opposite to a chameleon, she chose to
be always seen. More than that, she chose to be always the
only thing your eyes would permit you to see.

She waved again. Not enough people were paying attention to her. Where had she installed that lover-boy she'd
dragged along on this trip? It was part of his job to make
sure she was constantly the centre of someone's attention.
Why, for that matter, wasn't she off in the city shopping
somewhere? The excuse she gave Mabel for avoiding that
Kabuki play had been a desire to get into one of those
department stores where girls at the door bowed as you
passed by to go out. After being admired, her second favourite activity was buying things for herself: clothes, makeup,
and jewellery. Anything that glittered enough she was willing to hang on her body. With that white dress she was
wearing there would have to be silver: necklaces, bracelets,
even (he could see the light glint off it from here) a silver
chain for her ankle. When they packed to go home she'd
throw everything she'd brought with her into the garbage,
or give it all to a maid, then fill her suitcase with all the stuff

she had bought. When she stepped off that plane in Vancouver she'd make sure that anyone looking would know
she had been to Japan. Pearls, cameras, oyster-shell dolls,
she'd even got one of those expensive kimonos that girls
here bought only once in their lives — for their wedding.
Weins doubted that she'd have the nerve to wear it off the
plane, but considering the frequency of her own marriages
she was probably smart to have it on hand. A woman like
her must eventually get tired of trying to think up something new in the way of a wedding dress.

She'd given up on trying to lure him down. In fact she
was making a point of not looking in his direction. Something much more interesting, her posture implied, was going
on down the street. It was enough to make him decide. If he
went down now to talk to her he would be saving time when
Hiroshi came along, which ought to be any minute.

But crossing the lobby he was spotted by her gigolo, her
whatsisname, who sat behind one of the little low tables in
the tea room. His companions, a pair of boys who could
have been any age from fourteen to twenty-four, turned to
look. "Jake! Hey Jake!" Half-rising from his chair, Conrad
waved an arm. "C'm here!"

Weins cringed. Nobody called him Jake. No one had
called him Jake since childhood until this fool had taken
it up. Within fifteen minutes of meeting Weins he'd announced that Jacob was too old-fashioned a name to be used
today. They weren't living in Bible times. He couldn't call
him "Weins" like other people, of course, that would be far
too normal; he had to make it sound as if they'd been pals
for a hundred years.

Aside from cringing there wasn't much else to do. Stepping out of sight wouldn't help since Conrad (what the hell
was his last name anyway?) came out to the lobby after him.
"Come in and meet my friends."

If Conrad had friends, Weins was a giant carp. He couldn't
imagine anyone standing him for longer than twenty minutes, let alone calling him friend. "I haven't got time. I'm on
my way out. You go on back to your pals."

"Going out where?"

Had Conrad spent the afternoon drinking? His eyes were the colour of fish's innards, his breath like rotting hay. "To a wrestling tournament. I'll stop in for a drink with you later, when I get back."

Another fatal mistake. And stupid besides. Naturally, wrestling was something this creep had done in college. "A champion too, it was the only thing I lived for." He expanded his chest inside that golfer's shirt. "Ontario champion two years in a row. I'll come along." And hooked both thumbs into the pockets of his skin-tight jeans.

Weins could sometimes be stupid, but he was also quick to recover. "And leave your friends? Come on, I'll join you for five minutes before I go." Steering the Ontario champion back into the tea room wasn't hard — wrestler or not, he was loose and light as a girl. With his build he might have been a tennis star but Weins didn't believe for a minute the guy had ever been on a mat. The only thing he'd ever been champion at was talking.

Of course Weins had already discovered, from just a few unavoidable meals together, that Conrad never just talked. Like Eleanor, he preferred to put on a show. People at other tables would stop their conversations to watch. Talking, he bugged out his eyes, he threw out his arms, he clamped his hands on his head. He delivered each sentence like a small boy relating the most outrageous tale. "Do you *realize* what I just *said*? Do you have any idea what this *means*?" He wept, if necessary; he sweated, he pretended to faint. He threw his hands over his round boyish face, peeked through his fingers, stirred up his dark hair until it stood out in tufts all over his head. He acted out his stories and reacted to them at the same time — performer and audience both — a wide-eyed incredulous little boy who was wetting his pants with excitement and horror and anticipation and delight. Some people found him entertaining, but Weins couldn't stand to be near.

"Oh it isn't fair, it isn't fair," he was saying now. What wasn't fair was left for Weins to guess. The two youths already seemed to know. They nodded sympathetically and sipped their tea and looked at Weins with grave compassionate faces when Conrad asked why it was that North America had never adopted an official initiation rite for manhood. Was Weins supposed to supply an answer? He wasn't even sure he grasped the question. "What we're talking about here is a manhood ceremony, one of our own so we could *know*! A simple initiation rite, so that a guy like me doesn't have to be wondering still at the age of thirty-three!"

Wondering about what? Weins didn't want to imagine. The guy had deserted a wife and two kids in order to spend his life in the sack with Eleanor Barclay-Broune. To some, that would be proof enough that he'd entered puberty at least. Maybe he wanted proof that he'd survived it. Why should Weins, who had better things to do, provide the reassurance? Let Conrad confront his doubts alone.

And doubts of some kind was what he was yammering on about. Did an African pygmy have these doubts? The youths didn't know. A head-hunter in New Guinea knew, and had the scars to prove it. And what about that Amazon tribe that stuck a wooden disk in the boy's bottom lip? "Just think how much simpler adolescence would be for everyone if all you had to do was kill a rhinoceros with your own two hands and eat its testicles raw!"

What would this jerk say next? Weins made no effort to hide his disgust, it was time he got out of here. No one seemed to be paying him any attention, no one had come to take his order, no one seemed to care about anything except what this fool would come out with next. What was taking Hiroshi so long?

"Now I want to tell you people something true." This happened, he said, when he was working in a logging camp as a youth — "in your part of the country, Jake. There was this huge bohunk chokerman, I can't remember his name, this big lummox with dirty *filthy* longjohns rotted out at the armpits . . . oh good Christmas did he *smell*!" The little-boy face was both disgusted and delighted. He drew out the important words as if they had a taste he loved to roll around in his mouth. How much of this made any sense to the boys across the table Weins couldn't guess, but they seemed satisfied just to watch the performance itself. "What the hell was his name?" A hand slapped itself down on top of his head to help him remember. "Seven feet tall, a gorilla — Christ I admired anybody who could *stand* to be so *foul*. I wanted to be just like him — big and ugly and stupid and oh, to smell so foul!"

His bugged-out eyes were waiting for Weins or someone to say they couldn't believe a person like Conrad could ever have admired such a pig, but he'd wait until hell froze over before Weins would co-operate. Let's get this done with was all he was tempted to say.

"I remember" — whatever it was he remembered it was enough to make him bounce in his chair, and bubbles appear on his lips — "I remember one morning, I was standing beside him at the sink, both of us shaving, I felt nearly faint from that delicious *hideous* smell, that stink, while I scraped off my few weak little whiskers — I probably had about six of them at the time. And he let the water out of the sink . . . and there . . . at the bottom . . . was this filthy sludge, this *mat* of whiskers, each one as wide as it was long for Christ sake!" In disgust he leaned his face away from the imagined mess on the table. The two youths moved forward, as if they expected to find something hideous on the table-cloth. "HEY — he nudges me with his elbow — HEY, LOOK AT DOT! WHAN YOU LEAVE SINK LIKE DOT THEN YOU KNOW YOU ARE MAN!" Horror! Conrad's arms flew out, his head leapt back, one hand returned to slap on his forehead. "Oh my god I'll never make it, I'll never make it." He sat upright again, his eyes wide. "Do you realize what I just said?" He meant all of them, and looked at each in turn. "Do you realize what I just said? Do you know what that must have meant to me? I just *knew* I would never make it, never!"

The youths shook their heads, in sympathy, and started to rise. This seemed like a perfect time to escape — exactly what Weins himself was thinking. You leapt when he took a deep breath or you waited — who knows how long — for another. This creep had gone on long enough for him. But Conrad was letting no one escape, not yet. One hand clamped down on a youthful shoulder, the other rested on Weins's right knee. The expression on his face turned from public horror to confidential wonder. He came as close as he was capable of to whispering. "My god, I guess you never know. Thirty-three years old, married twice, with two children, and you still don't know." The two youths might have been watching a madman; alarm was as strong as amazement in those eyes. "You take your first cigarette and you think, *Is this it?* You smash up your first car. You get pissed. You shoot a beautiful moose. You go behind the bushes with Knockers McKechnie, and even while you're zipping up your pants *you still don't know for sure.* It isn't fair. They should send you out into the mountains for a month in the dead of winter, stark naked, and when you come back with a cougar's eyeball between your teeth, they should give you a certificate to hang on the wall that says *you are a man now, so stop torturing yourself.*"

What did Mabel's sister ever see in this guy? Though she'd demonstrated over and over again that her taste in men was disastrous — feeble old crocks and vicious bullies and momma's boys and dozens of others that Weins could barely recall — all of them had something to explain the attraction — money or power. What did this fellow have? Not money, that was for sure. The guy hadn't paid for a meal since they'd arrived. And it couldn't be a glamorous career — he was a salesman of some kind in Toronto. Lord knows it wasn't brains. Could it be simply that he was younger than she was, and apparently healthy? Every time Weins picked up one of Mabel's magazines he saw another article on this new trend of older women taking up with young men.

Making fools of themselves, as far as he was concerned, but every old gal who thought she was somebody was getting herself a young stud. Magazines exaggerated everything, naturally, but take a look at Eleanor. She'd started herself out with a series of old goats who croaked, luckily, just as she'd planned, then worked her way down the scale until now, with this latest turkey, she'd got someone who was fifteen years younger than she was. Forty years younger if you wanted to take his behaviour into account. Even Jill, who wasn't much past thirty herself, was shacking up with a boy — something her mother hadn't known about until they'd arrived here. How much of it would Mabel have to see before the idea started to appeal to her as well? If one old gal could make a fool of herself, why not another? Would she wait until he was dead, or dump him here?

The youths climbed out from behind the little table and made it clear, in their English, that this had been a most enjoyable and educational conversation thank you. The taller one even added that he wished he could stay but could not do so. Then they made their escape. Weins stood up to follow, before the opportunity passed.

"But wait . . . " There was something more that Conrad wanted to tell them yet. His hand reached out to stop the boys but both slim bodies neatly side-stepped it. Weins was not so lucky. Alone, he was Conrad's only audience now. It was clear that it wasn't enough. "I wanted to ask them if they had anything like that here. In an ancient culture like this, surely there are old ceremonies. Something that's never told to outsiders."

The only ancient ceremony that could have been applied to Conrad with any success was beheading. Weins himself would offer to wield the sword. In ancient Japan this baby would have found the manhood test that he'd been looking for when he was ordered to kill himself while a witness stood over him waiting to lop off his head the minute he'd cut into his gut.

"Nice boys," Conrad said. And drank tea. "These people are so polite. But dammit, I was hoping they could fill me in on the local customs."

The nice boys, Weins could see, looked back over their shoulders and heaved with giggles. A local custom? Free of that restraining hand, and those eyes, they could laugh at the fool in the corner. Or was it fools? When their hands touched one another and then closed in what looked like a lover's clasp, he suspected it was fools. All this talk of manhood rites must have been more entertaining than Conrad could ever have hoped. Weins laughed. "Those boys probably thought you were trying to pick them up," he said. Oh, it was good to laugh at this creep! At them both! "They probably thought you wanted to make it a threesome."

"Huh?" Conrad's mind was obviously still on his uncompleted quest. "Whaddaya mean?" With his back to the youths he saw nothing but what was going on in his own busy mind. "If we're still going to catch the wrestling we'd better get moving, I guess." And drained his cup.

Again Weins had waited too long. He should have broken his neck to get out before those boys had escaped. Now he could be stuck with this talking machine for the rest of the day.

The man at the counter, however, provided another chance. With his till taken apart, he asked them to wait while he fixed it. Since it was Conrad who needed to pay, Weins made for the door. Out in the steam-bath heat he hoped for Hiroshi but had to settle for Eleanor. On her bedsheet she reclined with her blonde head against the trunk of a tree while she watched him crossing the street.

He almost didn't make it. An old man stroking by on a bicycle nearly ran him down before he reached the farther side. The handlebar grazed his arm. Had the old geezer done it on purpose? It was hard to tell. Without even missing a stroke he pedalled on by, and didn't seem to be aware that Weins existed. A pair of flapping white pants was all he wore, and a yellow towel around his neck.

Eleanor, who'd screamed and stood up, sat down again when a second cyclist turned out to be more alert. Pulling in to the curb and stopping, she put one foot on the concrete to steady her bike. "So sorry mister. Are you okay? Were you? Damaged?" Her voice was high, and thin. Each of her words seemed to tilt up at the end a little. A pretty voice. A pretty face too. Not a girl, exactly, but young.

"It is! My grandfather!" she said. And flashed those snow-plough teeth at him. "He sees! Nothing!" Looking off down the street in the direction the old man had gone, she shook her head. With amusement or sadness — it was somewhere between. She even included Eleanor in her smile. "He rides like that, all day! He never! Stops! He follows the edge of the moat!"

Weins laughed. Of course she was stretching the truth. "Never stops?" The old man's tires had already bumped up onto the narrow park and he'd started around the curve. Weins could imagine him circling the moat — round and round the imperial palace all day. With this woman right behind.

"From morning, until night! He never stops! Except for sleeping. Not since last Carissimassa!"

More than eight months had gone by since Christmas. "And you — surely you don't have to follow him everywhere."

"Oh yes." She nodded her head rapidly, several times. "Oh yes. It is not! Safe! For him!" Then, perhaps noticing Weins's doubt, she saw that her English had failed her. "Oh — not only I! All my family! We take turns! Otherwise, he may never! Get home! Safely!"

Already she appeared to be restless. The old man was far around the curve of the moat, pedalling furiously. Another minute and he would be out of sight behind trees. Maybe that was his intention. Weins saw the poor old man cycling like mad all those months, hoping eventually to shake his pursuers and escape. But escape to what? How long could an old man survive unwatched in this Tokyo traffic?

"So!" the girl said, pushing off from the curb. "I must go! So happy to see that my grandfather did not wound you!"

The short conversation had given Conrad time to catch up. Typically, he wasn't interested in finding out what had gone on, he was still obsessed with his only topic. "Listen," he said. "In the modern world it's not easy to know these things. I read in the paper about this guy that went way up north — up to the Yukon — on a hunting trip. You know — one of those lifetime dreams — and shot himself this beautiful albino caribou. An *albino*, Jake. Can you imagine how excited he was?"

Eleanor sighed a ribbon of shredded smoke. "Oh Conrad."

Did he talk in his sleep as well? When an older woman looked around for someone younger to latch onto, was she willing to settle for *this*? Weins tried to imagine the pimply youth who would inhabit his side of the bed. If Mabel was willing to put up with his talking her ear off, would he in return be willing to wake up at five every morning to exchange sides of the bed with her? Her shoulder demanded it once a night. Would he be prepared, like Weins, to stumble in the dark around the foot of the bed to dive under the covers on the other side?

"No kidding, this really happened." Conrad was ready to act this out too, given a chance, right here in the open air. "A beautiful big white fellow like something in one of those books — y'know? But do you think anyone understood what it *meant*?"

Eleanor used the tips of her scarlet fingernails to rearrange the folds of her skirt. "Of course not, darling. Nobody understands these things but you."

"That poor guy, he was so pleased with himself too. He draped the animal over the front of his pickup and drove it down the main street of this little town, but the kids went nuts!" Out went the arms, down came the hands on the top of his head, out bugged the eyes. "Do you know what I'm saying? The whole town went crazy, they nearly wrecked his truck. They threw rocks, they jumped up on the back and hammered on his roof, they chased him with clubs. He was so scared he got out of there as fast as he could to save his own neck."

"Good for them," Weins said, and raised an eyebrow at Eleanor, who smiled. "You can't get away with things like that any more, he's lucky they didn't throw him in jail."

"What's the matter with you?" Conrad was shouting now. "That's just the point. Nobody understands the importance of these things. What's happened to ritual?"

Weins couldn't resist. "I heard about one of those Australian tribes that knock a front tooth out of a boy at a certain age, to show he's a man. And carve pictures into his chest."

Conrad gaped.

"Well, there are days when I could happily perform that front-tooth ceremony myself," Eleanor said. "Today is one of them. And if you decide to go Australian, don't forget the tribe that drills a hole in the base of a boy's penis when he reaches puberty."

Conrad's face lit up. Was this more to his taste? "A hole? They do that? My god!" His hand came down on the top of his head. In all his research how had he missed this goody? His eyes wide, he searched the world for someone who was equally impressed.

"Get out the electric drill," Eleanor said to Weins. "We'll put him out of his misery."

If this was what Conrad was looking for, there was nothing left on his face to show he had found it. His excitement had somehow turned to distaste. They could knock out his teeth, carve up his chest, put a disk in his lip if they wanted, but nobody was going to monkey with his dink. And it was all, to judge by the furious scowl, the fault of Jacob Weins. He turned and walked away with his hands jammed down in his blue-jean pockets. Was he hoping they'd call him back?

"He used to be fun when I met him," Eleanor said. "Why do I pick such duds?"

It was a question worth wondering about. With so many men to choose from, why did Eleanor always pick out the worst? Didn't she have any taste? What she had was a talent for finding them in the damnedest holes and then discovering when she'd dragged them into the light of day they weren't all she had hoped. Weins had no idea where she'd found the first half-dozen or so, or even the first one or two she'd married. He did recall a Frenchman with a nasal drip she'd met on a Pacific cruise. In France, they were told, he'd been a teacher with a reputation for beating students. Deprived of students, he took to beating her, until she kicked him out. One husband was a fellow she'd brought back from a week of gambling in Reno. She hadn't exactly won him in a slot machine but she called him the One-armed Bandit and joked about pulling his lever. He was a farm-machine salesman from Arkansas with three little hillbilly kids who said *yawl* if you asked them to, for a laugh. The four of them lasted a year and a half in her house before heading back to the States. Conrad's background was pretty conventional, if you believed what you were told: for Eleanor he'd deserted a job, a wife, and two little kids Back East. Nothing else seemed to matter a damn. She'd found him in a neighbourhood pub somewhere. Lined up with others on a makeshift stage, he was a contestant in a wet-jockey-shorts contest, on a Friday night. While all the others wore colours from mustard yellow to blue, Conrad wore pristine white, bought by his wife back home. The colours had nothing to do with whether you won or lost but something else did — and Conrad, Eleanor said, was something else. Whether this meant he had won was something Weins didn't know, and he didn't intend to ask.

For Eleanor, Conrad's sulking was apparently an excuse to break into song. It was her habit, anyway, to thread snatches of music through the gaps in her own conversation. Opera songs were her favourite, though she'd been known to stoop to Country as long as it was mournful enough. For the purpose of this trip she was naturally specializing in *Madama Butterfly*, though he wouldn't have known if Mabel hadn't asked. Weins had never seen an opera in his life, nor wanted to.

Perhaps singing not only screened out the noises other people made but helped her organize her thoughts as well. And line up accusations. "And so?" she said now, cocking an eyebrow at Weins. "You left poor Mabel watching that play by herself?"

When he nodded she put on a stern-actress face and shook her head. "Poor woman. Poor any woman in the world with a husband retired!"

Was she joking? He couldn't tell. What would she know about husbands who'd been retired? Any of hers who hadn't

died before they got that far she'd divorced while they were
still young enough to work for her alimony payments.

Whether she knew what she was talking about or not, it
was an excuse for another performance. "I swear they retire
on purpose in order to shackle you with chains of guilt and
fear!" Was this a speech from a play she'd acted in once?
The way her exaggerated hand movements seemed to take
in trees and even the passersby suggested practice. "They
shake off the single career of their lives and hand you your
own last full-time job, which is to watch their every move
for the first sign they are falling apart. Don't take your eyes
off me now, they say, not for the rest of my life! If you look
away for a minute I'll go into the final decline and it will be
nobody's fault but yours."

Weins swallowed a temptation to ask if that was the
reason her taste in men had shifted to a taste for boys.

Eleanor's script did not take Conrad into account. She
confronted Weins, face to face, with both hands on her hips.
"How could you leave her there? Do you think she's enjoy-
ing the play? All she can think of is that you're out here
somewhere." Weins could tell from the look on her face that
the actress in her was winding up for a knock-out line. And
here it came, in a stage whisper, with her face pushed close
to his. "She's probably wondering, darling, how long it will
take you to find yourself at the bottom of somebody's lake."

Oregon. Weins turned away and walked to the fence that
ran along the drop to the moat. It was in that sand-dune
park, he remembered, that Mabel had discovered people
were eager to pay her for her new-found hobby, they wanted
to buy her drawings. In *his* retirement, she said, she'd found
herself a career. Together they laughed at the thought. After
selling a dozen sketches of dunes and half-buried trees to a
woman from Austin, Texas, she got the giggles. The whole
business seemed so ridiculous. How did it feel, she said,
to be married to Grandma Moses? In bed that night they'd
giggled and snorted together. When she was rich and famous would he mind being one of those men who were
kept, those gigolos? They'd laughed so hard at that the

springs of the truck protested and they'd had to duck their heads down into their sleeping-bags. Inside, they'd laughed even harder, they held their breaths and exploded like a couple of kids. Worse than a couple of kids, they decided they didn't care who heard them, they laughed out loud. People would think they were tickling each other, carrying on in the dark. Eventually Mabel rolled close and held his hand, she wanted to know if they could stay in that park for a while, instead of hurrying on in their usual way, as she could do some sketches of the dunes. They lay like that, on their backs, and held hands until the caw-cawing of crows in the trees shattered the quiet of dawn. He'd managed to stay in that campsite for several days for her sake before the urge to move on became something he couldn't stand. Faced with spoiling everything for her anyway, he found himself considering the little lake. The next thing he knew he was considering it from the bottom.

Forty or fifty feet below him now the water was thick with streaks of different greens, like Mabel's pea soup when you stirred it up. Was it true he'd ruined the play by walking out? He supposed it was. At the very least he'd made it less than she'd hoped. After giving her a scare like the one in Oregon you could hardly expect her to relax when he was on the loose. Was it honest concern for his good or only guilt? He'd never know. Mabel had always put his welfare ahead of her own — he'd assumed she'd done it out of love but maybe she'd had other reasons as well. If Eleanor was right he'd been guilty of a kind of blackmail, along with every other retired man in the world.

But Weins had no talent for brooding in public. Too easily distracted, he would usually decide to put it off until he was alone — and then forget. The distraction this time was a confusion of gabbling voices from up the path. Squinting, he could make out a half-dozen figures, bending, scooping, turning their raised rear-ends this way and that. Gardeners, weeding the flowers? They appeared, rather, to be sweeping up leaves. He wondered if they followed this tree-shaded path the full way around the moat once a day, going around in circles like the ancient cyclist. If so, were they ever invited across?

Here the moat was as wide across as a six-lane highway. On the farther side, a lush tangle of growth swept down the steep slope from the base of the trees to trail leaves and vines along the water's surface. "Thinking of swimming across?" Eleanor said, behind him. He wasn't, but now that she'd brought it up he was sure he could make it, if he survived the initial drop down the bank and guards didn't pop out from behind those trees to shoot him. There didn't seem to be any alligators around, or crocodiles. If he stripped and dog-paddled across, would the Emperor be willing to entertain an interloper shivering wet in jockey shorts? There were questions he wanted to ask. Would a man like Hirohito, for instance, ever allow himself to be retired — even by a cataclysmic force of nature?

"A few minutes ago a young man stopped to talk," Eleanor said. "Told me if you rent one of the little rowboats down there and get across to the other side you'll see it's crawling with snakes."

What kind of a moat was it where a person could rent a dinghy? This wasn't Disneyland. Naturally there would have to be snakes, and maybe land-mines as well. Otherwise His Imperial Highness might as well be living in an apartment block downtown, with his name on the door.

Beneath a weeping willow that hung over the shallow water where the moat widened for a sharp turn, a white bird walked with slow deliberate head-jabbing steps, as if he were sneaking up on something. "A crane?" Weins said.

"An egret." How did she know these things? She moved in close beside him and pressed her face against his arm. "Poor Jacob Weins," she said. "I think he's decided to dislike the person he used to be, and hasn't yet found the person he wants to become." Suddenly she put a hand on his shoulder, stood up on her silver-painted toes, and planted a warm kiss on his lips.

Weins felt his face getting red. This woman had always liked to leave him gaping foolishly. An eccentric from the beginning, she considered him far too square. But the arrival of the street-cleaners amongst them saved him from having to react. A little old bent-over woman, sweeping leaves into her metal scoop with a broom made from a handful of willow twigs, paused in front of Weins and looked up at his face. Grinning, she reached out to whisk up a leaf from between his feet. In this heat she appeared to be dressed for winter. Under her huge straw hat a towel draped over her head was pinned under her chin. Thick green wool socks were pulled up over her slacks, which were themselves beneath a heavy black skirt. One of her gloves was white, the other brown, both were dirty and worn.

"Kon-ni-chi-wa," Eleanor said. Trust her to have brushed up on the lingo. Enough to impress the natives at least. "O-gen-ki de-su da?"

The old woman bowed several more times, to Eleanor, to Conrad. But it was Weins she was grinning so cheekily at while she rattled off a long rapid string of Japanese sounds. "I don't know what she's saying," Eleanor said, "but it's you she seems to be taken with."

"One of her own generation," Weins said, and shrugged. Of course he didn't mean it — at least he hoped this wrinkled old face was a few years older than he was. But there were some things you wanted to say before someone else said them, or worse.

The old woman found him so fascinating that she reached up with one of her hands — the one in the soiled white glove — and touched his shoulder. What was she saying to him? Was there something she wanted him to do?

Eleanor laughed. "That's as high as she can reach. She's admiring your ears."

His ears? Admiring his oversize ears? If anything she was making fun of them. If she was, it must be because they were burning now, as they sometimes were, and red. Hadn't she ever been told that the Japanese were famous for being polite? Maybe she had, but someone else had told her old people could get away with anything, so long as they smiled while they were doing it.

Talking and laughing at the same time, she yanked on the towel that was draped over her head, as if she would rip it off.

Eleanor laughed and pushed her forehead against Weins's arm. "I think she's telling you if you wore a rag like that one over your head your ears wouldn't have got so burnt!" Turning to the old woman, who was evidently prepared to abandon Weins in favour of her fellow workers down the path, she said a few more of her memorized Japanese words from the guide book. Mouthing each syllable with separate effort. "Domo! Domo go-shin-se-tsu ni! Kan-sha shi-ma-su."

In case they should admire her linguistic talents too much, she added, for Weins — and for Conrad, who'd come back from his walk to nuzzle his face in her throat — "I wonder what I said. If my Japanese is as bad as some of the English I've heard spoken here it could be anything. This morning I asked a lady behind the counter of a jewellery shop what was meant by all the posters you see hanging everywhere. Was there going to be a vote? 'Yes,' she said, 'we are having a general erection!'"

What? What was she saying? Conrad seemed to find it so funny that Weins was sure it had something to do with *him*.

"They can't say their *ells*, Weins. They're having a general election!"

Could Hiroshi have taken offence at the joke? He'd arrived soon enough to have heard it. Well mannered as always, however, he showed no reaction. Rather he gave Eleanor a shallow bow. She found it an occasion for another cigarette, though Conrad fumbled at her hand, and went back to her sheet-covered bench.

With his T-shirt hanging from his belt loop, Hiroshi was naked from the waist up but Eleanor turned her eyes away from the tattooed woman whose elaborate kimono swept like a peacock's tail down his arm. Conrad edged closer to stare. He'd probably want one for himself before he went home.

When the youth grinned, his large black eyes were

reduced to slits. Had the old lady been flirting with Weins or offering him a job? he asked.

"Jesus," Conrad said. "Can you imagine being stuck with a job like that?" He forced the tips of his fingers down into his pockets and bounced a few times on the balls of his feet, like an athlete limbering up for a race. "Why doesn't she sign herself into an old folks' home? After a day of work she probably can't even stand up straight; I bet her family uses her for an ironing-board."

If he expected a laugh he was disappointed. Eleanor was preoccupied with arranging herself for the unseen photographers. And Weins was watching the little clutch of retreating street-cleaners. How did he know that she was really a woman? He didn't. In this place you couldn't be sure it wasn't a little old man. There had been no clues in the face. Everything else was covered. That skirt was all he had to go on. When you got to a certain age, maybe it didn't matter.

Hiroshi hadn't yet learned that you paid no attention to Conrad. "You will not find many old folks' homes in this country, although young people are beginning to say we should build them. Old people are not so welcome in families as they used to be." Delivering this news required a long and serious expression on his face. He raised his hand to slip off the twisted rag he'd worn around his head. His thick black hair — a little longer than most you saw in this city — was damp. He used the rag to wipe the sweat off his face, then shoved it into the back pocket of his jeans. "Besides, perhaps she likes to work. Surely it is better to be out here in the world than shut up in some special home?"

Enough of this talk, Weins was ready to go. "Should we take a taxi or what?"

"No hurry, no hurry, it goes on until six. The best sumo-otori don't fight until the end. If we get there too early you'll be tired of watching before we get past the beginners." He ducked his head into his red T-shirt and drew it down over his chest. "University College" was printed on it, and a faded gargoyle. The sleeves had been cut away.

"You've got the tickets?" Conrad said.

Hiroshi looked at Weins. "Yes? I have the tickets. For two."

"But hey, hey, what about me?" A kid about to be left out of a game. Would he start to cry? It wasn't impossible, if you judged by the look on his face. If he didn't cry, he'd throw a tantrum at least, right here on the street. Or drive his fist into a tree. "I'll get my ticket at the door, okay? I'll just go along and get what I can, I don't even need to sit with you guys, I'll look after myself."

From her bench under the tree Eleanor sighed. "Conrad shut up. I want you to come shopping with me this afternoon — while I look for your birthday present." The look she gave Weins meant that she expected to be rewarded for this. "Then Jill promised to take us both to a concert."

"And there's little chance of getting in," Hiroshi said, "without a ticket."

Stabbed from every angle, Conrad confronted his assassins, his eyes accusing them one at a time. One hand was a fist, striking his other palm. Instead of crying or throwing a tantrum he chose to stomp off in a huff. "Screw the bloody concert!" And started towards the hotel. "Screw the bloody concert! Screw the bloody shopping! Screw the whole damn city!" On the edge of the street he turned and confronted them again, his arms thrown wide, his face the mottled-red colour of strawberries. "Screw the whole damn bunch of you, I'll find my own amusement!"

III

Sitting on the bottom of that lake in Oregon, Weins had decided to leave certain things to fate. If he drowned, he drowned, too bad, but if somebody rescued him in time he'd take it for a sign he was meant to live, at least for a while. When a pair of muscular youths had pried him loose from the bottom and dragged him up to the surface, he elected to see the experience in a different light. What he had done, he decided, was earn the right to indulge. From now on he could afford to follow his natural instincts just wherever they chose to lead him. That they'd chosen to lead him here to this cramped arena stall was surely a cause for rejoicing. Down on his knees he was sure — so what if his legs were in pain? — that this sumo business was all he had hoped for and more.

The two fellows up on the raised clay platform might not be Grand Champions yet but to Weins they were good enough. Especially the closer one, an obvious winner. In his purple silk sash with its long stiff tassels, he turned so the crowd on all sides could admire his incredible stomach, his enormous thighs. That bare glistening backside alone was enough to make you think of a hippo. With its heavy nose and puffy eyelids, his face was the face of a killer — there wasn't a dainty thing about him, except for those seashell ears. A sure bet to win, especially against the flat-faced sourpuss in green with the bandaged wrists. With all his tiny features pulled to the middle of a pudgy face, he looked like an ugly baby, ready to cry or pout. You could tell by the way he refused to look at his opponent that he was already doomed.

Crammed into the fifth row from the front, Weins thought he could hear their breathing, the rasps of excited beasts. He could be wrong. In the general noise of this packed arena it was hard to tell one sound from another. Row after row of squeezed-in kneeling people sloped up on all four sides, and no one seemed to feel the need to be quiet. At least not

yet. Weins thought of Mabel in her red-plush seat in that
theatre. What a contrast. Here all that separated him and
Hiroshi from the rest of the crowd was this narrow rail
about six inches off the floor. And a rather tubby neighbour
— perhaps a sumo wrestler himself in an earlier life? —
spilled over into some of Weins's space.

The referee's clothes would be more appropriate for the
kind of thing Mabel was watching, not this affair. In a white
kimono and a black hat, did he think he had come to take
part in a play? The way he postured, pointing his white-
socked foot like a dancer, his hand on his hip, you'd think
he was planning to give you ballet. Whisk whisk, you could
hear the rustling kimono as he changed his pose, and swept
his fan up into air. The names he'd whined out meant
nothing to Weins, just collections of meaningless sounds.
The Purple Hippo was the name he gave to his favourite; the
other was Sourpuss, it didn't matter — the man was too
obviously a loser to deserve a name of his own. You could
already see the shining smear of sweat across his shoulders
— a sign of fear.

Out by the nearest edge of the platform the Purple Hippo
squatted and tipped up a mouthful of water, which he spat
into a hole in the sandy floor. With a piece of paper he
wiped each armpit. Was he afraid of B.O.? "Purifying himself," Hiroshi said. "Before the battle begins, all evil must
be killed." Weins had no idea how a piece of paper could
wipe out evil, nor how this handful of salt tossed out into
the ring was supposed to do any good. But the contemptu-
ous look on the Purple Hippo's face as he flung the salt was
justification enough. His opponent, clearly intimidated, drib-
bled only a few grains and turned his back. People screamed.
A man with a camera down in front of Weins stood up,
crouched for a picture, and knelt again. The two warriors
suddenly squatted, facing each other from opposite edges of
the platform, and clapped their hands.

"To summon the attention of the gods," Hiroshi said.

Having summoned the gods, both men held up their
opened hands, palms outwards, and turned them in every

direction. To show that they hid no knives. Again they
threw salt — the Purple Hippo tossing such a huge fistful
that Weins could hear it land, while the other sprinkled
even less than before. They waddled towards each other —
the Hippo with a lip-lifted snarl on his face, the other with
his glance turned away — and then bent over, nose to nose,
with their fists on the ground. Like two runners waiting for
the starting gun they twisted their feet, tested their grip.
Weins could imagine the impact when they moved — two
sides of beef hurled at one another. The green one was
bound to give way, or fall. Once he was out of the ring he
was done for, or if he let anything but the soles of his feet
touch the floor. It would be good to see — in some strange
way it would serve him right, for having that big stupid
mug of an ugly face.

But nothing happened. Bent over and breathing heavily
they refused to move. Waiting for perfect silence from this
crowd? If they were, they got what they wanted but still
didn't charge. Both pulled back suddenly, stood up, and
retreated to the sides. New cries broke out. The man at
Weins's shoulder slapped his hands on his own thighs and
roared. The Purple Hippo turned his back on the other,
faced in Weins's direction, and lifted his left leg — grabbed
it by the ankle and raised it out and up higher than his own
head as he tilted his body away, turning the dirty sole of his
foot towards his opponent — then brought it down *slam* on
the floor. Enough to shatter bones, or crack open a weaker
mound of clay. Weins felt a needle of pain shoot up his own
leg and lodge in his hip. If he ever got himself straightened
out from this cramped position, which was doubtful, he
could be partly crippled for life. A good thing there was a
four-minute limit on all this warm-up business, these two
looked as if they could hold out until midnight at least.

Poised again like runners, face to face, this time they
seemed to mean business. Hiroshi elbowed Weins to look
at the referee, who'd dropped his fan to his forearm. Both
wrestlers leapt forward, as if a race was exactly what they
were starting (in opposite directions), and immediately

slammed into each other. For a moment nobody gave. The crowd howled. The photographer leapt to his feet again, ran around the ring and took a picture from a crouched position, then stood up and bashed into another photographer doing the same thing. Unlike the wrestlers, they both gave ground immediately, and scurried back to their kneeling-places on the rough hard mat.

What would Conrad think if he were here? That these two giants were acting out some important ritual. Only the winner, perhaps, would be allowed to call himself a man. The loser? Who could guess what Conrad did with losers, being one himself?

The Purple Hippo was a thick bare straining back, a greasy topknot, a slash of purple silk between his buttocks. The Green Sourpuss was a twisted face, tilted up and grunting. All those little features had clamped down into a tiny knot like a single twisted muscle, a tightened spring. Perhaps it would fly apart. Why were his hands groping all over the heroic belly of the Purple Hippo?

Things got worse. The tightened muscle of the face's features flew apart, the head disappeared, the whole body ducked, and those hands were into the sash. One hand slipped under the purple silk at the side, and the other hand hooked into the front, the face and head became a battering ram that pushed into the Purple Hippo's chest and drove him backwards several steps. Hippo or not, after the backwards steps his feet left the floor. The Green Sourpuss thudded forward, the giant's weight on the back of his neck and his shoulders, then lifted the helpless body up in a swinging arc and heaved him out of the ring. On the edge of the platform he teetered for a moment, then fell, like a collapsing house, and rolled into the lap of the photographer. Around him the crowd went crazy — you couldn't tell if you were hearing cheers of triumph or jeers of scorn. Probably both. The woman beside the photographer leapt to her feet, and offered her hand to the wrestler. He ignored it, of course — hadn't he been humiliated enough already? — and got to his feet without help. Not a trace of emotion in his face. These people were trained to hide what they really felt. He bowed to the strutting winner up on the platform, then turned to walk away. Before he left the arena, however, he turned and bowed again. Was this the usual? Weins didn't know, but he was sure there was a trace of mockery in that second bow. Self-mockery or hero-mockery, either was possible here.

The winner paid no attention to the loser's bows. He squatted to receive his prize from the referee and turned to leave the ring in the opposite direction. How had any of this happened? The obvious winner had been thrown right out of the ring by a baby-faced slob with only half the stomach, half the strength in his thighs. Astounded, Weins looked at Hiroshi for an explanation.

"Speed," he said, and grinned. "Weight and muscle are not everything. Back in the earliest days of sumo our friend in the purple might even have been killed by such an agile opponent. This was not such polite entertainment then. The victor might easily have kicked him once he was down, and stomped him to death. If you had bet on the loser you would know by now that your next crop was destined to fail."

Weins found himself looking at an assortment of food someone had placed by his knees. Was he supposed to be eating this stuff? People around had been feeding their faces ever since he'd arrived but he didn't know whether he felt up to it himself. The pickles he could swallow if he had to, and the oranges, maybe even the little cakes of rice. But his stomach still wasn't ready to tackle those bits of raw fish. As for the blushing squid — you didn't know whether to eat it or apologize and shake hands. It lay there in his cardboard carton, all its tentacles stiff, and waited. If Jill hadn't served him a meal or two of meat and potatoes, Weins would have starved to death by now. Bowls of rice he could stomach, and after some practice he could almost enjoy a bowl of seaweed soup if he didn't think about what he was doing. But he drew the line at chomping on creatures that looked more intelligent than certain people he knew.

Hiroshi, of course, was digging in, and slurping the sake

out of his little cup. "A good thing you are not in training for s'mo," he said. "With your small appetite you would never make a Grand Champion." He gestured to the giant portraits that stared down from the rafters, above the people in the balconies. "Those guys are expected to eat as many as ten bowls of rice every meal, and to stuff themselves with stew."

Weins made a face. "Does the stew have rosy squids looking out at you?" One of those portraits was bound to be of Taiko the Great, but how could he tell the difference? Careless Kashiwado the Cast Iron. Kirinji the Disjointed. Where was Wajima?

Weins pushed his food away. Maybe later. "How heavy you figure that fellow was? Three hundred, four hundred pounds?"

"Somewhere between. Do not think their training is only eating to get fat! That's not just lard you are looking at, it is muscle too. They walk up and down stairs carrying a man on their back, or haul a tire uphill with a man sitting in it. Exercise. And the stable boss thinks nothing of beating them with bamboo rods, or a broom handle. It toughens them up. I played the part of a *jo-no-kuchi*, a beginner, once in a movie. Not very realistic for a man of my size, but never mind. I stayed for a few days in one of the stables here in Tokyo, to see what goes on. And met the champion whose younger days I was playing. It is a difficult life."

If it was a difficult life, the afternoon's contenders seemed eager enough to get on with it. Maybe it was all they knew. One pair had hardly left the spotlight when the next were already climbing onto the platform for their encounter. Meanwhile their own successors were coming down the aisles to sit cross-legged on cushions in the front rows and glare at one another. How many tons of human flesh performed before Weins's eyes? One pair of moon-faced blimps battered each other so long the referee made them rest. One got more out of the rest than the other and immediately picked up his opponent by the sash and deposited him outside the ring. Another pair were only medium weight but concentrated all their efforts in their legwork. Each tried to trip his opponent by wrapping a leg around the other's but the tangled mess sent both of them toppling. The one who landed last was declared the winner. The biggest man that Weins had ever seen, with a belly like a cast-iron stove, ended his bout in less than a second by whacking his opponent in the back of the neck. Face-first in the sand, his victim would undoubtedly agree with Hiroshi. It was a difficult life.

An old man in a tight grey cap came pushing his way between the rows of spectators until he could whisper something into Hiroshi's ear. His own ears were even bigger than Weins's. His nose was considerably smaller, two nostrils and a tiny bump. Under his arm he carried something that looked like one of Mabel's sketching-pads. Was he someone Hiroshi knew? The jabbering that went on between them appeared to have something to do with Weins. They looked him up and down like an object for sale. Not only for sale, but comical as well; the old man opened his mouth and chuckled loudly, shaking his head. It was the doubting laugh of a farmer who refuses to believe that the price someone wants for a cow is to be taken seriously.

"He says he is an artist," Hiroshi explained. "He says he has been watching you and he would like to draw your face."

The old man bowed but still wasn't able to take things seriously. Maybe the sound of his own words turned into English struck him as funny. He sucked air and chortled, and continued to shake his head. What a joke the whole world was, he seemed to suggest, and slapped a bony hand against his teeth.

Draw this face? Weins had had his photo taken a thousand times, but no one had ever offered to do a portrait. Maybe this would be something a person could use — in an autobiography some day, or a history book, if the historians ever got around to writing the story of Port Annie.

Weins shrugged. "Hell — if he wants to. Tell him my wife does sketches too but she's never had the courage to tackle *this* mug. If he's got the stomach for it he's welcome. But tell him I'll understand if he gets scared off and runs away."

At Hiroshi's translation the old man laughed again, shaking his head from side to side, pausing just long enough to bow a few more times in Weins's direction. Then he scrambled away on his knees as far as the aisle and hurried with little shuffling steps across the space in front of the platform and squeezed into his own spot facing this way. He held up his pad and grinned, bowing again, then raised the other hand with a piece of something in it — charcoal? — which he slashed down across the paper in a dramatic gesture to show he was making a start. Too bad Mabel wasn't here, she'd get a kick out of this.

Weins imagined the picture in a history book. There would, of course, be a caption under it. *The portrait above was drawn by a famous Tokyo artist, shortly before Jacob Weins made the decision to enter the Foreign Service.*

The Foreign Service? The idea had never entered his head before. Was it a natural choice for a man who couldn't sit still? Maybe it was, but was it a natural choice for a man who couldn't eat foreign food? The world was full of countries where people ate things as bad as they did in this place, or worse. He looked at the squid. He'd starve.

But it didn't hurt to consider these things. "Do you think I'd make a diplomat?" he asked.

As if the shape of his body would provide the clues, Hiroshi looked him over. "Ambassador Weins?" He seemed to be tasting the words. "Your Excellency, External Affairs is the only sensible choice. I can see you eating jellied lizard with the King of Saudi Arabia. Munching ants with the Chief of the Oogabooga tribe. All this, of course, after you have whizzed through university, zoomed up through the ranks of the foreign service, and spent seven years arranging concerts for touring pianists."

Perhaps he'd been a little too hasty. Obviously he'd read the caption wrong. Even for a man who intended to live for a long time yet, it was one hell of a lot of training. He needed something he could jump into right away. *The portrait above was drawn by a famous artist while Jacob Weins was visiting Tokyo, shortly before he became a motion-picture star.*

Well, why not? He was a natural for that as well. "How about a movie actor, Hiroshi, just like you?" Pretending he meant it as a joke was the safest way.

A joke was precisely how the youth decided to treat it. He laughed. "Of course. We could become a team. When I am offered a role that calls for a bigger man I will send for you. Naturally you would have to be prepared, like myself, to put in an apprenticeship in porno films."

Weins saw himself undressing in front of a camera. A beautiful Japanese girl lay naked on a bed, waiting for him. When he stood in nothing but undershorts she started to giggle. At what? At his bulging stomach, or the mat of hairs on his back? When he stepped out of his shorts, the actress went into hysterics. He was not a tremendous success.

What he needed to find was something that required no training and demanded no qualifications. A politician! A politician was perfect, but wasn't that only more of what he'd already been? He was looking for something new.

The artist raised his pad again and grinned, to show perhaps that he was making progress. Hiroshi dipped his head. "That old man told me you seem an important man to him. Perhaps in your country, he said, you are a wealthy businessman or a judge. I told him you were once the mayor of a town, and he said he could see it in your face. He said too that he can also see you will not stop at being a mayor but go on to higher things. Obviously he is preparing you for a portrait that will be terrible. With so many compliments surrounding it you can't be disappointed."

"Higher things?"

"Perhaps he means that when you get home your Prime Minister will invite you to be — what is it called? — the Governor General?"

Hiroshi *was* teasing but there was no question he could carry it off with class if the chance should ever arise. With

class and considerable colour. It would be wonderful to have
that uniform at first, with all those decorations. But he'd
soon get tired of the repetition and set his imagination to
work dreaming up some creative eye-catching alternatives
to wear on public occasions. Wherever the law permitted it,
of course.

And meeting the Queen. He would take the job just to
see Mabel entertaining the Queen. If anyone in this
world could handle the job she could. And love every minute, he was sure of it. He, of course, would be forced to wear
regulation dress for royalty, no original inventions for her.
No room for showing individual style in a case like that. In
fact, it would probably be a frustrating job for a man like
Jacob Weins. No allowances made for originality, or an
active imagination. Since he'd probably get fed up and quit
within the year, there was probably no point in taking the
job in the first place if he were asked.

As if anyone anywhere knew he was still alive!

A sudden roar from the crowd reminded Weins that he'd
neglected the action up on the platform. Several pairs of
wrestlers had tested themselves against each other while he
was preoccupied with that artist. Maybe it was because
these fellows, unlike their cousins in American wrestling,
didn't try to make things worse than they were. You weren't
expected to hope that somebody would die, or scream out in
terrible pain. "There is very little here that is done just for
the show," Hiroshi said. "Everything that is done is done
for the sake of the gods or for intimidating the opponent,
nothing is done for the sake of the spectator." No need for
acting, he added, the pressures were already enough. "This
man in orange, now, must win this next match if he does not
want to be demoted again. Things have been going badly for
him, soon he will be forced to retire. He's getting old."

Weins looked at the two wrestlers stepping up onto
the platform. The one in orange had white tape wrapped
around one wrist and more around one ankle but he looked
as young to Weins as any of the others. "You call that old?"

Hiroshi grinned. "Over thirty. In this business that is
old."

The wrestler in orange went into the fight exactly as you might have expected from a man on the brink of unwanted demotion, or retirement — impatiently. The spitting, the wiping, the salting, were all disposed of quickly and the two opponents froze in their crouch, refusing to turn away. They stared, glared, made enraged murderous faces at one another. The audience, screaming, smelled blood. They knew that much was at stake.

"And to make it worse," Hiroshi said, "our friend is top-heavy. Look at that chest and those big shoulders. He is a different breed of man from this squat fat thing he is facing."

The opponent, whose furious Buddha face was as red as his sash, pumped his nostrils like a fish's gills. In his little eyes, even from this distance, Weins was sure he could see a passionate need to destroy the man in orange. If the rules of the game forbade mutilation and death, he looked forward to the next best thing — ending a career.

When it looked as if the two of them had revved up enough rage to burn the arena down, both leaped, and shuddered at the impact. Using his heavy shoulders, the man in orange ducked and pushed against the Buddha, driving him back a few steps. But the fat man used his mountainous stomach like a battering ram and bounced his chesty opponent towards the centre. Quickly, he jumped in close and pushed the flat of his hand in the other's face, pushed again, slapped this side of his face, then that side, over and over, driving him back. Alarmed, the man in orange dug in his heels and braced against the attacker, but the blows on his face continued. The hands were too quick to be caught, and trying to grab them only made him look silly. The slaps to the face, the hand-heel thumps to the jaw, drove him back. One hand dipped down and yanked on a tassel, pulling the apron off to drop to the sand. The man in orange was all but naked now. And his foot, one foot, was perilously close to the straw at the edge of the ring.

Weins could hardly stand it. If he had a gun he would shoot that piggish bastard. If he were close enough he would throw this sake in his face, or jab a vicious elbow into that belly. "Fight back, goddam it, fight back. How can he let that blubbery slob do this to him?"

Hiroshi shrugged, and broadened his grin. It was clear he found it more fun just watching Weins than watching the match itself. "He is trying."

You could tell by the snorts and grunts he was trying — what you could hear between swells of audience noise. His back leg quivered, planted like a tree in the sand, bulging with desperate muscles. Its job was the job of a piston, to stop everything where it was and then push back. So far it had done only half its job. The rapid hands continued to slap, the belly continued to thump, the Buddha face, still furious, continued to show its contempt.

Then the foot slipped, only inches. You didn't even have to be watching to know what was happening now. Ten thousand people groaned. The foot slipped back in sand until it touched the straw. The referee sang out something and the wrestlers fell apart. Weins, who'd been upright on his knees, fell back on his heels, exhausted. He'd pumped more sweat than both of those wrestlers combined. Now what would the poor bugger do? "If you retire in your thirties, what do you do for the rest of your life?"

Was Hiroshi squeamish? He looked as if something he was about to eat had spat at him. "What does he do? He suffers from ulcers, liver trouble, kidney trouble, and diabetes." It was serious enough that he put a hand on Weins's arm. To hold off a blast he could see coming, or to express sympathy for something that hadn't been said? "I know one who has lived into his sixties but most die around fifty."

And while he was suffering and waiting to die? "I hope he lives like a king on a big fat pension. He's a hero after all, or does he have to go out and look for another job?"

"The sumotori have no pension plan." Poor Hiroshi was beginning to look as if he regretted bringing Weins to this thing. "They do what every man must do when he retires if he wants to stay sane, he looks at himself to see what talents he has developed in the course of his career and then he does what he can. A few become coaches, naturally. But most of them open up restaurants."

Weins saw his big-chested friend sweating over a stove. Wiping tables. Punching a cash register by the door. While his muscles turned to flab and his insides painfully ate themselves away.

"Restaurants. Cafés." Hiroshi's voice was sad. "All those years of training they are forced to cook and serve the stew for their superiors. They become excellent cooks. Or at least careful and respected hosts. The man whose youth I portrayed in the movie runs a restaurant in the city now. Perhaps you would like to meet him?"

It wasn't as if the poor guy would be doing it for long; apparently he could count on dropping dead before he got bored, Weins thought. Burned or buried before customers of his own age even started planning for their retirements.

"Of course our friend's retiring will not be without ceremony. At an exhibition tournament he will be taken to the centre of the ring to have his topknot cut off, snip by snip. It is very sad — all his friends and colleagues will come up and cut off a piece of his long hair to remember him by."

Weins could see in the posture of the retreating wrestler that the man could already hear those scissors cutting his hair. His own stomach rebelled. "Let's go," he said, and tried to stand up. But his legs had lost their strength. Would he be sick right here in this crowd? The box of food tipped over. The sake spilled. His shoes had to be dug out from under the cushion. One foot, with a mind of its own, kicked the man in the neighbouring stall, provoking a great deal of bowing and chatter. The other, dead as a chunk of wood, had to be lifted with both hands out of the way, and pinched back to life. He crawled past bodies to the end of the row (women giggling at him from behind their fingers), then limped, with his weight on Hiroshi's shoulder, up the aisle.

Out in the lobby, among the busy employees of the tea-houses, Hiroshi asked if he wanted to use a washroom or just to rest on one of these stools with a cup of tea before going back. Alarmed, he appeared uncertain what he had on his hands. A sick man, or an old fool who was losing his marbles? "Some visitors find the crowds oppressive," he

said. "A few minutes out here where there is more space
and you will be ready to go back in for the rest. The Grand
Champions should be coming up soon."

Squatting to slip on his shoes, Weins could see through
the entrance to the arena that already things had changed. A
fat wrestler in a thick, brilliantly embroidered apron that
hung almost to his feet was up on the platform going through
what looked like a slow-motion dance. A white rope, thick
as an arm, was tied around his waist, with an enormous bow
at his back. When this was the one experience he had
wanted to get out of his trip, why was he so anxious now to
escape? His stomach would not have permitted re-entry to
that arena even if he'd still desired it. But the fact of the
matter was that he didn't desire it at all. He'd had enough.

"Let's go," he said. "We better get home so Mabel can
see I'm not drowned in somebody's lake. She'll be so pleased
to see me alive that she'll rupture her voice-box giving me
holy hell."

Somebody was trying to shove something into his hands.
The old man, the artist, was jabbing a rolled-up piece of
paper at him and Weins was supposed to admire it. Admire
it? When it looked like no one he'd ever seen? Certainly not
himself. "Dammit, he's made me a Jap . . . a Japanese! Look
at those eyes." They weren't exactly slanted — a long way
from being slits like the artist's own — but they had a
vaguely Oriental look about the eyelids. He'd given them
mongoloid folds.

Hiroshi's grin threatened to bubble into laughter. "Now
you know how you look, to us. Or to him at least."

"What? A Japanese with big ears and a long nose?"

"Perhaps to this old man all the rest of the world is
populated by Japanese people who are hiding behind masks
— only some have more successful masks than others."

Apparently taking all this talk to be complimentary, the
old man chuckled, sucking his teeth, and held the portrait
up for the other to see. "Ahh!" Ladies in kimonos compared
it with the original and found it perfect. Congratulations
were offered, along with bows and titters. To everyone the

artist bowed his gratitude, and shook his head. Did he believe he'd pulled off a miracle here? He seemed amazed at his own display of talent.

Before that amazement turned to greed, Weins rooted in his pocket for some change. Small pieces were worth less than big — that was all he could tell for sure without looking. Even looking he would have to have given it some thought. Instead, he used his thumb to push the larger coins off the cluster in his hand, drew the rest out of his pocket, and handed them to the old man. Once the old man had gone, however, Weins wanted to know what he should do with this stupid picture. "Where's the garbage can?"

Hiroshi studied the charcoal face a moment, then looked up at Weins with eyes that were threatening mischief. "I think you should take it home. You can tell people you found a cousin who lives in Tokyo."

Weins squinted at the face in the drawing. It *did* look half Oriental, half himself. "What is the bugger's name?"

Hiroshi closed his eyes to think. "Jacobichi, uh, Weinsanaka?"

Weins whooped. His mood was lifting already. Even that waitress with the silver teeth was laughing.

"Yes," Hiroshi added. "Famous sumo wrestler of the Yokojuna rank. Undefeated. Winner of the Emperor's Cup, the Prime Minister's Cup, the Fighting Spirit Award, and the Pan Am Trophy."

Weins displayed the picture for the waitresses who were peering curiously at this strange pair. "Jacobichi the Big-Eared!"

Where did Japanese men learn how to laugh. Even Hiroshi had his hand over his mouth like a girl. "Jacobichi the Iron Belly," Weins added. People probably thought they were drunk, they were getting far too loud. "Will they hoist this picture to the rafters do you think, to hang with the other champs?"

"Not big enough. We will have to call old Rembrandt back for another sitting. Something life-size this time, please."

"To hell with that." Weins looked at the portrait again,

struck by a sobering thought. "Gentle Jacobichi the Eye-
gouger. He isn't retired, I hope."

Hiroshi, too, gazed at the face with some fondness. His
voice took on a sombre tone. "They tried to retire him but
when they started to cut his lovely locks he made a sudden
come-back. Broke thirteen arms and tossed bodies through
the air like matchsticks. He will last forever."

Weins pushed through the door to the street and held it
open while the youth went through. "Forever?"

Hiroshi assumed a mock-indignant tone as he scanned
the street for taxis. "This is no ordinary man we are talking
about. You can tell your people back home your grandma
visited Tokyo once, where she was mistress for a short while
to the Emperor. Jacobichi the Gentle Marauder is a descend-
ant of that fortuitous mating."

Why was it foreigners learned English words that Weins
had never heard? "Does that mean I should be dropping
over to visit cousin whatsisname at the palace before I
leave?"

"If you don't, you will hurt his feelings. When he learns
you are a cousin of Jacobichi the Man of Steel he will insist
on honouring you with the position of carp-herd in the
imperial moat."

"If I give him this picture do you think he'll hang it in
the royal privy?"

Now he was being silly. Worse than silly, childish. For
all he knew there might even be laws in the country against
making fun of the royal family. To suggest on a public street
that the Emperor went to the toilet like normal people could
be considered treason.

If it was, Hiroshi didn't seem to mind. As a taxi pulled up
to the curb he bent to open the door. "Naturally that is where
he will hang it. To gaze on this handsome face every morning is bound to relax his rigid muscles, just exactly what he
may need." When he looked up at Weins he winked.

How many people had winked at Weins in his life? Not
many. Maybe that was why he felt this flood of gratitude.
He'd been caught by surprise. Ducking into the taxi while

Hiroshi held the door, he wondered which he'd found: a youthful friend or a son. God knows he needed both, though he hadn't thought of it before. And hadn't dreamed of finding either in this place. "Domo. Domo," he said, his first attempt in the several days he'd been here. If he'd got it wrong, or mispronounced it, Hiroshi didn't correct him. "Do itashi mashite," he said, and shut the door.

IV

In retirement this man had taken the name of Soseki. Weins was supposed to call him Soseki-san. In his present mood, when he considered the restaurant owner's appearance, he couldn't help thinking there was much to be said for an early death. In the case of heroes, that is, and giants. According to Hiroshi this man had once been both. Weins wasn't proud of entertaining such callous thoughts but he hadn't asked to come here either, had he? It had been Hiroshi's idea, not his, to phone the others and arrange to meet here for dinner. Apparently Hiroshi had played the part of this man in some movie based on his youth. Weins assumed his back hadn't been so twisted and bent-over then. Now his flesh, which had once inspired both fear and awe in the ring, sagged like runny dough at his neck and jowls. His skin, poor fellow, might have been stained with piss from a pregnant cow.

Not that you saw very much of it. A three-piece suit hid most: a sunken chest, a soft round belly, two short and skinny legs. Since Weins had witnessed Mabel's stretch marks at their worst, he imagined what couldn't be seen. Not beautiful. Even his face had the sad and wrinkled look of a melting mask. If Weins still wanted to meet a sumo wrestler after the failure of his visit to the arena, this wasn't a face that could cancel his disappointment. He found it hard even to look. Compared to him, the woman in that play was a raving beauty, even after her ruin.

The only English word the old man seemed to know was "where-come", which he repeated several times as he showed them into a private room at the back of his premises. "The western room, he calls it," Hiroshi said. The reason was fairly obvious. A large dining-room table, regular chairs (a relief for these aching legs), and several covers from the *Saturday Evening Post* on the walls. When he spoke to Hiroshi in Japanese he leaned close and muttered something through his teeth, as if he were afraid or ashamed to be heard by the others. Maybe he didn't like the way Eleanor lowered the silver lids of her eyes when she was trying to figure you out.

"He says," Hiroshi explained, "that a young lady will be with us in a moment to bring us something to drink, but in the meantime we can enjoy the view."

The view of what? The room was a windowless box. Weins wondered if you were supposed to imagine your own view, staring at a blank white wall. But the old man dragged a sliding panel open to reveal a garden — a stretch of gravel so white and clean you could see the perfect patterns of a rake's tines circling a single lump of rock. Reminded Weins of a fresh-mowed prairie field from the air, where the farmer had had to manoeuvre his combine around an immovable boulder. You didn't plant or weed this kind of garden, Jill had explained to him once, you only changed the patterns of the rake occasionally, then sat to enjoy it. A good idea, when you thought of Mabel's fights with weeds and rain and reluctant begonia plants. In boxes along the edge of the garden there was a row of short and snaky trees, but none that Weins could name. Some flared, like wind-blown hair, some hunched in poodle-cut puffs. All perched on the brink of that sudden drop above — here it was again — the moat. Wherever you went in this city, it seemed you were confronted with the Emperor's big ravine and its thick green nearly motionless bottom of water.

From here (wherever here was) you couldn't see anything more of the other side than you could see from in front of the hotel. A bank of green leaves, a thick jungle of trees, and a glimpse of tiles on a pagoda roof. You were told the Emperor worked outside in his garden just like a regular farmer but no one had ever gone so far as to suggest he might be sighted climbing around in the trees at the edge of his moat. Weins could hope. The slightest flash of movement over there and he would wave.

Mabel would know how he felt, if she were here. She would also understand why. But Mabel hadn't arrived. Finishing a little nap, according to Eleanor, who'd stepped out

of the taxi with no one but sulky Conrad in tow. "You know
what she can be like. Too much excitement and she's got to
get her feet up above her head before her temples start to
throb and drive her crazy." She sent word that the play had
been so wonderful she could hardly breathe, but that fifteen
minutes with her eyes shut ought to revive her. She would
come along on her own.

Where other people simply let themselves wind down
as the day wore on, Mabel was in the habit of reviving
herself as often as she found it necessary. A few minutes
with her feet on a table could do it. Running cold water over
her wrists might help. A minute of sleep over a hand of
whist could work a miracle. When others were played out
and ready for bed, Mabel would be lively and fresh. If it
weren't that things got dark and quiet at night, encouraging
the habit of sleep, Mabel could have survived on a life of
occasional catnaps around the clock. She often threatened
to do just that. But what she would do with those extra
hours was never clear enough to risk it. Fifteen minutes of
rest and she'd arrive here as good as new, ready to rave
about her Kabuki play and explain the plot. If she saw
Weins looking across the moat at the Emperor's private
grounds she might not stop her excited chatter, but she
would understand how he felt. He wouldn't have to explain.

Nor would he have had to explain it to Jill, if she'd been
able to come. But Jill, Hiroshi'd explained, was escorting an
octogenarian pianist from Montreal to his first Tokyo performance. You could count on Jill to be tied up with somebody weird. Above fashions, concerts, and even foreign
culture, her greatest passion was for genius, wherever it
could be found. Hiroshi, she said, was a genius on the
screen, whenever they gave him a chance. Her boss was a
genius of the diplomatic kind. The artistic geniuses who
passed through her hands on their tours were her favourites,
especially if they needed some pampering. From ballet danc-
ers to potters, if they came from back home to show off their
talents, she was the one who arranged things for them, and
held their hands. She was a person who understood these

things, she was a person who would understand immediately how Weins was feeling right now, about the man who lived on the farther side of the moat.

To expect Eleanor to understand at all was a different matter. Guessing people's feelings was not her strength. With Conrad you wouldn't try. He'd skulked and scowled around at everyone since he'd stepped out of the taxi, as if he'd been brought here by force. When the sliding wall opened, letting in light, instead of admiring the view he cringed and turned away. To preserve his sense of aesthetics or protect his eyes? You didn't have to get closer than this — ten feet away — to guess from the smell how he had spent his afternoon. His fiery eyeballs provided a second clue. If Hirohito appeared on the opposite bank and called them over, he'd be too tipsy to take along.

He pushed past Weins and stepped out into the garden. Ignoring the row of stepping-stones, he walked through the white raked gravel, leaving footsteps, and stopped to peer unsteadily over the railing. If they were lucky, maybe he'd jump. It was only a short drop to the grass and then the long steep roll down the bank of the moat to the water.

"That green crap down there looks thick enough to walk on."

Was he planning to try it himself? Weins followed the stepping-stones out to the trees and looked down. The water was farther down than he'd thought. "To walk it you'd first have to fly."

Conrad's laugh was a hiccup that jerked his shoulders. Weins said that one of the men in this book he'd been reading had tried to walk on water in his youth but failed. It ruined his life. "You might say it forced him into retirement when he was hardly more than a boy."

It was a fact, but Conrad squinted at Weins as if he thought he was making it up. "A book?" He made it sound as if reading a book was one sure sign of senility.

Maybe it was. Maybe it was a sign of senility if you tried to make sense out of anything, let alone books. Mabel said she chose this one because he had a lot in common with

someone in it. She couldn't have meant the fellow who tried
to walk on the water. The difference between them was that
the man in the book had *tried*, while Weins had not. In
Oregon he'd dived for the bottom straight off, like someone
who knew his place. The other fellow might not have known
his place but at least he'd made an attempt. The man who
dived straight to the bottom of water instead of trying to
walk on its top was a man who'd had the stuffing knocked
out of him by early retirement. Weins knew people who'd
died of boredom within six months of retirement because
they couldn't dream up anything compelling enough to get
them out of a chair. He suspected the old man on the bicycle
felt much the same, pedalling round and round the imperial
grounds without change. He never dared to strike off into
the traffic of Tokyo streets where he would almost certainly
be killed — or might, on the other hand, escape.

Hiroshi called them inside. "Soseki-san wishes to know
if Jacob Weins enjoyed this afternoon's *basho*. He would
like to know which wrestler was your favourite."

Weins hated speaking to someone through a translator.
He didn't know who to look at. With everyone else in the
room looking at *him* he would rather be quiet, but that
would be hardly polite. "Tell him if I had to have a favourite
it would be that poor fellow who'll get demoted now and
quit." It was true, his legs still ached from straining to help
that poor bugger from being pushed from the ring.

Conrad's sneer was audible. A hiss. "What's the matter,
Jake, you think wrestlers ought to stay in the ring till they
die, an old man's division?" The notion was apparently
so silly that Conrad had to blow out a mouthful of air.
He opened Eleanor's giant purse on the table and rooted
around inside until he came up with a bottle of Scotch.
Uncapped, it sat while he searched the room for a glass.
There wasn't one.

"Soseki-san says you should not worry about the defeated one, it is Soseki-san himself who should worry since
the defeated one will probably open up a restaurant just like
this and become the competition!"

The old man watched Weins's face eagerly for a response. Obviously, he was expected to laugh. The old man thought it was such a funny thought that the minute Weins cracked a smile he banged his fists on his knees and shook his head. Boozy Conrad burped. Eleanor hummed a bar or two of her opera and lit a cigarette. Hiroshi moved closer to Weins. "Soseki-san is considered a freak to have lived so long," he said. "It is very unusual."

"How old is he?" Eleanor asked. The restaurant owner might have been a chair or a vase to her. Weins guessed the man to be eighty, if he judged by what he could see.

"Sixty-one."

"The same as you!" Eleanor said, turning to Weins. "Exactly the same age as you!"

He could wallop the side of her head. If there were a mirror in the room he would run to it. How could he be sure that when he looked he wouldn't be faced with a wrinkled old crock like the one across the room? Born the same year, maybe they'd aged at identical rates and he'd just never noticed before. A cold fist twisted his gut: he recalled the look of surprise and dismay on the face of the woman down on her knees on the stage.

Hiroshi slipped into Japanese for the benefit of the old man, who nodded gravely and offered a few words back. His eyes, nearly buried in the folds of drooping skin, shifted from Hiroshi to Weins. "He says his liver will kill him off soon, but he is happy all the same to have outlived his own expectations."

"Something to ask him," Conrad said. "Ask if it's true what we've heard, that sumo wrestlers are trained from boyhood to hold their testicles up inside their bodies."

"Conrad." Eleanor's eyes flashed warnings from across the room. Weins had never heard of this; was Conrad making it up to shock them?

"You didn't know that?" Conrad looked delighted. "Jesus." He shook his head, as if he'd never met such a dummy before. "Well doesn't it make some sense? You saw what they do to each other. Did you think they were wearing jock-straps inside those fancy loincloths maybe? Ha ha!" His red eyes were ready to pop. "Ask him, Hiroshi, ask him. Jake here wants to hear it from the horse's mouth."

"When I've already heard it from the horse's ass? Don't bother." He didn't want to hear it from anyone, he'd already heard enough. Maybe Hiroshi guessed it, he looked embarrassed. Wasn't it enough that in this bloody country you were encouraged to sympathize with women who turned out to have a man's equipment inside their clothes? Was it necessary, now, to discover you'd been cheering for men who *didn't*. He could never have guessed that such an upside-down confusing place existed in this world. He was going home.

But not, apparently, without first doing something about this tiny cup put into his hand by a young woman who'd come into the room with a tray. A quick sniff confirmed his suspicions: warm sake, like the stuff he'd spilled in the arena. Weins would happily have turned it in for a tall cold glass of beer, but it looked as if Hiroshi was making decisions for them all tonight. "I have ordered a special Japanese dinner I think you will like," he said.

Weins doubted it. His stomach doubted it as well. Hiroshi, however, was getting to know him better. "No squid, my friend, I promise."

The young woman smiled as if she understood, then moved on to offer a glass to Eleanor, who was unable to take her eyes off the pink brocade kimono. Was there anyone in this city who wasn't dressed up in a costume? Besides himself that is. It seemed to Weins that what he'd been seeing since he set foot in this place was a parade of them. The actors in that play were no exception — everyone seemed to have something that suited a role. Joggers, street-cleaners, workmen with their hard hats and towels, businessmen in their white shirts with the rolled-up sleeves. Even the visitors knew what they ought to wear — all except Weins. He wore these baggy pants that felt like something he might have put on by mistake in a public changing-roon. While someone like bloody Conrad, when he pulled on those skin-tight jeans, probably felt more like himself when dressed than when he was not. To borrow the jerk's own words: it wasn't fair.

Once the old man had gone off to supervise their meal, Weins asked Eleanor why they hadn't gone with Jill to the piano recital. What did they do instead? "Are you kidding?" Eleanor said. "We went over to Jill's but he plunked himself in front of the television set and drank his way down through a bottle of Hiroshi's Scotch. There was nothing left for me to do but go shopping and buy these pearls."

She struck a pose, with one tanned hand laid out against the necklace at her throat, and waited for something to be said. Weins didn't know what it was. Hiroshi, who was an actor himself and therefore more used to the type, apparently did. "And very beautiful pearls too," he said. "Obviously of excellent quality."

Eleanor closed her silver eyelids a moment, treasuring. Then pouted her lips accusingly at Weins. "You see how a gentleman notices these things." Leaning against the end of the open wall she crossed her ankles and arranged the folds of her skirt with the crimson nails of one hand. "I am even thinking of taking a Japanese lover. Jill knows what she's doing." She slid a look at stinko Conrad. "Besides their beautiful manners, darling, they also have lovely behinds."

Oh hell. Was she trying to provoke Conrad into a fight? He looked dangerous enough already. Scowling up out of those reddened eyes he appeared to be blaming them all. But it was Weins's name that he barked. "Jake." His own head jerked back from the force. "You knew I wanted to go!"

Everything, it appeared, was Weins's fault. Was a reputation for deserting people his fate? It was time for Mabel to arrive and add her two bits' worth. The bunch of them could put together a case: the man who let others down.

Eleanor lighting a cigarette kept her gaze steady on something out over the moat. "You sat and watched the same damn thing that they were watching. For Christ sake, cut it out, you're becoming a bore." She shifted her gaze just enough to give Weins a look that begged for sympathy.

"Back home I thought I'd made one hell of a catch this time but get him over here and he acts like a dork. Conrad, try to be civil."

Hiroshi's gentle voice was almost a shock, after Eleanor. "Well, at least you saw it on television. If you had come with us you would have been disappointed, the place was packed, you would not even have got in the door."

Conrad shrugged. He almost smiled. "Did you see that sonofabitch crack the little fellow on the back of his neck? What a bastard. And that pig that used his stomach like a battering ram."

So Conrad had been watching when his man in orange was defeated. The end of a career meant nothing at all to him, of course, how could it? Just one more loser cast aside, it was part of the sport. "Oh Jesus those bastards remind me of that bohunk in the logging camp. I told you about him, Jake. Seven feet tall with a gut — shit, I'd like to've seen him take on one of those guys!" He was nearly back in his normal form. His eyes bugged out, his fingers raked in his hair, the beads of sweat were glistening on his upper lip. "One day — oh hell, he was a mean and filthy man — one day he sees this greenhorn whistle punk having a snooze behind a tree and he takes offence. A friend of mine, this was, who liked a siesta after lunch. Well this big bugger lets out a roar and practically flies through the bush and lands feet first right on top of the kid. Holy shit, what a way to wake up!"

At that, Conrad ran out of steam. Or lost interest. He dropped his gaze to the floor and seemed caught up in some other thought. Whatever it was it called for another drink.

"And then?" Apparently Hiroshi considered part of his role as host was to keep things going. "And then what happened? When the boy woke up with this giant on top of him — what happened next?"

Conrad narrowed his rosy eyes. At Hiroshi. At Weins. At Eleanor who looked away. "I don't remember." *Wouldn't* remember was probably what he meant. The puzzlement on his face was part of his act, he thought he would punish everyone here by withholding the end of the story.

Well he couldn't. Who cared? "It doesn't matter," Weins said. "We can imagine the rest."

Naturally it would end like all of Conrad's stories. The youthful snoozer was a city boy like Conrad, his first time in the bush. Whether he was beaten to a pulp by the bone-headed bully or turned the tables and broke the bastard's neck, he would go home from his summer's job having proved himself a man. That was the point. Conrad, on the other hand, would not. He'd go cringing home, more uncertain than ever before. For the rest of his life he'd wish that it had been himself the big logger had jumped on behind that tree. A black eye, a few broken bones — a small enough price to pay.

"You *knew* I wanted to go, goddamit." Conrad was back in his sulk.

Before he had time to find something new to say, however, Mabel and dinner arrived, both at the very same moment. Naturally it was dinner that had to wait. Mabel was in a mood not only for talking about the play but acting it out as well. The rest of them could sit, they could look at the food, they could even sample a bit here and there, but nobody dared to dig in as long as she was in action.

Oh, what they'd missed, she told Weins, she told everyone. They'd just never know! "It was wonderful. That poor murdered woman literally hounded her husband to death before the story was over   marvellous!" To show how marvellous it was she dug a number of sketches out of her purse and passed them around the table. When they'd come on without her she'd done more than just put her feet up and rest, she said. Here was that peacock husband terrified, the woman's misshapen face floating bodiless in the air. Here was the husband again, dragging her corpse up out of the water. "Oh, she had a delicious revenge. Before the fellow was killed at the end she chased him with the flaming balls of fire into a monastery where he tried to hide. He couldn't. She refused to leave him alone."

One of the sketches was of the woman herself, before her

disfigurement and death. Down on her knees she raised that pitiful doll-like face as if looking for help. Weins shuddered, and passed it on. As if she weren't already printed indelibly on his brain.

"So you see," she said, tossing the end of her long white scarf back over her shoulders, "I didn't miss you at all."

"Bravo!" Eleanor clapped her hands. Just once, before a look from Mabel, who was the older sister after all, made her stop. "That's not quite true, you had my stomach in knots when you left. My nerves were jumping. I saw you . . . I imagined you out there doing, well *something* foolish. Then after a while I got caught up in the play and I thought, why should I use up my energy feeling guilty? To hell with that." She looked defiant, like someone who'd dared to utter an obscenity for the first time in her life, then bent to kiss Weins's forehead. "You're old enough to look after your own darn self. I wanted to enjoy that play and I did."

She nearly joined them at the table, ready to eat, then squealed — remembering something else. "Oh, you should have seen it . . . this one scene . . . the whole stage from one end to the other was a canal. Great long strips of blue paper were the water, waving and drifting like the current, you even saw stuffed paper fish. Then along comes the murderer husband, with a fishing pole."

"The food's getting cold," Conrad said.

"So eat," said Mabel, who refused to cater to any of Conrad's moods. "Along comes the husband with his pole and stands on the edge of this high stone wall above the canal and throws in his line. Like this." She imitated a pompous male, tossing his line in the water. Her face was flushed. "He catches a fish." Anyone could tell Mabel had never caught a fish in her life. Anyone could tell that she'd never been trained for the stage; her idea of acting was to exaggerate as grossly as you might if you thought all your audience were dimwits. She was even worse than Eleanor. "Annoyed by some excitable old lady, he throws her into the canal, where big ugly water rats grab her and drag her down out of sight. A very nice man this is."

Eleanor looked at Weins as if he were the man in question. Weins chose to contemplate the collection of little dishes laid out before him. Was there anything here that he knew? One was a bowl of rice. That much was safe. Another when he leaned closer smelled like seaweed. Probably soup. He could handle that as well. But the rest might easily have been dropped on the table from Mars. Bits and pieces of things in some kind of batter. Dark suspicious-looking sauces. Where were you supposed to begin? He watched Conrad drive the ends of his chopsticks into his bowl of rice, dig out a wad, and lift it up to his lips. It fell to his lap. "Shit." He put down the sticks, looked into his cup, and filled it up from the bottle. Then he tossed it back. He stared at his collection of food dishes as if he thought they were plotting against him. He filled up his cup again.

"And then," Mabel said, "along came this wooden door that was floating on the water. My goodness, Hiroshi, I've never seen such imagination put to use in a theatre. How do they do it? And on the door was the decomposing body of his wife. If you thought she was in bad shape *before* she died," she told Weins, "you ought to have seen her later. Yuk. What a mess. The door is caught on his fishing line but he certainly doesn't want to reel it in. Oh, the look on his face!" If it was anything like the look on *her* face, he was worse than terrified, he was thrown into a convulsive fit. "But it floats right up to him anyway and — I can't even begin to imagine how they do these things — just as he's hauling it up the stone wall, all the flesh drops off the body and there he is faced with a skeleton!"

Aieeeeeeeee! Mabel turned in circles, shaking her hands. As if she'd touched death and it stuck to her fingers. Aieeeeeeeee! Sitting through five hours of melodrama had affected her mind. Maybe she'd snapped. Even Conrad looked mildly alarmed. Eleanor ducked her head. The smile that Hiroshi reserved for Mabel, the woman who disapproved of him, had died. Weins decided to devote his attention to seeing if he had any better control of his chopsticks than he'd had in the last restaurant they'd been in. He hadn't.

"I am happy that Mrs. Weins enjoyed the Kabuki so much," Hiroshi said, perhaps to Eleanor, who was on his right. Perhaps to Weins, who was the next one down the table. He picked up a piece of the mystery food with chopsticks, dragged it through a dish of sauce, and popped it into his mouth. "Maybe when she is settled in Ottawa, she can persuade the people in charge of cultural events there to arrange for Kabuki to be performed at the — what is it? — National Centre of Arts?"

"Ottawa?" Eleanor said. "Why would she want to live there?"

Exactly the question that must have occurred to Mabel, who halted her spin in mid screech and nearly toppled. Weins suspected he knew what they were about to hear.

"Well, Ottawa is surely where they will be making their home, once Mr. Weins has been elected to Parliament?"

"Parliament?" Mabel said, and dropped into the chair where she could look Weins in the eye. He could read in her face what she thought: the minute he was out of her sight had he planned his whole future without her? What happened to the notion of consulting the woman you lived with? "Don't look at me," he said. "Down there is the man who suggested it. What do I know? I thought my days in politics were over."

"They are," Mabel said, in a tone that declared the discussion closed. She picked up her chopsticks and, with the help of her other hand, arranged them between her fingers. She had not, however, managed to engineer any food up as far as her mouth when Soseki-san re-entered the room. She lowered her chopsticks for the introduction.

Some hasty conversation in Japanese, then Hiroshi said, "I explained to Soseki-san that you have returned from a performance at Kabuki-za and that you seem to have enjoyed the ghost story much more than Mr. Weins enjoyed the sumo this afternoon. Soseki-san says perhaps that is because Kabuki allows the defeated to seek a delicious revenge while in sumo the vanquished must bow politely and disappear." Hiroshi looked at Weins and grinned. "Of course I told him that when you are an elected member of your government you will undoubtedly take whatever action is necessary to have Kabuki and sumo matches both make regular visits to your country."

Was he making fun? God help him, his heart had been racing madly since the topic had come up, no kidding either. There must be something in what the boy was saying or why would he feel this way? No sooner had Ottawa been mentioned than he'd seen himself going in the tailor shop tomorrow. He even knew what he wanted. A business suit, or two. For formal occasions, or banquets and speeches in front of huge crowds, you needed a three-piece suit. When they made him minister in charge of — would it be Culture, or Industry, Trade and Commerce? — he would need a variety of first-class dressy suits for the meetings he'd have to chair, the big-shot businessmen and scholars he would need to meet, the functions he would be expected to open.

"Soseki-san says he could have guessed you were a man who would be much in the public eye, an important official. Just like that gentleman who drew your picture."

Mabel wanted to know what picture they were talking about, an edge of indignation in her voice. As resident artist, did she think it an act of betrayal to turn to a stranger? He reached for the rolled-up paper he'd propped in the corner behind his chair and unrolled it for her. "They've got the ears right, anyway," she said, and made it clear there was nothing else on the piece of paper which deserved a comment.

Soseki-san leaned forward for a better look, and said something to Hiroshi. "Soseki-san says the retired man has very few choices, unfortunately. To die. To wallow in self-pity. To paralyse himself with fear. Or to live in the way his own life has prepared him to live. At sixty-one years of age, whatever talent has surfaced is surely meant to be used."

"But he *has* no talent for politics," Mabel protested. She looked at the old man as if she would ask him to mind his own business. "He proved over and over again that he has no talent at all for politics." She looked strained, her face looked drawn, would she soon be fishing around in her purse for pills? Perhaps she saw herself and Weins slipping back into patterns she thought they had left behind.

Hiroshi translated Mabel's observation for the old man, then hastily switched to English. "I did not say he had any talent for politics — how would I know such a thing? Jacob Weins appears to me to have the instincts of an actor."

Eleanor put her hands up over her face and groaned. Weins felt his own face burn — not just his ears this time, but everything from throat to forehead. Mabel, whose face expressed astonishment, looked at Weins as if he were some new curiosity just installed before her. "Well I could have told you that, I guess. Being a mayor was only an excuse to wear your closetful of costumes. And to organize performances. That wasn't politics. You'd have been better off acting in that play I saw, for all the good you ever did as a politician." She smiled, and squeezed his wrist. In case this was disturbing news.

"Exactly my point," Hiroshi said. Weins was beginning to feel invisible. They were talking as if he weren't even here. "In my country," Hiroshi said, "the place for an actor to best make use of his talent is on the stage or the movie screen. But in your country . . . " He paused to watch Conrad concentrate on raising a piece of food to his mouth between the pinched ends of his chopsticks. It fell before he could nab it with his teeth, and dropped to the table.

"In my country, as I said, an actor would just naturally go onto the stage, or into the movies, but after a few years living in your country I saw that things were quite different there. In your country the best way for an actor to make full use of his talents is not on the stage — who would bother to notice him there? — and certainly not on the screen, since that is reserved for foreigners, I understand — but as a politician. Who else has so many opportunities to command an audience? Who else is measured by the amount of success he has at playing a role, at wearing a mask? In a country of stuffy legislators a genuine actor would shine!"

"You mean as entertainment," Weins said. "Like the

clown who dances around in the bullring?" He was thinking of that book again, and how the clowns distracted the
bull while the matadors jabbed in their knives, or made
their escape. Was Hiroshi suggesting he become a diversion,
a public clown who distracted the voters while the crooked
politicians robbed them blind?

Hiroshi laughed. "No, no, no, not that at all. I mean as a
colourful source of energy and life, which is something
quite different. Is there a country in the world that can
afford to turn down that?"

A different outfit every day in the House of Commons.
How could he stop these thoughts from crowding in? He
saw himself as Sir John A. Macdonald, he saw himself as a
coureur-de-bois, he saw himself marching down the stone
hallways of the Parliament Buildings dressed in the impressive costume of a Viking. Surely there weren't any rules
against being colourful! Television cameramen, bored with
dreary speeches and dull identical suits, would just naturally lavish most of their attention on him. No matter what
topic had been discussed on the floor that day, newsmen
would be sure to seek him out for a comment, confident that
whatever outfit he'd chosen to wear, it would be something
that would catch attention in homes across the country.

At that moment a wad of boiled rice which had got all
the way to Conrad's lips dropped off the chopsticks to his
lap. He tossed the sticks to the table, dipped his hand into
the bowl, and scooped up a lump which he shoved into his
mouth. That much swallowed, he looked at his greasy hand.
"Shee-it. I've had enough of this crap." He pushed back his
chair and gulped down one more cup. "Also enough about
politics. Who gives a shit?" He seemed stricken, suddenly,
by a brilliant idea. "Tell the old man I want him to show me
some sumo moves. Tell him to show me some of those
winning techniques."

Eleanor gritted her teeth and groaned his name. Hiroshi
looked down at his hands. "It would not be very polite," he
said, "to ask such a thing in the middle of this meal he has
prepared for us."

"I'm not in the middle of my meal," Conrad said, standing up. "I've eaten all of that stuff I can stomach. Tell him to show me some of those ritual things." He clapped his hands and raised one leg as high as he could to the side before slamming it down.

"Please," Hiroshi said. "Please sit down."

"You're being a turd," Eleanor said.

Conrad seemed to think being a turd was funny. He stomped his foot again and laughed, his face a tomato red. He started to unbutton his shirt, then swayed and had to put one hand on the wall to steady himself. "There's hundreds of grips, I know there's hundreds, just tell him to show me a few. Tell him I want him to show me how that big fat pig in purple got thrown out of the ring."

The old man looked confused. You could tell he knew that all this talk had something to do with him, but no one was telling him what. Poor man, if Weins could speak his language he'd tell him Conrad was a worm that should be ignored. As it was, he was ashamed to be here himself. Ashamed to have the old man treated like this. Ashamed to see Hiroshi exposed to such horrible manners.

With his shirt tossed over the chair, Conrad looked more ornery than ever, strutting about indignantly while he flexed the muscles in his arms and puffed out his chest. A salesman maybe, but he was one of those men who spent their spare time lifting weights. What did they like to call it, the jocks? Pumping iron. Naturally he never missed a chance to rip off his shirt. "Why the hell won't you tell him, goddamit? Just a couple of moves." He came around the table towards the old man, and hunched forward into a crouch, as if he were ready to leap. "Come on, old grandpa-san, let's see how this thing is done."

"Please leave him alone," Hiroshi said, standing up and putting a hand on the nearer arm. "He may be old but still he could break you in pieces if he wanted to. You are insulting him. He is not stupid, he can guess what you want, you are trying to make him look foolish, he thinks, instead of respecting his position as owner of this restaurant

where we are guests. If you do not sit down immediately I
will call a taxi and send you home."

Conrad blinked. Was he so tight that he couldn't recognize Hiroshi's threat was real? He seemed to think it was
funny. "I'm not trying to tangle with you, little man, I just
want this old fellow to show me something. What's the
matter with you bunch of shits, staring? For crying out loud.
If he was such a goddam big-shot champion in his day why
shouldn't he want to show a younger guy how it's done?"
He scowled at Hiroshi. "It's you," he said, pushing against
the youth's shoulder. "It's you that won't tell him. I bet he'd
be glad to help if only you'd ask, but you've decided to be a
goddam bastard about it."

When he gave the shoulder a second push Hiroshi looked
down, as if to hide his embarrassment. It was Mabel who
stood, "You sit," she ordered, and brandished her chopsticks as if she intended to throw them. In front of outsiders,
however, even her threats were issued in a strained pleasant
voice. She would give you a chance to avoid unpleasantries.

Weins saw that Conrad was not in a mood to appreciate
such subtleties. Something had to be done. He stood up
himself and started around the table.

"What's the matter, Jake — you think I don't know how
it's done? I watched the whole thing, don't forget. You think
I don't know how they do it?" He backed off and dropped
into a crouch, his fists on the floor. "Come on, here's the
line. Come on."

Was he mad as well as drunk? Weins didn't know where
to look. "Don't be a fool, put on your shirt." Soseki-san had
lowered his gaze to the floor, and backed away.

But Conrad seized one leg by the knee, lifted it slowly
up as far as it would go — just horizontal — then brought
it down.

Mabel grabbed at a dish which tottered. "You'll be
breaking things."

Again Conrad went into his crouch and snarled at Weins.
"Come on, you. Come on. You think I'm just somebody to
leave behind. You think the whole world is holding its

breath while you decide what to do with your stupid life.
You think nobody else around here matters. Come on, let's
see what division they'd put you in. Or if they'd toss you
right out."

Hiroshi came up and put a hand on the nearer shoulder.
"Perhaps we should wait until later, after we've eaten our
dinner."

But Conrad threw himself forward like a football player
going into a tackle and rammed his shoulder into Weins's
chest. Staggering back from the sharp pain, Weins had to
struggle for breath, while Eleanor shrieked and dishes crashed
to the floor. Now Conrad had his hands into Weins's belt
and was trying to hoist him. Was he about to be cut in two
by the crotch of his pants? There was nothing that Weins
could do but push with both hands against the head that
pushed into his chest. The dark hair stood up in spikes like
a little child's. Grunting, snorting — just to lift his weight
up off the floor? Weins felt anchored safely enough, but
wondered how long he could keep backing up. A few steps
more and he'd be against the wall and bring those pictures
down. He wasn't prepared to hold his ground forever —
surely someone else would help, instead of gawking. When
Conrad jerked to strengthen his grip on the belt, he twisted
his head and laid his face against Weins. It was red, un-
naturally red, and covered with sweat. If he ever managed to
lift Weins up off the floor would he toss him outside on the
gravel, or over the edge?

Hiroshi broke them apart. How, Weins couldn't tell. The
gesture was far too quick. It flipped Conrad flat on his back
on the floor as if he'd been shot with a few hundred volts of
electrical power. Bent over and gasping for breath, Weins
wondered how something could happen too fast to see.

But Conrad was quickly back on his feet. "Bastards," he
hissed. And turned to rush out through the open wall onto
the garden. Now what? Now what? Would the damn fool
jump?

If so, he stopped first to pull off his pants. At the edge of
the garden he let them drop down his legs and kicked with

one foot then the other until he was free. In socks and jockey
shorts did he make Eleanor think of the day she'd met him
in that pub? There was no understanding what a woman
would find appealing. To Weins this creature looked like
anyone else in a catalogue underwear ad, except for the red
furious face.

The underwear ad climbed onto the rail, then turned
and dropped onto the grass. He headed towards the flag-
stone walk along the bank of the moat. Was Weins the only
one who knew what would happen next? Nobody said a
word. Eleanor's only contribution was a groan when Conrad
leapt the fence and started down the steep stone side of the
moat. Out of control, he leapt, slid, flailed his arms, and
finally flipped into a dive that took him into the water. The
green velvet surface rippled in circular waves.

Had he dived for the bottom with the intention of staying
awhile? Weins's own hands were clutching at remembered
weeds. He knew how it felt. Everything in him was straining to rise while he strained with his will to stay down. It
wasn't easy. He doubted that Conrad would have what it
took to hold on. A fool going in, he was bound to be more of
a fool coming out.

Had he looked this much of a fool himself perhaps?
Only Mabel could tell. Conrad, surfacing, spluttered and
yelled for help. Why? Since he was already on his feet and
the water came only as high as his thighs, he could easily
walk to the shore. His body streaming greenish clots of
slime. Like a baby he chose to stand where he was and
holler. If Eleanor was reminded now of the jockey-shorts
contest she wasn't letting on. If she felt any pity for the
boy-man in the moat she was hiding that as well. With one
hand over her mouth she asked for the ladies' room. No one
was left who could tell her. Hiroshi and Soseki-san had
bolted when Conrad dropped. They reappeared on the grass
below, leading a posse of excited, jabbering people. Customers or employees, they huddled a moment, then sent
two of their crowd along the path to the top of a staircase
that led down the face of the bank.

What in the scene below would show up in Mabel's sketches? He would bet on Conrad's sagging underdrawers for sure, his stance of a helpless child, his wide-open mouth. He didn't know what to do with those slimy hands. If artists saw what they wanted to see, as Weins suspected they did, you could expect her to draw a few dozen snakes on the water's surface, and give the outstretched rescuer's hands the look of skeletons, so that you wouldn't know if he was being rescued or coaxed into the arms of something worse. If he himself were given free rein with a pencil on an artist's sketch-pad now, he'd have the Emperor down to watch the commotion from the opposite shore. Standing amongst the bushes, he would raise a hand in greeting to someone he thought he recognized on this nearer side. "If we go to Ottawa," Jacob Weins said, "we'll fix up one of the rooms in our house as a studio."

"What?" She wrinkled her nose. Preoccupied with Conrad's rescue she may have thought this had something to do with that. "What do you mean?"

"For you." Should he have kept the sudden idea a secret? "I'd have an office in the Parliament Buildings to work in, but you'll need your working space too." He would be famed not only for the colour and originality he brought to the country's politics, but for his talented wife as well. At formal balls she could be pursued by the artsy type, even people from the National Gallery, wanting to talk, wanting to buy her work, asking when she would have another public display. Already he could see it happening, her very first big-city show. "We'll rent a hall when you're ready. Classy, with chandeliers. With guards at the doors and waitresses carrying trays. Dignitaries and politicians and embassy people from other countries will come dressed up in their furs to admire your work, to sip at a glass of wine while they decide which sketch to buy to hang on their walls."

"So it wasn't only a joke. It wasn't a joke at all." If it wasn't a joke, why did she find it funny? Or was she laughing at Conrad, being coaxed from the greenish mud. When he reached the bank would his flesh fall away from his bones, like the rotting corpse in her play?

"Maybe I'll give it a try and maybe I won't. We'll see."

She raised one eyebrow. "And maybe I'll just refuse to go with you if you do."

A teasing edge to her voice but still, the idea had never occurred to him. "What do you mean?" Would a woman who'd let herself be dragged from campsite to campsite all over the continent be likely to balk at a chance to live in the nation's capital, as the wife of an elected official? If she was going to claim that play had changed her life he would tell her to get some sense. What could an ancient ghost story have to say to a woman today?

"Well never mind now," she said, and put her hand in his. "There's plenty of time to talk." She even rested her head against his arm. "And there's always the chance you won't get elected at all."

That wasn't true. She squeezed his hand to show she was making a joke. He knew the voting habits of the Island. If he showed up at campaign rallies dressed as a Haida chief he was sure to be voted in, no question about it. If he went to public functions as a samurai and spouted a word or two in Japanese he'd be in by a mile. If he went on television to tell the story of Port Annie's tragic disappearance off the map, dressed in a newer version of his Captain Vancouver costume, he'd be in by acclamation. It was only a matter of deciding whether he *wanted* it. There were other ways of being the person he'd been learning how to be for sixty-one years. Maybe he could find some television company that would snap him up and give him a part in plays. Or turn him into one of these colourful interviewers or a news announcer. It didn't matter *what* he did, the important thing was that now he knew he had to do something quick or die, he had to find something to do that used the gifts he'd spent a lifetime of instincts and choices developing.

Even in this whirring racket of cicadas and the tangle of voices, the oversize ears of Jacob Weins could pick up the familiar hum of bicycle tires on pavement. Around the curve of moat came the ancient cyclist who'd nearly run him down, pumping down the track beneath the trees. Still wearing the same white pants, still carrying the yellow towel around his neck, he strained ahead as if he saw his goal at last and feared it would elude him if he wavered. Not a glance at the bawling boy-man in the moat, not a peek at Jacob Weins in the garden, not even a flicker of interest in the direction of the crowd that jabbered excitedly along the bank, or those that hurried out of the building to join them. He stroked right through it all as if this type of thing happened every day within his field of vision. And maybe it did. The streets of Tokyo could be crawling with tourists who were destined to end up in the moat or gawk in horror from a garden at someone else who did. If you spent your whole life circumnavigating the Emperor's palace grounds, it stood to reason that sooner or later you were bound to see everything there was worth seeing in this world, if you bothered to look, and plenty more besides. If you raced unstopping like this man with the certain knowledge that some worried family member was on your tail, you might become blind to things that happened within the range of your vision and obsessed with things that were not — the invisible finish line ahead, for instance, or the constant hiss of the pursuer's tires behind you. Weins knew *that* as well.

This time the pursuer was not the pretty young woman Weins had talked to, it was a child. A boy. Unlike the old man, he hadn't seen everything yet. A man being fished from the moat by a noisy crowd was a reason to stop. He even swung off his bike and walked to the edge for a look. When two men up to their knees in green slime were trying to drag a third one out of the muck to the staircase and up the bank, a boy could quickly forget an eccentric old man. Especially now that police had arrived, and seemed to be hollering orders. And a photographer snapping pictures.

"Hey, kid!" Weins shouted down. Left unpursued the old man would probably escape. Weins saw him whirring off forgotten and lost in the world. "Hey, kid!" But his voice, even if the boy understood English, was lost in the confusion of sounds.

Too late, too late. By now the old man was half a mile down the track. The boy would never catch up. Just about now the old cyclist would become aware of his pursuer's absence. You could sense these things. Would a grin break out on his face, as if he'd accomplished something? Or would he start to worry? Weins, whose heart was pounding for him as it hadn't for Conrad, guessed he would leap on the chance to escape. The slightest turn of the handlebars and over the grass he would go, across the sidewalk and bump, down into the street. Into the heavy traffic. Cars would honk, arms would wave, drivers would yell out their windows. Unused to paying attention he would cycle care-lessly through. Did he know what traffic lights meant? It didn't matter. His chances for survival once he got off his track were practically nil, but that wasn't something that mattered to a man who was free.

And yet it was Weins, his supporter, who continued to warn the boy. "Hey, kid," he shouted. "Hey, somebody tell that kid to get back on his bike." Nobody paid attention. The boy continued to stare at the spectacle unfolding below. While somewhere out in the largest city in the world — Weins could imagine it — the old man went whizzing down a busy street of traffic, pedalling fiercely, hearing nothing but the child's heavy absence behind him, seeing nothing but his far-off impossible goal, whatever that was.

Given a choice between being a Conrad dripping slime and being an old man pumping pedals through hazardous traffic, did he know which choice he would make? He'd choose the old man's chances, no question of that, but he knew how Conrad felt. Being a man of similar experience himself, he could hardly avoid the knowledge. Between the moment he broke the surface of that lake in Oregon and the moment Conrad dived to the bottom of this, surely some-thing important had happened, surely something had changed. If nothing else, he could afford to feel some — what? com-passion? — for this fool, having once been there himself.

What good would it do to give a name to what had changed? Instead he would give it direction. For a man who'd spent a lifetime becoming an actor, he'd spent his retirement being an audience instead. He'd been nothing more than audience since he'd arrived in this city. It wasn't natural. It wasn't natural, at least, to him. Standing here in this garden he was being an audience now. When was he going to act?

"Have you got your camera here?" he said.

Mabel glanced back at her purse. "Of course. You know I have."

"Then get it out. I want plenty of pictures of this."

Plenty of pictures of what? Mabel looked ready to panic. "Now use some sense."

Of course he wouldn't use what she liked to call sense. He had something better than that. And it didn't matter whether she took pictures or not, that photographer was still below, with his fancy equipment. No doubt he would be happy to take a photo of this, several photos in fact. Jacob Weins on the edge of the Emperor's moat. A photograph in a Tokyo daily was bound to be reproduced in every paper on the coast when he took it home. Port Annie's colourful mayor, the captions would read, still had his well-known flair — look what he was doing now. Given to wearing unusual costumes in public, he'd made this newest one of nothing more or less than his own wife's scarf. Tied at the waist it was just big enough to suggest a loincloth and cover his undershorts. A splendid series of photos. Jacob Weins on the edge of the moat, the imperial palace gardens in the background, the Emperor himself could be imagined in the trees and looking this way, just as curious as the reader of the newspaper was to find out what was going on here. The other half-naked fellow would be identified as someone that Weins had only moments before helped save from the moat, someone nameless. What Weins and this stranger were doing for the sake of the crowd, for the sake of this camera, was having a little fun to celebrate the rescue, a very close call. In the middle of one of the largest cities in the world they were bent over nose to nose with their fists on the ground, prepared to demonstrate for all this laughing crowd — which incidentally included a former sumo champion — that North

Americans could have some fun with this sport so closely identified with Japan. A sport that every boy who wanted to call himself a man could engage in — and every man who liked to risk looking a fool. Upon his return to Canada, the story would say, Jacob Weins had announced his intention to begin a new career immediately. Not as a sumo wrestler, of course, he was a little too old for that, but something more in keeping with his well-known gift for cutting a colourful figure wherever he was in the world. If his grin in the photos reminded you of a little kid, it was probably because he was sure, like a child, that his future was securely gripped in his own two hands.

7

The Plague Children

Maybe this youth is dangerous and maybe he isn't, nobody knows for sure. What's known is that he's running up the entire length of the Island, end to end. With his track shoes dipped in the Strait of Juan de Fuca he is pumping knees and elbows towards Port Hardy. If he isn't dangerous maybe he's just plain crazy. A sweat-band keeps that long pale hair from getting in his eyes; a beard that looks like rusty wire fans out across his chest; a wrinkled cotton shirt, embroidered like a table-cloth with daisies, flaps and flutters around the waist of his track-suit pants. Whether you see him flicker past behind a screen of trees or catch him stroking head-on up the highway, the effect is much the same. The rhythm of his footsteps never changes, his bone-jarred breaths maintain an even beat, no sweat breaks out across his forehead or soaks that flapping shirt. Maybe this youth is dangerous and maybe he isn't; there are some who even think he may not be human.

Here in Waterville they think they know this youth and what he means: a spy, a scout, an advance guard for a swarm of others. While those legs and elbows pump him north,

those eyes are reconnoitring, the brain behind the sweat-
band taking notes. In Port Hardy where the highway ends
he'll catch his breath and make a phone call south to launch
this year's attack. These people have seen it all before.
When he passes through this small community of farms
they brace themselves for war.

    Yet only Frieda Macken acts. Even before the youth is
out of sight, she hurries out to the lean-to shed behind her
house and roots around in a clutter of rusty machines and
broken tools for a sack of lime. In all that settlement of
part-time farmers, only Frieda Macken and her husband
Eddie get out in their fields to spread the harsh white
powder with their hands, squinting into the dust that burns
their eyes. The others, seeing that youth thump past with
his covetous eyes and his rusty prophetic beard, move inside to wait for what they know is about to happen and still
refuse to believe. Not only scout, this youth is harbinger as
well. The invading horde is only a day behind.

Read the papers. Find out where they're from. Holland,
California, Rome. The Philippines. Some from as near as
Vancouver, others from Katmandu. All of them could be
here from another planet. A few every year get caught by
police and fined. Copenhagen, Tallahassee, Nome, nobody
wants to believe the addresses they print in the papers.
Nobody believes their names.

    For the people who live in Waterville there is something
a little incredible in all of this. The place has never wanted
to be part of anyone's map. This collection of thirty hobby
farms along a four-mile stretch of highway has never wanted to be anything at all but what it is: a General Store and
Post Office, a community hall, and houses you pass on your
way to somewhere else. They don't even ask you to reduce
your speed as you're driving through. Everyone here has
been here for fifty years at least, everyone here is middle-

aged or older. It's not easy for them to believe that people in Holland, Colombia, Rome, when they hear the name of this settlement, pack their bags and immigrate in order to take part in this annual assault.

And yet in Saskatoon, in Florence, and in Oslo, they wrench up whatever roots they have and join the converging exodus around the world towards this place. Word has gone out on some invisible global network that the September rains have come to this part of the world, the magic mushrooms are pushing their way through the ground in record numbers, and a fortune is waiting to be made by those who get here first. Bring your family, bring your friends, bring anyone with a pair of hands and a pair of legs for running away from the law. Fresh air, fresh fruit, and plenty of gardens to raid; a hefty profit and a month of incredible highs.

Dennis Macken sees them first. They lean their bicycles into the ditch outside his field, hide their motorbikes in the bush, and hop off hitch-hiked rides onto the gravel shoulder of the highway. Then they climb over, under, through his strands of barbed-wire fence. They stretch it, twist it, leave bits of their own patched sweaters snagged on it. One fat bearded man in leather shorts grabs a cedar post and levers it back and forth until it breaks off beneath the ground like a rotten tooth. Now he and his long-skirted woman and their four small children can walk unmolested onto Dennis Macken's nearest pasture and start their bent-over search in the damp September grass.

Dennis Macken watches with a hand on the telephone, his tongue exploring a cavity. Unlike his brother and sister-in-law he's done nothing at all to avoid this confrontation. Perhaps he even welcomes it. At any rate he doesn't stop himself from grinning. When it appears that no more of them will be coming this morning he calls the police, then moves out onto the step to watch. A woman with a baby strapped to her back pauses to wave, and smile. There is no one out there who is even half his age.

When the police arrive, he laughs out loud at the sight of that pack breaking up and scattering like panicked cattle — pails emptied, skirts hoisted, long hair flying, children screaming. Through his second fence, or over it, into the bush. By the time the Mounties have crossed the ditch and entered the field there's no one left in sight. The two of them stomp bravely towards the woods and disappear in alder. They come out again pulling a girl who kicks and screams and finally goes limp while they drag her back to their car. At the car she turns and shouts out something, a curse perhaps, at Dennis Macken, at those invisible pickers, at the world. Her words, of course, are in a language he cannot understand.

When the rest have come back to spread out over his field again, Macken moves inside his house and watches from a window. He knows that something is happening here but he doesn't know what it is. He only hopes they will have left for the day by the time he goes out for his evening chores. At sixty-three years old Dennis Macken still believes in the law. These people are trespassing on private property. They're tromping on the field he cleared himself with his home-made tractor. They're breaking down fences he worked hard weeks to build. He imagines himself with a rifle, picking them off from his window; he imagines his pasture a battlefield strewn with bodies; but he still believes in the law. He will phone the police every hour through the rest of this day. And tomorrow. And the day after that. Those young buggers may get their mushrooms in the end, but they'll get plenty of exercise, too.

His neighbour Angel Hopper doesn't believe in waiting for the law, he believes in fighting his battles himself. The sight of the second-day wave of pickers upsets his stomach, gives him migraines, sets his teeth on edge, but he doesn't phone the police. What Dennis Macken has is foolish faith, he says, what Angel Hopper has is a Hereford bull — a thick-necked, thick-shouldered, thick-legged miserable son-of-a-bitch that even Angel Hopper is scared of. A people-hater from birth. He rolls his bulging eyes and swings his head and paws at the ground at even a glimpse of something human, no matter how far away. In a small high-fenced corral behind the barn, he stands up to his knees in muck and swings his tail at flies while he munches hay and dreams of destroying the two-legged race. Sometimes just the sound of Angel Hopper moving around inside the barn is enough to make him circle his pen, work up some speed, and smash his head into the wall.

Hopper isn't half so mean as his bull but he can't help chuckling over what he knows will happen. A treat like this is worth a day off work — no logging company ever went belly-up just because one second-loader stayed home to protect his land. It is also worth the effort of doing it right — which means giving that ragged pack of youths some warning. He waits until all the young men in their crotch-patched overalls and pony-tails and the women in their ankle-length flowered skirts and the children with their pails and paper bags of lunch have crossed the ditch, have cut the strands of his fence and spread out over the field. Then he swaggers down into their midst with his twenty-two in his arms and approaches the only person who looks up, a girl in a purple velvet coat who reminds him of the runaway daughter of Frieda and Eddie Macken. "This is my property you're on," he says, as pleasantly as he knows how, "and I'd like to see you people off of here right away." He pauses and looks at the others, who don't even know he is there. "Please."

The girl frowns into his face as if she sees something at the back of his eyeballs that even he doesn't know is there. "Haven't you heard?" she says. "Nobody owns the earth. You got no business putting up fences and trying to keep us out."

"Thank you," Hopper says and heads for the barn. When the bull has been released to the field Hopper stands on the rusty seat of an abandoned hayfork to watch. Faced with so much humanity all at once, the bull hardly knows where to start. He bawls, drools, trots forward. He lowers his head and flings up dirt with his hoof and trots in a wide curve around the edge of the crowd. At last he charges. He seems to have chosen someone right in the middle. People scatter in all directions, screaming. Angel Hopper hoots and slaps his leg. No one would ever call him a sadist, but he is having a wonderful time. "Scare the hell out of them all, old Bull!" But Bull is intent on only the one original target, a youth with a rusty beard and a sweat-band who refuses to move. From this distance, Hopper thinks it may be the marathon youth. But marathon youth or whoever he is, this fellow has only to lift his arms and the bull nearly breaks his neck trying to put on the brakes. When he comes to a stiff-legged halt, his head lowered, he appears for a moment to be bowing to the youth. From their positions on top of fence posts and in the lower limbs of trees, the scattered pickers laugh. A few applaud.

The bull backs away from the youth and swings his head as if in apology. Then catching sight of Hopper on the seat of that rusty hayfork, he snorts and tosses his head and starts to run again. This time there's no indecision, the curve in his route is simply because his target is moving, is running towards the house. The bull cuts right through the fence like someone going through spiderweb, drags wire and broken post and several strands of honeysuckle vine behind him across the yard. Unhampered by so many accessories, Hopper is the first to get to the house. He even, for some reason or other, locks the door. While Hopper turns his basement upside down looking for strong enough rope to do something about that bull, the bull discovers a strong desire to travel. Out on the yellow centre line of the highway, he trots northward with his tail switching at flies. Perhaps he has an appointment he wants to keep in someone else's field. Perhaps he has simply developed an ambition to run the length of the Island.

Now all the world is draining into Waterville, it seems. There are people here from Taiwan, Turkey, and Tibet.

There are people off the plane from New South Wales, from
Ecuador, from Greece. Families of Alabamans. Couples from
Japan. Four youths on motorbikes from California, migrant
workers on the look-out for a crop more profitable and fun
than grapes or beets or oranges. The fields are crowded. The
woods are full. No one can escape them now. They hide
behind the cattle in the pasture. They camp in the bush and
sneak out after dark with miners' lamps beaming from their
foreheads. Alan Powers finds a family sleeping in his hay-
loft. Ossie Greenfield discovers a naked couple making love
in the attic of his house. All night long Grandma Barclay
listens to the sounds of running footsteps, whispering voices,
bodies brushing one another outside her bedroom walls.
Strangers sleep in tractor sheds and pick-up cabs and cel-
lars, children's voices cry from under trucks, the air at night
is alive with whispers like the rustling sounds of rats.

Dennis Macken wakes at dawn and knows that someone
else has slept beside him in his bed. The colour of his
dreams has changed and the sheets are strangely warm and
limp. Some of his forty-seven hats hanging around the wall
are rearranged. He believes it is the marathon youth himself,
who intends to push him off his place and use it as a
headquarters for his operation. Being a long-time bachelor,
Dennis Macken has the neatest house in the district, the
most expensive furniture, the newest truck, the cleanest
barn, and by far the biggest garden. Naturally, that rusty-
bearded runner would choose it for his own. Macken is
used to people wanting what he's got.

One of the things that people used to want was Dennis
Macken himself. He had his turn as heart-throb for the
entire district, years ago. Nearly every woman in Waterville
once dreamed of catching him. Star pitcher for the valley
baseball team, a heavy drinker, and a player of practical
jokes. He also played the field since the field was so willing
to be played, then in time chose Frieda Barclay out of all the
rest. Amongst other things, he liked her turned-up nose.
Frieda, however, liked the stronger, thicker nose of Eddie
Macken and gave Dennis back his ring. Her choice was to be
his sister-in-law instead of wife. His choice was to make no

second choice at all from the well-played field but to travel
twice around the world and hope to forget her. By the time
he stopped his running she was pregnant and he settled
into bachelorhood to watch her raise a family. Even after
forty years of watching, her nose still drives him crazy.
He keeps his place so spick and span not only because it is
where she grew up, the Barclay dairy farm he bought from
her widowed mother, but also because he knows she des-
pises dirt. He's the only man in the community who can
match the floors and windows of her spotless home.

But it isn't Frieda Macken's home that he feels is most at
stake. It's his. If he doesn't do something soon to stop that
plague of mushroom-pickers from overrunning the settlement they'll soon be crowding him off this earth.

Yet it appears that nothing can stop them now. Everyone
knows that police arrests are a joke. These people are happy
to forfeit their airline tickets to Norway or Egypt and high-
tail it back to the fields. Someone is making a fortune and it
isn't the Waterville farmer. His cattle huddle in corners. His
garden is picked nearly bare. His wife is afraid to step
outside her own house. Coming from town with her station
wagon full of groceries, Lenora Desmond finds her house
overrun; people in every room. Something they ate has gone
bad in their stomachs and they've converted her house to a
hospital: people are in her beds, people are throwing up in
her toilet, people are wrapped in blankets they've hauled
from her closet. The whole house stinks of some foul con-
coction of weeds a girl is boiling on her stove. "Who is the
doctor here?" she says. "Why are you in my house?" But
they turn up their sad forgiving eyes and pity her for this
bitter uncharity and refuse to move.

Aside from Eddie and Frieda Macken's silent farm, the
General Store and Post Office is the only part of the community not alive with strangers. By the fourth day of the
siege it is full of residents who've come in for the mail and
won't go home. They buy groceries to justify a few more
minutes of talk, then stand at the door until Em Madill
brings out more chairs from her kitchen. Display shelves are
shifted to one end of the room. Counters are cleared. Lenora

Desmond moves every loaf of bread to the top of the meat counter so that Angel Hopper can perch to smoke his pipe and Em Madill has somewhere to set up her coffee pot and cups. Women's jaws are set. Men's eyes refuse to see the eyes of other men. They prefer to read the tiny print on the labels of the canned tomatoes.

"It's really very simple," Frieda Macken says. "Nobody picks on our property. Nobody tramples our fences. Nobody scares our cows. You spread lime and the mushrooms don't grow."

"Not that you're gloating," they say.

And she isn't gloating, she understands that no one has followed her lead simply because they can't believe this thing until it's already started to happen. She smiles at a time like this, and almost sings, as if what she's got to offer is astonishing news. "If you gave all of your fields a good dose of it now, would those people still want the mushrooms?"

"Probably yes."

"Those people are crazy, Frieda. They'll find some way of hallucinating on a mixture of mushrooms and lime. They're very young, they're capable of everything."

"The police are trying but they haven't got a hope. That helicopter of theirs nearly scared my pants off, they thought I was one of them and chased me right across my own field. I thought that noisy rig was going to land on my head."

Ernie Butcher tells everyone he fixed up a forty-five-gallon drum of liquid manure on his tractor and chased these long-legged freaks all over the field, spraying them. "I even sprayed their car, but damn if they didn't come back the next day and I had to do it again." He's getting his field fertilized, he says, but he isn't doing anything else at all.

Ella Korhonen says she heard that flooding your field with sea water would solve the problem, too bad this place was too far inland and all uphill.

Uphill or not, a couple of miles of pipe would be worth it if it didn't ruin the soil. Ernie Butcher says he's keeping his own hands off from now on, he saw a bunch of the pickers on Alan Powers' field yesterday and stopped to holler at them to get out of there. "They never paid me no attention so I starts out onto the field myself to give them a piece of my mind and then old Powers comes roaring out of his house with his shotgun in his hand and stops on the top of his well-head to fire. I yelled and waved my arms all over the place but he blasts off just the same and cripes, you shoulda seen me run! I heard some of that buckshot whining past my ear. Somebody's going to get killed if we don't do something quick."

"It's got so's a person can't even protect what he owns. Yesterday I heard that Grandma Barclay — Frieda's mother, eh, and Lenora's — how old is she now? I heard she . . . "

"Eighty-four," Lenora says. "And I know what you're going to say. Yesterday she came across one of them smoking in the doorway of our root cellar when she went past to get me some spuds and without even thinking she hauled off and hit him with the fork. This morning the guy comes around with the police and wants to charge her with assault! You can imagine how far they got with me in the door."

Hell, Alan Powers says, he don't have to worry about that any more himself, this big fat fellow moved onto his property and thinks he owns the place, him and his gang, they chase everybody else away with sticks and even get into fights. "That bozo had the bloody cheek to tell me he made sixty thousand dollars off my place last year and he don't intend to share it with no one now! I told him, maybe him and that Back East Mafia is making a fortune off of this farm but they're tramping down my winter silage as well, which is the same as taking the money right out of my pocket. He laughed in my face. You think I'm going to tangle with him? Forget it."

"It isn't just that we own this land," says Ernie Butcher. "We put a lifetime of sweat into working it. Who do they think they are? If somebody shot just one . . ."

"It wouldn't make any difference," Frieda says. "You'd go to jail and the rest would move into your house."

At the age of sixty, with her white hair and determined jaw, she has the air about her of a woman judge. People will balk at everything she says, but in the end they listen. Her smiling eyes and singsong voice give her an added advantage: she can deliver a judge's orders and pass a judge's sentence as if she's dispensing news that delights and surprises even herself. "We'll go in to town and buy every sack of lime we can find," she says. "Then we'll spend tomorrow spoiling their obscene fun!"

At six o'clock Dennis Macken wakens and feels the heat of a second body in his bed. He knows the heavy breathing isn't his own. He knows the odour of unwashed feet is not his own. Beside him the marathon youth is laid out on his back, asleep. His hands are behind his neck. The hair in his armpits is as bushy as the rusted wire of the beard which rests on his skinny chest. Macken opens his mouth to holler. Then closes it. Who would he holler *for*? Instead he grunts, and moves to the edge of the bed, ready to leap. He wonders if he left his rifle loaded. He wonders, too, if he's left his senses altogether and taken a step into madness. Who is to say at this time of the morning whether the youth or himself is the intruder? How does he know for sure that this is his house?

Something he knows for sure is that the language he hears is not something he understands. Thick, European, full of sounds in the throat. The youth is awake, grinning. Without taking his hands from behind his neck he stretches his long skinny body, arches it right up off the sheet like a footbridge, then lets it collapse. "Jesus, I overslept," says the youth, in something a little closer to English. And sits up to swing his feet out onto the floor. While Macken still searches for words, the youth crosses the room, and bends to pick up his clothes from the rug.

"Just a minute," Macken says.

The youth drops his flowery shirt down over his upstretched arms and pushes his head through the neck. He pulls the track pants up his muscled legs. He crouches to lace his shoes. Then, running on the spot, he takes the sweat-band off his head and begins to comb his hair.

"What are you doing here? How the hell'd you get in?" The youth, still combing, laughs, then takes one of Macken's forty-seven caps down off the wall and tries it on. It's a little small for all that hair but he keeps it anyway.

Macken leans back on his pillow and pulls the covers up to his neck. "Who are you?" he says. He is cold. No, he is frozen. His hands are blue. Ice-water runs through every vein, out to the ends of his toes, his fingers.

The youth dances like a boxer across the floor to Macken. "That don't matter," he says. "But who are you?"

For a moment Macken doesn't know. His name is a foreign sound that people used against him years ago. He can't recall it now. If this stranger should ask him his age, however, that is a different matter. Macken suddenly knows that he is old. "Get out," he says, too weak to put any force in the words. "Get out." He closes his eyes until he is sure there is no one in the room but himself. Even then he doesn't get out of bed.

Not even the sight of Frieda Macken in his bedroom is enough to raise him up. Not even the devastated look on her handsome face, or her plea for help. What are they going to do, she wants to know. She's learned, from people in town who claim to know these things, that lime kills every kind of mushroom you can think of except this psylo . . . psylo . . . whatever it is, this thing. There is no antidote that will stop this plague amongst them. What she and Eddie have done, she supposes, is wasted time and energy spreading lime on fields where none of those things would have had the inclination to grow anyway. And made fools of themselves with their smugness.

Dennis Macken is not surprised to discover that the mushrooms are indestructible. He sees them in his mind's eye multiplying undeterred until they carpet the entire valley, until they are the only crop that grows in this part of the world. All he wants to do is look at his hands. They're old.

They're wrinkled and old and covered with splotches like some terrible disease. He's caught it, he thinks, from that youth who slept in his bed, but how can he tell that to Frieda without sounding insane? He can't. He'd rather be silent. He rests his hands on the top of his blankets and hopes she'll notice. She doesn't. His hands look no different to her than her own. It's his eyes she's worried about. His eyes look as if they've seen something they can't accept.

Dennis Macken knows that finding something that will kill the mushroom has nothing to do with anything, that even if every mushroom in the community turns to poison, the plague will not go away. It will increase the energy of its attack, like a horde of starving rats; it will overrun the district, destroying everything in sight. That's why he stays in bed until he's heard Frieda Macken's car pull out of his yard. That's why he listens until he is sure that the pickers are again at work, and gets up to watch from a kitchen window until everything he can see is alive with people. His own fields, Desmonds' fields, Powers' stumpy pasture. Down on their knees with their noses only inches from ground, they part the grass as if they've been told there are diamonds amongst the roots. He knows what they're after, he's seen it himself, a small pointed cap of flesh on a long wiry stem. The first few they find they will eat, to start the day off feeling good, the rest they will hoard in their tins or their plastic bags. He's heard three thousand dollars a pound is what they're worth. Having tasted one once, he can't understand why. All it did was give him a dizzy head.

A dizzy head is what time has given him too, with its incredible speed. Why has it gone so fast? One day you look out a window and dream of all you can do once you've grown into a man; the next, so it seems, you look out the window and find yourself wondering what you've done with it while it flew by. In his case, he wonders what *Frieda* has done with his life, the one he offered her years ago. Given it back. Having returned it, she seemed to have left everything else up to him. Some travel, a job, this little farm, helping his neighbours a bit — is this what they like to call life?

A pick-up truck slows down and parks in the shallow ditch. Close to a dozen people hop out of the back, and two more out of the cab. On the gravel shoulder they pause for a moment to look over his field, then climb through his fence and drop to their knees to start combing. One of them wears something that looks like pajamas. One is a child with a crutch. They haven't been there for even a minute when the people who got there before them stand up and converge to a knot in the centre of the field. Some carry sticks, a few swing their pails, all of them seem to be shouting. Macken sees, when they break apart and start walking towards the intruders, that the marathon youth takes the lead. Face to face the groups engage in some conversation. An arm is raised. A short piece of lumber is swung. The bodies convulse in a brawl. Even inside he can hear the sounds of their yells. One of the newcomers breaks free and makes for the truck. Others follow his lead. Waving their fists from the back of the pick-up they make their escape, while the rest go back to their work.

Once he is dressed, Dennis Macken crosses the yard and climbs on board his tractor, a monster he's made from a hundred scrapyard wrecks. Big as a tank, it has back wheels that stand higher than he does and a bulldozer blade on the front. Its motor rattles windows. Its tracks cut patterns of three-inch holes in the ground. Its exhaust pipe stretches skyward like a flagpole, and flies his flag — a flowered rag that whips about in the blue exhaust as if it wants to tear free and have a life of its own. A life of his own is what Macken wants too, and up on this tractor he'll claim it.

He starts the engine and manoeuvres out onto the grass. Selecting a cluster of adults down on their knees like pilgrims worshipping their god, he opens her up. Oh holy terror, the screams! Bodies leap up, fall away, scatter. Macken rattles on through. They yell at him, in thirteen different languages. Someone throws a jam tin that clatters against the hood. Someone throws a clod of grass that barely misses his face. He laughs, he laughs, he feels almost young again.

And now he is off to new encounters. This time they haven't the sense to scatter, they run in a pack, and he can't

resist the need to give them chase. He stands, he hollers
insults, he whoops like a cowboy. He follows them down
the length of the field, as close as he dare on their heels.
When they turn, he turns. Hair flies. Rags ripple and flap.
The girl in a purple velvet coat who looks like Frieda Mack-
en's runaway daughter trips and screams, crawls ahead of
the blade, gets up in the nick of time. Macken swings to the
left and heads for a new cluster of pickers, he won't be
happy until he has them all stirred up, he won't be happy
until he's given them all a scare, until he's made their lives
so miserable they'll be glad to leave, get off his land, and
spread the word that Dennis Macken's not a man to take
advantage of. Off to one side he sees a car on the highway
backing up for a better look, he sees Angel Hopper getting
out of his truck, he sees Frieda Macken running in this
direction across the Desmonds' field.

One youth alone stands upright, steady, refuses to move.
Macken decides to run over him. But the youth doesn't
move, doesn't leap, except onto the top of Macken's blade
where he rides with his rusty beard whipped up across his
face, his powerful hands on the bar. He is wearing a Macken
cap on his hairy head.

Macken stops for no one, not even this wild-eyed youth
on his nose. Not even the crowd of neighbours that's collected along his fence. Let them gawk, let them admire his
pluck. He sets out on a new crusade. "Get off my field you
pack of bastards, git!" But the marathon youth crawls up the
engine hood towards Macken's face. "Get out of my way,
you creep, I can't see where I'm going!" The eyes are so
deep and frightening that Macken can't bear to look at them.
The youth pushes his face up close to Macken's face, his
breath in Macken's breath, his nose against Macken's nose.
He says something that Macken can't understand, some
foreign sounds, but he tastes their meaning with his teeth.
He won't get out of this alive. Nobody will.

When the youth pulls out the key and rides the tractor to
a stop it's already far too late. Behind them a child is lying
in the grass and screaming. People are yelling again. People

are running to see what Macken has done. Someone hauls him down off his tractor and shoves him towards the commotion. The girl who looks like Frieda Barclay's daughter stops in front of him and spits in his face. Terrified by what he sees, Macken is almost relieved when the marathon youth pushes the others away and hustles him forward towards the child. The crowd from outside his fence is running this way, all of Waterville seems to be here. Macken can hear someone calling his name.

Some faces in this crowd are familiar, some are not. That could be Frieda Macken trying to get to him, but it could be someone else. Macken can't tell his neighbours from these children of the plague. A confusion of bodies. He thinks he sees Angel Hopper pushing someone, he thinks he sees Alan Powers. How carefully does a plague select a territory it will attack? Macken thinks that maybe it doesn't strike blindly at everything in its way, as people believe, he thinks its victims probably select themselves. The magnetic force it can't resist is fear.

The magnetic force he can't resist is that fallen girl. People move back so that he can be pulled towards her. A youth in wire-rimmed glasses is down on his knees in the grass with his eyes squeezed shut and his hands clasped together beneath his chin. A young woman is down in the grass beside him, holding the child's head in her arms. An arm, crushed by one of his wheels, is bleeding. Her mouth is open and her scream is so high and loud that Macken's ears are unable to bear it. He thinks, instead, that he's hearing the sirens that announce the end of the world.

A few of their names are appearing in the papers even now, along with their exotic addresses. Mexico City, Marseilles. Most of the pickers, however, have gone. Like other crops, the magic mushroom has its time and disappears. The marathon youth buys an Oh Henry bar in the General Store and sets off running down the road with his even pace. And where will he go to now? Does he scout for other causes? Will he lead his herd into department stores and onto beaches, will he usher them into picket lines and protest marches and demonstrations? Few have the time to wonder. They pick up liquor bottles and plastic bags and peanut butter jars in the fields. They examine livestock for signs of abuse. They bury smouldering campfires with shovelled sand. Some start giant bonfires of their own to burn up everything those hands have touched. Everyone is fixing fence. Lenora and Albert Desmond scour their house and scrape dried vomit out of corners with a paring knife. Grandma Barclay announces she wants to move into an old folks' home in town. Eddie and Frieda Macken lock up and head for the ferry, in order to spend some time with Frieda's sister Bella in North Vancouver. No one wants to believe what has happened. This collection of thirty hobby farms has never wanted to be anything special at all, except what it's always been. Nearly everyone has lived here for fifty years or longer. Rumour has it that Angel Hopper has decided what he'll do next year when the pickers return, if he hasn't sold out first. He'll sit by the gate and hold out his hand. For a hundred dollars a day — adult or child — he'll let a person pick on his private land and promise not to cause trouble. So what if he's lost a war? Dirty money or not, it's better than breaking bones, it's better than crushing children under your tractor wheels, like somebody else he knows.

Dennis Macken still believes in law, but not the law of the courts. He believes in Macken's law, which will have something to do with magnetic force when he finally figures it out. Watching that youth pump past his fence-line heading south, he knows that some day someone will drag him out of his house and try to convince him with speeches and legal documents and perhaps with a gun that these forty acres don't belong to him any more, or to anyone else that he knows. They'll tell him that everything belongs to this entire race of children from another planet who follow that bearded runner in a swarm from place to place throughout the universe harvesting their crop of drugs. Maybe this youth is dangerous and maybe he isn't, nobody knows for sure. What Dennis Macken knows is that there's much he's never thought of in this world, and plenty more to be found. What Dennis Macken knows is that before that plague of mushroom pickers returns he has eleven months to find some way of stopping clocks or step outside of time.

8

Ladies and Gentlemen, the Fabulous Barclay Sisters!

Don't think my father didn't warn me. I knew what was likely to happen if I didn't stay clear of my mother's sisters. He said marrying into the Barclay family was like getting a lifetime's pass to the movies for him. You just never knew what that pack of women would be up to next; there wasn't a one of them could tell if she was living a real life or acting it out on the screen. It was entertaining to say the least, he admitted, but hardly good for an impressionable growing boy.

Of course he didn't hold much hope for me. "Clay's already tarred a little with the same damn brush," I heard him tell my mother. "Keep him away from that bunch whenever you can." He believed her sisters' exaggerated sense of melodrama was catching.

My mother didn't believe for a minute in his "catching it" theory. To her, things were born right in you or they weren't. In her they weren't, or so she claimed. Of seven sisters she was the only one who didn't thrive on histrionics. She liked to think of herself as the sober one, like her father. When her sisters reminded her of the three engage-

ments she'd broken with other men before she settled on
one, she said that wasn't a sign of an eccentric nature at all,
it was just that she'd always had trouble making up her
mind.

Yes, my father said, and she'd also had trouble making
up her mind whether it was T.B. or pneumonia she was
dying of every time she caught cold. She'd had even more
trouble making up her mind whether to name my little
sister Marie Antoinette or Joan of Arc or Scarlett O'Hara
Desmond. Don't tell him she hadn't caught the family weak-
ness, he was there when she managed to fall off her horse
and feign a twisted ankle on their wedding day. He'd known
as well as she had that all her limping and wincing and
show of bravery were bound to get their picture onto the
front page of the weekly paper instead of buried on the
Women's Page amongst the other brides.

Of course, when she said she was level-headed, she
meant only in comparison with the others. Lenora Barclay
Desmond had little use for the way her older sister Frieda, a
married woman like herself, liked to tell deliberate lies at
the General Store and Post Office just to see people react.
That her husband Eddie had demanded a divorce, for instance, on the grounds that she'd stirred horse buns into his
porridge in a fit of rage when he refused to buy her a motor-
bike of her own. Or that she'd just heard on the radio that
the provincial government had plans to expropriate one of
the farms in this very community to give to some Germans
for some kind of factory. "A sauerkraut factory," added her
younger sister Christina, who loved to see people upset.
"You can imagine the smell." When the entire settlement of
loggers and farmers and housewives had got themselves all
in an uproar — planning letters to the nearest paper, design-
ing petitions to send to Victoria, calling meetings to organize a protest — Frieda brought in some updated news that
set things right again. But Christina, who hated to see people calm, said yes she'd heard it wasn't the Germans it was
the Japs, who wanted to locate a factory for canning seaweed. Sauerkraut would have smelled like roses, she said,

compared to rotting kelp. Then Frieda and Christina would snicker and snort about how gullible everyone was in this hickish dump of a place. My mother, on the other hand, failed to see what humour there was in making fools of people.

Making fools of people was precisely what my mother's sisters liked to do best. It was Mabel's habit to mimic people behind their backs. While making people laugh was all very well, my mother said, how did you think old Mrs. Morris would feel if she ever turned around and found Mabel behind her, imitating her limp and rolling her eyes and running her finger under her nose while she made grunting sounds like a pig? But cheeky Mabel with her freckled face and frizzy red hair had already won herself a reputation as the life of any party, called upon whenever things got dull to do her imitations of local eccentrics. She admitted that there was little fun in it for herself unless the person being mimicked was right there in the room, however. The challenge was in doing it when people didn't expect it, and not for long, so that every person there except the mimicked one knew who you meant.

There must be better ways to put all that energy to use, was my father's word on all this nonsense,. He said if he ever caught me up to Mabel's kind of tricks, he'd send me off to a private school in Victoria, where vicious teachers with English accents would beat it out of me with a wooden cane. He said he didn't know how my grandfather could live with that crazy bunch without going crazy himself. That quiet man must be some kind of saint. No wonder, when the family had moved out here to the coast from Alberta back when they all were young, he'd chosen to ride in a railroad car with the pigs rather than sit with his family! My father said that if he himself had had to live in an eight-woman household for long he couldn't promise he wouldn't resort to murder.

When tragedy or even sickness struck one of the homes in the community — an accident in the logging camp, say, or chicken-pox — the aunts were happy to spread the word themselves, since telephones hadn't yet been installed in private homes in the 1940s. They were happy to embroider the details with morbid speculations while they were at it. But my mother grabbed a couple of loaves of bread from a drawer and managed to arrive at the stricken house before anyone else, ready to dig in and work. You could tell by the way she grimly set her lips that she got a certain amount of pleasure out of being the charitable workhorse, but she never complained or tried to make herself out a martyr. "A waste of energy," Frieda warned her. "Don't think for a minute it's appreciated. If anything ever happened to you they'd stay away in droves."

"Either that," my grandmother said, "or you'd have fifty loaves of bread delivered to your door and swarms of people trying to do your work for you, and doing it wrong. Personally, I'd rather they stayed away."

Two weeks later my mother would still be worrying about the victims but the aunts would have written them into a three-act play which they staged in the garage of the Barclay dairy farm, two miles down the highway from our place. Neighbours, relatives, people of all ages paid a few cents for a ticket and sat on a kitchen chair or a block of wood to see what tales these crazy sisters had managed to spin from local events. Loggers would have been transformed into knights, and housewives into elegant ladies of the court, but you could tell, if you knew anything, that beneath all the melodrama was a story manufactured out of their neighbours' lives. An invasion of privacy? Nobody seemed to mind. Suffer today, people said, and then watch yourself suffer all over again a week from now when the chenille bedspreads were parted on that piece of clothesline in the Barclay garage.

Not that my mother objected to putting on plays. That was the one thing they did, in fact, that she found acceptable. Sometimes she even joined them. When they staged a medieval romance based on stories people told about Dennis Macken's self-inflicted bachelorhood, she played the part of her own sister Frieda, the girl who'd turned him

down and broken his heart and set him off on a career of
escaping one unsatisfactory female after another in a trip
around the world. Mabel and Gladdy and even timid Bella
had roles as the other girls, though Gladdy could never be
trusted not to add her own coarse observations, just to show
she was different from all the others. Christina played the
part of a rumoured African princess who kept him captive
for several months for her own convenience. Mabel made
faces at the audience and mocked the other actresses behind
their backs and tried to steal the show. Frieda, of course,
boycotted the performance and spent the afternoon with my
grandfather out in the barn. It was Eleanor, sweet young
innocent Eleanor playing the part of a dying invalid, who
captured people's hearts. Which demonstrated, my mother
said, that there was a big difference between making fools of
people and entertaining them. Eleanor now, she said, was
an example of someone with a healthy attitude. Though she
was the youngest in the family, with all those bad examples
to follow if she'd wanted to, she did it all for fun and never
meant people harm.

She didn't know, she didn't know. Being the youngest of
the family — in fact just a few years older than myself —
Eleanor with her fluffy curls and her Shirley Temple dimples had already perfected the art of appearing innocent
amidst the chaos of her own inventions. She was practising
up, even then, to outdo every one of her sisters. How was it
possible for my mother to forget the time Eleanor dressed
herself up in torn clothes and smeared herself with ketchup
to lie moaning out in the middle of the highway on a
Saturday afternoon? Old Joseph Macken had driven straight
into the ditch in order to avoid running over her. The whole
neighbourhood came out to poke at her body to see if she
was alive but eventually she roused herself and said she felt
much better now and thought she'd just walk home.

It was Eleanor who told it around the district that she'd
found out she was actually adopted, not a Barclay at all like
the rest of them, but a Polish princess. When people laughed
and said they remembered my grandmother's pregnancy,

she narrowed her eyes and challenged them to ask about the
baby who'd died and been replaced on the sly. Sometimes
she slipped into a thick foreign accent, as if she thought
that would reinforce her claim, and developed a taste for
jewellery.

A day without a manufactured crisis of some kind was a
day sacrificed forever to the grey world of dullness, according to Eleanor. My parents, she claimed, were dull. And if I
weren't careful I too would grow up dull. If I watched her in
action and picked up a few tips, on the other hand, there
was still some hope that I might create myself a life of a
little interest. For a boy.

"For instance," she said. "I bet you've never even put a
box out on the highway on the end of a piece of string."

"Never," I admitted.

"What a poop!"

To give her credit, she never entirely dismissed me when I
confessed my innocence. She taught me instead. You put a
box in the middle of the road, she said, and when someone
stopped his car and got out to pick it up you pulled the
string and stood up in the ditch to laugh at him. "Only I've
got a better idea."

Her better idea was to fill the cardboard box with cow
manure from the barn and wrap it in wedding paper topped
with a bow. We spent a good half hour getting it to look just
right. It might have been an electric kettle or a waffle iron.
We even stole an envelope from my grandmother's drawer
and wrote two names on it — Sam and Janet Evening — to
make it look authentic. You could see by the way Eleanor
admired the results that she hated to part with the parcel, it
looked so pretty. She clearly thought she'd created a masterpiece.

And so she had. At least that seemed to be the opinion of
the drivers of three cars that stopped all at the same time
when they saw it on the pavement just up the hill a few
yards from the gate. Ducked down in the ditch in the thick
tangled broom, Eleanor held her breath. Two men and a
woman got out from their cars and stood over the parcel.

"Someone must have dropped it on the way to a reception," one of them said.

"When are we going to jump up?" I whispered.

"Shut up," she said, and kept a hand over her mouth, perhaps to stifle her giggles.

The drivers argued over what to do with the thing. One wanted to take it into my grandparents' house, and one wanted to take it up to the General Store. The woman was all for tossing a coin and keeping it. Obviously none of them trusted the others.

"Now," Eleanor said.

"No," I said. My heart was pounding. "Think . . . if they take it to the store . . . and it sits on the counter, smelling."

She looked at me and grinned. "You're learning, kid." The important thing, she had told me more than once, was not only to manufacture excitement but to sweep up as many unsuspecting people in it as possible. Then you knew you were living at the heart of drama.

Yet once the drivers had settled the matter and driven off with the box, she decided that my brilliant idea was more the result of fear than superior talent. She and Gladdy rolled me up inside an old carpet and left me behind the dairy for nearly an hour. I couldn't move. Inside that dirty thing I could hardly breathe. When they came to see if I was still alive they said they'd unroll me if I agreed to let them practise a home-permanent kit on my hair, but I refused. They sat on my head. When they asked me again I told them I was nearly dead and they would both be hanged. They rolled me down the slope to the edge of the creek and said they would drop me in if I didn't agree. They wouldn't hang, they said, because they would bury my body under the manure pile and no one would ever find me. For that matter, Eleanor said, no one would even miss me. I said they could use my hair to practise on, but only if they confined themselves to the ends, where it could be cut away.

"Don't you try and tell me this was entirely Eleanor's fault," my mother said. "Did you or did you not sit still while they did it to you?"

I'd sat still, I said, but what choice did I have when they'd allowed nothing out of the carpet except my head? My mother said she guessed it was born right in me to be as bad as the rest. It couldn't be helped. My father didn't agree. I was a boy, he said, and there was still some hope if only I'd spend more time at home with my brother and sister, or doing chores, instead of hanging around with that bunch.

But how could I take his advice? It wasn't possible. Should I have refused to play the part of a rhinoceros in the Barclay Family Circus? Pacing on my hands and knees inside an overturned baby crib, I had little to do but ram my horny nose at the kids who poked their hands between the bars. Hardly melodramatic. Not when you considered that Mabel was dressed as the fat bearded lady you had to sneak into a darkened tent to view. And not when you considered that Eleanor, innocent Eleanor, set up business in the root cellar where she looked into an overturned fish-bowl and told children about futures so horrible that half of them left in tears. "Don't go to sleep tonight," she told Cornelia Horncastle. "Your mother is looking for a chance to slit your throat." Cornelia Horncastle got her money back, but Eleanor continued to indulge her imagination. My brother and sister were the Headless Twins. They mingled with the crowd in outfits that were built up on the shoulders to hide their heads, each with a papier mâché skull under an arm. When things threatened to get dull they picked a fight and rolled on the ground, puncturing bags of watered ketchup that splashed on people's legs and smeared their clothes.

The climax of the circus was a garage performance of a play in which a beautiful Polish princess, maddened by the loss of her prince in a noisy offstage battle, murdered the entire royal family before turning the gun on herself. Written by Eleanor, it was an obvious parable based on Noolie Dahlburg's crazy behaviour when her husband Homer ran off with Greta Trent. Eleanor, of course, had the leading role. My mother had no lines to say this time, she was the servant who handed the princess my grandfather's shotgun to do her dirty work with and was then rewarded for her loyalty with a blast of buckshot in the chest. My mother took advantage of her moment at centre stage to take longer to die than anyone else in the play. She staggered, groaned, gagged, rolled her eyes and stuck out her tongue, she slammed against first one wall and then the other, she pleaded with the audience for help, and dragged herself on her stomach across the floor to expire, at last, at the feet of the first row of spectators. The audience responded with a round of applause and she thanked them with a few more life-like twitches before she lay still.

To put everyone back into a happy mood, the concert ended with what that cardboard sign promised would be "the mellow sounds of a sister act, imported at great expense from Hollywood." From behind the hanging bedspreads a voice announced: "LADIES AND GENTLEMEN, THE FABULOUS BARCLAY SISTERS!" And there they were, when the makeshift curtains had parted, all seven of them lined up in a row, dressed in long slinky dresses glittering with sequins. One at a time, from oldest to youngest, each stepped out from the line, dropped a curtsey, and introduced herself. "I'm Frieda." "I'm Lenora." "I'm Christina." "I'm Mabel." "I'm Bella." "I'm Gladdy." "And I'm Eleanor the Tramp." They hummed a note, then broke into a seven-part harmony version of "Apple Blossom Time" that called for swaying from side to side, kicking one leg out this way and the other out that. My father, who'd built the concession booths out of packing crates but refused to stay for the show, came early to pick us up and caught the last few minutes of the singing act by mistake. He closed his eyes and backed outside the garage, then went off to find my grandfather's hiding-place. At least he could see that I had nothing to do with this. Dressed in my rhino costume I was sitting innocently there in the second row.

The men in those women's lives were going to have one time of it, my father said. Being one himself he ought to know. The men in those women's lives would have much to endure. If my mother thought the worst crime was making fools of other people, my father thought the worst crime was making a fool of yourself. To him, drawing attention to yourself was virtually daring fate to drop you on your face, and bring you down to size. How did you think it felt to be married to one of these show-offs, and have to stand by and watch? The thing that saved my mother was that she restricted her bouts of exhibitionism to when she was with her sisters; the other six kept it up all the time. "Life at your place is so dull," Eleanor said. "I don't know how you can stand it."

I began to wonder myself. My parents were fairly quiet and sensible people. Everyone trusted them. Everyone counted on them to keep their word, to do the honourable thing, to be consistent. Eleanor warned me that if I continued to live in that household I'd become like them, honoured and trusted and dull. Life would be much more fun if I lived in the Barclay house.

If only it were possible for my grandparents to adopt me! If only I could live like my quiet, unshakable grandfather in that house of eccentric women, at the very centre of their exciting chaos, then I would be able to witness dramas unfolding before my eyes every minute of the day. If I'd been living there, Eleanor said, I'd have seen the looks on my grandparents' faces when Christina announced she'd been secretly married to Eric Maclean for nearly a year and was probably carrying his child, or somebody's. I'd have been right at the centre of things when Jacob Weins got engaged to each of the girls in turn, from oldest on down until he came to the one he really wanted (Mabel) and lost his nerve. I'd have been there when my grandmother fell down the back verandah steps, breaking her leg, and could have helped spread word around the district that she'd been jumped from behind by a whiskered prowler in a bowler hat. And of course I'd have had a ringside seat when Christina decided to go mad and carry a knife in the top of her dress while she waited for the most dramatic moment to do herself in. "Any minute now," she'd say, and flash her mad eyes at someone, anyone, to keep the household in an uproar, expecting bloodshed. "I think I shall simply wander off into the woods," she said, pushing back from the table in the middle of a meal, "and never be seen again." If I'd been there, if I'd been inside that family, I could have been the one they sent to follow her, at a discreet distance, to wrestle the knife out of her hand at the very last moment and save her life.

"But you'd have failed," Eleanor said, "because they're bringing you up to be so ordinary and dull. You have no flair."

To have flair was the thing that mattered. The aunts had flair. The young men they spent their time with all had flair. Frieda's husband Eddie Macken drove a salvaged hearse, painted yellow and black like a swollen wasp. Jacob Weins showed up for his dates with whoever he happened to be engaged to at the time in period costumes — one day Cyrano de Bergerac, the next day Henry the Fourth. Eric Maclean owned a whiskey still somewhere back in the bush that the police were trying to find, and had once been almost married to a girl who'd moved to Hollywood, perhaps a star by now with a different name. Gladdy's boyfriends liked to drop hints about life behind bars, and drunken fights with police.

In the life they led, no incident was allowed to pass without someone turning it into an event. A drive to the Union Bay dance became a Ben Hur race, with cars side-swiping cars and wheels falling off in the ditch. The most ordinary movie became either a masterpiece or a bloody riot, depending on who was reporting. When Frankie Laitenan's two-door Ford went off the road and sank to the bottom of the river, you can be sure that three of the aunts were in it, screaming their lungs out. How they eventually swallowed their panic, how they rolled down the windows and struggled out into the water, how they floated to the surface and shouted for help in the direction of a truckload of soldiers in uniform was the subject of long, embroidered tales for several months. The soldiers, who were on their way back from a day of practising how to kill people in the mountains, demonstrated by the way they kicked off their boots and dived into the river that they had more than mere courage — they also had flair. I, on the other hand, had neither. Barclay Philip Desmond was in mortal danger of becoming as dependable, consistent, and sensible as his parents.

Consistent and dependable were hardly the words that came first to mind, however, when I came home from school a week before my eleventh birthday and found my mother standing in the middle of the living room loading shotgun shells into my father's double-barrel 12-gauge. Was she going to shoot herself, or me? Maybe being in Eleanor's play had put ideas into her head, I'd heard of mothers going berserk, I'd even picked up the information somewhere that it was the quiet ones you had to watch, the sensible ones. If she shot me now she'd have a two-hour wait before my father came home from work so she could shoot him too. Maybe she'd only tie me up for now, and plan to shoot us both at supper-time. I assumed my brother and sister were already dead. Either that or tied up behind the woodshed waiting their turn. "You don't need to go telling anyone, either," she said, and levelled a warning eye. She couldn't have guessed how relieved I was to hear her say that. If I were going to be in a position to tattle, then I could hardly be marked for death. Maybe she had plans to simply maim me. At that moment I'd be grateful for a couple of blown-off legs.

"That pheasant there in the garden is out of season for another month," she explained, "but I'm not about to turn down a chance like this."

The pheasant? It took a while to register. I was looking at the thing but hadn't been able to make the connection. Strutting, he dragged his long narrow tail-feathers between the rows of peas, not fifteen yards away, and held his brilliant head up high on his white-ringed neck as if he owned the place. If my father were here he'd have blown that head off in a second, as he'd done to dozens of others, and handed it over to my mother to clean for supper. Wild pheasant was his favourite game, in or out of season.

"If I don't get him somebody else will do it," she said. "Stand back a minute, you know how I hate doing this kind of thing."

Shooting some dinner was better than shooting me, but I felt a little sorry for that pheasant. At such close range he hardly stood a chance. My mother leaned on the front-porch rail and aimed. With her feet apart and her mouth screwed to one side, she sighted down the barrel with concentration and prepared to do something she'd never done before — kill a living thing.

The gun, it turned out, had other plans. When she pulled the trigger I heard the explosion but saw the pheasant run and beat his wings up into the air. When I looked at my mother, she'd dropped the gun to the floor and thrown her apron up over her head. I could see blood already soaking through the cloth and smeared on her hands.

Was she dying? My mouth was dry, I was afraid to go closer to see. This was much more drama than I'd ever bargained for. My mother had shot herself by mistake, she was bleeding into her hands, she was staggering back inside the house to find a place to fall. She chose the chesterfield, and slumped back with her wadded-up apron pressed against her forehead. "Shall I get help?" I said. "Shall I go for a doctor?"

She looked stunned for a moment, as if she couldn't make out what I was saying. "The damn . . . gun . . . backfired," she said. "I've never heard of anything so . . . stupid. But it's only a scratch. Just wait a minute and see."

I couldn't help it, I felt as if I had been cheated. Here we had this real-life tragedy unfolding in the house, something that could rival the theatricals of the Barclay household any day, and no one was around to witness it but me. If Mabel had been there, think what she might have done with this. Or Eleanor. If the whole lot of them had been in the house at the time this happened, the incident would already have taken on the importance and excitement of a royal assassination. The world would be talking about it for years. As it was, I was the only witness; whatever was to be made of this thing would have to be made by me. Dull and sensible me.

I was not so dull that I didn't recognize the gift I had just been given — once it was clear that no one was in any danger. Not only had my mother just shot herself before my eyes (how many ten-year-olds could boast of that?) but she'd done it in the course of breaking the law. My sober reliable mother was an outlaw! A gun-toting suicidal heroine, if you stretched the point just a little. A person could even say that her life still hung in the balance at the moment, and that everything depended on me. They made movies of situations like that.

"Maybe you better hop on your bike," she said, examining the forehead scratch in the mirror. "Phone the doctor. I should have this looked at at least. I don't think I should try to drive myself in."

"You'll be okay?"

She was okay, I could tell by the way she levelled that threatening eye again. "Just don't go telling the doctor I was breaking the law. As far as he needs to know, it could just as easily have been a grouse." Grouse, unlike pheasant, were already safely in season.

The only telephone in the district at the time hung on the wall inside the door of the General Store and Post Office a mile and a half down the highway. No time to put on shoes, I told an invisible audience, when my mother could be dying. I stood up on the pedals of my balloon-tire bike and pumped as hard as I could out the gravel drive and down the blacktop highway to the store, where my aunt Frieda was already shouting something into the phone. Behind her, Big Glad Littlestone in a purple hat thumbed through the pile of Star Weeklys on the counter and licked at an ice-cream cone. They were about to discover that something truly exciting had happened in the world.

"Get off that thing and call a doctor," I yelled. "My mother's shot herself."

I'd never before seen words I'd spoken cause such dramatic results. Big Glad dropped her cone on the floor, and Frieda stopped in the middle of a word to gape. I saw fillings at the back of her bottom jaw. "Which doctor?" she said, and swung her eyes at Big Glad Littlestone. "Are you sure it isn't too late?" Her hand pressed the cradle down and then let it click up again. "Glad, you get on up there and see what you can do. And you, you get home fast."

The fastest way to get home (mostly uphill) was to keep on going downhill to my grandparents' farm, where there'd be a car, and plenty of people to drive it. Now that I'd taken the plunge into this world of excitement I wasn't about to pass up the best audience of all. "Don't you go telling the police," I panted at the door to my grandparents' house. "They'll only throw her in jail — if she lives."

Mabel leapt up from the kitchen table, where she'd been sewing something. "Is that blood on your face? What are you talking about?"

"My mother," I said, and collapsed into the nearest chair. "Don't you tell the police. She's been shooting up the countryside with my father's gun."

Mabel groaned and put a hand on the table to steady herself. This was easier than I'd hoped. "She's snapped at last," she said. "I knew it would happen some day." To Christina, who appeared at the door from the pantry, "Lenora's finally snapped, I knew she would, she's gone crazy as a loon and is threatening to kill people."

Christina looked blank for a moment, then let out a scream that brought sisters running from every part of the house. "He says that Lenora's gone mad and tried to kill him," she said, and threw her hands over her face.

Another day of drama in the Barclay household. Only this time I was the centre and the cause of it. While Bella went whimpering out the back door to get my grandmother in from the dairy — my grandfather was off at a cattle auction — Mabel streaked out the front door to tell the neighbours across the road, so they wouldn't miss out on this. I was left with Christina and Eleanor staring at me. "There's blood all over the house," I said. "She's gone and shot herself."

Christina leaned back against the wall and closed her

eyes. Eleanor said she'd been suspecting for quite a while that my mother had been seeing another man and now she was sure of it. A case of love gone bad. Maybe she thought my father was getting suspicious. Christina opened her eyes and told her to shut her face, that was no way to talk in front of a boy. Suppose it were true? She said that Eleanor must have left her brains somewhere, to talk like that, and gave her a swat on the arm. Eleanor, swearing, narrowed her eyes and bunched up her fist and threatened to hit Christina in the throat.

I began to wonder if I hadn't made a mistake in judgement. This fighting, this talk of other men, made my stomach uneasy. If it was excitement I'd wanted to cause, I was seeing plenty but somehow I had the feeling that things had got out of control. When my grandmother appeared at the door I was sure of it. She was frantic. Things had already gone too far.

Riding home in the Barclay Dodge I began to see just how far they had gone. Dennis Macken waved us over to the side of the road just outside our gate and suggested we park where we were. The driveway was already clogged, he said, and people were finding the field a little too soggy to trust. Gordon Selby had already sunk his Hudson to the axles.

My grandmother stuck her head out the window. "What is it that's going on?" Beside me, Mabel snivelled, and Christina chewed on her bottom lip. Sharp cramps stabbed my innards.

"Oh pardon Mrs. Barclay, I didn't realize it was you. Just go on through, right on down to the house. Naturally you want to get there fast. Right on through, right on through." He was waving us on with one hand and already pulling someone else over with the other. "Just park 'er right over here sir, you'll only get stuck or jammed into the crowd if you go any farther."

"This is outrageous," my grandmother said. "Haven't these people anything better to do?"

You'd think it was an auction sale, or a wedding. Down either side of the driveway cars were parked in the grass. I

saw Mrs. Korhonen hurrying across the pasture from her
house with a Pyrex pot of coffee in her hand, and a loaf of
her braided bread. I saw three of the Grenoble brothers
riding their bikes around and around our house, stretching
their necks to see in the windows. I saw an ambulance
parked by the door, and people talking in clusters out in the
yard. Mabel shoved her handkerchief into her mouth to
stifle her threatening sobs.

"Vultures," my grandmother said. "Pretending to be
good neighbours but they're really a bunch of vultures."

Obviously the telephone company didn't need to bother
installing phones in all the houses of this community. People were proving they could manage just fine without. Couples, families hurried down to the house, cutting across the
garden where the pheasant had almost met his end.

Oh how I wished he had, to avoid all this. If only that
gun had gone off properly and blown off his head. What
was the sacrifice of one feathery life compared to the trouble
I'd caused? If running hadn't been an obvious admission of
fault — as well as a cowardly public escape — I'd have lit out
for the bush immediately, I'd have run until I found a boat
that would take me off this island to another world. "Maybe
I'll stay in the car," I said, when we'd come to a stop. "I
don't really want to go in."

"Why not?" My grandmother clutched at my arm. Did
she suspect that things were worse than I'd said, perhaps a
body too mutilated to look at a second time? Or was she
suspicious? Living with those daughters of hers she could
hardly have been naive. Her fingers dug into my flesh.
"Why not?" she said again, and dragged me by the arm
towards the house.

"You!"

The voice belonged to Frieda, who stood on the top step
with one hand against the wall as if she would block our
entrance.

"What is it?" my grandmother said. "What's going on in
this house?"

But Frieda's eyes were on me. "You! Do you see, you

little creep, do you see what a fool you've made of . . . of everyone?" With one helpless hand she gestured weakly, towards the cars, the people, the whole world. "Do you see?" Then she sat down on the wood-box and pushed the hair back from her face. "I could beat you, I could kill you." Yet she made it clear that she had energy for neither, that she was a wreck. "Your poor mother," she said.

"Would someone explain what is going on in this household?" my grandmother shouted through the door.

She found out for herself soon enough. Once she'd elbowed a path for us through the people who blocked our way, she could see for herself that the woman standing with a Band-Aid on her forehead was in no immediate danger of dying. She could hear for herself as well that my mother was trying to convince people to settle down, to go home, to believe her when she said nothing serious had happened. The cakes, the pies, the flowers, the offers of help were all unnecessary, she said, though much appreciated. It was wonderful to discover how generous everyone was but someone, she said, seemed to have got the story just a little bit wrong. She caught my eye at that moment and I felt the blood rush up to my face.

My grandmother raised a threatening hand. "If this was my kid I'd paddle his backside until he couldn't sit down." She wouldn't, though; only my father was allowed to hit and he wouldn't be home for another half-hour. Whatever happened to me would be up to him. I expected the Victoria private school. My grandmother sat on a chair and held the hem of her dress up to her eyes. Her shoulders trembled. "Your grandfather," she said to me, "would be ashamed."

"That wasn't bad," Eleanor told me. "Maybe you've got more imagination than I gave you credit for."

"Imagination!" Mabel, who pulled her freckled face into what must have been an imitation of my own confused and shocked expression, said that I ought to be dropped down a well. "He's got enough imagination to dream up a way to give us heart attacks but not enough to see that he was bound to be caught in his lie."

Christina agreed. "He's a bloody little liar is what he is."
The heads of neighbours, friends, relatives all around me,
nodded agreement. A bloody little liar was what I was, no
question about it, and look at the trouble I'd caused.

My mother didn't speak to me until all the others had
gone — my grandmother, her own sisters, the neighbours.
Some left their gifts behind, some took them. All of them
gave me a parting look that was meant to sizzle me there on
the spot. None gave me a look, however, that came anywhere near the look my mother gave me when we had the
kitchen to ourselves. The fury I could have handled, I think,
but there was pity in it as well, and something else. "Don't
you ever pull a trick like that again," she said. "Do you
realize, now, that no one will ever again believe a thing you
say? I hope you're ashamed of all the ruckus you stirred up
with your nonsense."

As a matter of fact, behind the fear I was not entirely
unproud of all the ruckus I'd caused. For a dull and sensible
boy I hadn't done badly at all; when people calmed down
they would say I was cut from the Barclay cloth. It was clear,
however, that if I continued to live at home I'd have to keep
this new-found talent under wraps, or find a safer outlet.

"Talent?" Eleanor said the next day, and laughed. She'd
been thinking it over, she said, and decided I hadn't all that
much to be proud of after all. "You've got to know how to
control it." The way she shook her head I could see she
didn't believe it was something I'd ever learn.

The private school hadn't materialized after all, except
as a repeated threat. But I was sorry to hear, I told her, that
no one, ever again, would believe a thing I said. It didn't
seem fair.

She shrugged. Who cared about fair? "If no one is going
to believe you anyway, you may as well tell them lies from
morning to night." It was a notion that appealed to her, I
could see. "You can tell them any old thing that goes through
your head. Or write it down in a book, where people will
assume it's the truth."

To give me a start, she suggested I write a play. "About

this beautiful gun-slinging outlaw woman. At the end of the play she learns that her true love has been unfaithful to her and turns her gun on herself." It was to be a jazzed-up version of my mother's escapade. Another invasion of privacy? Of course, Eleanor said. All fiction was an invasion of one kind or another, or it had no point. We would stage it in the garage, another Barclay Family Theatre enterprise, and splash plenty of ketchup all over the place at the climax. The audience would be in tears. She, of course, would play the heroine herself. And she could see no trouble convincing the other aunts to co-operate, once they got wind of the juicy roles. Even if they thought quite rightly that I was a little creep, they'd break their necks to play the parts of the faithless cowboy lover and the treacherous barmaid and the sheriff. Naturally there'd be no role in it for me; I'd be billed as just the author. Which was, Eleanor said, the perfect job for a person who was — let's face it — basically dull and uninteresting and totally lacking in flair.

ACKNOWLEDGEMENTS

Some portions of this book appeared in slightly altered versions in *Saturday Night*, *The Story So Far*, *Weekend Magazine*, *The Journal of Canadian Fiction*, and *Toronto Life*.

As implied by the style and content of the story itself, "The Sumo Revisions" is an exploration of some questions raised by a reading of Wright Morris's novel *A Field of Vision* and by a performance of Tsuruya Nanboku's Kabuki play *Tokaido Yotsuya Kaidan*. I wish, as well, to express gratitude to several generous and imaginative hosts in Tokyo: John Sloan, Bruce Barnett, Makiko Dochi, Mutsuo Ueyama, and Akira Assai.